WHERE THE WOLF HUNTS

TYLER FLYNN

WHERE THE WOLF HUNTS

PAPILLON
PRESS

WHERE THE WOLF HUNTS

Copyright © 2021 Tyler Flynn

Imprint of Papillon Press

ISBN paperback: 978-0-578-93771-7

Cover design by: Patrick Kang
Back author photo credit David Sherman Photography

Proudly printed in the United States of America

www.tylerflynnbooks.com

For my mother and father,

Thank you for always believing in me.

&

In memory of my grandparents,
George and Alice Moskalik.

"Now this is the law of the jungle,
as old and as true as the sky,

And the wolf that shall keep it may prosper,
but the wolf that shall break it must die.

As the creeper that girdles the tree trunk,
the law runneth forward and back;

For the strength of the pack is the wolf,
and the strength of the wolf is the pack."

-The Law for the Wolves
Rudyard Kipling

Part I

The Stalk

1

He should have checked under the car.

It was only one mistake, but Mathieu Bertrand would realize it too late. If he was honest with himself, though, the mistake was getting involved in the first place. He should have cut his losses and run when his wealthiest client met the wrong end of a gun months earlier. It was obvious he was out of his league.

As an attorney who prided himself on billing at a thousand euros an hour, Mathieu could conjure up magic from time to time. He did not, however, specialize in handling sensitive intelligence dossiers.

He should not have gotten involved in affairs beyond his usual scope.

The Parisian attorney turned from his office window overlooking the City of Lights. To his left, the Eiffel Tower sparkled on the hour for the twenty-second time that day. Straight ahead, the lit dome of Les Invalides stared back.

His grey flannel chalk-stripe suit felt stifling, so he tossed his jacket on the leather chair behind his desk. Mathieu picked up his crystal Baccarat tumbler and drained the last of his Blue Label. He needed courage. Simply remembering the earlier telephone exchange with the man he was to meet made him weak in the knees.

"How will I know what you look like?" Mathieu had naïvely asked, desperate to protect the flash drive he had been entrusted with from falling into the wrong hands.

"Doesn't matter. I know what you look like," came the reply.

The caller identified himself as a DGSE officer—*Direction Générale de la Sécurité Extérieure*, or the French CIA—and requested they met that evening at the Hemingway bar at the Ritz Hotel at 10:30 p.m.

Mathieu had waited anxiously for the office floor to clear. He was normally the last to leave in an effort to rack up billable hours, but tonight warranted the solitude to protect the valuable intelligence. No one could know where he was going nor what he was doing. It wasn't every day your client entrusted you with the details of Iran's efforts at selling nuclear enrichment.

He turned off the lights in his office as the Eiffel Tower still sparkled in the background. With his leather briefcase and coat in hand, he took the stairs from the seventeenth-floor office in the Tour Montparnasse to the parking garage. The stairs avoided run-ins with building staff on the elevator—a necessary precaution.

The underground parking structure was built like a bunker and haphazardly organized by thin yellow lines. The fluorescent lights were harsh, splashing white light across the cold, smooth surfaces. It smelled of old rubber and burnt oil, as if someone had kept their engine running for a while before peeling away up the steep exit ramp.

The drive to Place Vendôme would take only fifteen minutes this time of night, when most of Paris was at bars or cafés busy celebrating the end of another workday. Simple enough.

Mathieu checked the surrounding lot, peered into his Peugeot 3008 SUV's back seat, and checked over his shoulder to ensure no one was following him. Then he made his mistake.

I should have checked under the goddamn car.

He opened the driver-side door and stepped in with his right foot when he felt a searing pain in his left heel.

The attacker sliced Mathieu's tendon with a sharp knife, lashing out like a coiled serpent. Collapsing into a crumpled heap of an immaculate bespoke suit stained by blood on the dirty garage floor, Mathieu grabbed at his ruined Achilles, hollering in pain.

His attacker slithered from underneath the SUV, dusting off the black windbreaker he wore. He straightened up and tidied his long black hair back into place.

"Where are the files?" the man asked, his accent subtle, his stare intense. A severe face squared by a trimmed beard.

"I don't know what you're talking about," Mathieu cried out, hoping someone would hear him.

The man snapped the switchblade knife shut with a flick of his wrist. He dragged Mathieu upright and shoved him into the driver's seat. The man then leapt into the back seat.

"Drive," the man ordered in accented French. His breath smelled of garlic.

Mathieu didn't respond until he heard the steel hammer cocking on the gun.

"W-w-where?" he stammered, the pain blinding his senses.

Again, the man growled. "Drive." Mathieu felt the cold steel press against his neck, a little more firmly this time.

Mathieu did as he was told, shifting the car into gear. He left the parking garage, turning onto the one-way road.

He cursed himself and gritted his teeth in pain. Why didn't he check under the car? He had thought himself paranoid, but his anxiety had just been vindicated.

Driving north on Boulevard Raspail toward the seventh arrondissement with a gun pointed at the back of his head. Mathieu continued to bleed profusely from his left heel.

"Take a left here," the growl commanded.

Mathieu proceeded onto Rue de Grenelle, heading west while staying south of the River Seine. Tucked behind a block of four-story Haussmann buildings, the Eiffel Tower loomed in the distance. His captor's dinner breath filled the car. The man seemed relaxed, bored even, terrifying Mathieu. Adrenaline surged through his own body, compensating for the white-hot pain in his heel.

Mathieu was all for following orders. Then again, following orders had led him into this current dangerous predicament. The man had gone straight to violence. There were no threats or blackmail. A worker bee, Mathieu reasoned. He was either being taken to the queen, or he was about to be dropped from the nest.

The streets were still; no one out for a stroll on the narrow sidewalks or leisurely passing away the night in a windowsill. Streetlamps were scattered every few hundred yards with no definitive spacing; rather, it was as though someone plotted them with indifference. The street his attacker had told him to go down was residential, quiet. Mathieu realized it was a perfect route to take: no witnesses. His attacker was well prepared, but you can't prepare for the unexpected.

But Mathieu wasn't about to lie down and accept his fate. No, he had a job to do. He had to get the flash drive into the authorities' hands. It was his client's dying wish. "*In case of my untimely death under suspicious circumstances, please deliver this to the proper French authorities.*"

Mathieu clenched the steering wheel as the man in the back seat shifted his position and moved his head between the seats, the gun still tucked into Mathieu's neck.

"Pull over on the right and park the car."

Playing along, Mathieu nodded. He didn't know what was going to happen next, but they weren't stopping to chat. To hell with it. Mathieu had a job to do.

He began to slow the car on the narrow street. The Peugeot took up most of the road, and he figured there would be no parking spots on a residential street open—parking spaces were like gold mines in Paris. Once you found one, you dug in.

If Mathieu hadn't been in agonizing pain, he might have smiled at his luck. Ahead was an open spot, not big enough for his car lengthwise but just wide enough so he could pull straight into the spot perpendicular to the street. It was a split-second decision, but Mathieu wasn't going to make another costly mistake.

He punched the accelerator and the man in the back seat was thrown backwards. The V6 engine purred. Mathieu snapped the wheel hard to the right and his front-right fender scraped the bumper of the parked car to his right. He aimed to wedge the car and trap his captor inside, leaving both rear doors pinned on either side by the parked cars. But Mathieu had miscalculated how much sidewalk space he had and smashed into a building. His head bounced off the steering wheel as the airbag deployed.

His attacker grunted in pain from the back. The gun clanged to the floor. Wasting no time, Mathieu grabbed his briefcase off the front seat and leaped from the car, pain pulsing from his bleeding left heel. He fell, hauled himself to his feet and dragged himself down the sidewalk. He didn't dare look back. He was a wounded animal; flight was better than fight. He hurriedly ducked behind the row of parked cars as he scurried down the street.

His sock was utterly soaked from the blood. His shoes squelched with every stumble. He fell to a crawl, and with his briefcase in one hand, attempted his painstaking getaway. Hoping to find the nearest lit building, he'd pound on the door until help arrived. But the street was shockingly desolate. It was as if he were the only person in Paris.

As he crawled, the harsh stone sidewalk wore through his suit fabric. He felt the cool stone on his knees through the ripped material. He turned to look back and suddenly realized the trail of blood he'd been making while dragging his foot—another mistake.

Behind the bumper of a small black Peugeot, he paused. The small hatchback provided cover while Mathieu faintly heard the distant traffic from Boulevard Raspail. Maybe he had scared off his captor, nervous about neighbors or the police showing up on scene. But one thing was for certain: someone wanted the flash drive, and they were willing to kill for it.

Grabbing for his phone from his jacket pocket, he sought to call for help, but the phone's screen was too bright. He cursed and clutched the phone to his person, extinguishing the light. It was only for a second.

He leaned out from behind the car to see how far his attempted escape had got him. The wreckage of his Peugeot was a surprisingly long distance down the row of vehicles. Mathieu turned back down the other way of the quaint Parisian street and saw nothing. Breathing a sigh of relief, believing he would fulfill his duty of handing over the intelligence after all. He slumped against the bumper and smiled. So much for being out of his league, he thought.

Then, from the other side of the car, Mathieu's peripheral vision caught the familiar shape of the gun. A sudden flash from the muzzle was followed by absolute darkness.

2

Paris, France

Stephen Palmer removed his silver-framed glasses to rub his brown eyes. It wasn't often the veteran spy was called into the office in the middle of the night. Besides the trivial lack of sleep, it was of no inconvenience to him. All he left behind in his apartments was a freezer full of peach ice cream, some beer and leftover Chinese takeout. He could sleep when he was dead.

He paced the windowless operations center abuzz with activity and the strong smell of dark roast coffee. The room, Stephen Palmer thought, was not ideal for pacing. The burly fifty-two-year-old had only taken a few steps to his left before he had to turn back on the crusty brown carpet. His tired eyes glanced at the three flat-screen monitors displaying live camera feeds and a map of Paris.

Under the monitors, stationed at a plastic desk, sat a young technician. Kelly Caruso monitored the feeds and police scanners. She wore a purple University of St. Thomas football hoodie and a mask of concentration.

"Didn't know it was casual dress around here now," Palmer quipped.

Kelly glanced at her hoodie. "When I get called into the office at three a.m., I'll wear whatever I'd like." She smirked.

10

"They have a hell of a football team too."

Palmer grunted in amusement. "Isn't St. Thomas the alma mater of that spy novelist? Vince something?"

Kelly Caruso beamed with pride. "Mitch Rapp's the reason I'm in intelligence."

Suddenly, her monitors began beeping with an incoming message feed. The young intelligence analyst put on her headphones. After replaying the clip several times, she carefully navigated the headset around her crimson ponytail. "Police are saying the victim died of a gunshot wound."

Palmer pushed the sleeves of his thin hunter-green sweater up to his elbows. He moved closer to the center monitor, tapping the screen. "What do we know about this neighborhood?"

Kelly flapped her lips, a learned French mannerism for *I have no fucking clue*. "Upper-middle-class neighborhood, quiet."

Palmer sighed and plopped himself into a leather chair at the lone conference table. He had been awoken by several messages from Pierre-Emmanuel Dubois, his French intelligence counterpart. The man said there was an urgent and ongoing situation that required Palmer's immediate supervision. Palmer had trekked from his apartment off the Champs-Élysées, where traffic still trickled at 3 a.m., to the American Embassy. Irritated by what the night might hold, he'd tossed on yesterday's outfit from the floor—a tweed jacket, khakis, and a thin sweater—for his late-night rendezvous.

He grabbed a sip from his preferred form of caffeine, Mountain Dew. He had bottles of the stuff flown in by the pallet as excess cargo on military transports. He was going to need the kick tonight. Closing his eyes for a moment, he once again cursed the sleep that escaped him. His day at the office had officially started at 3 a.m.

He'd been brought onto the joint task force against international financial crimes as part of a deal he'd cut for an innocent American banker. The kid had been implicated in a money-laundering scheme to finance terrorism. The naïve banker had been too distracted trying to appease his client to recognize a fraud and embezzlement scheme until it was too late. Palmer had gotten involved only after the scheme had funded a terror attack.

Claude Renard had gotten into bed with some nasty financial partners and needed an out. The American banker proved to be a convenient scapegoat for Renard, but only for a short time. The nasty partners put two bullets in Renard's head, who left a void to take the fall, thus leaving the banker to bear the charges.

The story, or the highly scripted version, had been splashed across the Parisian papers and the TV news cycle, feasting on the dramatics for readers and ratings. The motive and circumstances of his death a murky soup the media delightedly picked through.

At first, Palmer had been reluctant to help the naïve banker. His time in Paris was coming to an end. Still, he wanted to leave the preeminent post of his shadowy diplomatic career with a clear heart. Thus, he called in some favors to secure clemency while ensuring the United States suffered no embarrassment in a time when such plots promoting nationalism would have pushed the current administration over the edge.

Palmer struck a deal to keep the American's involvement undisclosed. Instead of jail time, the banker was banished to house arrest on an island on the Atlantic side of the

French coast, under close French protection, until the story went away. In turn, the French received access to American intelligence regarding Europe. Palmer filled in his French counterpart, Pierre-Emmanuel Dubois, with debriefings lasting over several months. They even agreed to create a task force together to hunt common enemies committing financial crime.

Palmer knew working with partners wasn't simple, but nevertheless, he was thrilled to have protected the innocent American. The young man reminded him of an asset he'd tragically lost years earlier. He had found redemption in the American, and the newly formed task force meant Palmer would stay in Paris. He had learned in his life of espionage that if fate ever gifts you a second chance, you snatch it and hold on for dear life.

Palmer glanced at the center monitor and watched a little red dot blink on a map of Paris. The monitor on the right showed night-vision footage from a local Parisian cop's body camera at the crime scene. There was no audio, but the officer faced down the street, allowing Palmer to see a small white tent set-up and police cars blocking the road in both directions.

He took his glasses off and scratched at his thick salt-and-pepper beard.

His phone began to vibrate and dance across the smooth, veneered table. He answered and started pacing again.

"We have a situation." Pierre-Emmanuel's practiced English was instantly recognizable to Palmer.

"I'm listening." Palmer drained the last of his Mountain Dew.

"We had a lead on intelligence from an attorney. He'd shopped it all around town, calling friends in the police force, searching for the right person. I'd heard through the grape-vine he'd been seeking a rendezvous, so I set the meeting for tonight, but our source never showed. We've had the bar and hotel under surveillance all day. No sign of him."

Pierre-Emmanuel paused for a beat to allow Palmer to jump in, but he pressed on when no questions were raised. "Two hours after the meeting was due, we packed up shop. As I was heading home, I heard of a murder in the seventh. I checked with police contacts and found out the victim was our man."

"So?" Palmer asked the night's loss of sleep, providing little patience.

Pierre-Emmanuel sighed as if unimpressed with his American colleague's bluntness. "The source is dead."

Palmer leaned back in the chair, the leather squeaking. "Why didn't you meet earlier?"

"I didn't know if he was credible. I can't chase down every tip—there are too many to count."

"So now we will never know what the intel was?"

Pierre-Emmanuel sighed. Palmer heard the clicks of his colleague's shoes pacing near the crime scene. "No, our source was quite clever. While we didn't find a briefcase in the street, the medical examiner did find a small flash drive taped under his forearm."

Palmer exhaled in relief.

"We still need deeper analysis, but on the flash drive, I've watched a video of the French tycoon Claude Renard. He alleges serious accusations while providing numerous financial statements, and samples of material associated legitimizing his claims. Which leads us back to the frontline of this fight. We will need more help." Pierre-Emmanuel let the statement float in the air for a moment. "I was thinking an agent with a history with Renard could be particularly valuable."

Palmer found himself nodding. "Your agent would be perfect. Who better to work on this than the asset closest to him before Renard died? I hear she's been training the American too. If there's anyone who's suited for this, it's the two of them."

Pierre-Emmanuel chuckled. "I'm surprised you agree."

Palmer let the comment slide. "Well, we'd have to find them first."

The French intelligence officer scoffed. "They will be easy to find because they're right where we left them."

Palmer countered. "We don't even know if they'll say yes."

His French counterpart's voice dropped an octave. "We won't give them a choice."

3

The sun was blistering. Only the ocean breeze provided relief, cooling the beads of sweat on Paul Hart's neck. He'd lost track of time and the shade to hide from watchful eyes.

Hart felt someone following him, staring daggers into his back, but he knew he couldn't shake them. Not yet. Espionage, he'd learned, was a delicate dance; while you might know you are being tailed, you must pretend to be none the wiser. Just like two people flirting across a dance floor; both too proud to be caught looking, both unwilling to make the first move.

Around him, beachgoers lugged plastic buckets and voluminous tote bags, all the while hiding under straw fedoras and behind chic sunglasses. The place he had come to know the past several months, Noirmoutier, suddenly felt like another world, full of perils, strangers, and perhaps most regrettably, fatigue. He was a long way from his former life as a banker.

Hart straightened up off the metal railing where he had been observing Bois de la Chaise's beach and strolled a short distance to a crowded café terrace. He pretended to browse the menu of langoustine, *moules-frites*, and grilled shrimp, but Hart couldn't stop. He had to keep moving.

Behind his Wayfarer sunglasses, his ice-blue eyes darted

left and right, racking his brain for anyone who looked familiar or out of place. He proceeded away from the café and the beach toward the narrow road covered by the thick overhanging branches of high trees.

At a leisurely pace, he traveled down the center of the road. This served two purposes. The first being if the individual or individuals following him were foolish enough to walk directly down the road behind him, they might as well hold up a sign. But the second reason, and the one Hart was counting on, was he would seem aloof.

Cross streets cut across the main road every fifty meters. They were neglected, evident by the vines and foliage spilling onto the roadway from the yards of grand houses, passed from one vacationing generation to the next.

Hart chose the second street to make his move. He'd familiarized himself with the island the way any newcomer should, by walking. His reconnaissance had identified the particular street as well hidden from the main road—the perfect place to disappear. He slid past a parked boxy Volkswagen van with tinted windows. He lengthened his stride, making it from the middle of the narrow road and across the sidewalk in a few steps. Once on the cross street, and out of the vision from anyone following him from behind, he pressed himself against an exterior brick wall overrun by thick vines spilling from the property.

He waited a moment, listening only to the distant rev of a Vespa and the rustling of tree branches in the wind. Hart steadied his breathing—one, two, one, two—in through his nose, holding for a count, and out of his mouth. His heart pounded, and his fists clenched.

The steps he heard were careful, only the loose gravel giving away their imminent approach. Hart pushed himself further into the vines, the dense foliage prodding at his back.

His pursuer rounded the corner, the thick foliage jutting out and causing them to slow. Pouncing from the vines, he bear-hugged his shadow from behind. The woman's skin was soft and moistened from the heat, her hair in his face was coarse, the blonde ponytail clouding his vision. Briefly, Hart was terrified he had grabbed an unknowing beachgoer on their way home. But when the woman shifted in his clutch, raised her right foot, stomping down, he knew he'd caught his watcher. He pivoted his foot just in time, but she countered, landing an elbow across his face, rattling his teeth. He tightened hold so she could no longer spin.

Hart then shifted his weight backward, lifting his attacker clear off the ground. He squinted as the woman raised her hands, repeatedly drilling him on top of the head. He threw his weight forward, spinning her to the ground. Hart rolled on top of her, pinning her arms under his legs. Just like she'd taught him.

Her wig came loose and with it the sunglasses she wore. Once her disguise was unveiled, Clara Nouvelle smiled at him.

"Seems you've been paying attention to my training after all."

Hart rolled off and helped Clara to her feet.

"We said the head and face were off-limits? What happened to those rules?"

Clara shrugged her hands on her hips. She wore jean shorts that displayed her sun-kissed legs and a grin which told Hart she enjoyed the roughhousing. She picked a few twigs from her loose-fitting dusky-rose-colored T-shirt. Her espresso hair fell to her shoulder, and her high cheekbones accented sea-green eyes.

"I improvised, which is what you will have to do constantly in the field."

Hart laughed. "No, admit it, you were mad I got the jump on you." He attempted to take her hand. "Seems like the apprentice has become the master."

Clara scoffed, pulling away from his grip. "There are no rules in the real world." She began to walk back toward the beach. "When did you first notice me?"

Hart smirked. "Might have been when you were behind me in town when I went to the boulangerie. Or maybe when you were on the café terrace, where I believe you ordered an Aperol Spritz, which I might add sounds like an excellent idea."

"*Merde.* You played it off well. I thought you hadn't noticed me at all."

Hart bowed playfully as they made their way back along the tree-lined road.

They had spent months on the island, Clara training him in the techniques of hand-to-hand combat, surveillance detection routes, and shooting. She had become his teacher, lover, and entire purpose.

However, recently Hart had begun to question the current state of his life. The further away he moved, mentally and physically, from his previous life, the one where his ignorance led him into disaster, the more he pondered it. What could he have done differently?

The shift from a promising career in finance, his former life in New York, and the ideals of the world he held were all shattered by others' ill deeds. Currently, he was sentenced to a life of certain luxury—safety, food, beautiful scenery, the company of a smart and beautiful lady—but the allure of his past life haunted him. Now, every day, danger lurked.

Days like these were Hart's life lately. Wake up early to practice a fighting method, analyze a case study in tradecraft, lunch, then an hour-long swim off the beach of Luzeronde in the frigid Atlantic waters. He recalled the challenge Clara had given him at the market. Twenty minutes to acquire a phone number of a beautiful woman behind the *boulangerie* counter, which had at least an impatient twelve-person line at all hours of the day. Nothing got in between the French and their baguettes. But Hart couldn't believe he'd done it, earning only a wry smile from Clara. After these lessons in tradecraft, they'd return together to the secluded bungalow hidden behind a sand dune on the island's northern beach.

Clara's phone rang.

"*Allo?*" She glanced sideways at Hart while answering, "*Oui.*" She spun away as gracefully as a ballerina, nodding along in conversation until she ended the call abruptly.

"Who called?" Hart asked, unsettled by Clara's suddenly sharp demeanor.

Clara looked past Hart toward the street. "Not here." She grabbed his hand and started walking, nearly dragging him away from the café.

"What about the Aperol Spritz? I think I earned it." He shrugged.

"We have to report back to the house and pack," she said over her shoulder, rushing on.

"Why? What's happened?"

Her green eyes flashed in annoyance, then softened. "Seems you've just passed your training course. And to celebrate, you'll get your reward at home."

Hart grinned and took off after Clara.

4

Paris, France

Pierre-Emmanuel Dubois exited the Métro station on Avenue de la Republique and checked his Piaget Polo. He was running ten minutes early for his meeting. The extra time he'd planned for the journey wasn't needed on account of the Paris Métro running on time—a rare occurrence. But as man always with a plan, he followed his accordingly.

The French intelligence officer climbed the staircase on Père Lachaise Cemetery's side entrance in the eleventh arrondissement. He was thankful for the old moss-covered stone walls providing cover from a brisk morning wind.

The location for the meeting wasn't his idea and not particularly a sound one either. There were thousands of headstones on the 110-acre plot of land to hide among, and the hush hanging over the somber grounds gave flight to even the faintest voices. But when a prominent senator in France and a fellow alumnus from Saint Cyr Military Academy, requested they get together immediately, Pierre-Emmanuel acquiesced. After all, as a government servant, he reminded himself, you always worked for someone.

Strolling over the cobblestone walkways, the leather soles of his brown suede derbies fought for grip on the weathered ground. The headstones and statues that adorned many of the burials came in various shapes and sizes; he imagined they were representative of the people buried beneath them. Some extravagant, others humble and unassuming. But what caught his eye wasn't the décor, but rather the names of those departed. The lives who had come and gone before him, the secrets he would never know, their stories unknown to him.

Pierre-Emmanuel found his mark under a chestnut tree on a small, crooked path winding up the hillside of the cemetery. The man was facing away, the collar on his khaki Burberry trench coat flipped up, revealing the iconic tartan pattern. His black oxfords expertly polished, and he spun on them when he heard Pierre-Emmanuel approach.

In his late thirties, Charles LeBrun still possessed the excitable energy of a man climbing the political ladder. Each day brought for him an opportunity to step on someone to chase his ambitions.

"*Bonjour,* Charles, to what do I owe this pleasure?" Pierre-Emmanuel stuck out a hand, but the senator had already turned back around to face the grave of Honoré de Balzac, the famous French writer.

The young senator remained quiet, then motioned with his head for Pierre-Emmanuel to follow. They made their way up the incline, further into the cemetery.

"A little bird from La Piscine told me you came across some intelligence yesterday evening."

Pierre-Emmanuel tried to hide his surprise. The senator had referenced the DGSE offices by its nickname, a reference to the large aquatic center on the same Parisian block. Evidently, word traveled fast.

The senator continued. "It is my understanding there was a mention of Iran from the recently deceased?"

Pierre-Emmanuel pursed his lips. "Not here." He paused

to scan the area to ensure no one had overheard. "You understand I cannot confirm anything."

Charles LeBrun's brown eyes narrowed with anger. He steadied himself by adjusting his red silk tie.

"What *you* must understand is how delicate this is. Iran is a partner with whom we want to work with, not agitate."

Pierre-Emmanuel seemed to consider this momentarily. "Again, I can't confirm what intelligence we found, but I can say it requires a thorough investigation."

"Ah…" The senator stopped and squared up to the taller intelligence officer. "But you are mistaken. It requires just the opposite. We cannot risk offending a country we are working so hard to build trust with again. If the Iran nuclear deal negotiations collapse because of intelligence we stumbled upon from a former criminal himself, how would that look? Renard was a con man, laundering money across Europe— his word or his attorney's doesn't mean shit to me."

"What do you wish, Senator? I've already told you. I cannot comment."

LeBrun scoffed and pulled a silver cigarette case from his pocket. Forgoing an offer to Pierre-Emmanuel, he lit one hastily. "This investigation is over before it began. If someone is going to bring Iran further down the international order, it'll be thanks to me. By diplomacy and negotiations, not some dead fraudster and his final good deed. Got it?"

"You want me to ignore this credible intelligence?"

LeBrun smirked. "Happiness requires ignorance."

"Actually, happiness requires courage and work, at least that is what Balzac wrote."

LeBrun seethed. "Drop the investigation, or you'll find yourself working desk security at the education administration for the rest of your career. Don't interfere with Iran or involve the Americans. It's my job. I control them, not you."

"We can't ignore this information. It could be—"

LeBrun glared at Pierre-Emmanuel and threw his cigarette onto the stone pathway and stomped it out.

"And give me the flash drive. I know you have it. Don't make me tell the press about your disastrous mission to take down Renard. This entire fiasco can be pinned on your failures."

The French intelligence officer felt his shoulders sag. LeBrun wasn't wrong; Pierre-Emmanuel had overseen the operation to take down Renard, which ended as poorly as his failure to secure the intelligence from the now-deceased attorney. Without another word, he handed over the flash drive.

"Thanks, old friend. Don't fret, I will have every business from the intel sanctioned and their assets frozen. Great catching up." LeBrun sauntered in victory for the exit.

But Pierre-Emmanuel would be damned if he was going to jeopardize the safety of his country. His team would remedy his failures. He'd see to it. He may have lost this battle, but he already had a plan to win the war, and thus he would follow it accordingly.

5

Noirmoutier, France

After sharing a shower to wash off the day's activities and celebrate Hart passing Clara's training, she'd told Hart to pack up all his things. Packing didn't take long as he only had a few clothes and toiletries. Clara, however, had been racing around the rooms, stuffing what she could into her lone duffel bag. Watching her, he'd felt so uneasy that he asked her if they were in danger, but she remained tight-lipped until the moment a dark Peugeot SUV pulled up into the driveway.

After months languishing in the drafty cottage by the sea, the goodbye was unceremonious. Hart felt a particular attachment to the house; it had given him the safety and space to embrace the love of a wonderful woman at his most vulnerable. So, it felt odd to depart as if it were just a hotel on some endless journey. Would he return? He had no idea. He didn't even know why they were leaving. Hart took one last look at the ocean through the kitchen window and said a silent farewell to the house and the memories it protected. He went through the creaky front door, its wooden frame made soft from years of fresh sea air, which said its own goodbye with a low groan as Hart closed it behind him.

Climbing into the back of the car, Clara solemnly nodded

at the men sitting in the front. Hart recognized both agents as Clara's colleagues from DGSE. Climbing in after her, Hart recalled the memories of the two men who had been his protection detail a few months prior. Antoine Gamot, the more senior of the pair, remained unchanged since their last encounter. The man's sharp features, crooked nose, bald head, and watchful eyes were always intimidating. But Hart knew the man and how much he cared for his job. There was a flash of disinterest from him as Hart gave a meek hello from behind the wheel. The doors slammed shut and Antoine slowly turned the SUV around the white crushed-gravel driveway. The coarse rock crunched under the car's weight before he punched the accelerator, sending the stones flying.

Lucas Locatelli, the tanned agent with frizzy brown hair, turned around in the passenger seat and held out a manila envelope for Clara. "These are your travel documents and itinerary. You must stay on schedule." He held her gaze for a moment, allowing for questions before breaking into a wide grin.

"It's good to see you both." Lucas smiled and tapped Antoine on the arm. "Right, boss?"

Antoine managed a noise somewhere between a stifled laugh and a painful grunt.

"Don't mind him—new father. He hasn't been sleeping much, and they asked him to come off paternity leave for you—special circumstances— he's not in the best mood." Lucas smiled, his round face beaming until a stern stare from Antoine.

"Thank you both for coming," Clara said as she began to open the envelope.

Hart eyed it, which might have caused Clara to pause, leaving it unopened for a few moments longer.

"Care to tell me what is going on?" He reached over to touch her hand.

She glanced sideways at him. "We've been recalled to Paris for an assignment." She cupped his hand in both of hers.

Hart leaned back in the plush leather seat. "Getting back to work will be good for you."

She turned her attention back to the passing countryside. The past few months had been hard for Clara. Hart had seen it firsthand, fighting alongside her, the raging battles of anxiety and stress. She struggled with the trauma of her career as an undercover agent collapsing and, most brutally of all, losing her mentor and boss in the process. Clara was strong and resilient, not someone seeking people's pity, but Hart knew she was anguished just as acutely as someone far weaker.

Not to mention the physical pain caused by a gunshot wound after blunt force trauma from a car chase, leaving her with a 40 percent chance of survival. To the disbelief of medical staff, she'd survived and traveled to find Hart during his home arrest on Noirmoutier until he was cleared of his fraud charges. She'd never left his side since. They'd had a few incredible months, but as time passed, they became all too aware of the unchartered waters they swam in. And ambiguity had been okay until it wasn't.

"You want me to come with you to Paris, right?" Hart shifted in his seat, tugging at his seatbelt.

"It wasn't an option." A hint of reluctance flashed across her green eyes. "But you're ready."

"For?" he asked, eager to understand the plans.

"Do you trust me, Paul?"

"Infinitely."

Clara smiled and leaned across the back seat.

"Tres bien." She kissed him full on the lips. Hart caught sight of Antoine watching in the rearview mirror.

The drive to Nantes would take just over an hour and then a two-hour TGV ride to Paris. Hart didn't mind tagging along with Clara, because he didn't much like the thought of being left behind. But in Paris, he could keep busy wandering through the narrow streets of Le Marais, window-shopping and perhaps actually spending his newfound fortune. Another silver lining of the torrid affair had brought Clara and him together. Sure, it had cost him his job, but the generous severance package he'd received, thanks to Stephen Palmer, who he owed many thanks, meant working for a living wasn't a concern for the foreseeable future. But Paris could be dangerous for a man with too much time and money on his hands. Instead, Hart mentally planned some sightseeing, maybe even a tour of Les Invalides. Tourism seemed like a good idea until he remembered what happened the last time he was under the view of the golden dome.

Hart took a deep breath to steady his nerve and pushed the past from his mind.

It was as if leaving the island had torn away his armor, the golden prison of relaxation, and the safety of their seclusion was left in the cottage they had shared.

He turned to find Clara watching him.

"What are you thinking so intently about?"

Hart changed his face into a crooked smile. "Just what I'm going to eat in Paris while you're working."

"Oh? You think you'll be on vacation?" She frowned.

Hart gave a small laugh. "I guess not then. But I could go for a cheeseburger."

Clara rolled her eyes. *"Ohlala,* the best food in the world, but you want a burger."

Lucas spun around in the front seat. "That does sound good, actually."

Hart grinned at his small victory, playfully prodding Clara's arm.

"We have a busy schedule in Paris. I'm afraid your burger will have to wait. It's straight to the safe house from the train station and then to the meeting."

"It's okay. I can find something while you're working."

Clara drummed her fingers on the windowsill. "No, Paul, you're coming with me. Time to put your training to the test."

6

There were three taps against the thick glass door. The man inside the office eagerly awaited what was to come.

"Sir, your appointment is here," said his middle-aged assistant. Her jet black hair was pulled back tightly, highlighting her green eyes under her thick-framed glasses.

Luke Darlington stood and buttoned his suit coat. Appearances are everything.

He was well under six feet but compensated for his lack of height with vigorous gym sessions mainly confined to the bench press. He still had a strong jawline for being in his late fifties, emboldened by unsettling blue eyes, which could turn to ice in certain moods, and snow-white hair. He'd lived a stressful life, so he forgave his hair for shifting from a refined gray to snow-white by his early forties. The look grew on him, and when admiring himself in the mirror, he often thought of himself as a snowy owl. Silent but ever watchful above the madness, until the moment he'd swoop and strike.

"Lovely, send him in." Darlington checked his red silk tie knot carefully, the Double Windsor, meticulously crafted each morning. He glanced out the window at the Thames; the muddy water was choppy with small white caps visible. He silently cursed the omen and hoped it didn't accurately predict his meeting.

"Luke, how are you?" A tall man with a deep tan that he somehow kept year-round despite living in London, entered the office. Darlington couldn't help but stare at the man's high cheekbones, trimmed beard and deep-set brown eyes. He carried himself with an air of confidence, perfected by years of flirty smiles and undressing eyes. He wore a black suit and white shirt without a tie.

Darlington gave the man a firm handshake and a soft smile. His assistant closed the door. Once the men were in complete privacy, Darlington spoke.

"Diego, mind telling me what the fuck happened in Paris?"

Diego Ramos had grown accustomed to his boss's lack of care for small talk. He'd worked for the man nearly his entire professional life. "I took care of the problem." He smiled and spread his hands. No worries.

Darlington winced at his young protégé's naïvety. It was true he did his job well, but hell, Darlington thought, he should do it well with what he was paid.

"I'm relieved to see you're unperturbed." Darlington's owl-like eyes narrowed. "But you were ordered to *not* kill him. Regardless of the circumstances. Your recklessness is why we will never know what he knew."

Diego ran one of his massive hands through his long jet-black hair, brushing it back behind his head. "There is nothing to be worried about. The threat was dealt with."

Darlington craned his head toward the river. The fatigue he'd been acutely feeling for the past several months had been festering for years. He lived a life of lies and deadly truths. The desire every morning to grab his leather Louis Vuitton emergency bag, stuffed with cash and passports, from under his plush king-sized bed and escape never ceased. It was a precaution he took when another critical player in the organization, Claude Renard, was found dead in a Parisian hotel. It was not a fate Darlington wanted to share.

"Diego, as you know, things are at a precarious point. I need absolute certainty the threat has been sufficiently dealt with. Nothing less."

Diego rolled his eyes.

"It won't. I didn't find anything in the lawyer's briefcase, so I threw it in the Seine." Diego shrugged. "The authorities never recovered any documents as far as I know. My Police Nationale contact said they're not investigating further because they have ruled the murder a botched robbery. *Todo bien.*"

Darlington set his elbows on his glass desk. He fought the urge to bounce his legs anxiously as he knew Diego could see them. Appearances are everything. "No, not *todo bien.* Just because your contact at the police says they are not investigating doesn't mean that the lawyer didn't possess the intelligence?"

Diego grunted and rearranged himself to get more comfortable. The leather chair was rigid, its back nearly at a right angle for any visiting guest—specially designed by Darlington.

"Yes, exactly." Diego offered a smile.

The smile was not returned, and the two men sat in the glass office in silence. A boat on the river let off a blast from its horn, a small picture frame on Darlington's desk rattled.

"I expect you to go back to Paris and ensure your lapse in judgment didn't put our organization at risk. Find out for certain if anything was communicated from the attorney. I'm not expecting you to go for some croque monsieur and burgundy. I want answers."

"The only thing I ate last time was garlicky *escargot*. Quite terrible. I'd rather not go back." Diego stood.

"It's an order. You have obligations to this organization and people you cannot afford to disappoint." Darlington ground his teeth. His ass was on the line just as much, if not more than, Diego's.

"You know, on second thought"—Diego straightened his suit jacket and cleared his throat, seemingly trying on a serious tone for the sake of his boss—"I'll go back to Paris to confirm the case is closed. I'm sure there's nothing but if there is an investigation, I'll intervene. Plus, there's always more fun to be had in Paris."

Darlington leaned back in his chair and nodded in approval. "You're almost as smart as you dress."

Diego waited for a moment before mumbling a goodbye and left the office. The glass door slammed shut. Darlington watched the man make his way through the foyer to the elevators, all the while, clocking his assistant's eyes closely following Diego's ass.

Darlington shook his head. Diego was an expensive but invaluable security consultant. Years in Interpol and a brief stint in the Spanish Grupo de Operciones Especiales, the Spanish equivalent of the British SAS, left him with a specific skill set. Darlington expected his man to get results, executed with precision, or face the consequences. But, at the end of the day, Darlington was pleased to have a blunt instrument like Diego.

But then again, that was precisely how he'd found himself in the predicament of second-guessing his life choices. He'd seen what happened to Renard, how things could spiral out of hand after someone inserts themselves into your life and demands the world and gives little room for maneuvering.

What concerned him was something he couldn't share with Diego. Darlington had made a mistake. One self-indulgent luxury he didn't need. But when had that stopped him before? He consoled himself with the notion, everyone does it—just a little cut of the action on the side, without company knowledge. He'd opened a small holding company, from which he used a subsidiary to buy shares in a few companies, piggybacking off intelligence he'd learned from the organization. His accounts were with the Cayman National Bank because they'd protect his anonymity with the ferocity of wolves protecting their pack. He never used the funds, but they were hidden away for the one day he would grab that Louis Vuitton bag and make for the Caribbean's horizon.

He rose from his desk and looked out over the river once more. The water, like all worries, would eventually flow by and pass with time. Perhaps he wouldn't have to run. It all depended on whether Diego really took care of the mess in Paris. If so, Darlington's involvement would be washed away forever.

7

Paris, France

The skies opened with heavy rain before dawn, pelting the sleepy city awake. Commuters hid in the Métro, under an umbrella, or in the comfort of the city's cafés. The streets remained quiet until early afternoon. when the storm passed. Just after lunchtime, the sun, rising high in the Parisian sky, burned off the dark clouds holding the threat of more rain.

Hart's favorite spot in Paris, Palais Royal, was just how he remembered it. Enclosed by iron-clad fences with golden tipped arrows and the wide buildings surrounded the grand courtyard. He and Clara entered the expansive garden from the south, passing underneath the canopy of two rows of lime trees.

Clara pointed towards a fountain surrounded by a scattering of green metal chairs. "Stay there. I have a meeting at the northwest corner of the courtyard. But you know the game now, keep an eye out." She squeezed Hart's hand.

"So now it's me keeping an eye on you?" He smirked.

She spun away, her long cream-colored raincoat tied at the waist, revealing tapered jeans down to a pair of crisp white Veja sneakers. Hart watched her leave for a moment, then found a chair dry enough for his liking.

He tried to observe the peaceful garden, but his mind had

other ideas. It raced with questions. He could have stayed at the DGSE safe house in Paris, but he was glad to be with her out in the field, entrusted with keeping an eye out. But for what, or who, he didn't know.

Hart checked his Baltic Aquascaphe watch, a gift from Clara, an inscription on the back read, *Time is a gift*, and the sunray blue dial read half past noon. Palais Royale grew busier by the minute with workers eating *jambon* sandwiches around the fountain, chatting animatedly or hunched over their phone. Hart tried to relish the scenery. Instead of potential threats, he only saw lovers tangled together on the green benches and laughing while taking selfies. He sighed and closed his eyes.

It was only after a moment of calm, he felt a hand on his shoulder.

Clara hadn't wanted to leave Hart at the fountain, but it was an order. While with Hart in Noirmoutier, there always was the nagging question when her old life would return to break their spell. She'd never left her former job, but operating solo on an island training your lover in counterespionage wasn't exactly what she called work. But being back in Paris, to the memories of her long undercover role with Renard and subsequent chaos, put her squarely back in her old life. She just hoped there would be enough room for Hart.

She caught Pierre-Emmanuel's hawkish eyes, then his lanky silhouette. He leaned against a pillar in front of Le Grand Véfour, checking the walkway corridors.

"Nice to see you." Pierre-Emmanuel saw Clara and pushed off the wall.

Clara smiled half-heartedly. "Why are we meeting here?"

"Ah." He folded his arms and drummed his long fingers

against his forearm. "I have your next assignment, but it requires discretion."

A ping of unease sounded inside Clara. "What's the job?"

"It seems your old friend Claude Renard had an ace up his sleeve. Left us a gift of sorts." Pierre-Emmanuel peered past Clara's shoulder into the garden.

"What does that mean?" Clara asked. While closure from her former undercover life was appealing, sometimes the past was best left alone.

He reached into his coat and withdrew a phone and headphones. Handing them to Clara, he told her to watch. As she did so, she saw Pierre-Emmanuel change into protection mode, scanning the surrounding area while his agent focused on the screen.

Clara instantly recognized the groomed features of her former boss. The same man she saw murdered in cold blood. The video was taken in his office. The man's usually bright eyes were nearly colorless and fatigued.

"Bonjour. I'm Claude Renard, the CEO of Renard Industries, but more importantly, I am a patriot. In the case of my untimely death, I find it necessary to unveil a threat I worked hard to sabotage at every turn. But now, evidently without me around, I must leave all the information I have to the proper authorities. Iran is trying to sell their nuclear program plans and export their power like never before, expanding globally to unknown countries. I do not know much else besides the financial documents I have procured and a sample of the plans left on this USB. It is my hope, perhaps my dying hope, that Iran selling nuclear weapons plans will never be the case. Bonne chance."

Clara's heart pounded. To hear the man's voice again was unsettling, like talking to a ghost. Another part of her was relieved though; she'd worked so closely with him for years, she couldn't believe he was purely evil. In death, he proved her right. The intelligence was terrifying. Renard realized it needed to be shared. Nuclear weapon plans? It needed to be stopped at all costs.

Her boss shifted his gaze back towards her. "There are some people worried that pulling on this loose thread could unravel something much larger. There's an unwillingness to disrupt the status quo, the ongoing negotiations. I made a copy of this video, knowing the original flash drive would be taken from us by bureaucracy." He stopped and made sure no one walking by was listening. "Which is why I want you to investigate this, off the books."

Clara felt she was in a dream. Closure seemed comforting, but going back to the dangerous life she once knew with something, or more accurately someone, to lose, was daunting. The alternative, however, was allowing for the most perilous weaponry to profoundly shake the world order the most since the height of Cold War.

"Why me?"

Pierre-Emmanuel scoffed. "You knew Renard. I know you believed in him—now, you can prove it. And technically, you're still on leave in Noirmoutier. Which makes you an asset for me because you aren't on the DGSE's books. I don't know who we can trust in the government. I've already been threatened by an old friend to shut this down. *Alors*, you make perfect sense."

"Is this intelligence even legitimate? And what if I don't accept the assignment?" She let the question linger.

He drummed his fingers on his chin before answering. "First of all, we are to assume it's legitimate. If you do not want to investigate this, fine. But I'm afraid your current arrangement would no longer work."

"Excuse me?"

"You know, the one where your boyfriend is free and not in jail." He paused. "But I think you'd be wise to get rid of him anyways at your next opportunity."

Clara couldn't believe it. An off-the-book assignment? Get rid of Hart? "Why do I have to get rid of him?"

"As long as he is around, so are the Americans. No one likes having another chef in the kitchen. Our cooperation and friendship has run its course." He sighed. "Just use your best discretion and report directly back to me on what you find."

"Does the request to lose the Americans have anything to do with those higher powers who have squashed your investigation, or is it just from you?" Clara narrowed her eyes. When Pierre-Emmanuel remained silent, she pressed on. "I need Paul. His knowledge of financial insights is unparalleled, especially involving Renard. He works the case, or I quit."

The French intelligence officer smiled and looked over Clara's shoulder into the garden.

"You know, I've always thought of you as a daughter. Or at least one I'd have liked to have had. You're determined and resourceful. I trust you, so I'll ask you one time only, and you better be thoughtful before you respond. Can you trust Paul Hart with your life?"

"Yes, with my life."

Pierre-Emmanuel nodded. "You might very well have to."

He placed his hand on Clara's shoulder. "Please consider dropping him. Don't make me regret my soft spot for you."

Then, the intelligence officer pulled a thin manila envelope from his jacket and handed it to Clara. "This is some of the information Renard left. I pulled together what I could before this operation was shut down. It should be enough to point you in the right direction. There also are several credit cards for your operational costs. And remember, report everything directly, and only to me."

Clara grabbed the envelope and, without another word, went to find Hart.

Hart had his eyes closed when he felt a hand clamp down on his shoulder. His heart nearly jumped out of his chest before recognizing Stephen Palmer, the United States Embassy delegate who Hart knew was really CIA. He hadn't seen the man since he visited him in Noirmoutier months earlier.

"How are you holding up?" Palmer smiled, his dark silver beard bunching on his face. He plopped down on a chair next to Hart and pulled out a bottle of Mountain Dew and a sandwich.

"What are you doing here?" Hart asked, the surprise poorly concealed on his face.

"Well, your old friend Pierre-Emmanuel is meeting with Clara, so I figured I'd keep you company." He took a large bite from his sandwich and washed it down with a gulp of Mountain Dew.

Hart did little to hide his confusion. There seemed more to the story than Clara let on, and with Palmer there, it was a certainty.

"Do you ever miss your old life?" Palmer asked, taking another large bite.

"I don't think about it. Just makes me mad."

"Mad?" Palmer continued to chew and considered this for a moment. "But you don't miss it?"

Palmer crumbled the paper from the sandwich he'd inhaled and sat forward in his chair.

"Yes, mad because I wasn't given a choice. Other people

took my life away from me. And maybe sometimes I do miss it."

Palmer grunted. "You want payback? Feel you've been left with unfinished business?"

"I wouldn't say that. Just doesn't seem balanced, that's all."

"Well, I'd say when you talk to Clara about your new assignment, you might just have an opportunity to rectify your perceived injustices." Palmer smiled, then wiped at his beard to rid himself of leftover crumbs.

Hart realized he'd been death-gripping the chair. He hadn't given much thought to his past. He was focused on the present calm with Clara, but he sensed that might be coming to an end. "What's the job?"

"There are bigger things at play from Claude Renard."

Hearing the name Hart had tried to forget sent a jolt of energy through him.

Palmer continued. "Renard left us intelligence. A video on a flash drive I haven't been able to see. But hopefully, with it, we can flush out what's really going on." Palmer paused. "But I'm sure Clara will fill you in on everything. Why wouldn't she?"

Hart didn't know what game Palmer was playing, but he wasn't going to let it slide. "What the hell do you mean?"

Palmer held his hands up in defense. "Oftentimes, the best relationships have the biggest secrets."

"Sounds like you've had some pretty messed up relationships."

Palmer grinned and smacked Hart on the knee. "You take care and contact me here if need be." He slipped Hart a thick business card with a number on it. "Call the number and hang up. I will track you down from there. Keep Clara close, and you two find these bastards so you can get whatever semblance of a life you've had back."

Palmer stood and began to walk away but stopped. "One more thing. Since you'll be working with Clara on this project, we can't have you running around like a cowboy. You work on my team now. Welcome to the United States Government, Paul."

"I work for you now?" Hart stood, a mix of anger and confusion clouding his mind.

"Yes, that's what I said."

"I didn't apply for anything. This is preposterous."

Palmer laughed, then sadly shook his head. "Paul, you're going to need to get rid of this naïvety. We're the United States Government—we arranged your deal to go free without consequence from the Renard affair, but paperwork can easily be misplaced."

Hart felt his cheeks flush with the threat.

"What if I simply don't want to?"

"Like I said, paperwork can easily get lost. I'd hate to have you caught up in an international investigation where your criminal record prevents you from returning to the United States. Not to mention, we'd probably have to freeze your bank accounts in the meantime." He patted Hart on the shoulder. "Cheer up, you might learn a thing or two."

"So, work for you, or else lose my protection, my money, and right to go back home?"

Palmer batted away Hart's summary with his hand. "You catch on quick, but you should focus on the honor of protecting the free world." He winked and spun around, his raincoat tails drifting through the throngs of people, before disappearing under the thick lime trees.

8

It felt strange to be back in Paris so soon. Diego had taken the two-and-half-hour Eurostar from London St. Pancras to Gare du Nord and walked south through the tenth arrondissement. His hotel was about a twenty-minute walk, but he didn't mind. He carried a leather weekend bag and enjoy the pleasure of flirting with Parisian women on the sidewalks.

During his most recent trip to Paris, on the other side of the Seine, Diego's stay had ended with a gunshot and a disappointed employer. He momentarily forgot his reason for returning as he eyed a pair of women with heavy black boots and tight leggings that reached up to their midsections. They wore cropped jean jackets, highlighting their shapely behinds. Diego admired them as they sauntered by. Perhaps it wasn't so bad being back after all. And while he didn't have friends in the Paris police, like he'd lied to Darlington about, he had other resources to call on.

In fact, he had texted her on the train ride down from London.

Magali Martin was a well-sourced reporter for *Le Figaro*. He'd met her months prior, on a steamy evening in Barcelona. They'd both had been with groups of friends, lost amongst the DJ sets and strobe lights of Playa de la Barceloneta. Diego with former special operations buddies, Magali with a bachelorette group. He had lured her into the shadowy corners of a beachside bar with talk of his passion for windsurfing, which he did not do. He could tell she knew he was lying but had let him anyway. Away from the watchful eyes of both their groups, they danced. She had raven-colored hair, and her olive skin darkened thanks to a week lying on the beach. Diego noticed she did not have a bikini tan from her loose-fitting silk top. He imagined her completely exposed under the sun, anxious to know if he was right. She had full lips to which she'd applied a shade of dark red. Her brown eyes with drops of honey gold had drawn him in. She'd spoken Spanish fluently, and it wasn't until the morning after he learned she was French and lived in Paris, working as an investigative journalist.

Memories of their night together made Diego smile as he passed a bustling *fromagerie*. Magali had first suggested they cool off from the warm evening by taking a shower. They left the bathroom lights off, only a stream of moonlight crept in from a cracked window. He'd seen her shapely figure and wanted to explore her every inch with his hands. Magali had been a lover he wasn't accustomed to, one who took control and showed him what to do, guiding him to all the places she desired. He often dreamed of another night just like Barcelona, and he felt the desire to repeat the experience deep in his stomach and elsewhere. She also was practical, having excellent sources inside the French police and intelligence services—two birds with one stone.

He began to worry he hadn't heard back from her, though. She was his best chance to learn if the attorney's documents were found or even investigated by authorities.

While Renard's dirty laundry didn't concern him personally, he suspected the men who employed him had secrets to hide.

Turning left on Rue du Faubourg Montmartre, Diego checked his phone. He'd picked a chic hotel in the nineth arrondissement because it was close to the Gare du Nord. But more importantly, it had an outdoor terrace bar frequented by plenty of women. Out of habit, or tradecraft, he'd booked two rooms in the city under his name but would only stay at one. It would throw anyone off his scent if he were to be followed.

Before he could pull up his map to see how far he had to walk, he saw her message.

Call me—M

It had been months since he'd seen her last, but they'd exchanged pleasantries several times over texts. They kept things casual. Both knowing how to play the game.

She answered on the fifth ring.

"*Salut toi,*" she said, her raspy voice as sexy as he remembered.

Diego smiled. She seemed in a jovial mood. "I'm in Paris for a few days."

"Oh really?" He could hear her drumming a pencil on a notepad.

"Want to get a drink?"

"What makes you think I'd say yes?" Magali said deadpan.

"Well, you said to give you a call whenever I was in Paris. It's the first time I've been here since we've met," Diego lied, his mind drifting back to when he pulled the trigger on a quiet street in the seventh.

"I doubt it's the first time you've been to Paris."

Diego scoffed, half enjoying the flirtation and half annoyed by it. "Calling me a liar?"

The drumming of her pencil in the background ceased. "*Non, non.* I am inquisitive by nature—I am a journalist after all."

Diego chuckled. She was playing harder to get than he remembered, but he was terrified he wouldn't be able to get a lead from her. Best to not chase.

"If you change your mind, I'm staying at the Hotel Panache in the nineth. Just getting there now. I'm looking forward to a hot shower."

The line buzzed as if Magali had hung up.

"Still there?"

Magali responded. "I don't live far from there. I'll text you the address."

Diego grinned. He was in luck.

"And, oh Diego," Magali whispered. "Don't shower yet. You can do that with me."

9

Paris, France

Hart watched Clara rifle through the cabinets looking for wine glasses. They'd walked thirty minutes north from Palais Royale to the safe house located in the nineth arrondissement. The furnished apartment was tucked away on a narrow street off Rue du Faubourg Montmartre. The apartment was bright, white walls lit by skylights stretching across the slanted rooftop ceilings. The old floors creaked with displeasure. It was furnished with a walnut kitchen table with clear plastic chairs, a blue corduroy couch, TV and a glass coffee table.

Clara, after seeing there was no food, had suggested Hart go pick up something to eat. He'd known the request really was an excuse for some alone time. After his meeting in the Palais Royale, he was grateful for the time to himself as well.

She had yet to tell him what she'd talked about with Pierre-Emmanuel, nor he about his chat with Palmer. Hart's intuition told him she needed to process her professional life coming back. Now they were off the island, into the cold and unforgiving world of intelligence. It was understandable she was tense. He too, was unnerved.

Hart strolled north towards the Saint-Georges and managed to find a Monoprix. He grabbed aged comté cheese, a baguette, and a frozen pizza along with two bottles of

Tariquet—a cheap sweet white wine he knew was Clara's favorite. To ensure he was well prepared to keep her happy for the evening, he also grabbed an enormous box of dark chocolates.

Hart took a staircase pattern back to the safe house, more so out of habit than necessity. Who on earth knew where he was? He was halfway around the world from where he was raised and had worked. He'd been living in the shadows with Clara, where he wouldn't bump into forgotten colleagues or friends, yet he enjoyed the anonymity.

Lately, Hart had barely recognized his life. Gone were the dreams he had when he lived in New York, just like his former career, but he had been gifted a life of intrigue. He reasoned it was all worth it because he had Clara. Losing her was the only thing in the world that scared him.

He turned onto the apartment's street, immediately noticing the white van across from their building's front door. The running lights were on, exhaust fumes boiling into the air. Since the sun had set, the city had gotten brisk, presumably prompting the people sitting in a van for hours to turn the heat on. He scolded himself for being paranoid but then remembered Clara's training. If something seems out of place, it is. He doubled back to take the long way around the block to approach the van from the front. Through the windshield, he could see two men, and cigarette smoke pouring into the night air.

He tapped on the passenger window, startling both men.

"Evening, gentlemen!" Hart smiled at Lucas and Antoine, the same men who'd picked them up in Noirmoutier.

"Are you out here protecting us or watching us?" Hart asked, feigning a smile.

"Always watching out for you." Lucas tried to give a reassuring thumbs-up while Antoine glared at him.

He gave a cursory glance up and down the block. "Well, I never know which it is with you. But I appreciate you regardless, but this evening we'll be occupied."

He held up the bottles of Tariquet and received a knowing smile from Lucas.

Antoine scoffed. "Figured you'd be working."

Hart saw an opportunity to try his hand at bluffing to get information and decided it couldn't hurt. "Clara is focused on this; she's upstairs crafting the plan. But what do you guys think?"

Lucas and Antoine exchanged glances before Antoine gave a slight nod that his subordinate could talk. "We don't want you ending up like the attorney killed in the seventh. It's why we're here. We've heard some rumors about the video, anxious to begin the investigation."

Hart tried to hide his unease. So, this was about Renard and some attorney? Was that why Palmer had brought the name up? Why hadn't Clara filled him in yet? Suddenly he was eager to get upstairs. Once she'd had the time to relax, she'd talk, he reasoned. The wine couldn't hurt.

"But there's no specific threat?" Hart offered the question up as casually as he could, realizing there was a reason the DGSE agents were on guard outside.

"No." Lucas shook his head. "But a pro killed the attorney, from what we've heard. We're not taking chances." He took a pull from his cigarette and blew smoke from his nostrils.

"Whether we want to be here or not," Antoine added.

Hart handed the baguette to the men through the window. "Looks like you guys could use this more than us."

Lucas grabbed the treasure before Antoine could protest. He simply offered a nod of thanks. "Pulled off paternity leave for a stakeout and baguette with Lucas—not exactly a holiday," he said while ripping the end of the bread out of Lucas's hand. "My favorite part," Antoine said as he took a bite.

"Well, boys, thank you for being out here protecting us, but you better not be watching us." Hart winked and bid the men goodnight.

10

Paris, France

They'd polished off the first bottle of wine and were well
into the second when Clara got up and left the room. Dinner
had been light and pleasant, conversation about food with a
French travel TV show in the background. Hart even momentarily forgot about their day, which they danced around,
just like the light from the flickering candle on the table.

When Clara returned, she'd changed into a purple ter-
ry-cloth robe, carrying a manila envelope that she set down
on the coffee table.

"This is the new mission," she said. "But it is still the old
one."

Hart opened the envelope and pulled a sheet of thick
paper from the inside. It was entirely in French with several
financial tables. While the financial statements were clear, he
didn't want to misinterpret the French.

"What does it say?" he asked, looking up to find Clara's
green eyes studying his reaction.

Clara moved over next to him, tucking her knees under
her robe. "Allegedly, it's a dossier Renard left behind after
death. He specifically identifies a company and says it should
be investigated if anything detrimental happens to him outside the normal course of health."

"Like getting shot in the head?" Hart asked flippantly.

"Exactly. The thing is, Pierre-Emmanuel wants me on the investigation because of my prior knowledge. But it's sensitive work." She paused and readjusted her robe swiftly, revealing nothing underneath. Her body taut from the daily Noirmoutier swims.

"What are we investigating exactly?" Hart asked distractedly, his mind running in the opposite direction.

Clara twirled a loose piece of her dark hair around a finger before settling on an answer. "Renard was convinced Iran was trying to sell nuclear weapon plans. He believed the transaction was going to take place soon."

Hart nearly choked on his wine. "Nuclear?"

"*Ouais*. We can't ignore this—the risk is too great. A rogue group with the blueprint for a nuclear weapon would shake the world. We cannot let this happen."

"This is serious stuff. Who are we going to pass this on to?"

"It'll be our job, or rather I should say mine. The idea of an investigation has ruffled some political feathers, so discretion is required."

Hart frowned and grabbed the bottle to refill Clara's glass, but she waved him away after only a small pour. "You know I have never told you, but I detest a full pour," Clara said, emptying half of her glass into Hart's.

The sweet white wine had gone down easy, possibly too much so, and Hart felt the romantic potion at work. He'd had several glasses to diminish the discomfort of ambiguity hanging in the air since their midday rendezvous. Still, even through the haze of the grapes, he could sense all wasn't right.

"I know how to pour wine. I didn't even fill half your glass?"

She laughed. "I said I prefer it another way." She lifted her glass and swirled her small amount of liquid gold. "If your glass is too full, it can be hard to handle, the wine splashing about. But if your glass is nearly empty, the wine is almost weightless, you can smell it better as you dive into your glass. It's why I detest large pours—I just want to take my time and enjoy it, sip by sip, not glass by glass." She ran her finger up and down the stem of the glass while she remained silent for a moment. "Small pours save more for later."

Clara filled her lungs with air, appearing to make herself ready for a discussion she didn't wish to have.

"Paul," she started cautiously, as if to gauge his reaction to her serious tone. Hart was relaxed, his eyes attentive with a hint of want too. "I think it would be for the best for us to have some distance while I investigate this lead."

The room was silent. No scooters zipped past or laughter from the street to break the veil between them. Hart could only hear his breathing, suddenly labored and shallow.

"What do you mean by 'distance'?" Despite his best efforts, he felt his voice shake.

"I don't want to put you in danger," Clara said, her sea-green eyes soft. Retreating from her original firm line, she took his hand.

Hart forced a small laugh. "There's no way I would leave your side. We're a team, an alliance." He leaned forward and took her hand in his. "A Franco-American alliance. We will always have each other's backs."

"Maybe too much of a good thing can ruin something beautiful. Small pours can be best sometimes. Things might be better if you just forgot about me."

Hart inched closer to her. "In the immortal words of Dierks Bentley, 'There ain't enough bourbon in Kentucky for me to forget you.'"

She threw her head back and laughed. "How romantic."

"I'm serious. I am not leaving you."

Clara smiled. "That's what I was afraid you'd say." She leaned in to kiss him.

"You know, once we start down this path, there is no turning back," she said between kisses.

Hart paused and pulled away to look at the sheet of paper on the table and read a name from the top. "Jupiter Holdings. We're in this together now. I know too much."

Hart smirked and pulled her close.

Surprising him, she took his hand and placed it on her derriere. He gently worked his way under her robe, feeling her warmth between her legs. Clara sighed and feverishly kissed Hart, slowly swaying her hips back and forth, helping along. The robe slipped from her shoulders. She pulled him into the small of her neck. Hart responded by kissing her there, slowly working his way down to her teardrop-shaped breasts.

Clara unbuckled his belt, took him in her hand, then bent across the table and blew out the candle.

11

The black Jaguar XJ apprehensively navigated several puddles as if unsure of their depths. Once it arrived safely at the curb, its rear passenger door swung open. Luke Darlington spilled onto the wet sidewalk outside the building designed for leisure but somehow always gave him bouts of anxiety. The dark red-brick structure was tucked between several shops and apartments in St. Georges Field, Westminster. Vines clung to the building, as green and manicured as the first day Darlington had visited. He'd know it by many names over the years, some official, others not so, but he had always affectionately referred to it as The Rock. A not so subtle reference to Alcatraz prison in San Francisco.

The structure had been rebuilt after World War Two. During the London Blitz, a Luftwaffe bomb had landed on the street and burned down the entire block. But the club, just like a good deal of London, was rebuilt.

Darlington entered the foyer, its dark wood and hunter-green carpeting masking its relatively young age. As far as he was concerned, the interior decorating might have been from the turn of the last century. He dropped his coat off at the front desk and pushed through the heavy saloon doors into the study. Several club members in chalk-stripe wool suits sat enjoying brandy on leather sofas in front of a raging fireplace. They ceased talking as soon as Darlington entered the room and casually watched him walk by.

Darlington continued through the room, past the portraits of hunting expeditions in the former British colonies in Africa, and finally down a narrow hallway, lit only by golden candlelight fixtures on the walls.

The weight of his blue suit suddenly felt suffocating, and it wasn't on account of cheap wool. It was one of his many Saville Row bespoke suits from Huntsman. The epitome of made to measure, it didn't even have belt loops.

Darlington dabbed his face with his Drake's silk handkerchief to compose himself. The dim lighting and the stale air made him want to run for the front door, but he had no choice. He'd been summoned. Steeling his resolve, he knocked in the required cadence on the nondescript door at the end of the hallway.

The door clicked opened and Darlington shuffled himself into an area the size of a small coat closet. The first door he entered through closed behind him, and momentarily he was in complete darkness. The second door, which he still needed to go through, was locked and would stay so until the night-vision security camera completed the facial recognition process. The deadman door was designed so no person could easily wander into the highly secure inner room beyond. At the same time, Darlington knew he was being x-rayed for weapons or any electronics, strictly forbidden on club grounds. Members could leave them at the front desk or be politely asked to "bugger off" if caught with anything forbidden.

But Darlington was a cut above the aristocrat level of importance compared to the rest of the members. He was entering an area only a select few knew about. And if he were to fail the inspection inside the deadman door, several actions would be set in motion. He'd heard the cramped, dark place he currently stood in could be voided entirely of oxygen, stopping an intruder dead in their tracks—literally.

After a moment that felt like an eternity, the soft buzz of the door clicking open told him he'd passed. Dull yellow light spilled from the inner room, cascading across the thick and square twelve-person conference table surrounded by leather club chairs. Darlington took his usual place in the middle of the table.

He slipped on his virtual-reality glasses sitting on the table and, without ceremony, joined the meeting. In his VR glasses, he saw an interactive map highlighting several stock exchanges worldwide and showing the percentage of the commodities owned.

"Thank you for coming," an accented voice said.

Darlington felt his blood turn ice-cold.

The virtual-reality glasses flickered, and a digital map of Europe appeared. The strangely accented voice spoke deliberately, sounding out the difficult words. The cold voice of his overlord started. "Do you know why you are here?"

Darlington squeezed the armchair to brace himself for a scolding like an unruly schoolboy.

"I have an idea," Darlington said meekly.

"Tell me the three ways in which my organization achieves what it wants."

Darlington swallowed while he wished he could muster the courage to dab his forehead with his handkerchief. He was annoyed that he could be reduced to a quivering puddle of anxiety while speaking to his master. But it was the cost of striking a deal with the devil. He reminded himself appearances were everything and fought to regain his composure. He focused on the map floating around in his VR glasses and calmed his breathing.

He answered, "Leverage, power, and death."

The voice grunted in satisfaction. "And which of those three means will you be using to find the intelligence left by the late Monsieur Renard?"

Darlington drew a sharp breath. "I have several resources working diligently to track down the intel, if it even exists. I have my doubts." He had to force out the last words, a bluff he hoped would buy him the good graces of his leader.

"Okay," was uttered, in the thick singsong accent he could never place. "However, might I remind you, any failure to procure said intelligence and stop any corresponding investigation will be monumentally disappointing."

"I understand."

The voice continued. "Do you? We cannot afford mistakes. The deal I've brokered, an exchange between great countries of influence regarding the sale of certain plans, is coming. However, it will be quite unusual, there will be a payment to take the plans. There's a considerable amount of risk involved, so compensation is required to offset those. Having a common enemy has united some otherwise distant countries. If the deal should shatter, we'd face catastrophic problems. One country will go bankrupt, while the other mad with rage. The world would descend into chaos, and while I appreciate the opportunities war brings, I'd rather make money during global detente."

Darlington shivered. He was dancing with the devil but unaware of the steps to the song.

"I have the utmost confidence any deal can proceed without issue."

"Not true. The accounts associated with Renard have been frozen, giving credence that his intelligence was real. Your man lost the plot and failed to get it back. Our clients, the two countries in this deal, are both under heavy economic sanctions. Therefore, we face a challenge."

Darlington was immediately curious about the monetary figure required, estimating it would easily be hundreds of millions of dollars.

"What will you do to secure the money? Can my bank be of service since the intended accounts are frozen?"

The accented voice squealed with laugher, terrifying Darlington.

"No, I don't need your help to provide the funds. I will contact you in a few days with further instructions."

Darlington found himself nodding amicably. "Of course, I'm happy to assist."

The voice spoke with what Darlington could only imagine was a wide smile. "Good, because, Luke, I will not hesitate to use one of the three means at my disposal, and you can be sure to which one I would utilize first."

Darlington pulled at his collar but caught himself and smoothed his silk tie instead. He thought of Diego, and wondered how he was getting along in Paris, knowing his life hung in the Spaniard's hands.

"Of course, that is why I won't rest until this matter is resolved. I have a good man on this right now. I am sure he is deep into the matter."

12

Diego groaned and fell onto his side. He was exhausted.

It was 5:09 a.m., or so his Vacheron Constantin Fiftysix timepiece appeared to say so. But it was hard to read on account of his blurry vision. He glanced to his left, towards the open window where he momentarily observed the Parisian sky drift by. A breeze wafted into the sweaty bedroom. Magali lay next to him, still wearing white panties that Diego had simply pushed to the side to not waste valuable time. Her short dark espresso hair was swept across her forehead, sticking to her sweaty olive skin. The white comforter was covering her chest, her flat stomach laid bare for Diego to admire. He'd teased her about how often she went to the gym, but she'd protested the notion, saying she simply had good genes.

After a few moments to catch their breath, Diego felt Magali leave the bed. She made towards the dresser where two empty Chateau Eugenie bottles sat. They'd finished one during dinner, which she cooked, consisting of roasted duck and fried potatoes. Diego had been surprised that the same woman who had sounded eager on the phone slowly teased his lustful advances. Magali drank with ease thanks to years of practice, and after a playful dinner, she took him into the shower as promised.

She took another sip from her glass and leaned against the far wall in her bedroom. The white walls were brightened by the streetlight teasing its way into the apartment from the cracked window. Diego felt her eyes on him as he felt his eyelids grow heavy.

"So why did you text me?" Her voice was lighthearted, not accusatory.

Diego fought his way through his cloudy and satisfied mind. "Because I missed you and because you do that thing with your—"

"Stop playing games with me. We both got what we wanted. Now, I say we start the business end of the conversation. Talk."

Diego scoffed and dug his head further into the pillow. "Can't this wait until morning?"

"It is morning." Magali crossed her arms.

Diego's mind was muddled, confused by the fact he felt used, but then again, he'd used her. It was a dynamic he realized he immensely enjoyed. The world spun round and round. He was just there for the ride like all the others, or more accurately, to be ridden.

"Remember the French businessman killed a while back?" He knew Magali had investigated the story, like all of the other major news outlets in Paris. There had been rumblings of nefarious activity, but no one reported the more incriminatory rumors, the story buried by higher powers.

Magali leaned off the wall and sat down on the edge of the bed. "Yes, we all know it was a cover-up."

He didn't acknowledge her admission. "I need you to look into something for me. A few nights ago, there was a murder in the seventh. Some documents may have been retrieved by authorities. I need to know everything you can find."

"You're Interpol. Why don't you just do this yourself?" she asked, not hiding her frustration.

Diego wished this conversation hadn't happened when he was drained both mentally and physically, but perhaps it was her aim. "It's a delicate matter. I just want to confirm what I've heard. You're my fact-checker." Diego wasn't selling too hard because he didn't need to. She'd recognize a scoop as a seasoned journalist and could use her contacts in the Paris police department or DGSE to figure out anything worth perusing.

"Bullshit," Magali responded, startling Diego. "What aren't you telling me? I know Renard was in bed with bad characters, but I never got to the bottom of it." She crawled towards Diego and playfully straddled him.

Diego liked where things were headed, evident by the rush of blood to his crotch.

While he had promised Darlington he would personally look into the matter, he didn't disclose his reliance on Magali. Perhaps it was inevitable she would become too involved, and it didn't appear from his vantage point she could be easy to fool. Then again, he was rather enjoying the current vantage point.

"*Señorita.*" He reached up and stroked her bare breasts, licking his lips while doing so. "I will give you the entire story, but first, I need you to find out what happened the other night." He pulled at her panties, but she stood and spun on her foot towards the door.

He sat up and watched her for a moment as she put on her bathrobe. "Where are you going?"

Magali smirked and grabbed her phone from the dresser.

"Evidently, I have to get to work. Why don't you do the same and go fuck yourself."

She left Diego with a quizzical look on his face.

Once in the kitchen, Magali made a Nespresso and worked out her next steps. She pinched the bridge of her nose to recall the number and code word she'd sworn to memory. At the far end of her apartment was a small terrace just off the kitchen, just large enough for a metal chair. She stepped out into the cool night air wrapped in just a thin robe. Magali dialed the number she was told to call if anyone came asking about Renard.

It was answered on the third ring.

"*Oui?*" The man's voice was hoarse, but it seemed he'd been awake.

Magali took a breath to steady herself. "We need to talk. Republique Métro station, one hour."

13

Clara woke early and slipped out the rear entrance of the safe house before the sun had risen. On Rue du Faubourg Montmartre she found a boulangerie, the smell of buttered croissants, and the drum of the espresso machine welcoming her. She bought a half dozen croissants, two *chocolatines* and a baguette before retreating home through the quiet Parisian streets.

She approached the van and gently knocked on the darkened window. The small Renault shifted; its shocks squeaked as she had startled the occupants with her the early-morning visit. The window clanked and begun to roll down; Lucas's curly head popped through, as did the smell of two men in a car all night.

"*Salut,* Clara." He rubbed his eyes. Across was his superior Antoine, who seemed none too pleased. She fought the urge to giggle.

"I brought croissants." She took out a small paper bag from the larger one and reached across Lucas to Antoine.

"Don't I get some?" Lucas chided her, snatching at the bag from Antoine.

Clara reached inside and unlocked the car, then opened the door from the outside. "Grab your computer; we need your skills inside. You'll get a croissant upstairs, with some coffee as well."

Lucas's eyes narrowed for a moment as if contemplating his options. Antoine nodded to his subordinate. "I'll cover the street. But you better bring me coffee."

The kitchen table was cluttered. Hart and Clara perched over Lucas's shoulders, staring at the open laptop screen.

"Where do we begin? We only have a generic business name," Lucas asked.

Clara took a sip from her coffee before answering. "We have to find a connection somewhere. We need a financial transaction thread to follow so we can find out who is allegedly looking to purchase the plans."

Hart nodded. "Let's start simple. Search for the business name through the internet and see what pops up." He exchanged a look with Clara to ensure she agreed.

Lucas pounded "Jupiter Holdings" into the search bar, and several thousand results popped up. The first several links were for businesses in the United States, primarily Florida. The proceeding results were no specific help. Lucas dunked a croissant into his coffee mug. Speaking with a full mouth, he shook his head. "This will take forever. We need authorization to get into the European Union database for businesses. We could get lucky there."

Hart glanced at Clara. "If Jupiter Holdings is based in Europe, the EU database will give us the single largest shareholder or owner in the company, even if the largest stakeholder is only half a percent ownership. It's been a European law since 2015. No matter how big or small the company is, at least one real person has to be signed for the account."

Clara folded her arms and began to pace. The apartment

floors creaked as if giving her internal thoughts a voice. "What if I know a username and password to access the database?"

"But you don't have clearance?" Lucas raised an eyebrow.

"True, but I know the details of someone who does."

Lucas considered this. "The user would know someone signed on. They get an email notification." He shrugged and dove back into the bag of croissants.

"If they don't check their emails, it could work?" Clara asked, casting a side-eyed glance at Hart.

"Who doesn't check emails?" Lucas made a face.

"A dead man," Clara said.

She was thinking of her murdered boss, Maxim. He had been trying to help Clara and Hart in his way, but his eagerness to arrest the scapegoated Hart on fraud charges, he had been blind to other threats. He paid that price with his life.

Lucas sighed. "There's a possibility his system access wouldn't have been stripped yet. Thousands of law enforcement officers around Europe have access, so it's hard to keep it up to date. Worth a shot, but eventually, someone will be notified of the irregularity that a deceased email account was used."

Clara didn't hesitate. "Let's try."

Lucas did hesitate, making eye contact with Hart for support. Hart in turn, looked to Clara. She was making decisions, dangerous ones, against her orders of discretion. But Pierre-Emmanuel wanted this investigation over quickly; if cutting corners was required, so be it.

"I will take full responsibility if they find out." Clara strode to the kitchen to refresh her coffee.

Lucas signed in to the portal under Maxim's credentials provided by Clara.

"It worked." He swore and slapped the table with enthusiasm. "The system may notice the old user profile is active and lock us out. We need to work fast."

Hart watched the monitor flicker for a moment and a list of business matching Jupiter Holdings popped up. There were a dozen hits, some partial matches while the one at the top was located in Paris. Under European banking laws, all member states, except Switzerland, share banking information on clients and businesses. The policy, in theory, provides law enforcement, banking, and regulators access to information across countries to ensure transparency.

Clara leaned over Lucas's shoulder and tapped the top result. "What a coincidence?" She turned towards Hart. "You're the one with a banking background. What do you think?"

Hart took the mouse and began navigating the page. He clicked on "Jupiter Holdings," and a new screen showed several grey text boxes without much information. "It's registered in Malta with offices in Paris. There's the incorporation date, but it's a decade old—before ownership requirements were law. Also, there are nearly a dozen smaller companies associated with Jupiter. While it's not uncommon to see layers, it's suspicious." Hart tapped the screen. "There's an address to check out."

"No such thing as coincidence." Clara playfully smacked Hart's shoulder. "That address isn't far. We can visit, talk to the owners of the property."

The three leaned in closer to the screen before it flickered, and an error message appeared.

You no longer have access. Please connect with your network administrator if this is in error.

"*Merde.*" Clara went into the kitchen and dumped out her

coffee in the sink. She knew full well the gamble had only partially paid off while exposing them. Only time would tell if it was worth it.

"We better get to that address. I'm sure whoever kicked us offline might check it out as well," Clara said, throwing on her coat. "Lucas, another angle I need you to check out. What was the attorney Mathieu Bertrand doing the days leading up to his murder? Check bank statements, debit card transactions, phone logs, social media activity. I want to understand this guy's life. Maybe we pick up a clue or anything out of the ordinary."

Lucas chuckled. "Sure, I'll research all that in my free time."

Clara glared at her colleague.

"I'll keep you posted," he conceded.

"Good." Clara nodded with her chin at Hart. "*On y va.*" Let's go.

14

Paris, France

The labyrinth of tiled hallways and warm air led Magali up three flights of stairs into the orange early morning sky. Paris Métro Line 8 had taken her east across the city to Place de la Republique. The grand square stretched out before her. Its eight acres touched the third, tenth, and eleventh arrondissements of Paris. Marianne, the symbol of France, representing liberty, equality, and brotherhood, stood tall in the center. At over nine meters high, she faithfully watched over her citizens. Magali fondly regarded the area, which symbolized French freedom. The irony wasn't lost on her that it doubled as the epicenter of protests routinely taken up to voice opposition to losing those freedoms.

She felt at home in the square because, as a Parisienne, Place de la Republique was the heartbeat of Paris. Not the shops of Rue Saint-Honoré, or the selfie-taking tourists under the Eiffel Tower, nor the magnificent gardens of the Left Bank. No, to Magali, Paris was represented by Marianne and Place de la Republique: a place to congregate, celebrate, protest, love, and mourn.

Just a few blocks away, Canal Saint-Martin cut its way through the dense neighborhood of the eleventh. Its main attraction was the nightlife: hidden bars, clubs, bustling restaurants fueling locals with booze into the early-morning hours any day of the week. It was there, years ago, she was partying with friends when the shots rang out, screams echoed off the canal walls and white stucco buildings. The shrill sirens cut through the city air. She still carried the helpless feeling, though fear never crossed her mind that fateful night in November 2015. Instead, she felt hatred for the evil killing of innocents.

She'd held her chin high, knowing her country was targeted because of its love of friends, going out, being lovers, carrying on with laughter and vigor for life. The tragedy is they were murdered for it. The attacks around the lively canal and the Bataclan stole the lives of 130 innocent people. The pain of that night stayed with her like a scar. The sidewalks slick with blood from people running for their lives, the yellow tape, the body bags. She treated herself by writing whatever she could to tell the stories of that evening, to let others' hurt be known. But perhaps more importantly, chanted like a prayer, was the oath she silently swore to herself to investigate and bring terrorists to justice. Terror to Magali wasn't only explosives and AK-47s, but rather anyone who preyed on the weak, abused their power, or sought to hurt others. Since November 2015, she'd broken stories ranging from politicians embezzling money from charities to corrupt arms deals, and had been tracking down what she believed was a cover-up of the activities of Claude Renard. But to what extent? She didn't know, but it's what drove her to the early-morning rendezvous. Gliding across the darkened square, she could see a few lost souls stumbling home while several more were sleeping off a rough night, or life, on the stone benches. She scanned the street towards République of Coffee, the same shop where they always met. She expected to find him at the back table as per usual, facing the door with a copy of *Le Monde* folded on his lap.

The bright neon lights of the coffee shop lit up like runway lights from a block away. The white-tiled wall behind the counter sparkled with the purple and green neons.

Magali reached for her phone in her purse when she felt a hand on her back.

"*Bonjour, mademoiselle.*" The tall man with hawkish eyes and slicked-back grey hair wore an easy smile.

"Pierre-Emmanuel," Magali said, composing herself not to give him the satisfaction of knowing he startled her. He hadn't waited inside, which told her, he was anxious to speak. "Thank you for coming on such short notice."

"When you called so early, I assumed it to be of great importance." He outstretched his long hand towards the café. "Shall we?"

They made their way into the café and unsurprisingly to her, Pierre-Emmanuel picked a table in the back, sitting flush against the wall so he could face the door. The waitress brought over a double espresso for Magali and a glass of fresh carrot juice for Pierre-Emmanuel. For several minutes they chatted about nothing, then his eyes met hers with an impatient glare. "*Alors?*"

Magali sipped her espresso and realized her hands were shaking. Pierre-Emmanuel's fingers deliberately drummed on the wooden tabletop.

"I was told to contact you in case anything regarding Claude Renard ever came up." She paused, registering no observable difference in the man's face. "Well, a source suggested I look into the matter. Specifically about—"

Pierre-Emmanuel held up his right hand. "Who's your source?"

She scoffed and craned her head in disbelief. "You know I won't answer that."

Pierre-Emmanuel took a sip from his juice and politely nodded his head.

She began again. "You haven't ever denied anything and the fact I was to call you if anyone ever brought Renard's name up confirms my suspicions. So, I want the truth, or you'll force me to knock on doors and talk to people you don't want me to."

His hawkish eyes narrowed. "That would be unwise and more than a bit brash."

She smiled. "Exactly the reason why I'd do it. There's a bigger story than the fairy tale you spun me months ago. I want the truth."

Pierre-Emmanuel drummed on the table and observed the sleepy café. By his furrowing brow and twitch of his lips, she could tell that he was thinking hard about what to do next. She hadn't been expecting much, possibly another juicy tip like the last time she asked for information and was gifted the story of an American ambassador who'd had an affair with a French subordinate. But while the accolades professionally for such stories were appreciated, she didn't dream of reporting on men not being able to keep it in their pants, but rather exposing crimes against the helpless.

Pierre-Emmanuel finished off his juice, delicately setting the glass on the table. "There are some people you should meet. I will set this up, but in return, you will refrain from reporting anything for several days and will not hint at your source. Deal?"

Magali shifted in her seat. Where there was smoke, there was fire. However, she had nothing to write on. His coyness told her to go along with anything he asked; it meant staying close to him. While uneasy of the deal she was making, the journalist in her recognized the risk of being purposefully misled down dead-end paths; her instincts told her this was too good to pass up.

"Fine, but I want this meeting with whoever to happen soon. Understand?"

The French spymaster stood, buttoned his raincoat, and bowed his head. Without another word, he left the café and joined the swell of early-morning commuters.

Pierre-Emmanuel headed into the Métro station right out the front door on Boulevard Saint-Martin. He descended the stairs, his derbies echoing off the damp walls. *Merde*, he thought, trying to piece the puzzle together. Someone had tipped off Magali about the attorney's murder and subsequent investigation, or lack thereof? He'd told Clara to be discrete. Surely, she wouldn't have contacted a journalist.

Furthermore, his own department in the DGSE had shelved it on his authority, because he knew what was best for his career. Thanks to LeBrun's threats, the investigation was under wraps. Perhaps amid his anguish over who else was in the game, he could use Magali to his advantage. Just like his freshly pressed juice, he would squeeze all the information out of her that he could. But to do that, he needed to keep her close.

15

Stephen Palmer glanced up from the breakfast sandwich he'd been feigning interest in for the past twenty minutes to watch Pierre-Emmanuel drift down the Métro stairs from the café he'd just left. It was fortuitous there had been a Burger King across the street where the American spy could surveil from. He'd found a window to watch his target conduct an early-morning rendezvous.

Palmer couldn't quite place his finger on his need to stalk Pierre-Emmanuel. He reasoned it was due to his professional curiosity—"trust but verify," the ancient Russian proverb often cited by Americans. But really, it was his desire to protect Hart at all costs. The last time he'd trusted his agent's safety to someone else, he'd suffered the worst loss of his professional career, if not his life. It affected him deeply, nearly cost him everything, and led him to seek redemption in Hart.

It was 2002, and the free world seemed trapped in a death spiral. The United States had been brutally and cowardly attacked by terrorists from caves in Afghanistan, the country where it had been said that empires came to die. As a veteran operations officer, Palmer assessed and recruited human intelligence, or HUMINT, assets across Europe. Palmer had been assigned in London, working closely with British Army intelligence at the start of Operation Enduring Freedom. He had identified a young recruit, a Pakistani banker. The young man had graduated from Oxford and worked in Canary Wharf before being transferred to a large German investment firm with offices in central London. Initially, he had come to the attention of intelligence services because of his Pakistani heritage and frequent travels back to Southwest Asia.

Palmer's superiors saw Farhad as a means to an end. He was Pakistani by birth, but educated in the West. Thanks to many of the Pakistani generals and elites who banked out of London, he worked closely with the powerful upper Pakistani class. The generals, industrial titans, and political leaders all kept their money, one way or another, in the comfortable confines of the European banking system.

After months of surveillance, Palmer knew Farhad Orakazi was clean, nothing more than a successful mergers-and-acquisitions banker who often traveled to Islamabad, bringing money for family. Palmer also learned from his financial intelligence briefs that Farhad had been facilitating deals between entities from Pakistan, mainly in the agricultural sector, exporting cotton to firms in China. Thus, prompting interest from intelligence officials who fancied recruiting a young, up-and-coming banker who brokered between powerful countries. Farhad was valuable, and Palmer hoped, impressionable. Palmer's job was to find out which of his buttons to push and the extent to which the United States could push them.

Palmer worked for months on the approach. It was the height of US military expansion into Afghanistan, pushing Al-Qaeda into the Hindu Kush mountains before many of them fled into the lawless tribal areas of Pakistan. The rules of engagement were clear. No US military was to cross the border into Pakistan for fear of upsetting a nuclear country that maintained, at best, a prickly relationship with the US and many of its allies, including India. Any inroads into Pakistan would be helpful for the Americans, hence Farhad.

Palmer bided his time in their relationship, posing as an American businessman interested in purchasing an entire Pakistani cotton supply chain. He discovered what made Farhad tick and knew how to exploit it. Farhad's family. Palmer showed his agent by following his requests, he would make the arrangement worthwhile. Farhad was promised juicy mergers-and-acquisitions information before anyone else—just enough time before as not to arouse suspicions, but also hit some home runs on returns. These spun off into further promotions, which meant more money to provide for his large extended family in Pakistan.

Pakistan had become increasingly difficult to work with. American forces were constantly frustrated by Pakistan's refusal to protect their border, significantly hindering the American's efforts in the Hindu Kush mountain region, allowing terrorists to come and go into Afghanistan at their pleasure. Eventually, Washington decided that a full-fledged covert intelligence assault on Pakistan was the proper course of action rather than a military conflict. Palmer, to his dismay, was ordered to put Farhad into action. He'd struck a cordial relationship with the young banker, learned of his love for cricket and London's own Arsenal football club. Still, Palmer never believed Farhad could produce enough intelligence to warrant fieldwork. However, Washington gave him orders, and like the good foreign officer he was, Palmer carried them out.

He directed Farhad to contact a Pakistani arms dealer fronting as a Persian rug exporter based out of Istanbul. The arms dealer ran a vast network of weapons leaving Turkey via the Bosporus. Palmer instructed Farhad to set up a potential buy to entrap the dealer. Palmer's higher-ups made it clear that Farhad had to complete the op, or Palmer would be on the fast track to a post in the middle of nowhere.

Farhad met the arms dealer at a small café in Istanbul, just up the hill from Hagia Sophia. Over apple tea and baklava, Farhad listened intently to the man speak in code about rugs; never once did he think he was meeting an exporter of illegal weaponry.

Farhad detailed how he could move money through the arms dealer's network into Europe or anywhere else in the world for that matter. This movement would expose the various wire transfers and subsequent bank accounts the money would bounce around. The sting went well, Farhad got paid, the Pakistani intelligence officers behind the dealer got identified, and Palmer got his superiors off his back.

Or at least until Palmer's asset was burned when the dealer smelt a rat after two of the accounts he used to layer the money in were abruptly frozen. Farhad's life was put in jeopardy, and Palmer sought to protect the innocent man, pulling him from his everyday life. Farhad blamed Palmer for ruining his career and life when he was told he might be in danger. Palmer couldn't blame the man. They'd both used each other, but the world still spun round.

It was on a fateful cold night, one with a dark purple sky and snowflakes lazily floating down, that Palmer lost all faith in his own judgment. His innocent asset had been left for dead without a second thought. The memories were too painful to relive, so Palmer had tried to banish them from his mind. But perhaps it was also why, when he heard of Paul Hart, the banker who unwittingly stumbled upon a terror-financing scheme, Palmer's dark past stirred inside him. He'd sworn to seek a chance to right the wrongs of many years ago. Paul Hart now was that chance.

His mission to protect his second chance put him on the path Palmer realized had led him to follow Pierre-Emmanuel to the coffee shop. He didn't trust anyone anymore because the truth was he had before, and it cost him a decent night's sleep ever since.

Palmer watched a woman leave the café. He crumbled up the breakfast sandwich and threw it in the nearest garbage bin on his way outside. What the hell was his French colleague doing having clandestine meetings before the sun came up? Palmer could tell they weren't lovers—the obvious lack of affection the giveaway—so who was she?

As he went outside, he got a clearer view of her. She was striking, with tanned skin and a purposeful walk. She blended in by standing out—another beautiful woman in Paris.

He followed her across the Place de la Republique, towards the Métro station, where she made her way down to the lowest platform to wait for the purple 8 train towards Balard.

The chase was on.

16

The streets during the late morning were quiet: too early for lunch, too late for breakfast. A cold hung in the air. Passersby hurried with their heads down as if hiding from the chill.

Clara and Hart found the address for Jupiter Holdings without difficulty. Registered to an office tucked away on the second floor of the Galarie Vivienne arcade. Lucas and Antoine had dropped them off. Clara and Hart found a table at Bistro Vivienne, a belle-epoque café with thick red carpeting and heavy gold-tasseled drapes. From their vantage point, they watched the staircase door to the second level of the building where the office was. For an hour they sat, Hart, ordering one espresso after the other because he didn't possess the patience nor the stomach to drink a cold one. Clara kept up her conversation with him and a close eye on the dark wooden door with a brass handle in the hallway.

There was a purposefulness to her that reminded him of when they'd first met. He didn't know it at the time, but she had always been on the job, measuring his capabilities. Their time on Noirmoutier had mellowed her, but gradually she returned to her former self. On the other hand, he had changed from his former self and didn't see how he could go back to the naïve man he'd been. His old life was outgrown, now his future saw him squeeze into a life of intrigue. Hart didn't know what it took to be good at this different life, the endless speculation, and ambiguity of intelligence. But he had his new mission now, his purpose, and it was the reassurance from Clara, as they laid in bed the night before that sharpened his determination. She'd said becoming a master of tradecraft wasn't a talent that could be quantified but rather a steady growth of skills, masterfully incorporated into an armor. His emotional intelligence, reading other people, thinking quickly without hesitation were learned with experience. Still, the fundamental criteria of success in his new line of work was measured by whether you lived or died.

After what felt like all morning to Hart, Clara finally motioned towards the door. Hart laid down some euros for his espressos and followed her down the tiled hallway. Without a moment's hesitation and the fluidity of a frequent visitor, Clara climbed the staircase to the second level. They entered the narrow hallway lined by several teak doors with frosted glass. Clara said aloud, 'Jupiter Holdings,' as if by magic it would appear. They paced up and down the hallway, hearing the occasional screech of a desk chair or soft voices emanating behind the closed doors. On their second pass, neither had seen what they were searching for.

"Maybe the name won't be on the door? If the business has some secret worth investigating, they would hardly be advertising," Hart said.

Clara dropped her chin, her green eyes flaring more than usual with specks of gold. "Thank you for that valuable insight, Paul." She pulled out her phone.

Hart smiled and offered a shrug. "Hey, that's why I'm here, to connect the dots, right?"

Clara smirked while she scrolled. "There." She pointed at

a door they'd previously passed. "This is listed as the address. Office nine hundred and twenty-five."

On the frosted glass window, gold lettering spelled out *Antiquities de Chartime Maritime* with a French country code +33. Hart thought the lettering looked worn, as old as the door.

Clara slid her phone into her back pocket, catching Hart stealing a peek at her behind as she did so. She pressed her finger to her lips. Shh.

She raised one hand to the door to knock; with her other, she gripped her Sig Sauer P226 pistol from her quick-draw rear holster. Hart backed up against the wall next to the door as she knocked.

Her knock was light, yet still the old door rattled against its frame. From inside, a chair screeched across the floor, followed by heavy footsteps. The door opened, and Clara's eyes fell soft, offering a soft '*bonjour*' to the woman who had opened the door. She was in her mid to late thirties, with bleached blonde hair pulled tight into a bun. She had on a thick green cardigan that fell to her knees. Her face was severe and taut, the intensity highlighted by her bright blue eyes.

She looked out in the hallway first at Hart, then refocused on Clara. "Yes, can I help you?" She asked in perfect English.

Hart cast Clara a look before answering. *How'd she know to speak English?*

"Yes, we are looking for a business at this address."

The woman leaned against the doorframe and pulled her cardigan tight as if a cold draft was rushing in her tiny office. "I see." Her square face, bare of makeup or suntan, didn't bother to hide her disinterest.

Clara stepped in front of Hart, who had his mouth open

81

and, by the look of his furrowed brow, was not going to be diplomatic.

"It's a friend's business, you see." Clara paused, trying to look past the woman into the small office, furnished only with a metal filing cabinet and a metal desk. On the desk sat a computer, but curiously to Clara, she could see the power cord hung unplugged into the wall outlet. A glass ashtray sat on the desk overflowing with Gitanes.

"I'm sorry, who do you say you work for?" The woman asked as Clara tried to scan further into the office, but the lady pushed off the doorframe, blocking her view.

The woman glanced at Hart.

"We've got to speak with the owners. Are you one?"

She held up a finger as if she were asking a question, then suddenly leapt forward, landing a swift kick to Hart's mid-section. He doubled over, the unexpected pain compounded when the woman drove an elbow down on his back.

Clara, unable to pull her Sig from her quick-draw holder in the tight quarters, blocked a series of blows while landing several of her own on their assailant.

Hart straightened off the floor and tried to bearhug the woman from behind. She was still thrashing, exchanging blows with Clara. He jumped, landing on her back, a sharp object under her cardigan cutting into his ribcage. She responded by throwing her head backwards, connecting with Hart's forehead. His world lit up as his head took the brutal knock, forcing him to relinquish his grip on her. He fell to the floor, grasping for anything to stop his fall; he grabbed onto her chunky green cardigan. It was then that the pistol she'd been hiding clattered to the floor.

Clara attempted a running rugby tackle, but the woman dodged her. However, Clara forced their assailant further down the hallway towards the back staircase. Hart and Clara were between her and the fallen pistol.

The woman stood at the end of the hall, hands at her sides, an evil smirk across her face. All three of them stared at each other for a moment. Whoever she was, she wasn't interested in talking.

The woman spun away, making for the exit to the arcade and into a maze of hallways. Clara drew her gun, but by then, the woman had vanished. Hart sprinted down the hallway after her, ignoring the pain from his beating.

Clara shouted at him to stop, then followed suit while yelling into her phone at Lucas and Antoine.

Hart, a good distance ahead of Clara, bounded down the staircase, leaping down half flights at a time. His momentum carried him into the landing walls, shaking the entire stairwell. Once he spilled back in the arcade hallway, he desperately searched left and right—catching sight of a blonde woman making her way unhurriedly south past the bistro. Hart started after her, noticing a discarded green cardigan on the hallway floor.

He burst out onto the street, overwhelmed by the crowded sidewalks and construction cluttering the roadway. Traffic, however, was sparse. Hart ran into the middle of the road, searching for the blonde woman. Nothing to his right, but to his left, she was getting into a blackened Sprinter van further down the road. Its sliding back door was thrown shut as soon as she'd hopped inside.

Hart began chasing after the van as it pulled out onto the narrow roadway away from his pursuit. He could see a roundabout circle maybe a hundred yards ahead, with a statue of King Louis XIV on horseback in the center of the roundabout. Hart pressed forward, memories of his painfully long swims in the frigid Noirmoutier water and early morning runs spurned him on. *You will catch the van*, he told himself.

Traffic began to snarl around the roundabout, the black Sprinter mounted the sidewalk to getaway. All Hart wanted was a license plate, an opportunity to investigate further who had attacked them, but more importantly, why?

Then the van passed the far side of the roundabout, his chance to see the plate seemingly lost. But the traffic at the far exit of the roundabout had a different idea, blocking the chance at an easy escape. Hart heard the van's engine wailing in reverse even at the forty-yard distance he was trying to close, pumping his legs as fast as possible.

Then the van straightened out of its quick reverse, executing a tactical 180-degree turn, and tore back the direction it had originally come. Hart stopped running, the distance between himself and the van now shrinking rapidly. The van hurtled towards him from the center of the road tightly lined with parked cars and scooters, rejected by the snarling traffic of the roundabout.

Hart pulled his phone from his pocket and desperately tried to pull up the camera. He figured that a photo would be better than his memorizing a plate of up to nine different characters. With adrenaline coursing, his hand shook as he fumbled, opening the camera app. When he finally did and raised his phone, he hadn't realized how fast the van had closed on him.

He fired off a photo, mostly out of reflex, as if it could somehow stop the van hurtling at him like a runaway train. The front grill was barreling towards him.

Hart closed his eyes and braced for impact.

17

Paris, France

The street rumbled as the massive black van hurtled towards Hart. The impact, however, surprised him. He thought the van would jettison him backward or perhaps drag him under the chassis, but instead, he landed sideways.

Opening his eyes at the howl of tires, he saw the van disappear down a cross street.

Hart felt pressure on his chest and looked up to see Antoine laying on top of him, panting. Desperation and anger in his dark eyes.

"*Putain!*" he exclaimed, his face reddening.

Hart patted the man who just saved his life on the shoulder. "*Merci*," Hart managed. "I didn't realize how fast he was going."

Antoine rolled off Hart, who stood and offered to help his savior up off the street. Antoine angrily pushed Hart's hand away and pointed back down the road.

Hart headed towards the arcade, ignoring the looks of stunned passersby. He did, however, catch Clara's sharp glare.

They walked hand in hand past the small bookshops, art dealers, and fabric stores of the arcade, heading north towards the safe house. Lucas followed several paces behind while Antoine went to get the car.

Clara was the first to speak. "I'm relieved you're alright."

"I was lucky to have Antoine around. He got there just in time." Hart offered a smile, hoping that Clara would take it easy on his recklessness.

"You won't always be so lucky. And you can't count on others saving you. Antoine just became a father, you know."

Instead of arguing the opportunity to get a picture of the van was worthwhile, he listened to her lecture him about the dangers he put the team in. But he didn't apologize. Rather, he switched subjects.

"Didn't you find this at all..." His voice trailed as he searched for the words "... odd?"

"What, the fact that someone knew we were coming, or the van that attempted to run you over?" Clara stopped and grabbed him by the arm. "*Merde*. Paul, you could have been killed."

He ignored her worry. "What did you make of the office?"

"I saw her desk with a computer on top, but it wasn't plugged in. Didn't you smell the smoke? It was like she was waiting for something, someone to come?"

"Clara, I know you want to get to the bottom of this as much as I do, but we don't have any clue what just happened. We need to review the photos I took of the van. I'm sure it's most assuredly been dumped by now, probably on some street in Saint-Denis with the keys on the dash. It'll be stripped or stolen soon, but maybe we'll get lucky."

"Again, that is the problem right there. We can't wait to get lucky again. The woman got away, and that's on us. We weren't prepared."

Hart let go of her hand and turned to face her in the

middle of the tiled hallway. The lunch crowd still filing back to work from the cafés and restaurants towards La Bourse, and it seemed nearly all of them were utilizing the cover of the arcade.

"I agree, but had—" Hart started before recognizing his fatal error as Clara's green eyes flashed with fiery anger. He held up his hands, then gently wrapped them around her waist. She stood tense with her feet firmly planted for a moment before falling into his grasp.

She gave Hart a soft kiss on the cheek then stepped away. "I need to make a phone call."

Pierre-Emmanuel answered on the first ring. "Just the person I was hoping for."

"Why is that?"

"There's someone I need you to meet."

"We have another lead on the intel, but we need to run a license plate first. I'll probably need a few hours to check it out."

"It can wait. There's a more pressing need."

"Okay, but it'll have to be soon," Clara responded, eager to find out whatever her boss had planned.

"I'll provide you the details. And—" Pierre-Emmanuel cleared his voice, dropping it to decibel as if he didn't want it overheard "—I'd lose the American first."

Clara looked at Hart, who was busy in front of a shop window looking at books.

"How do you know I haven't already?"

"Because if you had, Antoine wouldn't be risking his life, and Hart's boss wouldn't be following me around." With that, he hung up.

18

Paris, France

The sun broke through the grey layer of clouds after the lunch hour. A few determined tourists sat along Rue Montorgueil, huddled under heaters turned on in the late morning to battle the rising wind.

Magali paid neither the wind nor the tourists any attention as she headed north up the narrow cobblestone street lined with cafés and patisseries. She needed to think, and when that was the case, she walked.

She'd taken the Métro to Arts-et-Métiers, a fashionable district just northwest of Le Marais. The old buildings that once housed textile mills and factories were renovated into apartments and chic hotels, now accommodating the trendy locals the factories once used to dress.

Magali was emboldened after her walk. She'd get to the bottom of this story. She knew it. Winding her way up the white and cold spiral staircase of her apartment building, the familiar buzz of a scoop carried her onwards. Pierre-Emmanuel's promise gave her hope. First, Diego had come to her with a story she didn't dare believe, and then without hesitation, she was gifted a meeting with an agent of Pierre-Emmanuel to inform her further. Where there was smoke, there was fire. Perhaps that was on her mind when she unlocked and door, kicked off her shoes and felt her heart jump in her chest.

Diego sat on her bed. She saw him through the French doors that opened to the living room. Magali had expected him to be gone, chased away with his tail between his legs, but instead, he sat with crazed eyes peering out from his unkempt hair. She figured he was still very drunk as he puffed on a cigarette while drinking coffee.

Magali patted her chest to calm her beating heart and gently set the keys on the dark granite kitchen counter. Diego stood and polished off the last sip of his espresso.

"Where did you go so early?" He came forward and leaned against the doorframe of the kitchen, blocking her path to leave.

"I had coffee with a friend," she said dismissively and began to rummage through her purse. For what she didn't know. Diego made her nervous.

He grunted and handed Magali his empty cup. She grimaced. She wasn't a maid, especially not in her own house, which had become, to her annoyance, somewhat of a cheap motel since Diego came to town. "Where's my update on the investigation?"

"You only told me about it hours ago. I need time. And if you stay around my apartment uninvited and interrogate me, I won't be inclined to give you anything but a swift kick to your balls." She stood tall, her confidence rebounding as she thought of her meeting, the promised scoop, and the fact she knew more than Diego.

He smirked and grabbed his leather weekend bag that he'd set near the front door. "I am staying in town a few more days. Tell me what you find out. Immediately."

Magali nodded. "If I find out anything, you'll be the first to know." She rolled her green eyes.

"Don't make a fool of me." He opened the door and stepped out into the hallway. "Or you'll learn to regret that mistake." He looked her over as if recalling the night before and grinned.

She closed the door, engaged the deadbolt, and exhaled a deep breath. Her phone began buzzing in her purse, and when she answered the unknown phone number, she realized her hand was shaking.

The rendezvous was arranged for half past three that same day at Jardin de Luxembourg in the Sxth Arrondissment, or commonly referred to as Saint-Germain. The *jardin* was originally built in the seventeenth century, born out of tragedy. It grew into something beautiful—a thought Clara reminded herself of every time she crossed the sandstone-colored gravel. Marie de Medici, the wife of King Henry IV, had lived in Palais de Louvre until her husband, the king, was assassinated. Deep in mourning, the widowed Marie longed for the sweeping gardens of her homeland, Italy. She instructed the creation of Jardin de Luxembourg on the much quieter Left Bank of Paris.

It was often the case, Clara Nouvelle thought as she moseyed past the Medici fountain; a setback was followed by opportunity. But it was the requirement of the affected to seek the opportunity out, rather than wait for it. She hoped her effort to turn a series of unfortunate events—the attorney's murder, the damning intelligence, and the mysterious request from her boss to meet with a reporter—would be her version of Marie de Medici's jardin. Clara did, however, recall from her history class that although Marie made the best of a bad situation, it was her own son, Louis XIII that ended up exiling her out of France. Perhaps things would turn out better for Clara, and those closest to her would keep her safe.

The jardin usually had on any given day at any given hour crowds milling about—Parisians and tourists intertwined. The main attraction was people-watching, getting lost in a book, or waiting on a friend or a lover. Clara waited for her rendezvous under the canopy of thick trees overlooking the central pool. She'd told Hart to go back to the apartment to research the license plate, and she would take the meeting alone with the reporter, as Pierre-Emmanuel had requested. Hart didn't argue, but he did suggest Lucas and Antoine go with her. Clara had politely told the men away from Hart that she could damn well handle herself.

So, Clara sat alone on the lookout for a woman with a red scarf and a black backpack slung over her left shoulder. It took her only one glance to know she'd spotted Magali making her way around the pool in front of the palace.

They sat perched on two of the hundreds of green metal chairs spread across the garden, lined in front of the fountain flanked by the terraces, tennis, basketball, and *pétanque* courts to their right. Clara pulled a small bag of *macarons* from her Longchamp bag and offered one to Magali, just like two friends visiting the park. Within a whisper of each other, Clara began by asking her new contact what exactly she was looking for.

Clara caught a flash of annoyance in the brown eyes of her contact. "I was told you'd provide me further information on an investigation I've been conducting."

"Well, I, too, was told to meet you, so let me try and help. What are you investigating?" As Clara spoke, she scanned the park for people nearby who may be lingering out of place, but couldn't find any. It still didn't stop the sudden chill that was running down her spine. Something didn't quite feel right.

"Claude Renard. Ever hear the name?"

Clara tried to hide her surprise, but Magali's soft chuckle told Clara she'd caught the slight wince.

"Vaguely familiar," Clara responded.

"There's more to the story than the press reported of his death. I, for one, never believed any of it. I've spoken many times with the man who summoned you here, and he was desperate for me not to report anything."

Magali let the words linger and regarded Clara. Her face remained stoic. She was glad she'd left Hart back at the safe house. It was less complicated this way.

"What do you want exactly?"

"More proof and exclusivity."

Clara huffed in exasperation and took a bite from a caramel macaron. She chewed to buy time to map out her options, which she found frustratingly limited. "I don't have anything concrete for you right now. But if we make a deal that you'll hold off on this story a few days, I can get you something."

"What's the point in holding off? I have sources, suspicions, and carte blanche from my editor." Magali grabbed her purse as if she had already made up her mind that this meeting was a bad idea.

"You'll get a clearer view of everything. Such as Renard left us something so important his attorney was murdered for it. You'll get exclusives eventually, but in the meantime, I need to investigate this further without scaring anyone off. We are talking about the safety of France, Europe, and maybe the world, for that matter. We can't afford to have a reporter blow this. No matter how much I love the freedom of the press."

Magali sighed, "So do you expect me to just not do my job?"

"No." Clara moved to the edge of her chair. "I expect you to understand lives are in danger. No matter how important a pillar the free press is in a democracy, this must wait. You'll get your story, but I ask you to give us a few more days. That is"—Clara lowered her voice— "unless you want to reveal your source to me and why they are looking into this matter as well?"

Magali laughed and grabbed an orange macaron from the paper bag. "I'll give you forty-eight hours, starting after this meeting ends, to get me the story. I'll hold off on reporting anything until then, but if you don't deliver, I will leak the story of the connection between the attorney and Renard. If I'm forced to publish before you'd like, I can perhaps, point you in the general direction of my source as a mea culpa. But no promises, you understand—I have a job to do."

"As do I." Clara's face hardened.

Magali shrugged and popped the entire orange macaron in her wide mouth.

Clara turned towards the crowds ambling by in the park, taking pictures or strolling along with several orange bags from Le Bon Marché, one of Paris's most beautiful department stores that happened to be blocks away. Part of her longed for their innocence, the ignorance of what she was facing, but the other part of her was determined to keep them blissfully unaware, to see her job through, no matter the cost. The world was a dangerous place, but she'd do her job to keep it as safe as possible.

"Give me two days. Don't run anything. You'll have total exclusivity—I'll personally fill you in—but we need more time to investigate, but if you run it before, the element of surprise will be lost, and the world we think we know, could be changed forever. Understand?"

Magali nodded in agreement. Clara told her she'd call her in forty-eight hours. Magali left, skirting the central fountain until she disappeared under the tree-covered terrace.

Diego watched Magali leave from his perch across the jardin. He was hidden near the pétanque courts wearing a baker boy hat pulled low over his brow. The Montparnasse Tower loomed a few blocks away, filling him with pride from memories of the night he took the attorney's life. The man had tried to run. How foolish.

A pair of aviators hid Diego's eyes. Perhaps to passersby, the finely dressed man on the bench was simply enjoying the scenery. Surely none would have guessed from under the low cap and behind his dark lenses, he was a killer glaring at his target. And now, she had provided him a new subject to investigate.

His phone rang.

"They came this morning, but it didn't go as planned." He recognized the woman's voice. It was the same he'd spoken to earlier that morning when he called to warn her about the address in Paris. Via an Interpol database search alert, he knew someone was onto Jupiter Holdings. He'd called the number Darlington had given him for use in such delicate circumstances.

"The alert that I received about the address gave you plenty of time to plan. What happened?"

"There were two of them. A man and a woman. She was French, he wasn't."

Diego heard a pull from a cigarette on the other end of the line as he checked his watch. The call wasn't supposed to go past forty seconds in length. But he had more significant problems. This confirmed there was intelligence out there. He had failed.

"Why do you say he wasn't? English?" Diego's mind went to MI6 and Darlington. He didn't want a British connection further confusing the matter.

The caller took another pull from her cigarette. Then as if her voice steadied from the nicotine, her shallow breathing evened out.

"Because I know French men. He wasn't one, and he barely talked. Maybe American, but not British, although his shoes were nice enough."

Diego rubbed his face at his failure.

"You were supposed to kill them. What the hell happened?" He strained to keep a visual on Magali and rose from his bench to follow her.

"It was complicated. I didn't get any information from them, and they got the jump on me."

The second hand on his watch was sweeping towards the time limit. Diego wasn't interested in excuses.

"Time for me to do your job." He hung up, dismantled the phone, slipped the pieces into his coat pocket, and headed after his mark.

19

The pounds on the door reverberated through the room. Sitting in the open kitchen of the safe house, Hart, and probably the entire building, was startled by the visitor at the door.

Checking the peephole, he breathed a sigh of relief and allowed Stephen Palmer in. He wore a long puppytooth raincoat and a gruff smile. Making his way into the kitchen, he found the freezer and immediately poured some ice and Mountain Dew into a glass.

After his first sip, Palmer finally acknowledged Hart. He plonked into the metal barstool at the center island.

"What have you been working on?" Palmer smiled.

"Good to see you too." Hart quipped. "We've got a lead on a license plate from a van that tried to run me over after one of its occupants assaulted us."

Palmer didn't seem surprised, and Hart figured he already knew. "You okay? Did you get a photo or memorize the number?"

"A photo which almost cost me my life." Hart pulled out his phone and handed it over.

Palmer immediately pulled out his own and made a phone call.

"Kelly, I am sending you a photo. I need a full analysis. ASAP." He hung up without another word.

"Your team of crack analysts?" Hart asked.

"Only need the one." Palmer drained his soda.

"Which brings up a good point, why do I feel like I'm the only one you've got on this case? Shouldn't you have some more resources assigned to this sensitive intel?"

Palmer seemed to consider this for a moment. "Who says I only have you? Besides, you just heard me give your intel to my best analyst. Now there are at least two people assigned." He reached across the island and smacked a disheartened-looking Hart on the shoulder. "If we threw resources at every tip we received, we'd waste lifetimes. You and Clara are doing just fine, and when we need more support, I'll call in the cavalry."

Hart ignoring Palmer's nonanswer and walked him through the details of the excitement that morning, from the name search to the near-fatal van incident. Palmer was pleased with the progress.

"And Clara, what does she think?"

Hart shrugged. "She thinks we need to catch a break. I'm hoping the van will be just that. Worth a shot, I believe." He paused as he could sense Palmer observing him closely.

"Where is Clara exactly?"

"No idea, she is off on assignment this afternoon and told me it wasn't worth my time to go."

Palmer nodded and pursed his lips. "She didn't want your company?"

Hart felt his face grow hot.

"Lady troubles?" Palmer cocked his head inquisitively.

Palmer, undeterred by Hart's glare, pressed onwards. "I thought things were tense between you too, what with the sudden rush back into your new lives. But luckily for you, I know when I'm right, well ahead of time." Palmer chuckled, his thick beard bunching up underneath his tortoiseshell glasses. He reached into his pocket and produced a red box that fit into the palm of his hand. He slid it across the countertop to Hart who picked it up cautiously. Immediately, he recognized the gold-lettered label. Cartier.

"What's this?"

"It's a gift—for Clara, of course. But also think of it as a little gift for you and me."

Hart opened the box and examined the thin platinum chain attached to a beautiful circle pendant the size of a euro. The charm was dense but exquisite. Judging by the complete randomness of the gift, however, Hart knew he was missing something.

Closing the box, Hart glared at Palmer. "No. I mean, what is it?"

Palmer grinned. "It's an insurance policy, Paul. With it, we know where you two are at all times thanks to an impossibly small tracking device embedded."

"What am I supposed to do? Just give it to her?"

"That's the general idea with jewelry. Hell, it might even pay dividends." Palmer winked.

Hart scoffed, pushing the box back to Palmer. "Clara won't accept this, and even if she did, she'd assume I'm trying to buy her trust."

"Paul, we're always trying to buy trust. Everyone, at every moment, has an opportunity to build trust. Just make sure she gets it. I'm sure you can come up with a good reason."

Before Hart could protest further, Palmer's phone began buzzing. He stood and answered, listening intently for a few moments, then grunted thanks and hung up.

"That was Kelly."

"And that was too fast. Let me guess, the picture doesn't work?"

Palmer studied the ceiling and smirked. "I told you she was the best. The van was a rental. She figured this out by the department number under the F for France on European plates. All one hundred and one départments, regions, in France have a number assigned—Paris, for instance, is number seventy-five, because it is in the Ile de France department. Most rental cars in France originate from the sixty region, Oise, because the vehicle registration tax is the cheapest. However, it also means you cannot easily track which département the car was actually rented from... Unless you have access to said company information." Palmer pushed back the Cartier box to Hart. "So I'd imagine Kelly will get us an address by this evening."

He changed topics quickly. "Have you begun to research the attorney's last days?"

Hart stirred uneasily in his chair. "We haven't gotten far. We don't have the resources to do so."

Palmer buttoned his raincoat. "I can help. Send me what you have, and I'll get some of my people working on it." He put a hand on Hart's shoulder as he passed toward the door. Speaking over his shoulder, he gave a final order. "Make sure she gets the necklace."

He paused in the threshold of the doorway. "And Paul, say something nice—ladies like a compliment."

Before Hart could respond, Palmer was gone.

Diego followed Magali from the jardin. She was completely unaware of his presence, or at least he surmised so because she went straight to the western exit and made no effort of blending into the crowd. He found himself in a trance, watching her full figure slip away in light blue jeans and a short jacket.

Her pride was making him angry because she was wasting a beautiful thing. In life, Diego didn't have many vices, only the entertainment provided by a woman happened to be the epitome of his needs. There was a certain sexiness he found in her defensiveness that hid a fiery passion always threatening explosion that satisfied him in ways no one had before.

When he was wrapped up with her, only for brief moments—his life, his mission, the things he'd done—all slipped away. It wasn't love, he wasn't foolish, but she provided him a lustful escape from life. The wrongs he'd done while straddling the fence between his nefarious employer and his actual career at Interpol did cause him to toss and turn at night, but eventually, he could sleep. The cases he'd purposefully misled, the training he'd given to terrorists, or perhaps the worst of it all, turning a blind eye to the evil witnessed, was why he sometimes second-guessed his life choices.

Diego huffed and chastised himself. There was no time to get sentimental. He was a killer—a damned good one too. There were a million more women like her, and he could have any of them. It was time to focus.

Keeping in the direction Magali was headed, he opened a secure messaging app on his encrypted smartphone. The paradox technology companies offered with regards to privacy was amusing to Diego. The companies would sell people's most private information to market a product but conversely allowed exchanges via encrypted apps, thus ignoring government pleas for oversight, giving evildoers and illegal activity a breeding ground. As a member of law enforcement, the dynamic indeed would have made him furious, but as a member of a criminal organization, it was heaven-sent.

He messaged Darlington to update him on his progress. Diego left out the part that he was following the intelligence of an investigative reporter and not his own. He received a response within two minutes. "Do what needs to be done. Zero fail mission."

Diego reaffirmed his directive, evident by Darlington's urgency.

He pulled his cap lower, stuck his hands deep in his Harrington jacket, and took off in pursuit of Magali.

20

Clara had left the jardin and headed the opposite way to Magali to the east, through Place Edmond Rostand, making for the Panthéon.

She climbed Rue Soufflot, named after the architect of the Panthéon—the street's gradual rise one of the more noticeable gradients in the relatively flat Left Bank. Not once did she feel like she was being followed. She had no reason to. After scanning the jardin during her meeting with Magali, nothing was out of the ordinary. Nevertheless, she glanced sideways into the storefront windows to double-check she wasn't followed. Satisfied, she passed the gleaming white buildings housing coffee shops, bookstores, and ateliers as she made her way to the domed building that looked over the fifth and sixth arrondissements of Paris.

After a short queue for a ticket, she paid the nine-euro entry fee. She proceeded across the marble floors, feeling a sense of security inside the hallowed halls of one of France's most distinguished burial grounds. War heroes, writers, martyrs, and philosophers who accomplished extraordinary feats for their country were afforded the honor of being forever protected by the Panthéon's high ceilings and thick walls. Those same walls also provided the perfect setting for discrete meetings. The security cameras on the property were safeguarded by the French Government's firewalls, and if anyone were to try and gain access, they'd have to fight numerous layers of security and French bureaucracy, both seemingly impenetrable in their own ways.

Past the swinging pendulum and down the back staircase, Clara found the agreed meeting place. The crypt was in stark contrast to the spacious halls of the main floor, the high ceilings traded for a catacomb maze of statues and posters detailing the remarkable lives of those buried. The hallway was five paces wide and lit only by dim track lighting, which illuminated the coffins of Voltaire and Rousseau, who faced each other as if the Panthéon hoped they could engage in eternal dialogue. Clara cleared the room and entered a doorway on the far side that lead to three separate alleyways containing various tombs. She took the far left passage and found the memorial for Jean Moulin, the French resistance fighter who withstood Nazi torture for several weeks before dying, having never given up any information.

It only took a few moments of Clara rereading his placard when she felt the familiar presence of her superior. "Bonjour, Clara," Pierre-Emmanuel said, his face peeking from the red silk scarf wrapped around his neck. They stood against the wall opposite the tomb and eyed the hallway for lingering tourists.

Clara briefly recapped her meeting with Magali, observing his every reaction—complicated enough in normal times without the darkness of the crypt. Pierre-Emmanuel's lips tightened and his hawk-like eyes narrowed as he listened.

"You recognize the need to complete this investigation while maintaining secrecy the entire way through?"

"Well, Paul and I weren't discrete this morning."

Pierre-Emmanuel's scoffed in agreement. "Did we get any leads from it?"

"Paul got a picture of the van. I'm sure something is going to come of that. Maybe we can trace the payment information and possibly get an address."

"I told you to get rid of him."

Clara nodded. "You have placed quite a bit of pressure on me. First discretion, then the Paul directive, and now you're railroading a journalist who is acting like she has the scoop of a lifetime. You've had your hands full, but I'm not sure I agree with your approach."

Pierre-Emmanuel folded his arms and lightly tapped his fingers across his forearm. "There are significant ramifications if we fail. I am not just talking about a story that will run on the cover of *Le Figaro*. I'm watching out for all of us."

Clara sighed. "*D'accord*, but my definition of failure is not uncovering the truth. Maybe Renard had a change of heart and left intelligence for us, recognizing that whoever is a part of this deal could jeopardize the global order. Maybe this can stop an attack or the shifting of regional powers. Whatever comes of it, finding the truth is the most important thing to me."

Pierre-Emmanuel stared down at his black oxfords and brushed at the cool tile as if there was an upsetting coating of dust. "You have three objectives, Clara. Listen to them carefully. First, you need to complete your investigation of this alleged black-market sale. Second"—he grabbed her elbow and gently led her down the darkened hall back towards the main walkthrough that housed Voltaire and Rousseau—"you should get rid of Paul Hart. I don't care how you do it. If you wish to get back with him later, fine, but end it for now. And lastly, don't let the press run this story. If we find nothing, you can maybe give her an idea in a few weeks. But I'm under immense pressure from the government to keep this quiet. There are already significant sanctions on Iran, and combative discussions for reducing their enrichment program have tensions at an all-time high. Can you imagine if we uncover their involvement in a brokered nuclear weapon deal?"

A dozen tourists passed them like a mob. Clara was grateful for the momentary repose. She could feel her chest rising with a mix of anxiety and anger at her superior's mandates. Whose side was he on? She needed Paul, and also needed Magali to not report on the story for some time. She was left with little room to maneuver.

"The reporter doesn't know what it is we are investigating, just who it came from. But I need Paul and the Americans. Without them, it will be too difficult. I won't push him away."

He sadly shook his head in response. The silence between them lingered; only the footsteps of solemn tourists echoed faintly.

Finally, Pierre-Emmanuel spoke. "It isn't him I am worried about. Rather his handler, Mr. Palmer. I don't want him around. It's for your safety, which I care deeply about." He placed a gentle hand on her shoulder as he walked past. "*Bonne chance*, Clara."

21

Paris, France

Le Bon Marché was nestled between a small park and the narrow street Rue de Bac in the Saint-Germain neighborhood. The old street was home to a few chocolatiers, patisseries, candle ateliers, shoemakers, and several boulangeries. Dozens of pharmacies dotted the route as well, catering to the area inhabited by older people. A joke among Parisians is the more senior residents were the only ones who'd saved enough of a fortune to live in the postcard quartier. For Magali though, the best thing in the neighborhood was the multiple-storied department store Le Bon Marché and La Grande Épicerie de Paris, the fine food market, anchoring the block. It was just the type of distraction she needed after meeting Clara.

The truth was essential, as was her duty to hunt it down. It's what made her a great reporter. She'd catch small prey every now and again, letting them go to catch the deadlier game, but she always managed to hunt the truth down. Despite her resolve, she carried an unsettling feeling after her brief meeting in the park. She knew there wasn't enough to go on, and she couldn't publish a bombshell story without the punch line. But she needed to quell her thoughts swirling in her head. She knew just the place. The store she used to walk years ago as a poor student in Paris, dreaming of the silk scarfs, the high-heel boots and fabulously bright dresses, made her, if only for a moment, relax.

Once through one of the small lobby foyers flanking the store, she passed the luxury boutiques of Chanel, Givenchy, Gucci, and Louis Vuitton but paid them no attention. The draw of Le Bon Marché for Magali wasn't the clothing. Sure, the garments and handbags that had once caught her eye were gorgeous, but her taste matured into a love for the bookshop on the top floor. She took the escalator, three of them, to the top while looking over the cosmetic and fragrance stands busy at work. A stained-glass ceiling, complete with bronze framework, allowed the natural light of the day to filter in.

Magali arrived at the bookshop, housed under broad skylights, giving the teak wood bookshelves a brightness she found refreshing. Stands of leather-bound journals, pens, coffee-table books, and thousands of novels. The maze meant one could become lost, and that was precisely her intention.

A few people milled about the shop, namely tourists, given away by their cameras hanging from lanyards and their loud exuberance as they wrestled open the boxes of candles to smell the fragrances. The shop had a particular soundtrack to it; the creaking of the floorboards as patrons moved about, books pulled from the shelves, covers closing, the soft sounds bouncing off the steel pillars and skylights high above them. After browsing the biographies, she moved on to the travel section, searching for exotic islands far away from Paris.

At first, Magali didn't recognize the stillness, lost in the back cover of a book on the Exuma Islands in the Bahamas, but when she heard a door close loudly from somewhere across the floor, she was jolted into the present.

She stood still, listening for signs of the shop, laughter, or shuffling feet, but when she couldn't detect anything, a lump grew in their throat. She checked her watch to gather if it was lunchtime and the shop had closed, but she knew the notion was ridiculous because Le Bon Marché didn't close for lunch. Cautiously she peered out from her aisle of books, searching the main floor space. There were no patrons and no sales associates. Just a man leaning against a bookcase on the other side of the room, his baker boy hat pulled low.

The air escaped her lungs. She panicked at her sudden inability to pull in any more oxygen, short shallow breathes the best she could do. *Stay calm. You're in a public space.*

Diego pushed off the shelf, took off his cap, and sauntered towards her. He wore a wicked smile and offered Magali a small wave.

"You know, I grew up working. I can recall my earliest memories in the vineyard my family ran in Spain. It was in the Rioja region, a beautiful place to grow up. No doubt. But our vineyard was one where tourists would have to get lost down a dirt road to find it." As he walked by a bookshelf, he pulled out a thick leather book as if to feel its weight and held it with both hands. "I worked like a dog there. My brother, who was older than me, didn't. No, he was going to be a great equestrian, you see. Had the gift of a once-in-a-lifetime star, could talk to the horses, whisper commands to them to jump higher and further than anyone else, to be still and prance like a fairy tale. My parents were weak with him. They made me do double the work, especially during the harvests when tourists flooded in looking to drink the crap we sold. I slaved away harvesting grapes for my entire childhood, filling wine glasses, cooking in the hot kitchen for drunk German and English tourists even while my brother practiced lounging about and riding. I must have been thirteen or fourteen when the idea came to me." He drummed his fingers on the cover of the book.

Magali backed against a bookcase. She could feel the heavy gold cross necklace she wore bouncing from her the pounding of her heart. What did he want? Was he a crazed lover that didn't handle rejection well, or was it more malicious? She spun around the shop but couldn't find anyone, as if it had closed for the evening. Diego must have caught her looking around because he broke into low laughter.

"You won't find anyone on the floor. I flashed my badge and told the store's security of a terrorist threat. They evacuated the floor silently while I kept watch on you. Perks of the job, I guess." He shrugged and then continued on. "Don't worry, we only have a few more minutes before the police arrive, but this won't take long. But we digress!" Diego threw the leather book on the floor, making a resounding thud. "My brother never worked, and I despised him for it. I begged him to help me, but he never did. What made him better than me? I didn't understand. So, one day, I'd had enough. We were at our home where the horses were kept in the barn not far from the house, and an idea came to me. In the middle of that night, I crept from my bed, went to the barn, locked the doors, and lit the barn on fire with my father's cigar lighter. Before my parents and brother could run from the house screaming, the barn was up in flames. I just stood there watching it burn and registering my family's pain. I will never forget the cries of the horses or, perhaps worse, my brother's. It wasn't long after my actions—and everyone seemed to know it was me who did it, but they didn't want to admit it—that my parents sent me to military school. I have only spoken to them a few times since, and I don't go back to visit." Diego was steps away from Magali and held out his hand. He gently caressed the side of her cheek, her lips quivering in fear, as he moved his hand around her throat.

Magali put her hands up to defend herself from his firm grip, but he swatted her away with his free hand before putting both around her neck.

"So you see, *señorita*, if I was willing to end my brother's dreams and completely denounce my family because he wasn't willing to help me, what do you think I am willing to do to you if you do the same?"

Magali bit her lip to suppress the fearful rage building inside. She couldn't break free. Panic began to set in. Her arms were trapped under him, and her hands felt down and grabbed him by the waist to push him away. Instead, a crazed smile spread over his face, and he leaned into her more, pressing his hips into hers.

Magali struggled violently to free herself, but it was no use. She pushed harder against his waist and felt his wallet sticking from his back pocket. Trying anything to take his attention away from suffocating her, she grabbed the wallet. But Diego didn't notice or stop. He might get what he wanted, but she still would provide her own small act of resistance. If he choked her to death, at least the cops would find his wallet in her hand.

Her vision slowly fading, she willed herself to stay alive, managing to speak hoarsely. "What do you want?" Her mind was erratic from her lack of oxygen.

He smirked and suddenly relaxed his grip. "Tell me about the woman you just met in the park?"

22

They were up before the sun. Paris was quiet. Only taxis blazed through rain-soaked boulevards, the sidewalks vacant of pedestrians. Hart watched the city pass by from the rear window, occasionally finding dim lights from cafés where a few brave souls stood slamming espressos at the ungodly hour. Lucas drove them south across the nineth arrondissement, past the shuttered Galeries Lafayette, which wouldn't open for several more hours. On the wide Avenue de l'Opéra, Hart caught sight of a green-lettered Starbucks sign, and for a fleeting moment, he missed home.

At Gare Saint-Lazare, Lucas pulled to the curb, and Clara and Hart climbed out of the small Citroën. Hart wore jeans, suede chukkas, and an Officine Général hopsack blazer, a small Moleskin backpack slung over his shoulder. Clara wore high black Chelsea boots with skinny jeans, a silk cream blouse, and a black leather motorcycle jacket. A purple Longchamp purse in hand. They'd packed light since their return to Paris was planned for that evening. Check out the address supplied by Kelly and return home. There were no records online or street views of the address in question, so the lead required an in-person follow-up, just like the arcade fiasco.

It took a tremendous effort from Clara, but she persuaded both Pierre-Emmanuel and Palmer to allow her and Hart to go unaccompanied. After the ambush at the arcade, everyone was uneasy, but Clara was adamant, much to Pierre-Emmanuel's chagrin. Antoine had gone back home for temporary leave to visit his baby shortly after saving Hart from the van the day prior. Everyone understood the stress on the new father.

Lucas rolled down the window after dropping Clara and Hart off on the curb. "I'll monitor everything from the US Embassy at Monsieur Palmer's invitation." He smiled. "They have a few more technical resources, so we'll be with you in real time. Call if you need anything. *Bon voyage.*"

Clara then set off with Hart into the station to catch their predawn departure for La Rochelle.

Once aboard the train, and after several espressos, Hart felt emboldened enough to ask Clara about their plans. As she laid out where they were heading, he felt a strange sense of déjà vu. He thought back to their time on the Eurostar to London, where events changed their lives forever. But those challenging circumstances were also what brought them together, and Hart remained forever grateful. Suddenly he had a strong desire to run away with Clara, forget their current mission and find a hamlet to escape from the madness of their world. A foolish thought, he scolded himself. How long could that last?

While he appreciated her detailing their day, Hart simply wanted to know about the phone call she'd received the night before. After a quiet dinner of takeaway pho, the call had flustered Clara. Storm clouds gathered as her mood worsened, and Hart saw fit to give her distance. A short time later,

Pierre-Emmanuel knocked on the apartment door asking to talk.

Besides casting a nod towards Hart, Pierre-Emmanuel had ignored him. Just he and Clara spoke in hushed tones in the kitchen. Hart sat in the living room and managed to catch the final twenty minutes of a Paris St-Germain's thrashing of Marseille FC. While it was soccer, he was comforted by the familiarity of watching a game on TV. Probably besides a well-made burger, it was what he missed most about the US.

Finally, before bedtime, Clara undressed, shimmying out of her jeans, and turned the shower on. She pulled Hart from bed and led him into the bathroom. With a slight wave, she invited him into the cramped shower. They both maneuvered in the small space to get under the hot water. Clara's hair was wet and pulled back how Hart loved it, her makeup washed away, highlighting her green eyes, just the way Hart found her most beautiful. They spoke softly about the reason for her boss's visit, the shower providing cover in an abundance of caution from listening ears. She told him that an agent from Interpol was looking into the case and wanted to meet, asking where Clara would be the next day.

Hart recalled his confusion and the jealously of another man being involved in the investigation. It was his and Clara's to conclude, no one else. Clara had agreed to meet the agent, but she didn't want Hart to come. She said it was to protect him, keep his identity a secret, an asset, but he took it as though she didn't want to involve him, the amateur, the novice who might get in the way. He played it off as a good break for the investigation, glad they might receive Interpol support.

As the train sped southwest towards their destination, passing the flat green landscape of northwest France, Hart

113

listened to Clara explain their day. Kelly provided the address once she had hacked the van rental records. First, they'd scout it and later visit, before Clara's evening rendezvous with the mysterious Interpol agent.

"So, this rendezvous, he have a nice place picked out?" Hart inquired, feigning interest at his window's view.

He turned to find Clara frowning at him. "This isn't a dinner date, Paul. It's a meeting in a public place."

"Why not invite him to the address we're scouting?" Hart countered, itching for a chance to complain about their newcomer.

"Because I don't know if the lead is even worth our time. I'd rather we went about our business first. He said he'd already be down in that area of France, so it made sense."

Hart nodded and took notice of the elderly lady across the aisle from them who'd noticed their raised voices and had since been watching them. She turned away with Hart's glare.

"Yes, so you can meet with him alone."

Clara sat up and leaned forward on the table between them. "If you have a problem with the arrangement, you should have said so last night. But if not, I'll give you another chance right now." She stared at him, daring him to press the issue.

Hart felt his internal alarm bells go off and decided quickly to retreat with a shake of his head. He was upset about the meeting, but perhaps what weighed on his mind more was the seemingly constant reoccurrence of their feuds. Small things that added up, like tiny seeds of doubt that blew from distant places and settled in, slowly sprouting and rising to the surface.

He turned his attention back to the window and felt the

Cartier box inside his blazer pocket dig into his side. He was relieved to have the necklace now, the same one that Palmer had instructed him to gift to Clara. *So I can keep an eye on you.* He thought of a way to present it to her as not to arouse suspicions. Ironically, his stupidity of starting a minor tussle worked perfectly.

"You know, what bothers me is I want us to be a team. To figure this out together." He paused, trying to read her green eyes and their tepid reaction. "Our lives are intertwined because of the very things we are investigating come from our joint pasts. It is what has molded us, and it's us who should uncover whatever there is to find. No one else. This is *our* mission." His weak attempt at an apology didn't appear to have entirely won over Clara, who let out an exasperated sigh.

"Between the two of us," Clara began, "who do you think has more experience in this type of thing?" She smiled and reached for his hand. "You need to trust me."

Hart nodded. He knew he'd backed himself up a little from the mess he'd step into.

He pulled the Cartier box from inside his blazer and saw it grab Clara's attention. Smiling, he handed it to her.

After regarding the box, she looked up at him in astonishment. "But why? And when did you have time to—"

He gently cut her off, eager to avoid questions. "I have my ways. Plus, I don't need a reason to get you a gift, just I thought you'd like it. To commemorate our new chapter."

Clara opened the red box with more caution than delight. To Hart's relief, she grinned then playfully bit her lip. She lifted the necklace from the box, its platinum gleam catching the glare of the early-morning sunlight.

"You'll look fabulous wearing it." Hart tried not to over-sell it.

Her eyes narrowed as she tucked the necklace back into its box and slid it back onto the table. "You can't buy my forgiveness or affection, Paul."

"I-I-I…" Hart stammered, searching for his words and a grasp on the quickly deteriorating situation. What the hell did he care about fulfilling Palmer's wishes and getting her to wear the necklace? But then again, he thought, it might be helpful to have when she goes to her meeting alone. "It's not a bribe. I thought you'd look stunning in it. And I have the means since my generous severance package. Figured it was about time I got you a gift." He placed his hand on hers, attempting to add reassurance.

Clara seemed somewhere between acceptance and anger.

"Could I put it on you?" He stood, gently taking the necklace out of the box.

She swept her dark espresso hair to one side of her neck and held it in place. Hart delicately affixed the necklace and leaned in to give a soft kiss on her neck. "There. Perfect." He stood back to admire her.

"It is quite lovely," Clara said, absentmindedly fingering the necklace.

"Think of it as a token of my trust." Hart said.

She smiled, her eyes bright, and leaned across the table. She pulled him by the collar and kissed him. Her lips were soft and swollen with emotion.

"*Merci*, Paul."

The train rumbled along the French countryside and into the still sleepy city of La Rochelle. The ocean peeking out from behind low rolling hills. Hart, for the first time in quite a while, felt at peace.

23

The room was busier than Palmer ever remembered. In fact, the situation room, tucked away upstairs down a hallway, had never surpassed more than three visitors in the whole of Palmer's time in Paris. But that had all changed with the recent developments in the investigation. Ever since he'd seen Pierre-Emmanuel descend into the Métro after a pre-dawn meeting with a journalist Palmer had identified thanks to facial recognition software, he held suspicions about his French colleague. So, it went without saying Palmer took particular pleasure when he had surprised Pierre-Emmanuel by calling the night before, asking for a more prominent role in the investigation. "Bien sur. *Of course, what is it you'd like to be a part of?*" For starters, Palmer wanted the inquiry to be closer to him.

Lucas entered the US Embassy, not via the long queue in front of Jardin des Ambassadeurs for security purposes, but rather through an underground tunnel accessed through the Sofitel Paris Le Faubourg next to the embassy. Reserved for shy dignitaries, if there were such a thing, or for discrete entrances or exits by intelligence officials, Lucas slipped onto US soil unseen.

Once situated in their makeshift command center, Palmer

stood in wrinkled khakis and a blue oxford shirt, sleeves rolled up, eager to get to work. He brushed his gray-speckled beard to hide a wry smile. The pieces were in place to provide more robust resources to the French-led investigation. After all, he gave Hart his word that he would be keeping an eye on him. Lucas gave Palmer a play-by-play of Clara and Hart's plans, then went about finding a workstation. Palmer closely watched Lucas work, namely his efforts to detail the hours leading up to the death of the Parisian attorney Mathieu Bertrand. Palmer knew Hart and Clara were eager to uncover the attorney's movements the day of his death. The police investigation didn't warrant such detail, according to the Parisian detectives. They accepted that the murder was a result of a carjacking gone wrong, paperwork filed. Case closed.

Palmer was surprised Pierre-Emmanuel would let him pull Lucas closer into an investigation. He knew damn well the French didn't want him anywhere near. But maybe, the French intelligence man was clever. If French politicians wanted to squash the investigation, what better way to continue than having the Americans take it over? Why else would Pierre-Emmanuel meet with a journalist? It seemed he was leaking information. Palmer figured this was why Lucas had come. Nonetheless, it thrilled Palmer. He might eventually run the investigation, but more importantly, now he could keep a closer eye on Hart. His new agent was but a young duckling in a scary new world, whether he knew it or not. He would simply follow the leader, Clara in his case, anywhere she went, leading him into dangerous waters. Palmer believed it was his job to protect Hart, his de facto duckling. He wouldn't allow his history, or more specifically, the mistakes he'd made, to repeat.

Palmer stood over Lucas's shoulder, opening a new bottle of Mountain Dew as he read from the flat-screen monitor. There was a bank logo he recognized, and Google maps up in two separate windows.

Lucas turned around and smiled at Palmer. Then he eyed the man's drink for a moment. "Do you want one? I get them flown in especially."

Lucas shook his head in a mix of confusion and disgust, as if he couldn't understand drinking a soda during the morning.

Palmer shrugged. "So what have we got on the attorney?"

"I have the whole story of his last day, but unfortunately, I don't think it gives us any help right now."

"Tell me anyway."

"The day of his murder, Mathieu Bertrand woke at seven forty-three a.m., and we know this thanks to social media activity. He logged on to Twitter to scroll for approximately four minutes. I imagine he got ready for work then, and he left his apartment in the seventh arrondissement. At eight thirty-four, he stopped by a local café, Couleur Café, on his way to the office. We know this because his phone connected to their Wi-Fi, which we traced via its IP address, for sixteen minutes. It appears he paid cash because none of his debit cards were used. Once at the office, Bertrand spent the morning in various meetings as per his Outlook calendar. He did, however, leave the office for an extended period over lunch."

Palmer took a swig of soda and nodded at Kelly working away on her computer. Her hair was tied up in a bun, and she wore her now usual St. Thomas football hoodie. She rolled her chair to Lucas, who began again, albeit after a moment of checking out his new team member.

"At lunch, it appears he left his office and headed into Saint-Germain-des-Prés. He ate at Le Relais de L'Entrecôte, and judging by the debit-card amount cross-referenced with the menu online, he ate alone or at least only paid for himself. After he went to Café de Flore, once again joining their Wi-Fi network and sent several text messages to a female clerk in the law office. She appears to have joined him for a drink there." Lucas paused and looked over at Kelly, who had silently shouldered up close to see his monitor.

Palmer saw the two exchange curious looks. "This is Kelly Caruso. She specializes in electronic footprint tracking. Thought it'd be good to bring her in," Palmer said as he walked around and took a seat at the head of the conference table.

Lucas smiled and introduced himself. Kelly's brown eyes were focused, and not bothering with pleasantries, she motioned to the screen. "Let's keep going."

He continued. "After Café de Flore, where Bertrand spent a good amount of time buying several rounds of drinks, the couple headed east towards Jardin de Luxembourg. They entered the park via Rue de Bonaparte, where Bertrand got cash from an ATM. They wandered the park for a bit, taking a few selfies. The pictures were uploaded to the cloud, which is where I found them. And afterward, they walked back to the office. Bertrand went inside first and alone via the closed-circuit cameras feed in the lobby. The girl loitered at a bookstore nearby to make sure it wasn't obvious they were together."

Palmer leaned back in the leather chair. It squeaked in displeasure. All the furniture in the room was from the Cold War days, a forgotten cave hidden away from the opulent diplomatic rooms of the embassy. Only the computers and flat-screen monitors were of the current decade. Kelly

120

strained for his attention. He gave a slight nod in reassurance. She began peppering Lucas with questions.

"What about the car, the one he left in?" Kelly asked, tilting her head slightly.

Lucas seemed momentarily distracted by her brown eyes, which were vibrant with enthusiasm, and had to ask her to repeat the question. "Oui." He snapped his fingers. "I asked myself the same question. There are no records of his apartment in the seventh having a garage stall, nor any records or payments to a storage facility. He purchased the car last year, and through professional benefits, he housed the car at the office's underground parking facilities for free. Judging by how often he purchases petrol, which is less than once every two months. He didn't drive often."

Kelly seemed pleased by the answer and raised her eyebrows, imploring Lucas to continue. "Anyway, he spent the rest of the day in the office, making phone calls and attended scheduled meetings. He did have activity on a secure messaging app, but with encryption and an automatic-deletion feature, we don't know the subject of those messages."

Lucas paused as Palmer's chair creaked when he stood. He paced around behind the table, his hands clasped behind his neck, eyes to the ceiling as if the answers were written there. "So we know he was moving around quite a bit that day. But his car stayed in the garage. Is there footage in the garage? Someone could have staked him out down there and not on the street or building."

"Good thought," Lucas started, "but the car was parked in a dead spot in the garage. No camera footage, and only the garage exit has a camera, not the three staircase entrances. And the exit camera didn't get a look inside the tinted windows."

Palmer turned towards Kelly, who was already back at her monitor typing away. "Thoughts Kelly?"

She navigated through several touchscreens before finally looking up. "The good news is the guy had great taste. The places he visited the day he died are trendy. Lots of social media activity is tagged to specific locations, selfies, stories, location updates, and I can get any security cameras feeds on the route from shops or banks. I have an algorithm set up. It could take a few hours, but it'll comb through the entire route he took, minute by minute, and piece together a real-time photo and video journey for us to follow. That would give us insights if he was being followed because we'll scan the people in the photos and videos for facial recognition. We'll cross-reference that with known criminals or persons of interest from our NSA database, and it might give us some information on who killed him." She turned back around and began swiping at her monitors.

Lucas turned to Palmer. "Had I known there were resources like this, I would have done this work days ago." He checked to see if Kelly was watching and when she wasn't, mouthed, "Who is she?" at Palmer.

Palmer winked. "We enjoy having her around." He took a swig of Mountain Dew and watched his analyst go to work.

24

Their ride from Paris had been uneventful. They were only an hour from Noirmoutier, but neither Clara nor Hart commented on this. Now wasn't the time to revisit the way things had been left, the ambiguous conversations of their futures still undecided. Maybe Clara's quietness was due to the same reasons as his: professional duty. Regardless, they passed the signs for their island sanctuary without a word spoken between them.

The port city of La Rochelle appeared to Hart to be the same as any other French town at first glance. They passed through the impossibly narrow streets, parked cars hiding small light-stone storefronts—the insurance agents, *salons de coiffeurs*, and pizzerias. In their rental car, Clara drove through the maze of streets while Hart used his phone's GPS to follow their circuitous route to the expansive blue on the screen. Finally, creeping between two buildings barely wide enough for their Skoda Octavia to fit through, the sea appeared beyond the packed parking lot. To their left, a sand-colored fortress wall, which Hart guessed was at least forty feet high, ran along the water's edge until it reached two towers framing the port entrance and inner harbor. The tallest towers guarding the port stood at over 130 feet in height.

They parked next to the towers, and they followed the stone wall until a walkway appeared leading to the top of the fortress. Hart held Clara's hand as they strolled, taking in a beautiful day at the old port city. The sun had risen high in the late morning, and the strong winds from the sea had brushed away the clouds. A few seagulls floated lazily in the breeze high above the harbor in search of scraps of baguette or discarded breakfasts.

The Vieux Port de La Rochelle was striking. Dozens of boats were moored in the harbor. Tall sailing yachts, tourist ferries, and flashy speedboats dotted the dark blue water. Restaurant terraces expanded into the walkways surrounding the port, lined with vibrant green trees providing shade. Scanning the harbor, Hart figured there was only a little more than a mile to walk around the water, with as many places to eat as one could desire. Clara pointed out a fisherman in yellow waterproof overalls delivering a cart of freshly caught fish right up to the restaurant. A waiter met him at the door and immediately started putting the fish on the ice display case next to the terrace. Hart's stomach growled. From the fresh daily catch to the creperies offering sweet and salty delights, the plethora of options called to him. The bad news was, he would have to wait.

Clara guided them past the harbor into a jungle of narrow streets full of boutiques. The buildings were densely aligned, but no more than six or seven stories in the Haussmann architecture style. Hart felt an energy in the air of the city, a quiet confidence from its people who seemed to have combined the best of several French cities: the harbor of Marseille, the architectural elegance of Paris, and the cuisine of Lyon. Clara consulted her phone, then looked up to the street signs plastered on the white stucco buildings.

"The address is a few blocks from the water. It shouldn't be difficult to find."

"What's the plan once we get there?" Hart said, recalling the staunch resistance they'd found the last time they checked out an address. He had lobbied for just him and Clara without the added protection of Lucas or Antoine, but now, far away from support, he second-guessed himself.

"We'll be fine, Paul." Clara consulted her phone and then looked at him. "We can handle ourselves, can't we?" She winked and continued down the smooth cobblestone street.

They walked for some time, the winding streets making navigation of the unfamiliar town difficult. Clara stopped to check her phone again and Hart pulled up alongside her. As he began studying their surroundings, he heard a voice call his name.

"I found you with no trouble." Antoine smirked, showing the most emotion Hart had ever seen from the man.

"What are you doing here?" Clara stood, her green eyes bright with confusion.

Antoine's smirk on his leathery lips remained. "You know that I got some time off, again, to go see *mon fils*. I heard you two were coming to La Rochelle, and we don't live too far from here. I decided since Lucas was in Paris, I would supervise. But I'm happy because I got to spend last night at home. Left early this morning. It didn't take me long to find you."

The three of them stood facing each other, all momentarily lost for words. Finally, Hart spoke in mock disgust. "So, you didn't bring your wife or son to meet us? We're not good enough?"

Antoine laughed and held up a long, skinny finger. "No. I told her about the American who almost got me run over.

She was not too pleased." He playfully jabbed at Hart. "But while I can keep an eye on you two, I could also sneak a 1664 too."

Hart laughed at the reference to the popular French beer. He was glad Antoine was with them and happy for the man who was obviously in a jovial mood after seeing his family. Sometimes it was the best, and the only remedy required.

Clara rolled her eyes at the men. Then she embraced Antoine.

"Well, it's good timing because we are going to case an address. Later I have a rendezvous with a law enforcement source, so you can keep Paul company over beers on me."

Antoine nodded stoically, seemingly back in business mode.

Without another word, the three continued through the cobblestone streets until they found the address. Antoine was ordered by Clara to hang back; she and Hart would make the approach alone. A couple would be less conspicuous.

But the building wasn't what they'd expected. Hart, for one, wasn't sure what he did expect, but the decrepit two-story brick building surrounded by chain-link fencing and water dripping through the large holes in the roof certainly didn't come to mind. The street, in contrast, was sparkling, with pristine apartments on either side of the sorry excuse for a building. Further down the street there was a Saint Michel Bakery and a soap shop.

For what felt like several minutes, they all stood in quiet contemplation. Clara was fuming, their day seemingly wasted. Antoine stood regarding the crumbling building like a work of art in an exhibition. Clara consulted her phone to confirm the address, glancing back and forth at the numbers on the unhinged front door that lay singed on the ground.

Antoine stepped into the soap shop next door to the abandoned building and stuck up a conversation with the middle-aged shopkeeper. When he came back out to Hart and Clara, he shrugged in defeat. "Owner says a fire broke out late last night."

Hart steamed. He considered the building once more, thinking it was a miracle it hadn't yet fully collapsed.

"Someone tell me what the hell we are looking at?" Clara squinted in the harsh sunlight that flooded the pedestrian street. They were several blocks from the main port, where the sun baked the air, but only now the intense heat was finding its way to them.

"Easy, the business address related to the ownership of the account paid for the van was tied to this building here. It's a dummy address—oldest trick in the book. If we dug hard enough, we could find the endless string of corporations that own this. That isn't the question, though." Hart paused and shifted towards Clara, lowering his voice even from Antoine. "Why would someone go to all this trouble to burn it down? I mean, the van didn't need to be rented. They could have stolen or owned one, swapped plates. Why bring us here? I get the feeling we're chasing our tails." Hart turned from the building while Antoine kept his eyes on both ends of the street.

Clara paced for a moment. "You may be onto something. Let's try and get out of here sooner than later." She waved for Hart and Antoine to follow as she headed back towards the port.

"I am going to call my contact—guy's name is Diego— and hope he'll meet sooner, so we can catch an earlier train home."

Hart agreed, pleased Clara shared his concern. Their time

could be better spent in Paris, driving the investigation. He was anxious to know more about the attorney's final hours, and he figured Lucas was hard at work on the subject. There was something they were all missing, and Hart needed to find it to stop the burning feeling he'd had in his stomach for the past few days. *Solve this investigation, and you're out.* Palmer's promise rang in his ears. Hart carried a burden on his shoulders, not just what he had at stake personally, but the potential danger the world would face if nuclear weapon plans were for sale. *If,* he reminded himself. It was their mission to find out.

They made their way back to the port, which was filling up with the local workforce and a few tourist ferries during the lunch hour. He regarded the ballet of waiters dancing from table to table on the terraces surrounding the port and was about to offer the idea that they stopped for lunch when Clara held up her phone. She dialed her contact, and to Hart's displeasure, she took a few steps away towards the water to give herself privacy.

The gentle rock of the boat put Diego at ease. He regarded the busy port of La Rochelle, pleased he'd slipped into town with ease after driving nearly all night. Resources had to be marshaled, and through the vast network that he operated in, he called in several favors. Those manifested in the form of a Sessa Marine twenty-eight-foot speedboat, with a small cabin below deck and two trusted Italian men he'd served with in joint Special Forces operations. The men were costly but professional and when the time came, they would do what was required without hesitation. Just like how they'd burnt the building to the ground last night. No questions asked.

His face had begun to sting from being on the water for

the past hour. Diego scratched his beard and was about to start on the *jamón ibérico* sandwich he'd found on board when he noticed a familiar face on the walkway surrounding the harbor. For a moment, he watched her, immediately taking notice of her slender frame, the shapely curves in all the right places, and the soft bounce of her dark hair. He had, in fact, been so consumed with committing her shape to memory that he almost didn't notice the men trailing her. One reddish-brown skinned man, probably Algerian with a shaved head and long arms, another man with wavy blonde hair was dressed smartly in a blazer and jeans. There was, however, something about that man that told Diego he wasn't French. He couldn't place what it was, but the man looked neither English—he didn't have the air of confidence about him—nor American, on account of he wasn't wearing sneakers, a fanny pack, and a windbreaker.

The harsh vibration of his cell phone in his jeans pocket rudely interrupted his train of thought. He relished the familiar thrill of excitement that ran through his veins when he knew danger was close. Answering the call on its fifth ring, he looked up and across the port to the woman he would meet later that day.

"*Bonjour,*" he said and saw her turn away from the two men, putting more distance between them. Good, he thought; the fewer people who knew, the better.

Diego slipped below deck to avoid her hearing the seagulls and boats passing by. He listened to her request to meet earlier than planned. No, he thought, it was important they meet at night. He couldn't rush this part. He apologized for inconveniencing her, but as he explained, he wasn't in town yet but would be there tonight. He peered out from a porthole and caught a glimpse of a restaurant right near the dock on the far side of the port.

"Again, I am sorry I can't make it earlier, but we need to meet. It's vital to the investigation. How does dinner at Le Bureau, a café that faces the port, at seven p.m. sound?"

She'd said yes and told him she'd be at a table wearing a red scarf.

Diego crept up on the deck once more, staring across the water at Clara and her two companions. *Yes, I already know what you'll be wearing.*

"*Parfait, a bientôt.*"

Diego ended the call, and from a distance, he smiled at his prey.

25

The sun had started to dip under the horizon, the last rays of sunshine fighting to light up the sky in pinks, purples, and oranges. A sailor's sky, made for a clear night, where the stars would dot the darkness. The sunset splashed off Portimão's white cliffs, sculpted into beautiful rocky shoreline long ago by the sea.

Farhad Orakazi watched the sun slip beneath the ocean. He remained on the helicopter pad of his 111-meter yacht, *No Good Deed*, for a moment longer than the sun had, letting the sea breeze wash over him. The simplest moments in life became his sanctuary, where often he could find a sense of peace. But not on this evening. In a few hours, on the same helipad, he would bring chaos onboard.

His life revolved around stress and anxiety, but he'd managed to leverage these sensations and build himself an empire. He sold his services, those of security, access, but above all else, the peace of mind his clients treasured as their money man. He worked hard to build his clientele, from corrupt politicians and businessmen and women to cartel leaders and terrorists living in caves. *Yes,* Farhad thought, *I created quite the empire.* Although it had lived in the shadows. Until tonight.

Life for Farhad was an extravagant affair. After all, everything was a bonus to him. He was living on borrowed time. At only five foot four, he made up for his lack of stature in width. His hair was thick and jet-black, always brushed straight back, held in place with copious amounts of shiny pomade. But to Farhad, his most attractive feature wasn't his bushy mustache or thick mane, but his eyes. The same color as a tiger's, brown with a swish of honey. His tiger eyes took in the sky before heading inside the cabin for dinner, but his mind remained elsewhere.

Farhad's life before the luxury yachts, silk suits, and endless amounts of young, eager women had been challenging. Born in Karachi, in the Sindh region of Pakistan, his childhood memories were buried deep in his subconscious. He remembered the Arabian Sea, the smell of the naan, the unsightly smash of colors from his apartment block, and the constant smell of oil from the nearby garage. Then, when his father died, his uncle living in the United Kingdom filed the correct forms, in the proper buildings, at the correct times, and brought Farhad and his mother to Redbridge, just outside of London. There he grew up in a 30,000-strong Pakistan community, where he learned to play cricket and speak English by watching the BBC. His uncle got his mother a job in a clothing mill in the city, stitching collars on dress shirts, while Farhad worked with his uncle, a buyer for the mill. Having a Pakistani man deal directly with his brethren from one of the world's largest cotton exporters was advantageous. From the age of thirteen onwards, Farhad learned from his uncle the craft of negotiating, sealing deals, and cultivating relationships. This birthed in Farhad the soul of a capitalist. Eventually, he graduated as a business major with honors and found an analyst position at a global bank in Canary Wharf.

But it was during his first year at the bank when eighteen hijackers attacked the United States on September 11th. Subsequently, Afghanistan was invaded to wipe out Al Qaeda. The markets reacted for a short time. The uncertainty of a new age marked by war was not a solid foundation for financial stability. Farhad didn't pay much attention to international geopolitics but instead found himself affected by the global war on terrorism in odd ways. He recognized the looks of disgust as he walked to and from his office, his Pakistani skin undistinguishable to simple-minded Westerners that couldn't tell nationalities and religions apart. It was around that time when he noticed a nondescript saloon car often parked across the street from his apartment building. Some days it would be a silver Volkswagen, but other days it would be a Ford, but Farhad always saw the faint glow of cigarettes giving two shadowy faces away.

He told himself he was imagining things, swept up in the hysteria of the new world dynamics where anyone with dark skin was a threat. He reasoned the surveillance car was for someone else, maybe a local who was the distant cousin of some freedom fighter in Afghanistan.

But one morning at the coffee shop he frequented before work, a man with thick dark hair, a clean shave, and tortoise-shell glasses took a seat at his table. The American's approach was straightforward, blunt even, Farhad would learn later. Approaching an asset cold was an aggressive move, but then again, those days were bold times, and the Americans weren't patient.

The offer, or more accurately, threat, was that Farhad work with the Americans to provide details about sensitive clients at his bank. In return, he'd get fast-tracked for a grand career in banking. The implied alternative was to ruin his reputation in his neighborhood by being outed as someone who had been passing information to Western intelligence services. Professionally, if a rumor spread that he worked for foreign governments, it would be a death sentence, but socially, Farhad would become a pariah. No longer would be able to call London home. The American had even smiled during the offer, the audacity Farhad would later reflect on. The agreement was Americans would pass insider information from various business circles in London to assist Farhad at his job. Perhaps a company was about to lose a government contract, Farhad magically would be the first to know and correctly speculate on the situation. Farhad surmised the information sharing wasn't out of American's goodness, but rather, part of the plan. Farhad moved up the corporate ladder, two promotions in two years thanks to his adept reading of the markets, undoubtedly influenced by the American's intelligence. But with his burgeoning career, his access to delicate client information and the darker corners of the bank became easier to come by. His American handler indeed was pleased with the arrangement, often looking cheery at their monthly meetings held at various hotel rooms around the city. Their investment had paid off.

Several years into Operation Enduring Freedom, as the theatrical Americans called it, Afghanistan was a mess. It was known as the graveyard of empires for a reason. Sure, America might have made progress, but vast pockets of the country were unstable, especially its border with Pakistan. Diplomacy was required to not anger the nuclear-powered neighbor. On whose side Pakistan would join was anyone's guess. Farhad had long suspected this dilemma is what led his American handler to put him in jeopardy. He was thrown into the cauldron of fanatics and zealots. At least, that is how he once viewed them, but after working with so-called zealots for many years, it was no longer the case.

One man's terrorist is another man's freedom fighter.

Farhad often contemplated what would have happened had he simply said no. Most likely, the Americans would have disowned him, his life vanishing with a heartless goodbye, rumors spread, his neighborhood turned against him, an outcast. Perhaps an older version of himself would have happily taken those punishments if given the chance, knowing what he would face in the years following that fateful arrangement. But Farhad had grown in the past fifteen years since his entire life abruptly changed course. On a purple evening in Southwest Asia, when the snow listlessly fell, was the start of his new life. One he believed was destined for greatness.

The assignment was simple, follow the money. There was a tremendous amount of cash pouring in from numerous countries funding terrorism, namely from Pakistan during the war. The Americans wanted to get the actual bills because many of the Taliban, local warlords, and community leaders would be paid off with American bills in exchange for their cooperation to allow allied forces hunting down Al Qaeda. Through intelligence, it was learned some of the marked bills had physically made their way to London. Western intelligence agencies were furious. If money could be transferred, what else could be smuggled into the UK, or America for that matter? And furthermore, what was money marked for paying off Taliban leaders doing in London?

The Americans arranged for Farhad to insert himself into the banking community responsible for the laundering operation on British soil. He was perfect: a highly positioned Pakistani banker loyal to the cause.

Farhad had been told by his handler to meet a man in Istanbul, where intelligence sources had traced the bills. In a small restaurant near Hagia Sophia, over burning-hot apple tea, Farhad met the man he would later learn was an arms dealer. He was tall, his tan suit hanging off his lanky frame. Farhad remembered being struck by the man's face, pitted with dark spots, a wispy grey beard, and black pits for eyes.

The man's network used second-generation Pakistani's living in England as pawns for moving money. Farhad explained that working through a large bank meant the money would be hidden among hundreds of thousands of transactions every day. The man's black eyes flashed with greed, and an agreement was reached to meet in Pakistan in a few weeks.

Farhad debriefed his American handler in a nondescript musty hotel near Waterloo station across from Big Ben. He was instructed to prepare for Pakistan and began, in the meantime, receiving instructions for monthly deliveries of funds into an account he oversaw at the bank. While he longed to be done with the work, he was unsure how it would end. The war in Afghanistan was escalating, as were the rumors that another Arab country was to be invaded imminently. Then his mother became ill. The American offered treatment in exchange for the continuation of his project. Farhad had no choice but to agree. That is when Farhad felt that fate had taken over. It wasn't soon after he became a slave to the Americans in order to ensure his mother's health. He was ordered to go to a place he hadn't been for many years. Pakistan.

Farhad slipped off his deck shoes and walked fifteen paces across the plush red carpet through his saloon and into the dining room. He was angry he'd reminisced about his past, noticing his clenched fists. Then again, it was a helpful reminder of his purpose. He would right the injustices done to him.

A cream-colored tablecloth and porcelain plates accented with gold tigers were set at the middle of the table. Farhad likened himself to a tiger, a beautiful creature with so much to offer but so often wrongfully captured by a formidable opponent: man. He had escaped with his life, if only just, but now he meant to be true to himself, to his inner tiger.

Farhad took his usual place at the head of the table. He had no family, and the women he kept weren't meant for conversation over dinner. One of the ship's crew, a stout man with arms the size of a normal man's thighs, placed a satellite phone and a laptop next to Farhad. It was during his first course of bouillabaisse with muscles and blue prawns, the phone rang. He let it ring while he finished taking a sip from his chilled glass of Corton-Charlemagne chardonnay.

"Is it done?"

The voice on the other end of the line was familiar, English, and edgy.

"My man is in the process of it right now. Should only be a matter of minutes."

Farhad was curiously nervous and felt the bouillabaisse tossing about his stomach like the seafood was once again alive. But he knew nerves came only when something worth having was close enough. He quickly checked various social media platforms and news blogs, finding nothing of interest. *Patience*, he reminded himself. He'd waited for decades, and now, in only a few more days, he'd have his payback. He must act confident. After all, appearances mattered.

"Send confirmation when it's done. I want this to be clean, professional."

Luke Darlington responded. "Of course. That is what he's paid to do."

Farhad, without another word, ended the call.

The hunt was in its final act, like a tiger stalking its prey, preparing to pounce. All the effort, all the pursuing through the jungle had led to this moment. The kill was just there for the taking. Soon, he would unleash hell on all those who'd wronged him.

26

La Rochelle, France

Clara, Antoine, and Hart sat at a café near the port's opening, under the shadow of the towers. Their location ensured they could see anyone arriving via the car park to their right while soaking up the view of the energetic port to their left. The nightlife was picking up, the terraces playing a symphony of conversations and clinking silverware. As the evening wore on, the three of them made small talk on the wicker café chairs under a white-and-green checkered awning. Clara had an espresso, and at Antoine's insistence, Hart ordered a demi-peche, a lager with a touch of peach syrup.

According to Clara, her contact could only meet later in the evening, and she was dead set on meeting the man to bring clarity to the investigation. Antoine was happy after his family visit, but he channeled his energy into a heightened awareness, surveying each passerby.

Clara's meeting was set for 7 p.m at a restaurant overlooking the Vieux Port. Antoine suggested that he and Hart be at the café next door, but Clara declined. They were free to do as they liked while she went alone. Hart was reluctant, but the flash of independence in her green eyes and Antoine's excitement in getting another beer ended his protest.

When it was time for Clara to leave, Hart walked her down to the far end of the port where the meeting was to take place. The night breeze cooled the sweat on his temples. Hart couldn't shake the fatigue washing over him after a long day. He put his arm around Clara as they strolled. His hand brushed against her neck. What he wouldn't give to get a hotel overlooking the port and spend the night.

"You're wearing the necklace," he said.

Clara reached up to touch it. "I am. After all, you gave it to me." She smiled playfully.

"It's important to me that you have it." He regretted bringing attention to it, not wanting her to question him any more than she already had.

She hesitated and then stopped, turning towards Hart. "I know things haven't been easy for us the past few days. Our new lives will take some getting used to." She brushed a loose strand of her espresso hair from her forehead and searched for words as if they were on the smooth grey stone sidewalk.

Hart gently lifted her chin with his finger. "Every day is a challenge, but it's what brought us together. We face challenges, but we do it as an alliance."

Clara's eyes filled with emotion. She looked towards the incoming ferries. "But should it be? Should things be so hard after all we've gone through? I just want this job to be over so we can start our lives. No more orders or ultimatums."

The words were precisely what he wanted to hear, but he knew they couldn't lose sight of their mission. Palmer made sure Hart understood. *Complete the mission, then you're out.* He smiled, willing himself to appear happy. "We're doing something good here. We are making the world a safer place. There's good karma in that. Our lives are about enjoying these little moments, and in the meantime, we can take it a day at a time." He gently brushed the unruly stray hair from Clara's eye.

"That is harder than it sounds, though." Her voice fell into a whisper. "Nuclear weapon plans? Paul, this is life or death. It's hard to focus on little moments."

Hart surprised himself by laughing. He knew the dangers of their investigation, the ease in which the fear of failure could paralyze them. But they had to focus on the present, what they could control, and whatever would come, good or bad, they would handle together. "Well, someone wise once told me that small pours save more for later. It's about keeping perspective and just enjoying what's in front of you."

Her green eyes lit up, highlighted by the fresh golden glow she'd received from being out in the sun all day. She pressed herself against him with vigor as she kissed him. Their lips locked in a fiery kiss. Just as Hart began to feel himself react, she pulled away. His hands found the small of her back. Clara wrapped her arms around his neck for what felt like an eternity. All Hart wanted to do was spend the evening alone with her. The ideal moment for him to again say how he felt, but he couldn't bring himself to do it, not until she said it back to him first.

She untangled herself and made towards the restaurant, turning back to smile at him. Hart gave a small wave, and she blew him a kiss before she slipped inside the restaurant and out of view.

27

Paris, France

Lucas leaned back in his chair and stretched, letting out an audible groan. He'd been at the console for nine hours, and while he very much would have enjoyed an actual lunch break, the Americans had preemptively brought in sandwiches, so he didn't have an excuse to leave. Which was fine because it meant he could watch Kelly work on a detailed visual of the attorney's final hours. She expertly compiled his movements on a map. At any given location with high levels of social media activity, one could click the spot and view all the posted photos arranged by GPS positioning so that you could view nearly every angle imaginable.

Lucas clicked on the location dot of Mathieu Bertrand in Jardin de Luxembourg and rifled through the Instagram and Snapchat posts. The shots weren't of him in particular, but in his light grey suit, the very clothes he would later die in, he was clearly in the background, wandering through the park on a sunny afternoon. The man appeared calm, but what could Lucas tell from a few candid photos?

"Kind of creepy, isn't it?" Kelly stood behind him. He wondered for a moment how long she'd been watching him.

"Privacy doesn't exist anymore." He clicked through

several more photos of young teenagers posing on the Medici fountain with Bertrand in the background.

She shrugged. "I scanned them all and created a program that will cross-reference all the face captures with our facial recognition database, which has over two hundred million faces. As we speak, it's running through the photos."

Lucas spun around. "That will take us days, if not weeks." *Mon dieu*, he'd never leave the windowless room.

Kelly leaned closer in the chair next to Lucas. "Should be a matter of hours. We have strong computing power." She lifted her legs up onto the table. "I noticed the first round had produced only a few results. So, I thought if our man was followed, the pursuer might not be close behind. I added a search of each area up to thirty seconds behind his route, which is running simultaneously."

It took another hour and a half, but both programs spat out seven people who showed up multiple times in the circuitous route Bertrand had taken. Palmer rolled up to Lucas's workstation and clamped a hand down on the French intelligence man's shoulder. Kelly had positioned herself over Lucas's other shoulder, directing him to run facial recognition on the seven individuals that hit multiple times. Of the seven people, four were young females that seemed more interested in getting the perfect lighting for their social media posts than murder. They agreed to rule the ladies out quickly. Of the remaining three, work began to identify the woman, approximately in her mid-thirties, and two men, one who had a thick beard and bright neon sneakers. The other man Lucas figured was late thirties, with a baker boy cap and sunglasses. The man in the cap was always difficult to make out, turned just slightly at seemingly every camera lens that he came across. It was almost as if he was trying to remain hidden.

The door to the conference room buzzed and then creaked open. A uniformed Marine received a nod from Palmer before standing back. Pierre-Emmanuel entered wearing a double-breasted navy pinstripe suit with a thick royal-blue silk tie. He offered his hand to Palmer, who took it with a gruff hello.

"Lucas messaged me that we were making progress. I wanted to see if I could be of any assistance."

Palmer gave a toothless smile to his French counterpart. "About time."

Hart had waited down the walkway to watch the restaurant after Clara disappeared inside. Several patrons entered the restaurant during the dinner hour, with only two elderly couples leaving. When he saw a tall man, dressed in all black with the swagger of an apex predator, he knew who Clara was meeting. He sighed, irritated he'd been forbidden from joining her. This Diego looked like a piece of work. Hart trudged back to the café and Antoine. He was at a table at the edge of the terrace, half in the restaurant's light and half out, holding two-refilled demi-peches. Before Hart could get a word out, Antoine handed a beer to Hart. "She'll be fine. She can handle herself."

"Yeah, I know."

Antoine raised an eyebrow. "Do you, though? She's a badass. She doesn't need your help."

Hart took a sip of his beer and silently told himself that he was incapable of hiding his genuine emotions. Yes, he was thinking about Clara, and he knew she'd be fine; nevertheless, he wished he was there. Switching subjects, Hart pressed for more background on Antoine's wife, how they met, what the future held for the couple.

Antoine stared out across the old port, studying the ships coasting in and tying up before boatloads of passengers disembarked to enjoy the nightlife of La Rochelle. "You know I like my job. It's good but hard work. *Alors*, I think since now I'm a father, I want to be home more. Play *foot* at the park, watch my kid grow into a man before he heads off to start his own family." He polished off his glass and gently set it on the table.

"What's next then? You don't want to work with us anymore?" Hart playfully asked as he drained a third of his beer. Antoine glared at him for a moment. Hart mainly figured on his hurried drinking and not the question asked, but some habits die hard.

"I don't know what's next. Maybe I'll become a local *flic* in our area, keep an eye on the streets while being close to home. But other than this, I don't know what I'd do." Antoine watched an elegantly dressed elderly couple enter the restaurant and take a seat at a table facing the port. "What about you and Clara? How are things going?"

Hart blew air through his lips and took another sip of his beer.

"That good, eh?" Antoine laughed.

A pigeon danced under their table, and Hart shooed it away.

"No, we're good. It's just..." Hart picked at the white linen tablecloth, debating how much to disclose to Antoine.

"My friend," Antoine placed his hands flat on the table. "No words needed. I know things can be challenging with a woman like Clara and your new life, but the two of you are together. At the end of the day, you must remember she is a woman who needs a man who understands her fiery ways. You cannot forget this."

Hart was astounded by the kindness Antoine was showing. Ordinarily stoic, after a few beers, the man had changed.

"I seem to be reminded all the time."

Antoine laughed. "But this is okay because you are both young enough to handle it. I always like to say, young wine goes best with spicy food for a reason."

Hart grinned and was about to agree with Antoine when he felt his phone vibrating in his pocket. The number was blocked. "I have to take this."

Antoine raised his beer in acknowledgment. Hart walked around the corner from the café.

Clara had never heard of him, but then again, why would she? Her role with the DGSE didn't necessitate collaboration with Interpol. However, she would meet the man, identify if valuable information could be obtained, and extract it without giving anything she didn't want to concede. This was what she'd learned to do every day living deep undercover in her life as the right-hand woman to one of France's most successful and yet corrupt businessmen. She listened, gave counsel, but most of all, observed. It's what led her to be continually aware of her surroundings, and she was precisely doing this while she waited at the polished oak bar for Diego.

The restaurant interior was made entirely of wood, like the inside of an old boat. The décor of ship's wheels and fishing lines hung on the walls. Clara ordered a drink, not because she wanted one, but because otherwise, she might stand out. An attractive woman alone at the bar in a relaxed port town might as well hold a sign reading *Welcome to try your luck here*, but Clara counterbalanced that aura with a glass of Bandol rosé and a stone facade. She scrutinized every man coming towards her and fended them off with ease.

Finally, after she'd counted at least four men over the age of fifty wearing colored chinos and fake teeth smile at her, an attractive dark-haired man entered the restaurant. He wore all black, from his Chelsea boots to his black bomber jacket. He stood in stark contrast to the bright colors and stripes of the townspeople. He blew past the hostess stand, strode confidently across the dining room's plush red carpet to the bar where Clara sat among five empty green leather stools. She caught him take a glimpse of himself in the mirror behind the bar before smiling at her as he took a seat. Without introducing himself to her, he flagged the barman down and ordered a Ricard with a tiny splash of water.

Clara raised her eyebrows as he threw back most of the Ricard and motion for another.

"Been that long of a day?"

Diego wiped his hand across his mouth and smiled. Clara was momentarily drawn to his eyes, a deep reddish-brown. "I was quite parched. Been a long week, actually."

Clara took a sip of her rosé and did a cursory sweep of the restaurant. A few couples dined, wearing bibs and cracking crab and langoustines, while the faint clink of glasses and silverware provided the background music.

"Clara, I presume?"

"What have you got for me?" Clara began, forgoing small talk.

"So what lead are you working in La Rochelle?" Diego asked. He leaned forward as if he tried to come into Clara's vision.

"There was a business associated with our case here. But we didn't come up with much." She paused as a waiter raced by with a basket of bread. "But then again, you were eager to meet, so I thought the trip might be worthwhile after all."

She gave him a glance from the side of her eye, and with a woman's intuition, she knew he'd find it flirtatious.

Diego rubbed his beard stubble for a moment. "How far along are you in your investigation? Do you know who killed the attorney yet? Or who burnt the address down?"

Clara thought about answering truthfully, but there was something about the man she didn't want to satisfy. How much did he know? And for that matter, how did he know about the attorney? "We have some promising information."

Diego pulled out a small tablet device and handed it to Clara. She set her glass of rosé on the oak bar and looked at the photos on the screen with curiosity.

"Do any of these individuals ring a bell?"

Clara scrolled through the grainy photos of men and women. She had to admit she hadn't recognized one until she swiped past the blonde woman who attacked her and Hart at the Paris Arcade. It took her best effort not to stop and stare at the photo. Who the hell was she? Something about Diego, the intensity with which he watched her, told Clara to hide her reaction.

Clara scrolled until the last photo, about twenty or so in all, and handed the tablet back to Diego. "Where's that list from?"

"Some known associates and people connected to the case. That's all I can say for now." He slipped the tablet into his jacket, turning his attention back to his drink.

Clara welcomed the distraction and grabbed her own rosé from the bar, and took a sip.

There was something about the man she didn't like. Maybe it was his smooth demeanor or his devil-may-care attitude of slamming drinks while on assignment. Clara, nevertheless, knew when her inner voice was trying to tell her something.

She made to reach into her purse for her phone but thought better of it. She wanted to contact Paul and Antoine to ask them to head her way just in case she required a smooth extraction. But the idea of needing to flee from a fellow law enforcement professional gave her serious concern. Something wasn't right. She could imagine after several drinks the man being somewhat aggressive, and so far, he wasn't providing much help to her investigation.

Clara shifted on her barstool while Diego watched her with renewed interest. She could feel his eyes on her. She gave a sideways glance to catch him ogling her legs. That was it. Too many warning bells. She stood and excused herself, heading behind the bar and towards the women's room at the back of the restaurant. On her way past the kitchen, she smelled the delicious buttery whitefish, so it came as a surprise that she suddenly felt ill.

Her vision began to tunnel, and her heart raced. The floor lost its certainty. The hallway felt as if she was in the bowels of a ship being tossed at sea. With a worrying clumsiness, she burst into the ladies' room and found a stall. Leaning against the partition, she tried to steady her breathing and fumbled for her mobile.

Something was terrifyingly wrong.

What was happening? She tried to calm her mind and walk through the symptoms, asking herself what could have caused her sudden nausea? She thought back to the tablet, the distraction from Diego. Had she taken a sip of wine after looking at the tablet? In her panic, she reminded herself to breathe, but she couldn't steady her breath.

Terror flooded her mind, but Clara fought to focus on getting help. She fumbled for her cell phone, finally pulling it from her purse. The screen lit up, and with great effort, she squinted and scrolled through her contacts. Antoine's name appeared first, and without hesitation, she called for help.

28

La Rochelle, France

Hart immediately recognized the voice on the other end of the call.

"We got him," Stephen Palmer said, his heavy breathing audible through the phone. Hart couldn't make out whether his boss was ecstatic or furious.

"Great, but who?" Hart wandered down a cobblestone street away from the café. The street was wide enough for only one car, if such vehicles were allowed. The dark sky showed a few stars, but the lights of restaurants and a few streetlamps lit the winding street that led away from the port. Although he trusted Antoine, Hart figured a little bit of privacy was always a good thing.

Hart again asked Palmer what he was talking about, but his boss was distracted, speaking with someone in the background.

"The assassin who took out the attorney. We got him."

Hart peered into the closed boutiques and bustling restaurants along the street as he listened on his phone. Paris seemed a million miles away.

"In custody?" Hart asked

"No, but we know who he is." Palmer paused, and Hart heard the hiss of what sounded to be a soda bottle opening.

"We tracked his movements the entire day of the murder. Got a strong hit, one man tailed the attorney halfway across Paris."

"What do we know about the guy?"

"We have a name, thanks to facial recognition. The problem is, he's a cop."

Hart cursed. Just what they needed, another layer of political muck to an already messy investigation. "Who does he work for?"

"We need to tread softly, he's a member of Interpol, but all the evidence is pretty damning. We're starting to check the guy's bank accounts and do a complete intel pull, but it'll take some time." Palmer sighed and Hart could hear him itch his beard. "I had our analysts run a back-channel request, and turns out, this guy Diego had no business in Paris the day of the murder."

Hart felt a chill run up his spine.

"His name again?"

"Diego. Diego Ramos."

Hart stopped walking. "Send me a picture now."

In the background, Hart heard the animated voice of Pierre-Emmanuel. Palmer attempted to cover the phone as the two men started bickering. The senior DGSE intelligence man seemed livid.

"One second," Palmer shouted at Hart.

He'd neared the far end of the street, where the pedestrian cobblestone met a paved road. Hart turned around. The lights from the port spilling into the sky seemed far away. Quickening his pace towards Antoine, Hart opened the texted photo... The bearded man and his tanned skin. The man he'd seen enter the restaurant earlier.

A wave of nausea swept over him. Clara was in danger.

An animalistic instinct to race to her gave him a surge of adrenaline. He began to sprint back to Antoine and screamed into his phone at Palmer. "We have a problem!"

Diego took another pull from his Ricard. The drink had been mixed with too much water for his taste, giving the silver liquor a milky texture. Still, it would do the job. He'd need it for the long night ahead. Hell, drinks always made for a wonderful evening. He always operated better afterward. The volatile mix of Special Forces training and his penchant for staying alive balanced with a brashness he developed after a few. It gave him an edge of unpredictability. The drinking had also helped steady his hand, if only ever so slightly, so he could drop a little of the potion that was currently incapacitating Mademoiselle Nouvelle in the ladies room. Rohypnol, or "roofie," or as Diego referred to it as the "Forget me pill," performed wonderfully in small doses. First, the body becomes drowsy, the brain distracted by the thousands if not millions of electrodes firing to tell the mind something isn't right. Clara had noticed it and played it off well, with a fluidity that Diego had to admit he was impressed by. He'd been careful not to add too much to her rosé from atop the bar. He'd been known to over-drug in the past, especially one time in Venice where he didn't account for the low railing overlooking the canal. But that was a story for another time. He'd felt confident he'd done well this evening.

He went to drop a few euros on the bar and once again cursed himself for misplacing his wallet days ago. He hadn't lost any IDs or personal information. Still, the tools of his trade, cards connected to accounts he frequented for what he liked to call "special activities," were lost somewhere in France. Maybe it had fallen out while he walked around Paris, in a couch, or fallen behind his nightstand. It was an inconvenience and an amateur mistake, but he couldn't worry about it at that moment. He would get paid handsomely for this job soon enough.

He slapped a few twenty notes on the bar, not because he felt like paying, but because he didn't want some waiter running after him and ruining his plans. He set off back towards the ladies' room to take his prize for the evening. He glanced at his watch and was pleased with the time he was making. The other team would have met their mark by now, otherwise, they would have contacted him with a change of plans. Yes, Diego thought as he strode past the kitchen, none of the chefs giving him a second look. Tonight was going to be a wonderful evening.

Hart raced down the narrow street, his chukka boots thumping on the cobbled stone. He skidded as he turned towards the restaurant and made it around the side of the building when he heard the smashing of several glasses and shrill screams. He scanned the terrace, drawn to the man slouched in his chair, arms dragging on the ground.

Antoine.

His eyes were open as if he was staring at Hart, but the tiny dark red dot in his forehead told him the story. He leaped down onto one knee, ignoring the screams of the restaurant patrons, and stuck his fingers onto Antoine's neck for a pulse. He knew he wouldn't find one. Nothing could be done for the new father.

Hart fought the urge to vomit.

He stood, barely, his legs wobbling. Hart looked across the port towards Clara's meeting place. Several waiters in white coats whistled for his attention and pointed to the port.

"*La bas! La bas!*" Hart made out two dark shapes moving down the pier. The assassins had come while he was away, a brazen attack. *It would have been me too*, Hart thought. If Palmer hadn't called, he'd be sitting right next to Antoine, a dead man. Without giving the dark shapes a second thought, Hart took off, sprinting towards Clara, terrified of what was happening.

His brain processed the facts while his instincts cried out to him to protect the woman he loved, who was undoubtedly in peril. He had to make it to her before Diego could do anything. If he hadn't already. His fear pushed aside by purpose. *Get to Clara.*

Hart was gaining on the restaurant, only two hundred yards away when he heard, and then saw a long white speedboat racing to the back wall of the port. The boat cut its engine and expertly drifted sideways next to the port wall just in front of the restaurant Clara was at. Hart continued sprinting, jumping over a park bench when a large group of tourists blocked the walkway. Straight ahead, he could make out the entire block. There were crowds of people but no sign of Clara, or Diego. The boat, however, was there for a getaway. Intuition told him so.

He heard his phone ring again as it had been doing constantly since he'd hung up on Palmer. There was no time to answer. No one else could help Clara, no one but him. It was then he saw a massive figure emerge from around the corner of the restaurant. At first sight, it was as if a giant had stepped from the shadows, but upon the figure stepping into the light from the streetlamps, Hart saw it was Diego, with the limp body of Clara over his shoulder.

Before he could think of any strategy, he reacted emotionally, bellowing Clara's name across the port. Hart's voice echoed off the old stone buildings surrounding the water, but Clara didn't respond. Diego, though, searched for the voice until he met Hart's eyes. A sinister smirk slid across his face.

Hart gritted his teeth and ran faster. He was only forty yards away when Diego handed over Clara to one of the dark shapes Hart had presumably seen fleeing from Antoine earlier. There were three men on the speedboat, and Diego hopped down several feet off the port wall onto it. Within an instant, they jumped away from the wall and out of Hart's reach.

He skidded to a stop, staring at the boat as Diego and the others took seats in the aft. Hart's lungs burned, but he called out Clara's name once more out of desperation. He saw her hand first, a small wave as if beckoning him, and then she lifted her head, her eyes seemingly trying to blink away her obscured vision. It was the fuel he needed.

Hart scanned the port until the two looming towers that protected the entrance gave him an idea.

Without hesitation, he took off, sprinting back the way he came, toward the tower a hundred yards ahead. He kept watch on the speedboat, which was thankfully slowed by traffic of several large ferries leaving the port for the evening. The speedboat was not near the port walls, so Hart couldn't have run onto any of the docks and gotten close enough to jump on board. He knew he only had one shot of saving her.

Diego caught sight of Hart running and lifted a hand to block the light emanating from around the port. Hart saw him motion to one of the other three people on the boat. While he was still more of a dark shape than a person, Hart could tell the man had pale skin and a shaved head. He pointed at Hart and then…

156

Suddenly, the trees alongside Hart exploded. The bullets cut through them, smashing into the buildings behind, shattering glass and screaming panic rained. The only protection Hart allowed himself was his raised arm, which was more of a reflex than anything else; it certainly wouldn't stop a bullet. The gunman from the boat spat three-round bursts at Hart but he was too far away, and shooting from a moving position at a target in motion caused terribly inaccuracy. But Hart could tell from the muzzle flash and the bullets' solid whacks against the buildings, the weaponry was the first rate. These were serious professionals. Undeterred, he sprinted on, his legs burning and his lungs screaming for oxygen while his body pumped adrenaline to urge him forward.

Hart took one last look at the boat, which was nearing the exit between the two towers. The ferries had cleared, but now there was a fishing boat coming into port, lazily straying from its course, blocking the opening. Hart covered the ground to the tower and bounded up the first flight of stairs, climbing as fast as he could. From his elevated viewpoint on the stairs, he could see Clara curled up in the boat's aft, not moving. Racing up the second and third flights of stairs, he turned left and found the door leading to the top of the tower's lookout platform. From there, he could use the far window to leap into the water below. He had to find a way on that boat, and with its current lack of progress, thanks to the tight opening of the port and the fishing trolley blocking the way, he had hope.

He crashed into the door with all his might and tried the handle. No joy. He shouldered it once more, cursed out loud, and kicked the old wooden door with all his strength. But he was no match for the ancient steel padlock. Changing tactics, he ran to the far side of the wall facing away from the port and leaned over. A ledge went around the outside of the tower, just wide enough that he figured he could stand with his feet spread out to the sides.

A boat horn sounded as he climbed over the ledge. The sky was darker this side of the port. Gone was the light spilled across the walkways and terraces, instead replaced by the vast emptiness of the ocean. Hart shimmied across the ledge, his back firmly pressed against the stone façade of the tower. The water below was choppy. Small white caps lapped against the stone walls surrounding the port. Hart assumed he was about four stories above the water. He only had one chance to get on the boat that was only yards away from being out of the port and on to the open sea. He had one shot, and he couldn't afford to miss.

While he couldn't land on the boat, it would be like hitting the sidewalk from his high above. But rather, he figured he could get in the water, as close as possible to the boat and possibly hitch a ride on the back swim deck. He'd cut it close, and if he landed on the boat, he'd be badly injured, but so be it. He disregarded the thought of the high-caliber machine gun and focused on making the leap.

Had he been thinking logically, he would have told himself he was foolish, stupid even, to consider such an idea, but matters of the heart and mind differed. There was no choice. He had to do it for Clara.

Hart threw himself from the ledge into the dark of the night, a silent prayer whispered to an unseen guardian angel. Time slid by as he fell. The fresh night air rushed up to meet him, the black water seemingly still ready to swallow him whole while he fell like a bird with a broken wing.

Then he saw the speedboat break through the port opening and flash beneath him as its powerful twin engines rocketed it past. Hart caught a grin from Diego as the man watched Hart falling from the tower.

He was too late.

Right before he plunged into the water, he heard Clara scream from the vanishing boat.

When he broke the surface, the boat, and everything he held dear, was gone.

Part II

The Chase

29

She's gone.

I've failed her.

It was the only thoughts Hart had since the night before.

She's gone.

I've failed her.

Hart was back in Paris thanks to the quick actions of Stephen Palmer, who had sent the cavalry to help his shattered asset. No more than forty minutes had passed since Hart had watched Clara disappear into the vast sea, when the quick-response team showed. The woman in charge of his rescue from French authorities flashed a badge and diplomatic papers, making an appropriate amount of fuss, then took a shaken Hart back to Paris via helicopter. La Rochelle was a mess, with wounded civilians scattered about on the promenade, victims of the indiscriminate firing from the boat. Miraculously, there were no causalities reported. At least, no one other than Antoine, Hart had thought when he was told the news.

The helicopter had landed at Issy-les-Moulineaux Heliport, which sat on the Seine River in the south part of the fifteenth arrondissement. A short ride in an armored SUV brought Hart to the US Embassy, and by 5 a.m., several hours after Clara had been taken, he was in the conference room where analysts hurried in and out from their computer stations. He felt sick to his stomach. Having remembered Clara's necklace, he had tried to phone Palmer several times but was told simply, "We're working on it."

Hart tore through the embassy halls in an angry stupor, stuck in a surreal world where his mind could barely process what had happened. How could a reality exist where his own sense of loss outweighed the threat of nuclear weapon plans falling into dangerous hands? Damn it, he scolded himself. She wasn't gone yet.

He'd entered the conference room looking for Stephen Palmer, only to find Lucas with his head in his hands. Upon Hart entering, Lucas slowly stood and put a hand on Hart's shoulder. Without further acknowledgment, Lucas slumped back down. Hart had felt the man's hand shaking uncontrollably.

Hart went to the corner of the room and leaned against the wall. Analysts rushed in and out, a beehive of activity. He hadn't recognized anyone. Where the fuck was Palmer? He wanted answers, and his temper was boiling. He scanned the room insistently and wanted to take over for the analysts pouring over typography maps, and traffic camera feeds. He needed to talk with Palmer, to form a plan.

The sickness he left at being away from Clara left his breath shallow, his heart jackhammering in his chest. There seemed some poison in him, eating him alive. Worse perhaps, was not knowing where she was. He wanted to cry out, scream, put a fist through a wall, or better yet, hit someone—anyone—to get her back. But what could he do? He reminded himself of the necklace, hoping this ordeal could be over in a matter of a few hours. He couldn't be sanguine;

a happy outcome wasn't guaranteed. Who had her, and what did they want with her? Hart knew he was ready to explode. He'd put all his negative energy into getting her back. The problem was, where to even start?

It had only been a few hours since she'd been taken, but already the sensation of the last time her lips were on his was fading. He should have demanded to go with her. The profound sadness he felt was met only by his resolve to find her and never feel this way again. There was no comfort he could find, not until he got her back.

Where the fuck was Palmer?

After the dust had settled and a quick-response team picked up Hart in La Rochelle, Palmer went to work. He knew what he had to do, and it would be costly. No matter, fortune rewarded the bold. Palmer swore he'd never put an agent in harm's way by trusting anyone else but himself again. Hart should have been protected at all costs, but Palmer had failed him. Once again, the mistakes of his past returned without ceremony.

Palmer hurried down a wide windowless hallway in the embassy. The harsh fluorescent lights burned his tired eyes. He knew he was exhausted, eyes bloodshot, sleeves on his wrinkled white shirt rolled up in crisis mode. It had been a considerable amount of time since he'd used a mirror, but as a seasoned veteran of operations gone awry, he didn't give two shits about that. No, what he cared about was in his hand: a photo of Pierre-Emmanuel at the café near Le République. He was sure as hell going to find out what that meeting was about.

He'd separated his prey from the pack. Lucas was told to remain around the control room once Hart returned, while

Palmer requested a uniformed Marine take Pierre-Emmanuel to his office on the third floor. There was a little protest to the request. After his agent was taken, the French intelligence man seemed to stagger upstairs in a daze. Usually, had never taken orders from an American, but technically on US soil, the shellshocked man put up little resistance.

Palmer's office was more dungeon than a workspace; the perfect place to let someone stew for an interrogation. The office had no windows, memorabilia or pictures on the walls, only a clock to watch time slip by and a sign on the door that read Today is *September 12th, 2001*. Tucked away down a desolate hallway across from the emergency fire escape—for the veteran intelligence man, not by accident: Always have an out. He wished he had one now for the shitstorm he was in.

Pierre-Emmanuel had been waiting nearly twenty minutes before Palmer barreled into the room. The solemn French intelligence officer sat hunched at Palmer's desk chair, drumming his long fingers on the leather top.

"Let's not play games, Stephen." Pierre-Emmanuel stood and buttoned his suit. "What's the meaning of this?"

Palmer huffed and closed the door. "Did I ever tell you I was married?"

His colleague shook his head from side to side and tried to speak, but before he could, Palmer started again.

"Well, I've been married twice and divorced the same. The damnedest thing to me was both marriages were completely different. The first wife I loved, like a teenager with a crush. She was a redhead with the bluest eyes you've ever seen." Palmer took off his glasses and set them on a bookshelf near the door. "But that one ended pretty badly. She was stepping out on me with almost everyone she met. She'd deny it, which I allowed because I wanted to believe the lies. Which is quite ironic since I've worked in the intelligence business almost all my life. You'd think I'd have better instincts about lying."

Pierre-Emmanuel wrinkled his face in confusion and held out one of his long hands. "Stephen, I don't understand the point of this. We have a missing agent, and now we don't have a damn lead on these weapon plans. Time is crucial—"

Palmer interrupted Pierre-Emmanuel by picking up one of the two chairs facing his desk and heaving it into his office wall. "I'm not finished!" He barked, leaning over the desk and well inside the personal space of his counterpart. When Pierre-Emmanuel grew quiet, Palmer straightened up and continued.

"So there I was, a young man in love, with a wife I didn't know if I could trust. One night, she told me she was going to a café with a friend. I followed her because my gut told me to. I should have known the moment that sinking feeling struck that it wouldn't end well. Sure enough, she kissed some tall bastard outside an apartment building and went inside. It was that moment when I made a promise to myself. I'd always listen to my instincts. And I'm damn glad I did." He held up the photo of Pierre-Emmanuel and the reporter at the café. "I had a bad feeling about your meeting, and then next thing you know, my agent and yours find themselves in a gun battle, with one missing in action. Now I want you to tell me what the hell is going on, or am I going to beat it out of you?" Palmer steamed, he could feel the heat in his face, the rage burning in his eyes as he fought every impulse he had not to drag Pierre-Emmanuel from behind his own desk.

Pierre-Emmanuel cleared his throat and straightened his tie. "So, you followed me? Clever, but not what a spouse should do." He walked from behind the desk and made for the door. "That was a mistake. And now we will go about our business separately. I hope you enjoyed your hissy fit, but I won't dignify it with a response."

Palmer felt the swift breeze Pierre-Emmanuel made as he hurried past him, making for the door. He threw out his arm, grabbing him by the lapel and spun him so his fleeing colleague faced him. Using his smaller height to his advantage, Palmer drove the taller Pierre-Emmanuel into the far wall of the office, causing several picture frames to crash onto the floor.

"Get your hands off of me!" Pierre-Emmanuel cried out.

"Tell me her name. The woman you met." He shoved his taller colleague into the wall once more for good measure.

A lock of hair fell across the Frenchman's face. With his hand shaking ever so slightly, he brushed it way. "She's a reporter. I was trying to help, to cover our mistakes from long ago. She doesn't know anything."

"Name?" Palmer hissed.

"Magali Martin."

Palmer let go of the lapels but stuck his finger in Pierre-Emmanuel's face. "So, help me God, if you put my agent's life at risk…"

"We don't know whether—" Pierre-Emmanuel defended himself by holding up his index finger.

"Which is why you're going to go talk to her. Take Lucas and make it quick."

"Don't give me orders in my own country," the French officer snapped.

Palmer growled. "You may be in France, but know, there is no place on earth you could hide from me if I find you're to blame."

Without another word, Pierre-Emmanuel barged shoulders with Palmer and made for the door. Palmer didn't bother to watch him leave; instead, he headed towards his computer. He had a necklace to track and an agent he needed to talk off the ledge.

30

Hart stared at the red blinking dot in the middle of the blue. As far as the GPS tracking screen showed, the red dot was surrounded by hundreds of miles of water in every direction.

His eyes hadn't left the screen since Palmer had shown it to him twenty minutes earlier. He simply watched the red dot blink as it moved across the Atlantic Ocean.

Palmer stood next to him, but Hart had ignored him ever since he activated the tracking beacon in Clara's necklace. She was right there in front of Hart on the screen, but she couldn't be rescued, like a prisoner seen through impenetrable glass walls.

Hart unfolded his arms and hooked them behind his neck, trying to catch his breath like he'd just run a marathon. His heart pounded against his ribcage.

Palmer was the first to talk. "I know what you're thinking, and I'm sorry it's not that easy."

Hart scoffed. "Like hell, it isn't! We go and get her now. Can't you call up the Navy SEALs?"

Palmer turned to face Hart, and through his thick bushy beard, he could see the man's frown. "We can't get anywhere near that boat. They'll kill her if they see us coming."

"How do we know she…" Hart trailed off, looking back at the red bot blinking away on the map of the Atlantic.

Palmer seemed to ignore the train of thought. "The best chance we have at getting her back safely is to monitor from a distance. If the worst has happened, there's nothing we can do. But they took her for a reason, Paul. Our best shot to keep her alive is to see how it plays out. In the meantime…"

Hart turned back towards him and threw his arms up in the air. "In the meantime, what the hell can we do?" Hart shook his head and then snapped back straight up with another idea. "We can send a drone, a submarine, something to be close by."

"They're in international waters, Paul, I can't command the Navy to conduct an operation for a French national who may or may not be on that boat. Not with everything still up in the air concerning the sale of these plans. Plus, a drone might as well be a big sign saying 'We're watching and waiting.'"

Palmer skirted around Hart and plucked a manila folder from the outstretched hand of Kelly.

"We managed to get a satellite images, she was taken by speedboat to a large yacht, which is now sailing west, presumably across the Atlantic. The crossing will take over a week by Kelly's calculations."

Hart grabbed the folder and opened it to find several photographs inside. The yacht was enormous, with its hull half painted blue until just above the waterline. Behind the first grainy photograph from the satellite, Kelly provided several pictures of the interior and cabin spaces. It was as opulent as grand, all the modern amenities of a five-star resort—a sauna, gym, library, wine cellar, movie theater, cigar lounge, amongst more than half a dozen bedrooms. The yacht was a floating palace.

"Kelly's working on identifying the yacht owner. No surprise, it's hidden behind several shell corporations. Will take time to crack."

Palmer paused to let Hart leaf through the photos for a moment. "But you need to understand, any operation we could plan puts her at risk. We must be prudent. I'm sorry."

"Fuck you and your prudence." Hart threw the folder to the ground and bumped shoulders with Palmer. He threw open the door to the hallway to find two uniformed Marines turn to block his exit. He turned towards Palmer with a look of disgust.

"So, am I a prisoner now?"

"Paul, you have to trust me."

"Trust you?" Hart shouted, slamming the door shut. "Trust you?! You're the reason for this!" He banged his fist down onto the conference room table, causing Kelly to flinch. "I have to get her back. You've got to let me try."

"Paul, you wouldn't last thirty minutes on your own going after her."

"But it'd be thirty minutes well spent. I won't just sit here."

Palmer sadly shook his head and took off his glasses. Deliberately, he pulled a handkerchief from his back pocket and delicately cleaned his frames, holding them up to the light.

"We're going to get her back. I can promise you that." He paused. "I'll bet my life on it. We're going to get her back. Together."

31

Atlantic Ocean

The cabin rolled rhythmically, gently waking Clara from a deep sleep. It was one filled with vivid nightmares, the most prominent of which was of men in black hooded masks chasing her with guns, across a beach she recognized in Noirmoutier.

Her eyes snapped open. Her fears, sadly, were her reality. In a flash, she took stock of her surroundings. First, she noticed the streaks of sunlight sneaking in between the shutters, the tufted-leather ceiling, the polished wood dresser, nightstand, and door. She sat up, surprised to find no restraints, and noticed she still wore her clothing from the day before. The familiar sensation of being on a boat dulled by the sheer size of the one she was a passenger of now. Standing, she made for the window and lifted the shutters. The expansive ocean greeted her, and a hazy horizon a great distance away was lit by a rising sun.

Think Clara. She willed herself to steady her mind, but the drugs from the night before had not entirely worn off. She felt hollow, groggy, in desperate need of water. Pieces of her kidnapping came back to her, the bar, the dark handsome man, Paul running, the gunfire, the tower, Paul...

Clara felt her heart catch in her chest. Was Paul alright?

She'd seen him unarmed, racing after her. The jump from the tower... She had to find out his condition. But how? Who kidnapped her, and what did they want? Clara's mind swirled with a million questions.

She unsteadily shuffled to the expansive bathroom in the cabin. Marbled black-and-white ceramic tile covered the floor, the walk-in rainforest shower, and toilet area. The vanity cabinet of polished oak cabinet was stocked with bottled water, vitamins, Hermes toiletries, and several bottles of ibuprofen. She took two pills from the bottle but thought better of it. How did she know they weren't drugged too?

This is madness, she thought. Might as well check to see if the main door is even locked.

It wasn't.

Outside her room, Clara hugged the wall in the narrow hallway. The plush red carpeting led past several closed doors, which Clara checked were additional vacant bedrooms. At the end of the hallway, she found a staircase which she cautiously climbed. Voices came from the floor above. She crawled to the top of the stairs. As she peered over the top step into the expansive parlor room, no one could be seen. She'd have to make her way through it to get to the outside deck. And do what exactly? She hadn't a clue, but a small voice in her head told her to keep moving.

Always advance, Clara. Just keep moving.

She crawled up the stairs on all fours, staying low into the parlor room, and slid behind a black leather couch. The ornately decorated room had peculiar red-and-white wallpaper depicting what she could only guess as a samurai battle complete with tigers in a Japanese village. Under a grand crystal chandelier that gently chimed with the ship's movement, black leather couches and armchairs sat facing the far wall where a massive flat-screen TV hung on the wall as if it were floating. The ship, Clara realized, was even more massive than she initially thought. Questions swirled once again in her mind, but she pushed them away. *Keep moving.*

Sunlight filtered into the room from both sides through the picture-frame windows. Gold crown molding reflecting some of the rays gave the room a frightening glow from the red wallpaper. Clara caught sight of two crew members outside on the portside deck wearing matching red polos. They moved like killers, with big arms, beards, and sharp faces hidden behind oversized sunglasses. She let them past and silently moved further into the room. She noticed the staircase doubled back behind her to the bridge on the floor above. She could hear the voices more clearly now and with stealth, moved away from the stairs and hid behind the couch.

If she could manage to get to the bridge, there'd surely be a radio to call a distress signal on. But where were they sailing to? She didn't have a clue. Every window showed the deep blue sea. *Think, Clara.* There must be a lifeboat she could stow away on? No. She had no idea where they were, or even who was "they"? With no supplies to live on, and the almost definite certainty of being spotted as she made her escape, she likely wouldn't get far.

It was decided then. Advance. She'd charge the bridge, subdue the captain, send out distress signals and get back to the continent. Clara scanned the room. On top of a stack of nature photography books on the coffee table was a silver airplane paperweight. She took it in her left hand and was immediately surprised by its weight. It was about to become an unconventional weapon. She took off her shoes to quiet her approach. Even on the soft carpet, she wanted every advantage. She climbed the stairs with alertness, one at a time, as she strained to listen to the voices from the bridge. She heard English, spoken with an accent Clara placed as Italian, and the other she couldn't quite make out, but it had been a woman.

She heard a door slide open and shut, then silence.

All she needed was a minute, maybe less on the radio. She could send out her distress signal, and she knew they'd come for her. French, British, anyone listening. A few good swings with her paperweight, and she could clear the bridge, allowing her the time to send her cry for help. She knew teams would be looking for her already. Was Paul? She caught herself and took a deep breath.

She burst up the last few stairs, quick as a cat.

Clara was shocked by the captain's size, dressed in all white and with a tanned bald head. He faced the bow, eyes glued to the horizon. Momentarily, she froze, but surprise was her ally against the man's size. She swung the paperweight with all her might and connected the plane's nose with the back of the man's head. He fell forward onto the control panel, grabbing at the wheel as he went down. The large yacht responded to the mistaken command and swung starboard. Clara was knocked off balance by the yacht's maneuver and braced herself using the captain's chair.

The door to the bridge from the opposite deck banged open. Two of the large crew members jumped into action. The first righted the yacht, straightening the vessel, while the second stepped over the captain and raised his fists at Clara.

The radio hung above the steering wheel. She could almost reach up and grab it. But now there were two men in her way. She gripped the paperweight tighter and made like she was going to swing it. The man in front of her instinctively raised his arm to try and block or grab her. But instead Clara kicked hard into the man's knee with enough force to hyperextend it backward. He doubled over in pain, and Clara then brought the paperweight down on his back while she drove her knee into the man's face. He fell onto the ground, next to the incapacitated captain.

Clara was about to start towards the remaining crew member operating the wheel when she heard the unmistakable sound of a round being chambered behind her. She turned cautiously. There stood a blonde woman with her hair tied up in a bun, porcelain skin untouched by the sun, and sharp, cold-blue eyes. She had a rectangular face, but she was undoubtedly beautiful. Clara recognized her from the Paris arcade, where she'd attacked her and Paul.

"That's enough now," the woman said, with the same accent Clara couldn't place.

A light breeze meandered through the bridge. Clara dropped the paperweight and brushed the hair from her face. She looked at the radio and silently cursed.

She'd been close.

32

Paris, France

They took one large black SUV through the long and wide streets of the eighth arrondissement, past L'Opéra de Paris. Hart couldn't help but think of Clara, and the day they met. It felt a lifetime ago. It wasn't far from where they drove past now, the memories of the first evening out together with her best friend Justine, at a local bar with moody lights and strong drinks. The very first time he'd laid eyes on her, he wanted her in his life. Fate worked in mysterious ways. Now he hoped their story wasn't over. Hart continued to stare out the window but was struck by the sudden unfamiliarity of Paris. It wasn't the same without Clara.

The SUV traveled straight through the eighth towards the white-domed symbol of Sacré Cœur on top of the hill in Montmartre.

Hart sat alone in the back, with Palmer in the passenger seat alongside a mountain of a man who drove them. Palmer had briefly introduced Hart to their driver. George was deeply tanned, middle-aged with a shaved head and watchful brown eyes. He barely said a word, only nodding as Palmer gave him specific instructions while driving, his arms barely contained by the red Henley sweater he wore.

George wore a thin hiking vest which Hart assumed hid his sidearm. While George didn't exactly blend into the chic Parisian surroundings, Hart could tell he was a warrior, and he was glad to have the extra set of hands.

Palmer had pulled the men together into the empty conference room while Kelly gave them their briefing. According to Pierre-Emmanuel, the target was a reporter named Magali Martin, who had contacted both him and Clara. Kelly had pieced together intercepted communications from Magali and Diego. There were frequently in the same place simultaneously, and according to Magali's messages, they'd met up and spent a night together. Kelly told the men the reporter's intentions and affiliations were unknown. Magali was to be treated as hostile until proved otherwise.

Palmer hadn't decided either what side the reporter was on. Instead, he hedged his risk and rounded up the toughest man at his disposal for fieldwork.

"We're off the books," Palmer said, downing the last few drops from his Mountain Dew. "This reporter can't know we're coming, otherwise, she could tip someone off, or worse, run away. She's the best lead we got. Better make it count."

George uneasily navigated through a roundabout. "So our French friends, they know we are conducting an op on a French national, in Paris, I might add?"

Palmer grunted. "They'll get over it."

For the next thirty minutes, the three men watched Magali Martin sit on the steps of Sacré Cœur. Hart and George did a lap around the basilica and found no idle watchers or security elements out of place. Palmer watched Magali in anguish from the base of the wide stairs with a view overlooking the city. She could conceivably be at a drop or a meeting. The place was packed with tourists, providing plenty of cover. He knew he didn't have the luxury of time.

Kelly had traced Magali's phone and Métro card to the hilltop refuge overlooking Paris. The area packed with tourists taking in the sweeping panoramic of Paris below—the Eiffel Tower in the distance, to the spire of Notre-Dame resting on the Seine. Street performers were dancing, drawing caricatures, vendors selling cotton candy, a kid dribbling a soccer ball while hanging from a lamppost smiling for a few photos, and of course, tips.

Palmer took out his cell and called George.

"SUV in place?" he asked.

"Parked past the tourist shops of Montmartre and ready to roll at a moment's notice should we need to scramble."

Hart peered over George's shoulder, up past the steep steps in front of the gleaming white basilica. Even from his distance, he could easily see their target's beauty. She sat and smoked in a black leather jacket, a knitted brown shoulder bag lay by her side. Her dark hair was tied up in a makeshift bun, highlighting her bright and pensive eyes as she stared at the city.

Hart thought about walking up to her then and there but doubted George would let him take a step in her direction. As if George read his mind, he put a firm hand on Hart's shoulder.

"Don't rush into anything. We have this covered." He offered Hart a nod and smiled.

Hart realized his impatience was getting the better of him.

Palmer climbed the stairs to a spot behind Magali. He stood

directly behind her and watched the crowd. A minute later, Hart, with his breath held, followed Palmer as he approached from Magali's left. He was in stark contrast to the tourists in his muted clothing and thick-soled derbies, and if that didn't completely give him away, his sour look might.

Palmer didn't appear to startle the woman as Hart watched him presumably ask if he could take a seat next to her. The response drew a shrug of the shoulders and eventually, Palmer sat and began chatting with their target.

The steps were crowded, but there was ample space to be found next to his mark. Palmer steeled himself for the approach. His hands hung loosely at his sides as if willing them to stop from twitching. This was personal. He would find out what her relationship was with Pierre-Emmanuel and how their talk somehow led to his agent getting shot at and another kidnapped and taken to the middle of the Atlantic.

"Mind if I sit?"

Magali Martin didn't bother looking up. "I do mind." Her words were smooth. Not said with vitriol. Her accent was subtle.

Palmer chuckled in amusement. *She's got some fire.* He sat anyways and viewed the city under the late-morning haze.

He began to introduce himself when she interrupted. "You can fuck off."

"Now, that's no way to treat a stranger." Palmer offered a half-smile.

Magali smacked her lips. "I know why you're here, and I already gave you everything I had, okay? I don't want to be a part of your game. Leave me alone."

Palmer frowned. Had Pierre-Emmanuel already spoken to her? Told her not to cooperate? The thought angered

Palmer, but he didn't allow himself to jump to conclusions. Instead, he switched tracks.

"Why are you, a native Parisienne hanging out at one of the busiest tourist destinations on such a beautiful day?"

Silence hung for a moment between them. The crowd down the steps clapped as a young man surpassed one hundred dribbles with a soccer ball, weaving it over and under his legs, all the while wearing a blindfold.

"I've always wanted to move from Paris," she began, taking a cigarette pack from her purse. "Every time something happens that makes me want to leave, like an asshole boyfriend, the noise, the pollution, I come up here to watch the tourists look at my city." She lit the Gilante with a silver Zippo with a flaming heart logo and snapped it shut just as quickly. "Because to them, Paris is merely a dream. A place they'll visit once in their life. They'll stay for a week and tell their friends and family how magical it was for the rest of their lives. Maybe some might even complain it wasn't that great of a city. But they'll all remember it. It gives me the perspective that no matter what, I am still fortunate." She pulled on her Gilante and pushed the smoke out through her nostrils.

Palmer caught the light in her golden-brown eyes, which seemed more sad than anything else. He nodded in agreement. Her logic was quite sound, he reasoned silently. He might even take up the practice himself. His usual way of dealing with letdowns was a trip to the hotel bar down the street for an expensive negroni and fits of jealousy over the sumptuously dressed women.

Palmer glanced at the crowd, catching Hart standing at the bottom railing, George on his shoulder. His young asset was angry and impatient—a volatile combination. Palmer couldn't blame him. Clara was gone, and with her, seemingly Hart's purpose. But, Palmer couldn't afford to lose another agent, physically or mentally. But time was not a luxury they had, Hart was a rocket ready for flight.

"I need your help," Palmer said softly.

"I told you, I don't want to be a part of this."

"Pierre-Emmanuel gave me your name. I need to ask you some questions. We're in trouble."

Magali scoffed. "He gave you my name? That is ironic, to say the least."

"Why do you say that?"

She blew more smoke in Palmer's face and stubbed out her cigarette on the bottom of her boots. "Men always ask for things they know they cannot have. Goodbye."

Palmer scrunched his face in confusion. "I am telling you, I need your help. Please. This will be better for everyone if you cooperate. I'd rather do this the simple way."

"Last time I was in your little game, I was followed, threatened, and frankly, I don't care to learn anything else. I am done. No threats can change my mind. Now please leave me to my view."

Palmer slapped his hands onto his knees and made ready to stand. His groveling harshly rejected. He looked back over at Magali, her face masked with resistance. Another request seemed futile, but he tried anyway, receiving a one-fingered salute. He turned up the stairs and made towards the car.

George answered his phone, turned to face the city, and listened to the commands. The crowd's noise had grown loud since it began chanting in English the number of dribbles the performer completed.

Hart watched Palmer disappear above the stairs and turned back to George.

"What happened. Are we good?"

George shook his head. "Head back to the car. We have to roll."

"We got what we wanted, right?"

"Let's get to the car and regroup." George placed a hand on Hart's back and began guiding him up the steps.

He'd seen the exasperation on Palmer's face and watched the gait of a defeated man. What would they do now? Tap the woman's phones? Research her for endless hours before making another attempt at contact several days later? Or would more drastic measures be taken? Could Palmer be capable of throwing out the rulebook of diplomacy and intelligence gathering? The thoughts drained his energy. He couldn't bear the idea of being away from Clara more than he already had, her fate unknown to him, lost at sea. Could he allow himself to sit by and wait? No, he thought, no chance in hell.

Then a thought hit him. Just do what Clara would do.

He scanned his environment and crafted a plan. Hart moved purposefully up the stairs, bypassing tourists lounged about on the cool stone steps. He glanced at Magali up to his left. She was lighting another cigarette. Hart would have sworn he saw her hand trembling. Climbing several more steps, he was almost even with her. George's guiding hand still on Hart's shoulder like a worried father.

Then, Hart and Magali made eye contact. It was for a brief second, but they both knew and recognized it. Her golden eyes flashed away as she stood. Hart knew it was now or never.

"George, do you speak French by any chance?"

The man smirked. "Not a word other than *merci* and *oui*."

Hart suddenly jumped down two steps to his right and shouted at the top of his lungs to the Paris police watching the steps nearby. "*Il a une arme a feu! Aidez-moi!*" He has a gun! Help me!

George's eyes opened wide and his jaw slacked. Hart spun away from him, while the steps turned into a stampede of terrified tourists. The police blew their whistles and drew their sidearms while George raised his hands in surrender.

Hart bounded over several steps in the opposite direction.

"Get back here, you idiot!" George screamed while Hart scampered off.

Without missing a beat, Hart used the cover of the crowd to race over to Magali. She had turned to watch the drama while most of the crowd ran for their lives.

Their eyes met again, hers fixing a defiant gaze towards the man approaching her. He took her by the elbow and nodded forwards, imploring her to go. Magali shook free of Hart's grasp and squared up to him.

"What the hell do you think you're doing?"

"Getting out from under their watch. I don't have time to play games."

Her eye snapped to George on the ground covered by police and came back to meet Hart's once more.

"Why should I trust you won't hurt me?" She asked the question without any fear in her voice.

Hart could feel the internal clock in his mind screaming. Like a quarterback in the pocket, the defense barreling down on him, he was out of time. They needed to move before Palmer, the police, or anyone for that matter, could stop him. He hadn't planned it out, but if he could get her to trust him, maybe he could make progress. *For Clara.*

"Right now, you're the only lead I have in getting back the person I love most in this world. And so, help me God, I'll do anything to find her."

Magali smirked and threw her purse over her shoulder. "Then lead the way."

33

A fresh Atlantic wind washed over the ship deck. Clara sat on a couch at the yacht's stern, the spray from the ocean kissing her cheeks.

The woman who had stopped her remained close by, sat in a deck chair. She was still pointing the silver Beretta pistol at Clara. Every so often, the woman would stare intently at her prisoner before looking away with disinterest.

"You'll get tired carrying that heavy thing everywhere," Clara remarked.

Her captor's taut face simply turned into a smirk.

Clara glanced at her Cartier Santos watch. She'd been outside for less than fifteen minutes before she heard what sounded like a dozen people walking on the deck. The noise steadily grew, and from behind the bridge, she caught sight of no less than six crew members in their red shirts and a short man with a thick mustache. The men in red circled around her couch. The first mate, who wore bloodied bandages wrapped around his head thanks to Clara, approached her with a menacing pace. Clara stood to defend herself when the man slapped her across the face. Her left cheek stung and immediately felt warm despite the cold Atlantic wind. She temporarily closed her eyes to will the pain away,

187

then she faced up to the man. He wiped a hand across his mouth and smiled as he reared back to deliver another blow.

Out of the corner of Clara's vision, she caught the blonde woman stand and look at the mustached man. Clara turned her attention back to the attacking first mate, readying for his next parry. He began to swing when a loud crack resonated around the deck. The gunshot had made Clara flinch, and her heart stopped like she'd been hit with a sledgehammer.

She looked down to find the bullet hole and began patting her torso but found nothing. The first mate swayed for a moment before another shot ran out, this one slicing through the man's head, remnants of his brain spreading across the light wood of the deck. He dropped with a heavy thud.

"Thank you, Greta." The mustached man smiled and politely bowed to the blonde woman who sat back down on her deck chair, folded her legs, and laid the gun on her lap.

The man regarded the remaining crew. "I had given explicit instructions that our guest not to be harmed, regardless of the circumstance." He walked over to the dead first mate and made a face as if he were viewing unappealing options at a buffet. "This is what happens when you disobey me." He turned to the crew and expectantly pointed at the lifeless body on the deck. The crew began scattering to clean up the mess. He then spun towards Clara. "My name is Farhad. Please allow me to welcome you aboard *No Good Deed.*"

Clara was ushered inside after being introduced to her captors. She was led to a dining room at the stern of the yacht. The dining room was grand, with windows on both sides, dense maroon carpeting with gold flecks, and a crystal chandelier hanging from the ceiling.

Farhad watched his guest enter through the sliding glass

doors and then placed a hand on the arm of his right-hand woman, Greta.

"Now she believes she'll be protected."

Greta's green eyes flared with annoyance. "The bitch deserves to die."

Farhad squealed in a soft chuckle. "All in good time, my dear. But for now, see to it her stay aboard the ship is a living hell. She thinks of me as an ally now, but I don't want her too comfortable."

Inside the ship's dining room, a rectangular table covered in a white linen tablecloth was laid for three people. Soft jazz music played from speakers in the cream-colored ceiling. The rest of the room's walls were painted a slate grey. Clara was placed at the head of the table with only a plate and no silverware. After a moment sitting alone, Farhad and Greta joined her.

"You must be famished," he said, smiling from the opposite head of the table, Greta sat at his left side.

Clara managed a nod, more confused than anything else. Who were these people? What did they want with her?

Before she could formulate any questions, a crewmember appeared through the service door and set a plate of sushi in front of her, a pair of wooden chopsticks to the side. The service door once more swung open and more sushi for Farhad and Greta was brought out.

"While we eat, I thought it would be nice to get to know one another. After all, you did work for me at one point." He smiled and plucked a piece of bluefin tuna nigiri into his mouth.

"How is it that I worked for you?" Clara felt her voice shake before she found the resolve to build rapport with

189

her captors. She wouldn't needlessly make life difficult for herself. She was in the middle of the ocean; where could she escape to?

Farhad dabbed a napkin to his mustache and smiled. "Well, Monsieur Renard worked for me in a matter of speaking. Although, perhaps a part of him didn't think so, hence our current situation alerting the authorities to my plans to sell sensitive plans. But nevertheless, if you follow the logic, you worked for me because you worked for him." He let out a barely audible squeal of laughter.

He continued. "But now you see, there are other matters that need tending to. I do hope the drugs have worn off. We didn't see any other way to get you to cooperate with us." Farhad looked at Greta, who sat expressionless across the table.

"But Renard worked for his banker, who acted alone?" As soon as she said the words, it dawned on her.

Farhad shook his head and slurped soy sauced whitefish into his mouth. "And the banker worked for me. I have people all over the world, in fact."

Clara had realized that he'd just given away intelligence. She hadn't known about a larger ring consisting of anyone else. The white tablecloth and amenable conversation perhaps masked the lunch as an interrogation.

She stared at her sushi and felt her stomach growl in anticipation. Was it drugged? Suddenly, she felt lightheaded. As if Farhad were reading her mind, he leaned closer to her.

"I assure you the food isn't tainted. Nor is the water. We are at sea now, and there's no reason you shouldn't be treated as a valued guest. After all, where else would you go?"

There was a reason she was still alive. She reminded herself, don't give away too much because the status quo must be maintained.

Clara dug into the sushi with a ferocious appetite. She tried to take her time, one bite, a few breaths, and especially pay attention to the conversation. She couldn't afford to become distracted and give up vital intelligence. But she was famished, like she hadn't eaten in days.

She ate for a time in relative quiet. The ocean waves greeting the sides of the ship were faint. The yacht had clearly been designed for luxury high-seas voyages.

"So why go through all this, to what end? Selling nuclear plans to who?" Clara asked, dropping her chopsticks and sizing up her captors. The food had provided nutrients and a burst of energy. Greta, however, had never touched her food. Her icy eyes fixed on Clara.

Farhad placed both of his hands flat on the tablecloth and stared at the ceiling. He had several gold rings on his stubby sausage fingers and a watch Clara swore was the same size as her dinner plate.

"Is it for the money?" Clara opined. "No, too weak in my opinion. Plus, it seems you're doing okay, unless the gas for this thing is running you dry."

Farhad chuckled. "I didn't set out to be in this business, you know." He gave a toothless smile nearly hidden by his mustache.

"The business of kidnapping? Or selling weapon plans? You're going to have to be more specific," Clara said, glancing from Farhad to Greta.

He ignored the comment before continuing. "I always thought I was going to become a traveling salesman. And I suppose, in a way, I did. Sailing around, selling my services to others. I had wanted a simpler life. But fate had other things in store for me." Farhad trailed off, taking another piece of nigiri from his plate.

Clara's curiosity got the better of her. "Such as?"

He set his chopsticks down, and a sparkle came to his eyes. "I am so thrilled you asked. There's no reason we can't be civilized." He stood and shuffled around the table in red velour smoking slippers. "Living in London was a curse set upon me. But at the same time, a gift. I was whisked away in a world of enchantment, of more possibility and wealth than I could have imagined in several lifetimes. I also recognized the world after 9/11. My skin—a tint that scares Westerners—was an asset.

"I must say I never saw the approach coming. The arrangement was simple: feed banking information back to the Americans, a quid pro quo. I got tips that led to promotions, which meant more money and security for my family. Life was good. I'd take any bit of protection I could find. As I said, these were troubled times for people who look like me. And it all started because I tried to do a good deed to help others, but you know what they say, no good deed goes unpunished."

He stood watching the horizon at the window, and when he turned back to the room, his face was darker and his eyes strained.

"I wasn't given a choice." He paused and scratched his face. "My career was made successful so I would constantly be in influential positions for Western intelligence agencies to suckle off me. Then they sent me an assignment. I was to meet with a financier of terror in Pakistan. US intelligence services had me on a leash. I had become their puppet and I lost my own way."

Clara pushed around some sushi on her plate, now much too enthralled to eat.

"The day before I was to fly from Kabul, Afghanistan,

to meet with a group in Pakistan, there was intelligence I'd been compromised. Sources learned I was an American mole. You see, I was fronting as a financier of terror, but in reality, I was a banker who informed Western intelligence of everything I knew. If a suspected terrorist or supporter moved money from bank to bank, and certain countries or institutions wouldn't look into it for them, I could. I'd tell you the name of the account, the exchange rate, even what password they used. Being the man on the inside at one of the most important banks in Europe was helpful.

"But I was blown. Instead of throwing me into the fire as a marked man, my handler decided to pull me from the operation. And not just from the trip, but from my life, my job."

A crew member materialized from the kitchen and cleared the table. Farhad watched the waiter's door swing back and forth until the crew member returned carrying several desserts and a carafe of coffee.

Clara declined the cheesecake but took a coffee. She felt guilty about the refined service. Once the crew member left, Farhad began again.

"We were at an airfield in Kabul, of all places, because my handlers had decided I would be flown back home via private aircraft. Quicker and off the radar. This should have struck me as odd. A private plane declared itself a target for the militants, but then again, anything was a target. My handler was there to make sure we got back to London safely and gathered my belongings before setting off onto a new life. Where? I never found out." He sighed and leaned against the window.

Greta began eating a slice of cheesecake. Clara watched the robot of a woman for a moment. When Greta caught sight, she seductively licked the spoon while making eye contact with her prisoner. A shiver ran down Clara's spine.

Farhad gently cleared his voice as if to ask for Clara's attention once more.

"Westerners have a poor understanding of the weather in Afghanistan. It is a brutally cold place in winter, and the desert is unforgiving. The Hindu Kush mountains are awash with cold air from northern Pakistan. Oftentimes it snows. Heavy frozen snow packed tight to the ground. It snowed the night I was to fly out." He trailed off and checked his watch as if trying to keep on time. Clara regarded him closely. Something was practiced about the man, as if he'd emotionally detached himself from the story.

He continued on, deliberately walking back to the table. "We took off, the plane full of my disappointment and frustration at the failed operation. I'd never got the opportunity to complete my mission, and I let down the guys who had helped my career flourish. My handler was furious, years of work wasted. We fled home like a dog with its tail between its legs."

He took a seat back at the head of the table and bridged his hands together. The room was silent until Farhad began in a low voice. "But we never made it home. The plane shuttered first at about seventeen thousand feet. Then a blast of ice-cold air filled the cabin. I can still feel the tightness in my chest as my lungs breathed in the cold. A loud beeping emanated from the cockpit. The pilots pressed a series of buttons on the control panels rapidly. They shouted back and forth at each other, each putting on oxygen masks. Then the plane began to plummet like a pheasant shot from the sky. It was the strangest sensation; I'd never felt anything like it. I could imagine it's similar to the rides at theme parks, the impression of free-falling. Nothing has ever been as terrify-ing." Farhad stopped, rechecked his watch.

Clara took note of the man and how he routinely checked his watch. She thought about asking why he was telling her this but didn't want to throw off his rhythm. He wanted his audience on the edge of their seats.

He cleared his throat before continuing. "Our plane was free-falling, the wings dipping back and forth, the pilots screaming back to me in the cabin. I didn't do anything. Rather I was absolutely helpless, at the mercy of machine, of fate. The pilots tried to turn around, but the loss of cabin pressure—indicated by the cold air's arrival, I later researched—made the aircraft unsuitable for flying at the altitude we were. We dropped quickly enough to not lose consciousness, but the plane was in a death spiral. I don't know how, but the pilots managed to correct at the last minute to ditch us into a poppy field. I was told one of the engines was found over a mile away from the crash site, wreckage spewed everywhere.

"I must have been thrown too, because Pashtun farmers, whose poppy field we'd set ablaze, found me strapped to a seat. They recognized my dark skin, and my condition was quite poor, so perhaps they took mercy on me. Apparently, they did not find anyone else before military helicopters swooped to the rescue. We were in Taliban stronghold territory, on a field where they grew poppy for heroin. After some mending from the Pashtuns, I was given in a prisoner exchange between Pashtuns and the Taliban, many of whom lived in Pakistan's tribal region. The Taliban wanted to hang me, but I told them I could be of great service. You see, I'd made a choice to save my life. I'd lost everything I'd worked for my entire life because I tried to do the right thing and help the so-called good guys. But what did I get in return?

"It wasn't long after working in Pakistan, teaching them how to launder money, that the Pakistani intelligence enlisted me. Living in squalid caves, hiding from bombs delivered by the Americans who I used to worked for, I set my mind to use the skills they taught me to make them suffer. So, after many years of work, I control the money for despots with sanctions, make deals between countries—allies and enemies—that the world doesn't want to know about. But then, just a few months ago, an old lost friend returned to my life." Farhad clapped, and a crew member rushed from the kitchen to bus the table.

Clara's mind raced to put the pieces of the puzzle together. Perhaps she was sitting in front of the man responsible for funding many of the world's problems—the armed conflicts in Africa, North Korea's access to military systems, terrorist training camps, Iran skirting sanctions—Farhad was the man who managed all the money. A raging desire to leap from her spot at the table and choke him built inside her. But almost as if Greta could sense the call to action of their prisoner, she sat up and placed her silver Berretta onto the table.

Farhad smiled at the ladies in his company, sensing the tension. "As I was saying, an old friend appeared back into my life. It was as if fate put us in touch to work out all that was left unfinished. My handler, the one who changed my life, and put me on that doomed plane, was Stephen Palmer."

Clara gasped, surprising herself at the audible sound. She tried to keep her calm but also noticed she was white-knuckling the arms of her chair.

Farhad seemed pleased with her reaction and let out a tiny squeal of a laugh.

This isn't about me, Clara thought as she fought to control her breathing. *It's about Paul.* Her concern grew into a momentary panic. Why take her? Paul is closer to Palmer. Like dark clouds rolling in, ready to unleash their wrath, she felt the dread of her predicament settling overhead.

"What is it that you want?" She mustered as much courage into her voice as possible, not entirely sure if she could drown out her own doubt.

Farhad leaned forward and grinned. "Oh, my dear, you are the sun around which all the planets orbit."

The room was silent for a moment as the ship cut through the sea.

"I don't understand. Why kidnap me?"

"Because," Farhad said, as if suddenly bored, "Paul Hart cares about you more than anything in the world. And if my former handler is still the same man, he cares about Paul more than anything in the world. So soon, they will blindly run to your rescue out of love and duty. This means I can still complete the transaction I've arranged, even without access to the funds your government froze. But you're my insurance policy that nothing can happen to me in the meantime." He checked his watch, raised his eyebrows and stood.

"And finally, when the time comes for your assured rescue attempt, we will be ready and waiting. It has been a long time, but I will finally get closure by taking something Stephen Palmer holds most dear. Then, I'll allow him to live just long enough to watch his world burn, just like those poppy fields I crashed on."

34

Paris, France

The morning darkness had given way to an orange sunrise flooding over the maze of Parisian rooftops. It was forecasted to be a beautiful day with billowing white clouds blowing in from the English Channel. It was, without question, a perfect day for a river cruise on the Seine.

Such was the plan for *Les Jeunes Républicans*, to celebrate a successful round of recent fundraising with even more fundraising. The three-hour cruise would meander north up the Seine past the Eiffel Tower, Notre-Dame, and the Left Bank before swinging about and heading back to port. The boat was thirty-three meters in length, flat and rectangular with two levels. Its main level was surrounded by glass windows, where guests ate at tables while watching Paris pass. The top deck, which the group had privately rented out, provided for unobtrusive views of the city, and thanks to the favorable weather, endless sunshine.

There were young and old amongst French political supporters: professorial types in tweed jackets with suede elbow patches, quick to diatribe to the younger volunteers about the importance of 'history, national pride, and unity.' While *les jeunes* were quick to point out to the older members, it was best to adapt to the changing times.

In his early forties, Charles LeBrun moved about from donor to donor with bountiful energy. He had graduated what felt like a lifetime ago from Saint-Cyr Military Academy. There he studied military leadership and academics. After a brief three-year post as a commissioned officer in the French army, he'd gone into banking. The rigors and rules for which he left the military had once again comforted him in La Bourse as a currency trader, where he made plenty of money. Thus, he began mixing in the aristocratic circles to which, he always believed, he belonged. Passionate about several issues, chief among them making powerful allies and carrying good favor, he began to dream of a political career. Charles shook all the right hands and said all the right things—mainly not saying much of anything. He positioned himself for a seat in Sénat, an indirectly elected member of the National assembly's upper house.

So, it was there when American politicians and lobbyists alike tapped him to be the French hard-liner on Iran relations. He was happy to oblige. The way Charles saw it was that he wasn't doing the Americans' bidding. Instead, he was staking out promising positions for his political career. He held hushed lunches at cafés near the Sénat in Palais du Luxembourg, Café de la Rotonde by far being his favorite. Upstairs in a red-velour-walled room, politicians discussed various topics—farming subsidies, workers' rights, ever contentious rural-road speed limits—and even Iran. Casually, Charles would bring up the country's fondness of Airbus planes and French medical technology. Still, he'd also highlight Iran's atrocious human rights record and continually fanning the flames of the Middle East. Within a year of smooth talk over *tartare de boeuf et pot de crème*, he'd managed to single-handedly turn most indifferent politicians into staunch opponents of

Tehran. So, when the United States added more economic sanctions and France supported the measures, Charles felt vindicated by his journey. With his confidence peaked, he even went so far as to even lobby the Swiss to show support, who unsurprisingly did not.

Nevertheless, he became the preeminent voice on Iranian issues in the French government. So, when he heard his old military academy colleague had stumbled upon damning intelligence about Iran, he had to act. Charles LeBrun was going to make sure he was the judge, jury, and executioner, not Pierre-Emmanuel. It was the coup de grâce, delivered to Iran from Charles himself. He'd blackmail whoever he could with the intelligence to get an edge.

From the military, to commerce, and finally into politics, his future was now lined with red carpets, seven-course meals, finely tailored Italian suits, always blue, and occasional political discourse. He was a wealthy and powerful man, but with such status, many favors were asked from various people. However, one of these simple favors benefited him quite well personally for a change.

The favor Charles had begrudgingly agreed to was to hire an intern on his campaign. She was a wealthy donor's daughter who wanted in on the action of politics while she studied it at the Sorbonne. Charles had rolled his eyes during the phone-call request and dreaded meeting her until he saw her tall frame, and porcelain skin. He had wanted her from the moment she entered his office. The job, he reassured himself, was tortuous, and he deserved the rewards of a fun chase.

On the top deck, he excused himself from his chief economic advisor, who was still ranting about the European Union's decision to adopt a single currency decades ago, and headed for the bar. He was sure to smile at his staff and supporters alike, but there was only one thing on Charles's mind. He sipped his Aperol Spritz and regarded the Haussmann architecture of the sixteenth arrondissement as the boat cruised by. Then, he saw her.

She was leaning over the railing, admiring the Eiffel Tower. She wore a light-yellow sundress he longed to run his hands over and eventually, under. She was on the ship's starboard side, directly across from where he stood, separated by joyful and inquisitive partiers.

He made his move, swapping his Spritz for two glasses of Taittinger Brut from a passing waiter. But before Charles could make his approach, a staff member with a broad smile stopped him for a picture and a chat. By the time Charles had expertly offered an excuse to pick up the conversation later, she was no longer leaning over the railing or anywhere to be seen. He spun around, searching. Undeterred, he figured she'd ventured downstairs to the ladies' room, in which case would provide the perfect opportunity for privacy.

The commotion of the top-deck partiers watching the Place de la Concorde approaching the port side allowed Charles to sneak after her. His upcoming conquest dominated his mind. He never stopped once to think of his safety. Certainly, his leather-soled tassel loafers were suspect on the slick metal stairs, but, it was his party's security that he should have paid more attention to.

Deep in the political season, it could be forgiven to overlook the necessary precautions to ensure safety for a well-known member of the Sénat and his supporters. For instance, it was far too easy for a terrorist cell operating out of Molenbeek, Belgium, to be given the plans to strike a soft target in Paris.

There was little to no security around river-cruise ships and little strategic reasoning to defend such targets.

However, once a target had been communicated and a company's booking system was hacked and subsequently cross-referenced with a specific individual name, a suitable date and target aligned. In a grungy internet café, with a program designed to redirect the VPN from Belgium to South Africa, then to a network in Argentina, orders were communicated. Moussa Al-Bakari had the requisite bomb-making experience from his time in Syria, after making the trip through Greece via Istanbul then Italy before finally reaching his home country of Belgium, where he prepared for his mission.

After the sweat-inducing work of mixing the highly volatile triacetone triperoxide (TATP) in the basement of a Saint-Denis apartment in the *banlieue* of Paris, the purchasing a tourist-boat ticket, and the fortune of Charles LeBrun actually attending the boat party, Moussa knew Allah smiled on him. It didn't matter that he received his orders from individuals he'd never met in person, they had provided him with the resources to act.

Charles ventured towards the stern of the boat to find the yellow sundress he so lusted after. Carrying the two glasses of champagne, he passed through the narrow white corridor that smelled of bleach thanks to the constant scrubbing of the deck and spills from the kitchen. He turned the corner to head to the restrooms, only to find a pair of long white legs with bright white sneakers on the floor.

At first, Charles thought the young woman had slipped, or she'd had too much rosé on the top deck, but when she came fully into view, he caught her bright green eyes filled with fright and a red stain growing from her stomach.

Crouched over her was a man with dark skin and even darker eyes framed by a thick black beard. He was sweating profusely through his striped shirt. There was a kitchen knife covered in blood on the floor, his left hand over the young girl's mouth, and in the other, a plastic detonator.

Charles threw the glass in his left hand towards the man standing over the young girl. He smashed the glass he held in his right hand against the wall, leaving the unbroken stem in his hand as a makeshift weapon. He lunged forward at the man, his military training kicking in from all those years ago.

At the same time he made his charge, a smile washed over the dark man's face. He quickly stood, allowing the young woman to scream in terror, and stepped back towards the deck. The man began muttering something Charles thought familiar. Before his mind connected the dots, he was killed in an explosion of white light.

Black smoke rose into the clear sky from the stern of the boat, the thick smog blocking the view of Notre-Dame across from the sixth arrondissement. The barge groaned as its bow lifted from the water, and it began slowly sinking into the Seine.

35

Paris, France

Hart and Magali bounded down the long and steep stairs, past the sweaty faces of tourists brave enough to climb up them. Hart frequently checked over his shoulder, expecting to see the familiar faces of Palmer, set in disappointment, alongside George, chasing him like a runaway dog. But they were nowhere to be seen.

Having passed the Square Louise-Michel and the vintage carousel at the bottom of the hill, Hart was worried the SUV would cut them off on Place Saint-Pierre, the most extensive road in Montmartre, but still, he didn't see them.

Magali had stayed by Hart's side, not asking questions, just keeping up with him briskly. There was a resolve about her that Hart found both comforting and somewhat alarming at the same time. Was he doing the right thing? Could he trust her, knowing she was crazy enough to follow him? Palmer had asked Hart for his trust, but it was Hart who quickly broke it. Conceivably, it didn't matter. If he could get Magali to speak and learn what she knew, then all could be forgiven. All's well that ends well, right?

They scurried past the ice cream parlors and tourist shops, heading towards the nineth arrondissement. Hart knew where they could find plenty of dark bars and quiet cafés amid the winding moody streets in South Pigalle—or SoPi, as it was known to the locals. There he and Magali could talk, and hopefully, he could be one step closer to Clara. *No, damn it,* he corrected his train of thought. *I will be one step closer.*

Palmer took off his jacket and tossed it into the back seat of the SUV. To hide his wry smile from George, he tried not to look at him sat in the front seat. The man had just been released from questioning and a pat-down by the Paris police, and Palmer recognized the angry look of someone who wanted blood.

"You're just going to let him go?" George asked, rolling the front window down.

Palmer rolled his eyes. It was the third time in as many minutes that he'd heard the question from his irritated operator. "Did your feelings get hurt because he got the drop on you? I told you not to underestimate him." He took off his glasses, folded them, and slid them into the front pocket of his shirt. "He's a wounded animal. He won't act rationally. No telling what he will do next, but if I know him like I think I do, this could work out in our favor."

"How's that?" George snarled.

"Easy, Wojtek. Hart can get what we need from the reporter and come back to us. What else will he do? He can't go fighting the world on his own." He leaned against the window. "Patience, he'll come back."

The truth was Palmer was impressed, albeit a bit nervous too. Hart becoming irrational wasn't an unforeseen development; it just added to the already murky complexity of the mission. Find and stop the sale of nuclear plans, and get Clara back. They had become one operation, and it didn't matter much to Palmer which came first. As far as he was concerned, the mission's success came from both situations turning out favorably.

Maybe he wouldn't always be there to protect Hart and his country, but he'd sure as hell die trying. For the moment, though, he had to trust his agent.

All's well that ends well, Palmer thought, as he looked over the rooftops of Paris.

Magali stirred another sugar into her coffee and eyed Hart. He sat facing the glass windows that overlooked the street running alongside the bar. She sat directly across from him in the plush red velour booth in the corner of the café. Her spoon softly clinked while she stirred, which she hadn't stopped doing since she'd received the coffee several minutes earlier.

"What do you mean they took her?" she asked, almost to the coffee, refusing to look up towards Hart.

"Men took her onto a boat, headed out to open sea. The last I knew…" He paused, allowing the emotion of his words to fade until he felt his façade fall back into place. "The last I knew, she was headed across the Atlantic." Hart leaned forward, his elbows pressing on the table. "I need to know two things. First, who did you tell about Clara? Second, where is she going?"

Magali dropped the spoon. It clanked loudly onto the table. "Why do you put this on me? What did I do?" Her golden eyes lit with anger.

"You met with Pierre-Emmanuel, who fed you information you shouldn't have known. Somehow that information was used to arrange a meeting with Clara, kill one of our partners, and then she was taken. From where I sit at this moment, yes, I put this all on you."

"And who are you to even be upset? A lover? You're not French. You don't work for her. Maybe an American intelligence agent with a crush, yes?"

Hart realized Magali had turned the conversation around with ease and proceeded to ignore her. Damn journalists. "I need to know who you told about meeting Clara. Please."

"Ah, yes, a lover." A thin smile appeared. She glanced at Hart and then back to her coffee. "If I help you, what would you do for me?"

"Anything." Hart felt his chances rise. If there was any possibility what she told him could help, he'd listen. He would agree to make a deal worth the world and leave the formalities of delivering it to Palmer. It wasn't his concern. His only mission was Clara. Anything else was a bonus. "You can be kept completely up to date with the investigation, and I'll make sure you have exclusivity. There's something much larger at play—the world could change forever—but I need this information now." He attempted to smile, but his blue eyes gave away his intensity.

She took a sip from her coffee then set the cup back down on its saucer with a soft click. Ensuring the room was empty, she began speaking.

"I told an Interpol agent about her. I've seen this man on and off for some time. He called me out of the blue last week, wanted to meet, so we did." She stopped for a moment, appearing as if debating how much to divulge. "He wanted information on a murder a few weeks ago, about the man killed in the seventh."

Hart felt his temples pounding. "The attorney who was gunned down?"

Magali nodded. "The Interpol agent wanted to know if the authorities were close to apprehending whoever did it.

But more curiously, he wanted to know more about what was found on the victim. He inquired specifically about a Claude Renard, and that is when I called Pierre-Emmanuel, as per the instructions he gave me should anyone ever mention that name to me."

Hart was surprised by the turn of events. "So, you called a French intelligence officer?"

Magali shrugged. "He told me if any source was ever to bring up Renard, then I had to call him directly. I did, and we met to discuss. He wanted my source's name, and I refused to give it. So, he made me an offer. Meet up with Clara, and she would tell me some details about the case. It was his way of trying to get the source's name."

"When did you met with her?"

"The other day, in the Jardin du Luxembourg. It was actually right before..." Her voice trailed off as she turned to look around the room. Hart didn't press her, just sat silently and watched.

"Before," she continued, "he threatened me. He'd followed me, I think. My guess is he'd been tracking me from my apartment on the other side of the river. That isn't easy to do, especially since I look for people following me. I am not an amateur. It was horrible, you understand?"

"Who threatened you?"

"The Interpol agent I told about Clara. His name is Diego Ramos and he is the *connard* who wanted Clara. She was his mission."

Hart felt as if the velour booth was trying to dump him on the floor as his world began to spin. He squeezed his eyes shut and willed himself to focus. His mission was to get Clara?

"What happened next?"

Magali drew a deep breath as if steadying herself. "I told him you were going to La Rochelle."

Hart dropped his head into his hands and rubbed his face. It had all been a setup. Clara had been the target all along; it wasn't just a grab and run job haphazardly put together. Clara had walked right into a trap and he failed to stop it. Now she was halfway around the world on a yacht heading God knows where. He felt nauseous, like his stomach had shrunken into the size of a sugar cube. Where could they go from here?

He felt a warm hand gently take his hand on the table, and he looked up.

"The day Diego threatened me, with his hands around my neck, I felt my life slipping away. I was so scared, just like how I imagine you feel right now." She smiled as a single tear fell from her cheek.

Suddenly Hart felt not only sick to his stomach for learning that Clara had been ambushed without him, but he felt badly for Magali. She was just doing her job, albeit a bit too ambitiously for his taste, but what could he have expected her to do with the information she learned? She was following leads.

"I'm sorry, I didn't know," Hart managed, already trying to think of where to go next, what other leads to chase down. There were none he could think of. Magali had been it. He hoped that she was somehow more involved, but it appeared she'd told him all she knew. Magali had been at the meeting Clara had gone to without him, was the source Pierre-Emmanuel used, and the informant Diego had threatened.

Hart slowly pulled his hand out from under Magali's.

With her voice cracking with emotion, Magali started again. "I am so sorry to cause you this pain, but please know I want to help you."

Hart met her golden eyes, which seemingly weren't sad anymore, but alive with energy.

"I wish you could help." He sighed and began to stand from the booth.

Magali wiped the tear off her face. Then she dug in her purse and held up a thin brown leather wallet. "Well, I did manage to swipe this. Would that help?"

36

The door slammed shut and shook the room. Paul Hart faced forward, not wanting to look his raging boss in the face. Palmer stalked around the desk and thumped into his oversized chair. Hart knew he'd been summoned to the principal's office.

"Want to explain to me again what the fuck you were thinking?" Palmer started; his cheeks were unmistakably red, even obscured behind his thick beard. "In case you didn't notice, there was a terror attack in central Paris today! We had resources diverted to cover you. Maybe they could have been better deployed, ever think of that? Or are you too selfish to care?"

The room fell silent after Palmer let out a sigh, as if the man realized he'd been too harsh on his inexperienced agent.

Hart, however, spoke up. "We don't have time to complain about feelings getting hurt. I didn't take no for an answer and got results. Now we have intel and a source who can be helpful. I suggest we prioritize what information she has given us and stop this madness. Once we get Clara back, then you can chew me out."

Palmer grunted. "You sure have some balls on you, I'll tell you that. Grew up pretty damn quickly."

Hart threw up his hands. "Circumstances dictated." He didn't feel sorry for what he'd done. They needed results. He'd deal with the consequences of his throwing a teammate under the bus later.

Hart also doubted three American agents could have prevented the Seine attack, and his boss's anger was out of frustration than anything else.

"Do we know anything about the target?" Hart asked, not willing to connect the attack to their current situation, but his sinking gut told him otherwise.

"It hasn't been long enough for a proper investigation. The preliminary report we're getting from our French friends is a political party rented out a riverboat. The party leader is a hard-liner on a crusade against Iran. Lobbied support all around Europe for harsh economic sanctions."

"Iran would never be brazened enough to attack a country outright. Using a proxy only makes sense if we're talking Hezbollah and Israel."

"You're a quick study, aren't you." Palmer stood and headed towards the door. Hart followed suit, momentarily relieved his chewing-out wasn't worse. But, before opening the door, Palmer put his hand on Hart's shoulder.

"Don't forget, I am on your side. I want to stop all this and then get Clara back home just as much as you do. But we're a team—you mess with one of my men again, and I'll send you back to the States." The men made eye contact and held it while Hart decided on his response. There was no point in debating their purposes; their energy needed to be poured into sourcing every lead from Diego's pickpocketed wallet.

Hart motioned at the door. "Let's get to work."

The men took off towards the conference room where the team was gathered.

The room was a beehive of activity. Every computer station was taken up by an analyst, shouting bits of information back into the crowded audience. Hart noticed Magali sitting at the head of the conference table, her purse, phone, notebook and any other possible recording method had been confiscated. Still, it seemed fine by her as she took in the scene, watching in amazement as the information flashed on the large flat-screens on the walls. Lucas had returned, his focus steadfast on several maps.

Palmer paced the short distance between the back table and the monitors, wearing out the carpet. He listened to the analysts shout the latest intel derived from the wallet provided by Magali. George watched on from the corner, where he was leaning against the wall. Hart felt the man's death stare from across the room. But their beef would have to wait.

Kelly, wearing a Patagonia sweater, her dark red hair tied in a bun, commanded most of Palmer's attention. "Wallet contained four debit cards, all associated to various accounts under different names. Researching the banks now."

Palmer nodded and turned towards Lucas, who had his hand raised.

"Wallet also contained Métro passes for Paris and an Oyster card."

Hart recognized the name of the London Underground travel card.

"We're building house, folks. I want the foundation laid—who this guy is, what he does, where he works, gets laid, and even where he gets his tapas—I want it all." Palmer pounded the table.

Hart moved to Magali and took a seat next to her.

"Where is Pierre-Emmanuel?"

"Working the Seine attack."

She nodded in understanding, then switched subjects. "It is incredible to see. Taking a man's life apart with only a few simple items."

"Thanks to you. Don't forget that."

Magali smiled, and then as if silently scolding herself, she looked downwards at the table. Hart noticed her melancholy eyes as they darted around the room.

"I am not happy with myself. For trusting this man, for allowing him into my home, m-m-my bed." Her voice trailed off.

Hart leaned forward on the table. "What's past is past, and you're helping us. We couldn't make progress without you."

Magali shook her head, and the sadness from her eyes disappeared behind a curtain of fiery anger. "You are all here because of me. If I'd kept my mouth shut. if I hadn't called Pierre-Emmanuel, if I hadn't met with Clara, or been so naïve as to have given in to being threatened." She dropped her head into her hands and sighed in frustration.

Hart put a hand on her back. He could commiserate with how she felt. An overwhelming sense of guilt wasn't an easy cross to bear. But when he got Clara back, they could all have their closure. He was determined to put Magali at peace with all she'd done too.

Palmer turned to Lucas's station. "What do we have?"

Lucas pointed up to the monitor showing a map. "Several hits on one of the cards. Seems two hotel rooms and two train tickets were booked. One set for Strasbourg and one for Toulouse. Hotels appear to be pending room rates after cross-referencing the amounts with average nightly rates. These are reservations. There are no other transactions on this card."

"He has multiple fallback plans. The cities are on opposite sides of France. But wouldn't he have canceled the cards since he lost his wallet, making the reservations cancel out too?"

Lucas considered it for a minute and began typing vigorously. "True, the cities are far apart. But the cards canceling is not necessarily the case. The website he booked through is pay upfront, not when you check in. The hotels are paid for, so switching card numbers won't matter, even if he replaced them after he lost his wallet."

Palmer patted Lucas on the back and waited for the next round of information from Kelly.

"From the bank accounts I managed to get access to, I see another withdrawal from an ATM in Libourne, which is southeast of his last known location in La Rochelle, but west of Toulouse and his hotel bookings. Seems our man is on his way to Toulouse."

Palmer spun around to face Hart and stifled a smile. They had a lead.

"We might know where he is going, but I want to know what he is doing. Focus on why he could be going to Toulouse. We all agree this is the direction he's heading, right?" The question met with a series of nods around the room.

Hart spoke up. "But we need to find out why they took Clara and how it relates to our operation. Maybe Diego has some vast amounts of money dumped into his accounts? Any suspicious ones?" He was struggling with the group's focus on the granular transactions of Diego. He wanted the reason they were targeted, and to get that, he needed to find Diego. Follow the money, find the man.

Kelly snapped her fingers. "He's right. We need to pull the loose thread and watch it all unravel. We have cracked a few bank accounts, but we'll need to use our contacts for the more private banks to know what, or who, is behind the accounts and identify any patterns."

At that moment, there was a knock on the door. Hart looked at Palmer for an okay as he went to open it.

Standing outside with a look of contrition and angst was Pierre-Emmanuel.

"Perfect timing. Just after all the hard work has been done," Palmer shouted over his shoulder as Hart stepped aside, letting the French intelligence man in.

Pierre-Emmanuel brushed off the insult. "My old school friend was killed today in the attack on the Seine. I believe the attack is connected to our investigation. Now, I am here to offer my assistance. What can I do?"

Palmer opened his mouth to speak until he saw Pierre-Emmanuel notice, Magali. Palmer then merely smiled and turned back around.

37

Three o'clock was the time of the workday when Florian Deschamps felt most at ease. It was too late for his fellow *Français* to go to lunch and too early to escape the office for afternoon errands. This meant the bank was quiet, and he could fiddle about on his computer to look busy while he read the news.

Today's bulletins were littered with somber pictures of the Seine river, a boat's stern sticking up from the surface as smoke billowed from the burning wreckage. But, as usually is the case, the tragedy unveiled human resilience. According to reports, Florian was reading, Parisiens jumped into the river to help victims. There was even a photo of several Parisiens forming a human chain, lowering themselves down a stone embankment to fetch out a young boy who was clinging to a life raft. Yes, Florian thought anyone could be a hero. Prior experience wasn't required.

The day at the bank was otherwise slow and understandably so. Usually, the people of southwest France were more easygoing compared to the northerners who were used to the hustle and bustle of Paris. For Florian, the languid life, along with persuasion from a Frenchwoman with Moroccan blood, dark skin, and the bluest eyes he'd ever seen, motivated him to move to the pink city of Toulouse. 'Oui, mon lapin,' she'd purred. '*Of course, there are banking jobs in my hometown.*' And Florian had to admit she wasn't wrong. Airbus, French telecoms, space companies, and a cluster of European technology startups made the city fizz with a young, vibrant personality he had gotten used to.

Sure, he had to forgo his career as an economic analyst at Paribras Bank in Paris. Still, his new job as manager of a local bank branch of Crédit Agricole suited him just fine. It was less financial modeling and Excel spreadsheets, more consoling anxious grandmothers who had forgotten their online banking password. But oddly enough, it paid nearly the same.

His days were spent helping clients who still trekked to the bank. He helped with everything, from greeting customers when they came in to approving wire transfers and handling rental deposits accounts, all the while managing the cash inventory in the safe, which is never as much as anyone thinks. Florian also approved various transactions carried out by his staff of three bankers in accordance with European Union banking compliance laws.

In fact, it was one of these approvals from his bankers that alerted Florian to an unusual volume of activity in an account.

The account belonged to an irritable man who came into the branch the day before. The man had stumbled into the bank, dark beard and features wearing a Stade Toulousain hat on. Florian recalled thinking the man was trying to blend into the city because the hat appeared brand new, and baseball hats were unique fashion accessories in the southwest.

The customer's account hadn't been used in quite some time, more than several months. For the money to be accessed, it required he return to a branch to reactivate the dormant account in person. There was no other option. This was a new policy in line with regulatory compliances managed by the EU. It was enacted to prevent fraud.

The account was eventually reactivated after the customer explained he had to leave town due to his brother's passing. Now, he was back and account activity would ramp up significantly. The junior banker, a forty-two-year-old lifer, simply passed on her condolences and didn't bother asking more questions.

Except Florian wasn't so easily convinced.

So, it was during his favorite hour of the day that his curiosity got the best of him. After he'd read all he could stomach about the attack in Paris, his mind jumped to the man the day before. He looked up the customer's account once more, doing a thorough dive into its history. The account had five hundred thousand euros. When researching further, Florian discovered most of those funds had come via wire transfers in the past twenty-four hours since the customer had reactivated the account. Doing what he thought of as a fun way to pass the time, he pulled the wire information. He was surprised to see it originated from a holding company in the Cayman Islands with notes referencing "purchasing of daily business supplies."

After opening his internet browser, Florian popped a Nespresso pod into the machine hidden under his desk and fired it up. He pulled out a few Prince cookies, a guilty pleasure, and dunked them in his espresso while he learned more about this mysterious client. The first sip had already burned his tongue by the time he'd found what he was looking for.

Cross-referencing the business name on the wire, search results showed that the holding company that had paid out hundreds of thousands of dollars was a restaurant group. The information online showed they owned several locations around the resort area of Grand Cayman.

Florian dunked another Prince cookie into his Nespresso and contemplated what to do with the suspicious information he'd uncovered. It certainly was odd, the frozen account, the irritable customer, and the connection to one of the world's most infamous banking locales. Florian reasoned there was only one thing a good bureaucrat and banker could do in such a situation— file the paperwork to pass the information up the chain of command.

38

Clara woke in a cold sweat. For a moment, she couldn't recall where she was, and still half in a state of sleep, she rolled over to put her arm across Paul's chest. But the bed was empty. The stark realization snapped her out of her sleepy state.

The figure standing over her bed was shrouded in darkness. Clara gasped and sunk her head deeper into her pillow, convinced she was in the middle of a night terror. The dark figure sat down on the edge of the bed. Then, a callused hand stroked Clara's cheek.

She was too shocked to do anything; her torturer, however, sensed her fear.

"Don't scream. You'll wake the ship," Greta whispered, her face now inches from Clara.

"Wh-wh-what are you doing?"

"It gets lonely for a woman on a ship with only men." Greta's hand left Clara's cheek and slid down her neck across her shoulder.

"Get out," Clara managed, her heart racing.

Greta showed her teeth, her eyes still lingering over Clara's shape beneath the comforter. "Another night then... You never know when I might drop by." Greta leaned over and kissed the top of Clara's head. It took everything in Clara's power not to headbutt the woman. Then Greta stood, her billowing bathrobe covering her retreat.

When she was alone again, Clara lay still. Sweat dripped from her brow as she tried to steady her jackhammering heart. The room was dark, the shades open, no moonlight filtered in on what she assumed was a cloudy evening, but she longed for daylight. The crash of the seemingly angry ocean against the hull heightened her anxiety, but she willed herself to slow down her breathing. She stretched out, her silk pajamas comfortably gliding under the high thread count sheets.

Her thoughts shifted to Paul to calm herself. She wished he was here now. Their paths had intertwined in the way only fate could have fashioned. There had been days when she'd questioned herself, the craziness of it all, but then she'd remember the peace she felt with him and the hopefulness of their future together. Her anxiety washed away like the rescinding tide.

Her mind drifted to a specific night with Paul as she blocked out her late-night intruder. It was a special night on the island of Noirmoutier, where their story wrote another chapter. After the exhilaration and danger during their relationship forming, that night on Noirmoutier, she learned more about Paul. But wished she could go back to change her greatest regret with him. She prayed she could have the chance one day. Clara closed her eyes to remember every moment, every word as if she were there with him again.

The evening sky cast an orange flame across the marina. The sailboats' white hulls reflected the light onto the water, setting the sea ablaze with color. They had had dinner reservations at the Michelin-starred La Marine restaurant. Clara had made reservations weeks in advance on one of her daily walks to the landmark to inquire about any availability.

They had come to the marina the restaurant overlooked to watch the island's activities cease for dinner. Boats pulled in and tied off, the captains rinsing the decks to fight the corrosive seawater.

She had worn a yellow sundress, the color of a sunflower, with tiny blue tulips decorating the airy material. Her dark hair was braided and pulled back.

"You look stunning," he'd said, grabbing her around the waist and seemingly enjoying the soft fabric revealing her every curve.

"I'd think you could wait until after dinner before you start to get handsy." She toyed with him, the twinkle in her eye driving him mad. She knew because he told her so, just like he told her the truth all the time because, as he once had said, he only told the truth to her.

The dinner started with a bottle of Pol Roger champagne, a favorite of Winston Churchill who drank it religiously, which Paul acknowledged with his toast, "To our time together in London." He had smirked and Clara had playfully rolled her eyes at his boyish humor. It had been London where their love had first bloomed, late in the night. They'd been brought together by necessity to stop a scheme financing terror attacks, but they formed a natural bond that transcended both their worlds afterward.

The first course was several versions of *pommes des terres*, the local potatoes from Noirmoutier, covered in the *fleur des sel*, baked, mashed, and puréed for their pleasure. As they ate, Clara could feel Hart's eye's stealing looks at her, and she couldn't hide her smile. On the island on which she grew up, at a Michelin-starred restaurant, with a man she'd come to love, Clara felt entirely at peace. As her grandfather used to remark, if you want to make God laugh, tell him your plans. It was not the life she ever imagined having, but there she was, in the midst of it, loving every moment.

Since they'd been on the island that first month, she'd slowly recovered from her injuries, one-step forward every day, sometimes quite literally. At times she'd push herself too far, a hike along the Bois de la Chaise with Paul would require she spend the next day recovering from the soreness, but it would eventually pass. They'd spent their days teaching Paul about the finer aspects of intelligence gathering, from the simplistic counter surveillance routes to managing an asset and understanding body language clues to discern the truth. Meanwhile, Clara learned more about him, how he lived when he wasn't in the midst of a money-laundering scheme. He matured into a resolved man, changed by the events that transpired against him. She didn't know what to expect from their romance; a candle burning bright and hot, but for how long?

Their dinner that evening was exquisite. The third course, turbot, arrived in a carrot reduction sauce garnished with fresh herbs of thyme and rosemary. Clara watched Hart with amusement as he had taken a bite and put his fork down to savor every flavor.

"I've taught you well. I'm glad to see you're taking the time to enjoy it," she'd remarked, starting on the expertly crafted dish as if it were a work of art she was unwilling to destroy.

"You've taught me many things, among them the ability to enjoy what I truly love." Hart winked. Clara couldn't manage to stifle a loud giggle, the fault of the long-since-emptied bottle of Pol Roger and the new glasses of chablis accompanying the turbot.

"Clara." Hart leaned onto the table to get closer to her. She remembered how handsome he looked in the blue linen blazer purchased at a shop in town, the most formal piece of clothing they could find on the island, with a crisp white shirt. "I love you."

The words had resonated as if there'd been a detonation in the dining room. The calm enjoyment of their meal, the masterfully prepared fish, the wine, and light heartedness, were stolen away by his proclamation. She remembered her clash of feelings, heart and mind battling against one another. *He loves me*, she thought, struggling to hide her emotions, and what those were, she didn't quite know herself. Stealing a sip from her chablis, she'd tried to buy time, but it had been long enough. She could see it in Hart's eyes she'd hurt him by not saying it back.

He had fallen silent, choosing to focus on his plate. For some time, they ate without speaking. The awkwardness only interrupted when a nervous server stopped by to ask if anything was wrong with the dishes. Finally, after what seemed like hours but Clara was sure was only a few minutes, Paul put his fork down and spoke. "You may think it's too soon or that I'm foolish. But the thing is, I love you because you're strong. After all, you're a fighter, or else you wouldn't be here with me. Clara, you're smart, probably too damned smart for my own good, but you push me, and you're quite easily the most beautiful woman I've ever laid eyes on."

Clara had managed a smile, the corners of her eyes welling with tears, but she did not cry. She was touched by his words, upset with herself that saying it back didn't feel right. Perhaps it was too soon for her, or maybe it was because she'd never been in love. Sure, there were men, some of them more like boys, and she'd had relationships. The problem was she'd never loved any of them. Her career was her partner, but that had all changed when Paul had entered her life.

She reached across the white tablecloth and placed her hand on his. "I need time, Paul."

He stiffened and then offered her a smile. "I know, and I'm not surprised. You do what you feel is right at the time and make no apologies for it. You're a fighter, but defending how you feel isn't necessary. It's one of the many reasons why I feel the way I do about you."

She had squeezed his hand once more.

Clara lay awake, staring at the ceiling, her eyes moist from recalling the memory. It was as if he was speaking to her then and now. *You're a fighter.* The most unexpected turn of events had occurred in La Rochelle, and as she took his words to heart, she couldn't rest, the regret of that very evening gave her strength, but it also gnawed at her.

The truth was, she didn't know if she'd ever get the chance to tell him the words she couldn't say that night. The words she felt, but had been too reluctant to share. "I love you too, Paul," she whispered, if only to herself.

Would she ever get to tell him? The terror of the thought made her physically ill. All she wanted to do was be in his arms, wrapped up in a blanket on the beach, far away from the world's troubles haunting them.

Stop it. Clara remembered Paul's words. *You're a fighter.*

39

They quickly decided to mobilize. Palmer and Pierre-Emmanuel dished out the orders for equipment, personnel and hustled travel arrangements to get them from Paris to Toulouse. Within ninety minutes, they had boarded a Cesena Latitude at Le Bourget and gone wheels up.

Magali, who had demanded she accompany them to Toulouse, sat next to Hart. She had, however, reluctantly agreed to stay well clear of any operation. Hart owed her a debt of gratitude for helping and was the biggest supporter of her request to come along. He found her quiet resolve comforting as if he weren't the only one carrying a burden of regret around.

They sat facing Lucas and Kelly, who both vigorously typed away on their laptops. The bosses sat towards the front of the plane, in what Hart saw was deep in conversation. Way out back was George.

Hart glanced at George and tried to hide his failure at getting comfortable. After a run-in, and a deserved one at that, with George before boarding the plane, Hart's side ached. As they'd passed through the private terminal before their flight, Hart had made for the restroom. George followed him, and once inside the men's room with the door shut, he delivered a fierce rabbit punch to Hart's kidney, dropping him to one knee. George had lifted him quickly. "Ever play me again like earlier today, you won't walk right for a month. Got it?" He winked and patted Hart on the head before making for the door. Hart stood gasping for breath, his insides screaming out in pain when George stopped and turned around once more. "Oh, but I do like your spirit. So, keep that up. My friends call me Wojtek, but you can call me George for now." With that, he had left Hart alone.

Once the flight leveled off, Hart made his way back to the galley and offered coffee to everyone, but only Magali accepted, asking for a double.

"When will we have him?" she asked after her first sip.

Hart shrugged. It was hard to tell if they'd even be able to track Diego down. But he was their only lead to Clara. The tracking dot still had her steadily heading towards what appeared to be South America on their current course.

"If you do catch him, I am afraid I don't think he'll say anything." She took another sip from her coffee.

"We have our ways of making people talk." Hart's voice trailed off as he imagined what he would do to Diego if he were alone in a room with him. If only he could get the chance, he'd tear the man apart.

"The look in his eyes the last time we talked. He is evil, pure evil. I want to kill him for what he put me through." She paused, her eyes tight with anger. "For what he is putting you through." Magali put her hand out and rested it atop Hart's.

Her touch was soft, surprisingly so. Since Clara had gone from him only a few days ago, he hadn't had much contact with anyone other than a rabbit punch and a few pats on the shoulder.

"I know how much you care for her, and we'll find her. With or without Diego's help."

Palmer watched the countryside of Ile de France fade away from view as daylight slowly began to fade. He consciously told himself to relax and tried to focus on breathing. Flying had always given him anxiety since the accident, but he was determined to cope with it. After all, he hadn't been in the accident, but rather, in his view, he was responsible for it. But he'd be damned if a past event would control his life. He'd fly, whether it killed him or not.

He noticed Pierre-Emmanuel staring at him from across the aisle and fought off the annoyance he felt for the man. Palmer then tried for several minutes to ignore him but finally gave up, turning to his French colleague. Pierre-Emmanuel, in his light grey glen-plaid suit with a blue silk shirt, seemed to fit in comfortably to the luxurious surroundings. His long legs crossed to reveal purple socks and suede oxfords. A fish to water, Palmer thought.

"Stephen, I am curious," the Frenchman began. Palmer already dreaded where the conversation was heading. "Are we following up on a lead in regards to the broader investigation, about the weapon plans for sale, or is this merely the chasing down my agent, who your agent happens to be in love with?"

Palmer smirked and took notice of his quickened pulse. The stubborn bastard can't help himself, he thought.

"They are one and the same, my friend. Our joint task force can't have a proper investigation if we don't follow the clues. I'd say having an agent kidnapped qualifies as a significant development."

Pierre-Emmanuel nodded and drummed his finger on his

chin as if debating whether to press further. He did. "And the tracking device, was that meant for the investigation or to keep an eye on her for your man?"

Palmer swiveled in his chair to glance back at Hart, who was in conversation with Magali and paying him no attention. He turned back towards his colleague and leaned in, closing the space between the two intelligence men. "You can moan all you want about that, but the facts are I was right not to trust you. If she hadn't worn that tracker, she would have completely vanished off the face of the earth. In the end, the means were justified."

Pierre-Emmanuel sighed as if he were bored. "You Americans go around the world bossing people about with your ethics and codes, but when it comes to your friends you play by whatever means necessary. You and I both know the dirty little secret, don't we? She's as good as dead, if not already, then soon." He sat back in the chair and examined some lint on his trousers.

Palmer kept his face as relaxed as possible although he contemplated throwing Pierre-Emmanuel out the emergency exit door. He didn't want Hart to see them arguing. Instead he spoke through gritted teeth. "Talk like that again about your agent, especially in front of Hart, and I'll break your pretty little neck."

"With friends like you, who needs enemies?" Pierre-Emmanuel turned towards the window as Palmer did the same.

The fields of central France were covered by shadows from the passing clouds. Palmer had extensively traveled through the small villages and the quiet towns in the countryside before, always uneasy by the distance from the bustle of big cities. He long ago vowed never to go back, but from 30,000 feet, up they appeared serene, almost comforting, as if in the spots of shade, you could hide from the world. Maybe if he made it out of this mess alive, it's exactly what he'd do.

Sometimes, Palmer reflected as the Cessna jet made its descent over the outskirts of Toulouse, *all you need is a different perspective to change your mind.*

40

The landmass appeared on the horizon like a mirage rising from the sea. Clara could make out the lush green hills and felt a burning desire to be on them. Land seemed so close, perhaps a place where she could seek safe harbor. But how could she manage that? Jump overboard and hope to be rescued? It was a foolish thought. Hopeful, she granted herself, but ultimately foolish. Be calm, she steadied her resolve. Take in the environment, learn and come up with a plan.

She turned to leave from the front deck. The weather after their dinner was agreeable. The fresh sea breeze cooled the warmth on her cheeks. She decided to make her way to the bridge to ask where they were, or better yet, steal a glance at the ship's GPS screen. *Learn, and improvise. You're a fighter. Those mantras will set you free.*

The bridge was full of crew, milling about and pressing a series of screens, their functions lost on Clara. She guessed that with the first mate gone, they may have been operating by a committee. Greta had materialized and stalked behind Clara like a lioness following a wounded antelope across the Sahara, just toying with the fact she could sneak up on her at any time. The GPS screen showed the boat as an arrow cruising towards a set of islands Clara recognized as the

Azores. They were owned by Portugal and located some 900 miles west of Europe, nearly in the middle of the Atlantic Ocean.

Clara knew they had been sailing for days, but seeing their distance from mainland Europe was shocking. She leaned closer to the screen and was about to ask one of the crew when they would arrive at wherever their destination might be when the equipment began to crackle and buzz with static. She straightened up; at first concerned she touched a dial. The static faded as she stood, just enough that the equipment turned quiet once again. Clara glanced around the room, registering the confusion on the sun-kissed faces of the crew. They didn't dare make a move after the first mate's fate, but Greta grabbed Clara by the back of the neck.

"Seems the equipment doesn't like you. Why would that be?"

Clara fought back the urge to elbow the woman in the face. She was captive and needed to at least act like she knew it. "I don't know! Maybe I touched something." She offered, longing to be outside on the deck and away from this mad-woman.

"No, no." Greta pushed on the back of Clara's neck, shoving her face onto the bridge's electronic equipment. The necklace Hart had given her slipped from inside her sweatshirt and clanked onto a control panel. As if on cue, several machines began to buzz and beep, crackling as if they had a bad radio connection.

Greta, still holding tightly onto Clara's neck, leaned over and whispered in her ear. "That static is interference, *mademoiselle*. I think you're hiding something from us, like a naughty girl."

With force that surprised and infuriated Clara, Greta

pulled her backward, so Clara stood upright once more away from the electronics. Once again, the static ceased, and the machines operated silently.

Greta reached for the silver pendant and, at the same time, let Clara free. While Clara tried to distance herself, Greta pulled with all her might and broke the necklace chain.

"You bitch, give that back." Clara felt her chest heaving as she touched the empty space where her gift from Paul had just been hanging seconds before.

Greta smirked and walked across the bridge to a desk and dropped the necklace down on it. She pulled the silver pistol that had been wedged into her back and, without hesitating, grabbed the gun by its barrel and used the grip to smash the necklace pendant.

Clara watched in horror from across the bridge as her only physical memento connected to Paul was smashed to pieces. She fought to maintain her composure and not show the sadness she felt. Her heart ached from a place of loneliness. The most profound sadness settled in her stomach.

Greta marched across the bridge with her hands curled into fists; the heavy footing of her approach distracted Clara from the horizon. She raised her right hand as if she was going to swing on Clara, but her prisoner didn't flinch, but merely returned the death stare she was receiving.

Greta clenched her square jaw, the muscles in flexing with anger. "You lied. You were tracking us." She held out her hand; the Cartier pendant had been cracked into pieces, little green bits of microchip scattered about in Greta's palm.

The revelation brought a rush of panic to Clara. Her head began to pound. Abruptly, as if she hadn't noticed before, she felt the floor rock slightly in the waves. She grabbed hold of the center console to steady herself, weakness causing her legs to shake. Had Paul given her a tracking device? She thought back to the evening they shared in the Paris safe house— the conversation, the creaking floors, the wine, his touch. Then the train, he seemed nervous about the necklace. Did he know she was in danger? Would he have told her? Conceivably it was why he was so reluctant to let her go alone to meet with Diego. Her world came crashing on her like a tidal wave, its weight, and roll causing her to feel unbalanced. She didn't want to look weak in front of this heinous woman but already knew it was too late.

"I'd like to go to my cabin."

Greta smiled and titled her head as if to study Clara's reaction. "Of course, where else do you have to go?"

41

Toulouse, France

The team gathered in a part of the city overflowing with the youthful energy Toulouse was known for. The Capitole square was filled with cafés packed with groups of students drinking Perrier Menthes, overlooking the expansive city hall, built in the 1750s. The small pedestrian alleyways connecting into the square were just as old but now filled with trendy sneaker shops, handmade candle ateliers, chocolatiers, and tapas restaurants winding as far as the eye could see. The Spanish influence was strong in Toulouse, as the short two-hour drive through, or over, the Pyrenees to Spain inspired a tranquil and laidback lifestyle upon the city. Or the Pink City, or as the locals affectionately referred to it as, *La Ville Rose.*

Over the centuries, the buildings were fortified with vibrant pink-colored bricks, fighting the endless battle against age, and had thus far managed to keep their luster. The Capitole itself was as jovial as the people of La Ville Rose, shining brightly throughout the day, but it truly sprung to life when it lit up at night. The lifestyle reminded Diego of home, so it's no wonder why he decided he would stash many of his accounts there.

"Getaway accounts," as he referred to them. Enough money to slip away for long enough, if ever life got too hot.

Or if he needed just to quit. Although quitting wasn't a realistic option. He loved life too much. The power he had, the fear he could smell in others before he killed them. He was masquerading as a police officer looking out for Europe's best interests, but in reality, he was a hired killer. The money flowing into his accounts came from a simple untraceable arrangement, electronically, that is, from his employer. The amounts showed up as revenue from a holding company in the Cayman Islands. The holding company owned several touristy restaurants set right on the sandy beaches. But should anyone look hard enough at the businesses, no suspicions would be raised at the dollars flowing through since the wine cellars alone at the restaurants were valued at over millions of dollars.

Diego's accounts also functioned as the conduit for his kidnapping payment. Get the girl on the boat and be paid handsomely. Those had been his orders. He didn't know the real reason why she'd been taken or what Darlington was so eager to hide, but it didn't matter. As long as he'd got paid, he didn't give a shit about what happened to whom.

Begrudgingly he knew the time had come to take his money and piss off to a secluded island for the foreseeable future. Sure, eventually Interpol would come looking, but they knew he was an untamed spirit that floated from lead to lead, sometimes going days without checking in. Reasonably, he'd be long gone before they started looking.

All he had to do was wait until morning, grab the cash the bank would have waiting for him, and he'd jet off from Blagnac Airport to whichever continent he pleased. Darlington, or the puppet master, Farhad, would always know how to find him.

Diego sat on a purple suede chair in a dark room and

gazed out the window down the desolate street. All he had to do, was wait.

The team split into two mobile units. With Palmer and Pierre-Emmanuel leading from the frontline, Team One from the elite counterterror unit, *Groupe d'Intervention de la Gendarmerie Nationale, was* posted inside a sizable white Sprinter van parked near the Capitole. Team Two was stationed several blocks away in a hotel suite down the street from the bank Diego had last visited. In the suite, Hart and Magali watched on as Lucas and Kelly set up their electronics. The operation had been hastily put together in less than three hours from leaving Paris.

Through some digging, Kelly had learned of Diego's several bank branch visits in the area earlier that day. She had cross-referenced the banks with the accounts they'd found through his wallet and traced the transfers. Then, using a rudimentary phishing program, Kelly infiltrated the two different hotels' guest reservation software. It appeared Diego had checked into the hotel near the Capitole square. Kelly found his room number and learned their suspect had ordered room service, a jamón ibérico sandwich with fries and several beers. Palmer requested a Toulousian, with the proper twang of the Sud-Ouest, to call the hotel and ask if the guest staying in Room 517 was around. The guest apparently was in residence, but before the call could be transferred, Palmer cut the connection.

Pierre-Emmanuel seemed out of place in the van full of hardened gendarmes with balaclavas and black tactical gear trained for terrorist situations. Palmer had managed to ensure George could join in the operation, while Hart, Magali, Kelly, and Lucas remained at the hotel far away.

However, the orders didn't sit well with Lucas, who didn't want to stand down. In the room, Hart watched him pace like a caged animal for several minutes before Lucas left the room entirely. Hart crept to the peephole and saw Lucas in the hallway put his back against the far wall and slide down until he hit the floor, head in hands. Hart wanted to offer the man his sympathy, he knew how horrible he felt, but there was no time for softness. Yes, Lucas had lost his partner, just like Hart had, and the regret of not being there to protect them was excruciating. Hart knew because he faced the same demons. Still, he focused on action, not sulking. The operation needed to go smoothly, and if Lucas wasn't in the proper mindset, Hart didn't want him around. The entire team was tasked with capturing Diego. As challenging as it was to remain away from the action, they provided valuable support to the operation. There was no other choice but to ride it out.

With Lucas in the hallway, Kelly typed away on her laptop even more feverishly. Magali kept watch from the window. Hart gave up on Lucas, rejoining Magali.

"Anything cooking out here?" He nodded outside, slightly lifting the sheer white curtain.

She checked her watch - 8 p.m. "It's a bit too early for dinner here."

Hart cracked a thin smile, forgetting for a moment to choose his phrases carefully. He glanced down at the street and saw several people, high-top sneakers, tight graphic tees, and snug dresses, walking towards the city center.

The window had a solid vantage point up and down the street, at least a hundred yards in either direction. Directly across the narrow one-lane road was another set of buildings, apartments that were the same five stories above ground as the hotel. Hart could easily look into the kitchen window across the street and see colorful laundry, complete with a France rugby jersey and purple towels, hanging from a wire.

After several minutes of watching city life go by, Hart grabbed the room-service menu. The anticipation of capturing Diego gave him fits of anxiety, but unlike others who might lose their appetite, the tension only exaggerated his. "Anyone want anything?" He held the menu up. Both ladies looked at him, then at each other, and shook their heads collectively.

He opened the door to ask Lucas and stepped out into the hallway. But the French agent was nowhere to be seen.

Hart asked into the room. "Anyone know where Lucas went?"

The ladies answered in shrugs and looks of confusion.

"Shit," Hart said, dropping the menu and racing out into the hallway.

Hart ran through the varying scenarios like he used to do at his old firm, analyzing risk, weighing the different factors to predict the most likely outcome. Lucas had vanished, but in what frame of mind? Sadness, anger, hate? A volatile mixture. Lucas knew where and how the operation would commence because he'd helped plan it. He knew which room Diego had ordered room service to a few hours ago because Kelly found it, and he knew the building layout. Worse, he knew how the attack team would execute a raid.

Hart realized they didn't have much time. He tried Lucas's phone but found it off. He'd been gone for at least fifteen minutes, plenty of time to get anywhere in the city center. If Hart's gut was correct, Lucas wasn't walking around looking for a kebab or a *demi-peche*. He was hunting for blood.

Rightfully so, thought Hart, but not now, and certainly not at the cost of screwing up their operation. Hart wanted revenge just as badly, but he understood rage could jeopardize the operation already underway.

Hart raced across Rue de Metz with Magali beside him. She insisted on coming with, and he didn't have time to argue. Hart decided the operation must continue, but no formal communications would be sent to the team about Lucas's disappearance. Kelly had stayed back at the hotel to provide overwatch for the operation; if any attention was diverted from finding Diego, he could slip from their net and vanish, taking with him the only lead left to Clara.

Hart and Magali passed The Four Monkeys bar, across the street from their hotel. The bar was already packed with locals hanging outside, nursing beers and smoking.

"How about there? He might have gone for a drink?" She tugged on Hart's sleeve, but he ignored her. He was adamant they must continue their pace. He didn't know when Palmer and Pierre-Emmanuel would launch the operation, but it would be soon. While Hart would love to watch the life leave Diego's dark eyes, too, they needed him alive.

Diego leaned back in his chair, watching the streets below fill with nightlife. It was starting to get busy, a few groups here and there, people getting off work from the local shops, heading to get ready for a night out. He munched on his sandwich and finished several 1664 beers while he half paid attention to the security camera he had set up on his room's peephole. But he couldn't help watch the street outside, hoping to catch sight of a beautiful girl's dress lifting in the night breeze.

Then, a sudden movement caught his eye. The fisheye

camera view showed a man race past his room, appearing to read the room numbers, only to turn back around and stand in front of Diego's door. The hair stood up on the back of his neck, not out of fear but a primal sense of twisted excitement. They'd found him. He reached across the table to the Glock 17 and slid it into his waistband, then tossed on his leather jacket. Grabbing his to-go bag from the bed, Diego faced the door and steadied himself for what could lay on the other side of the threshold. He'd barely gotten any of the money he'd been promised, but undoubtedly the accounts were how they'd found him. Greed kills. He cursed at his stupidity. No matter, it was time to get out of the city.

And that to Diego, meant by any means necessary.

42

Toulouse, France

Lucas floated with adrenaline as he raced down the hallway. He was about to come face to face with the man who'd taken Antoine from him, from his newborn baby, from this world. He would make him pay.

He checked the Glock 19, dropping the clip and pushing down on the ammo to ensure it was fully loaded. Fifteen rounds plus one in the chamber. But he'd only need one to make it count.

There would be repercussions for this unsanctioned killing, but the guilt-laced pain of losing his partner pushed concerns aside. He should have been there, protecting him. Of course, he lost Clara too, but the Americans had a tracker on her, and since she was Hart's woman, they would move heaven and earth to ensure her safety. But what luxuries did Antoine or the family he left behind have? None.

Lucas was his only chance of justice, and he was about to fulfill a silent oath to his former partner.

The van was stifling. Eight men crammed into the back of the mobile unit while two measly AC vents on the ceiling pushed the hot air around. Two computer monitors showed the live surveillance camera feed from inside the hotel. It had been Pierre-Emmanuel who stood then uttered, '*Merde!*'

Lucas raced through the lobby of the hotel, his aggression visible by his agitated movements. He was hunting with force and speed, not tact and patience. Palmer and Pierre-Emmanuel knew they didn't have time.

Pierre-Emmanuel ordered the operation to commence. "*Allez-y!*"

By the time he'd uttered the command and punched the van wall in frustration, the force had spilled out towards their respected destinations. Teams of two tackled the rear service entrance, the stairwell, and the lobby elevator simultaneously. Palmer and Pierre-Emmanuel followed them, wading into the red-carpeted lobby, ignoring the terrified guests. Palmer found a plush lobby chair and sat down while his colleague stayed glued to the gendarme in charge of communications.

One swift kick from Lucas, and the door gave way.

The room was quiet. A service cart sat in plain view. There was a narrow hallway with a bathroom off to the right, but the bedroom was out of sight. He imagined Diego hiding against the back wall, ready to run for the door. The curtains were drawn, and there was no balcony or other way to escape.

He was about to enter when he heard the elevator ping. Lucas turned to see two heavily armored gendarmes sprinting towards him. The timing wasn't ideal, but he'd only need a moment to do what was required.

"*Arrêt!*" he heard them frantically shouting.

Lucas ignored their commands and swung his Glock into the room.

The door bursting open and off its hinges didn't make Diego flinch. Instead, he let out a sigh. He was intently watching the computer screen in front of him in the decoy hotel room he had set up the day earlier being raided. Thank goodness he'd ordered the room service, hung the do-not-disturb sign and made it appear he hadn't left the room—tricks of the trade. There had been just enough tradecraft to slow down his pursuers, to put them ever so slightly off his trail, hopefully, long enough for him to escape the city.

Diego knew the heat would be on him ever since he took the French woman, which was fine by him. Eventually, they would trace him to the southwest of France, and what mattered was hanging around the city long enough to get his money for his troubles. His money was now lost, but at least the insurance he'd taken out by having the second hotel room paid off.

Now he needed to get out of his second hotel room and Toulouse. Nothing of any value was left in the other room, other than a gift to ensure everything would be certainly destroyed.

Diego tossed the laptop into his backpack and placed the SIM card into the burner phone he'd bought at the bus station. He dialed the number he'd memorized by heart only that afternoon. Counted quickly to three in both Spanish and French, then pressed send.

Adios. Au revoir.

Lucas's initial shock of finding the room empty was quickly replaced by sheer panic when he saw the cell phone taped to a brick of plastic explosive lying on the nightstand. He turned to run from the bedroom at the same time the two commandos raced into the suite. Then he heard the chillingly joyful chime of the cell phone and looked in horror over his shoulder as the phone's screen lit up.

"Get back!" he shouted, charging into the armed men. They collided as the explosion's force sent a fireball and all three men tumbling into the hallway.

43

Toulouse, France

The rumble from the blast caused Hart to stop dead in his tracks.

Even several blocks away from the Capitole, he felt the ground shake. The subsequent pandemonium became a swelling mass of humanity as everyone ran, screaming. Magali's face turned ashen as she grabbed onto Hart for answers. The explosion had come from the direction of Diego's hotel. He took her hand and fought forward through the panicked stampede.

"It's gonna be okay." He offered reassurance, but even he couldn't believe his own words.

"Maybe we should go back," Magali pleaded, her dark eyes darting towards the billowing smoke of the explosion. Suddenly she looked like she wanted no part of Hart's plan.

The truth was Hart didn't know what the hell to do. He had been accustomed to taking directions for so long he had begun to operate at extremes now: either follow orders completely or utterly ignore them. He didn't know which tactic to take right now. Race to Diego's hotel and the siege? Or head back to their hotel and wait out the tongue-lashing he'd get for losing sight of Lucas?

The flow of people from the Capitole square was getting

stronger, the narrow pedestrian side street they were on becoming overwhelmed with hundreds fleeing from the blast.

He nodded with his chin back the way they'd came, hoping to find another route that wasn't like trying to swim upstream. Magali accepted the proposal by jogging alongside him.

They were just past The Four Monkeys, Hart trying to find a passageway through the maze of streets and people, when Magali grabbed his arm in a death grip.

"*Il est la bas.*" She muttered it a second time, just loud enough for Hart to hear. He is over there.

Hart's confusion dissipated when he followed Magali's terrified gaze and caught sight of Diego. He was half a block away, casually blending in with the unnerved crowds. He wore black jeans, a black leather jacket, and had a backpack swung over his shoulder. His dark features were prominent even from a distance, especially to a woman who knew them so well.

Before Hart could even formulate a plan or try to hail anyone for backup, his instincts kicked in. He took off in a dead sprint, the anger inside propelling him forward. His chukkas thumped down the narrow sidewalks, bounding over sidewalk book stands. He couldn't lose sight of Diego. He was the only lead to solving the past week's events but, most importantly, to finding Clara. The man had somehow escaped the raid, or worse, never been there at all. Worry flooded Hart's thoughts. Could Diego have lured the team into a trap?

At the end of Rue de Metz, Diego turned right, out of Hart's vision, past an oyster café filled with confused diners sipping rosé, watching crowds flood past. Hart raced after Diego and willed his legs to pump faster. He jetted out into the street to keep a wide-angle on his target, who'd skirted the corner. Hart hadn't even bothered to look back to see if Magali had followed him. Diego was his.

Rounding the corner past the confused patrons of the café, Hart scanned the street for the black-clad Diego. The small side street was perfectly placed to shake surveillance, sloping downwards towards the river to the left. The riverbank walkways overflowed with people displaced from the city center. Hart scanned the parked cars and scaffolding from the restoration of a church that was taking up the block's right side. There was no sign of Diego. Had he spotted Hart?

Thinking Diego might have ducked into the darkened confines of the house of God, Hart hurried up the stairs to the church and peered inside. But it was void of visitors, only bright light filtering down from the stained glass above the altar. Hart cursed and turned his attention back to the street, and by a miracle, Hart caught sight of Diego making his way down towards the river.

The evening sky turned bright orange with lavender clouds hanging over the Pink City. It would soon be dark, and the lengthening shadows would only help Diego to slip away. The several thousand people sat on the riverbank, stretching as far as the eye could see. Many of them were lounging around, watching the sunset, drinking, smoking, and playing music, while others sought safety away from the Capitole.

Hart dashed across the road, ignoring the passing motorcycle that almost ran him down, and bounded down the stairs towards the water after Diego. The man turned left, doubling back in the direction he had been traveling on street level. Soon he would cross under the bridge that lay at the end of Rue de Metz. Hart was now only some thirty yards behind him on the straight walkway. Ahead the underpass of the bridge was darkened. Hart decided he would make his move. Diego's features were more apparent now. The black bag slung over the shoulder looked heavy, the man's stride confident.

Hart figured that the guitar players using the bridge's underside for better acoustics would quieten the brash approach of his running. He just hoped Diego wouldn't glance over his shoulder.

But Diego kept his head down and walked briskly south alongside the river.

Hart was nearly ten yards away now, just under the bridge, his approach quieted by the blaring guitar. His lungs screaming for air, cramped with pain, but with a shot of adrenaline he got when he was within striking distance, he pushed the pain away.

He leaped and, with his left hand, grabbed Diego's shoulder and brought his right elbow down on the man's head. Diego spilled to the ground but recovered well, rolling and catching Hart with a flailing kick to the midsection.

The two scrapped like animals, rolling over one another, clawing at anything they could manage to get a hold of. Hart grabbed Diego's neck with both hands and tried to squeeze the man into submission. Holding onto Hart's hands with one of his own, Diego grabbed Hart's right ear with the other and pulled. The pain was blinding, and Hart let go, rolling off Diego.

He heard the unmistakable clink of a gun falling on the ground.

In the darkness under the bridge, Hart made out the wild look in his adversary's eyes. The glint of the knife came quickly, as if from a magic trick. The switchblade appeared from nowhere. Hart threw his body backward during the first onslaught. Praying he could recall all of Clara's combat training. He ducked when Diego thrashed the blade near his head. The man's jabs and slices were controlled and powerful. Dodging a thrust, Hart dove forward into Diego's legs, wrapped him up, and spun him into the ground. Diego hit the stone walkway with a thud. Hart was momentarily dazed since he'd slammed face-first into the ground as Diego fell on top of him. He opened and closed his eyes, trying to blink away the dark spots to clear his vision. He heard Diego grunt as he got off the ground and onto his feet. Hart managed to get to a knee and rubbed his eyes. His vision returned to the darkness under the bridge, just in time to see the knife catch the dying sunlight as it swung at him.

He pivoted to his left and raised his arm, redirecting the blow just enough so the knife sliced across his back rather than his neck. Hart howled in pain.

Diego stumbled from exhaustion and looked down at his wounded prey. "You know, I think she wanted to come with us." He sauntered around Hart as if circling before he went for the kill. "I was just angry you didn't get the chance to watch me caress her when I found her on the floor of the bathroom. You see, she had tried to run away, to call for help, but you were nowhere to be found."

The words filled Hart with a wave of anger. He'd always been triggered by slights and unjust circumstances, but for the first time in his life, he felt the red-hot glow of pure hatred. Revenge was on his mind. He wanted to kill the man.

He wobbled to his feet. Slightly hunched on account of the gash in his back, he stared into Diego's dark eyes. "I'll ask once. Where is she?"

Diego barked in laughter and wagged the knife back and

forth. "Tsk, tsk, tsk. I cannot tell you that, otherwise what fun would this game be?"

Hart felt the fires of hatred burning extra hot inside, as if his eternal engines were being shoveled vigorously with coal. His heart beat fast and the pain in his back subsided for the moment.

"Listen, I—" Hart sprung forward towards Diego from his crouched position. He caught the man momentarily off guard, throwing a vicious uppercut that he felt rattle Diego's head. The knife fell to the ground, and it skidded several paces away. The guitar player had run away at the start of the scuffle, and the bridge's empty underpass echoed with the men's grunts.

With Hart advancing, Diego staggered backward. Hart worked on his adversary's body, landing hooks and jabs on the man's ribs and kidneys until Hart couldn't feel his arms. Diego threw a defensive elbow that caught Hart's temple, stunning him. The Spaniard capitalized on his advantage and threw his body onto Hart, pinning him on his back. Diego pressed a hand onto Hart's face when he tried to reach for the fallen knife. Hart was now helpless, the knife too far out of reach.

A sudden sickening noise of knife grinding into bone and flesh, followed by a swift breath escaping. Hart felt the hand on his face relax. He tore it away, frightened and eager to find where he'd been stabbed. He must be in so much pain his body was in shock. But as his vision cleared, it was Diego's face that was frozen in shock, staring right towards Magali, who stood back, blood dripping from her hand.

Her fierce eyes were filled with rage as he stared at the knife sticking out of Diego's side. He gazed at her with disbelief and attempted to sit upright, feeling around for the knife sticking out of his side.

He pulled it from his ribs with little effort and wheezed in pain. Then he lunged at Magali, swiping in her direction with the blade. She dove backward onto the ground a safe distance away.

Diego, still on top of Hart, turned his attention back towards his trapped victim. He bent over and, with both hands, plunged the knife at Hart's head. Hart blocked the effort with both his forearms, catching Diego's assault only inches from his face. The man leaned harder as Hart craned his head to the side, desperately trying to use momentum to roll Diego off of him. From the corner of his eye he caught Magali rise to her feet. A familiar shape in her hand. Hart's mind began to panic, spinning the possible scenarios. Things were far from in control.

"Stop!" Magali yelled, her cry reverberating under the bridge. She held the Glock 17 that had fallen from Diego when Hart tackled him. Hart knew Glocks didn't have a safety mechanism that would confuse novice shooters; rather, the weapon had a simple trigger guard to prevent an unwanted discharge. Even if Magali had never fired a gun, she could figure this one out.

Diego glanced at her but kept the pressure on the knife driving towards Hart's head. "Oh, you were foolish to point a gun at me." He wheezed, blood evidently finding its way into his lungs. "I hope you remember what I did to my brother, because it will be worse for you, just like I promised."

Magali stepped forward, a wild look in her eyes.

Hart fought with all his might to not let the blade kill him. He pleaded to Magali through gritted teeth. "Don't shoot. We need him alive. For Clara!" His arms began to shake, his strength beginning to waver.

"He's going to kill you!" She moved closer to the two men, now only steps away. "I said stop!"

253

"You'd better do it because I'm going to kill you next." Diego sneered at Magali before leaning even further onto Hart. The blade nicked at his forehead.

Hart cried out in pain, his arms feeling like they would give way at any moment. He looked over at Magali once more, the wildness in her eyes replaced with a determination. "Don't!"

The shots boomed out under the bridge, the first hitting Diego in his midsection, the exiting of the bullet hitting Hart in his right leg. The second missed completely, but the third found its mark right under Diego's armpit, through his heart. He rose for a split second, his eyes frozen in the colors of the dying sunset like a stained-glassed window.

Then he toppled over onto Hart. Dead.

44

Luke Darlington had not heard from Diego for several days. The Interpol agent was on the job, orders straight from the top of command. Then shortly after that, Darlington's own directives came. Pay Diego half a million dollars. It seemed now, his Interpol agent had gotten a promotion.

Being the good company man he was, Darlington had deposited the money into Diego's specified account, deriving the funds from the Grand Cayman holding group saved for such payments. But Darlington got spooked when Diego seemed to disappear off the face of the earth. The little Spanish *mierda*. Constantly fucking up plans.

Darlington left the glassy confines of his office; his chauffeured Jaguar stalked through the dark and rainy streets of London until he reached his flat in Knightsbridge. He bid the driver farewell, utilizing his best poker face, and told him that he wanted to get a later start the following day, so to pick him up at nine in the morning instead of seven. With a tip of his cap, the driver was off into the night.

Darlington raced upstairs to his bedroom, lifted the mattress, then the bed slats, and pulled out his Louis Vuitton duffel. It was not exactly a discreet way to carry wealth, but then again, what banker wanted to be discreet about money?

His life had been one large bluff for the last several years since he'd gotten himself mixed up in this deadly game. His well-established bank had sprouted connections to nefarious individuals who otherwise couldn't access their money because of economic sanctions or terrorist ties. Darlington began making money hand over fist. The arrangement, however, always seemed destined for disaster.

The radio silence from Diego told him something was amiss. He was indeed a Spanish shit, but he'd always kept Darlington in the loop. Now, days of silence told another story. They'd had a good run, so there was no bitterness as he fled his home. Undoubtedly, Darlington would fondly recall his walk-in closet, dripping with hand-carved dark wood and cream-colored carpet, and his bedroom painted a rich eggplant and his bright yellow silk bed sheet as he lounged on some secluded island.

Dumping handfuls of clothes into the bag, Darlington figured whatever he forgot he could buy. He hurried into his closet. From a dresser resembling a central island in an expansive kitchen, a glass top revealed dozens of watches tucked into spinning contraptions designed to keep the automatic watch movements going. Picking a few of his favorites, including a Patek Philippe and a vintage Rolex Submariner that could easily fetch him a few hundred thousand dollars on the black market, he tossed them into the bag in alongside the bundles of cash.

He finished packing, poured himself a cognac with a shaky hand, and plopped on the floor next to the bed. Was he making the right choice to run? If he stayed, surely the mysterious voice on the headset would come for him. He'd failed him, or at least his man Diego had. Same difference. Perhaps the more accurate distinction, though, was he lied to them. The money he had tucked away still hadn't been found, otherwise, he'd be dead. Could he ride out his hand and hope they never found the money? Unlikely, especially with his man Diego falling off the map—where was the bastard? The payments to Diego's accounts could probably be traced back to his own with enough effort and rule breaking. The thought of armed agents of the crown storming his flat, arresting him for laundering money for sanctioned countries or individuals, scared the shit out of him.

They would eventually find out with time. Time was the ultimate teller of truths; give it long enough, and the truth would come out. Someone would find out, whether it be the government or the syndicate he ran with. Because he knew he'd eventually get caught. He was living on borrowed time, which was somewhat liberating.

He rang the private airline concierge and requested an immediate transatlantic flight to Grand Cayman.

It was time to make his move to cash in his chips and get out of the game.

Part III

The Trap

45

Toulouse, France

Stephen Palmer took off his glasses and rubbed his face. He sat slumped in a metal folding chair, ignoring the noise around him. He needed to concentrate on the next steps. Their best lead was dead, shot in the street after his agent made a hasty decision of playing the hero. There was a hole in the side of a hotel, and three men, including Lucas, in the hospital with severe injuries from the blast.

His skin felt hot, and despite the charged energy of the past twelve hours, he could go for a nap—a reminder of being too old to be a spy. It seemed long ago he was stuck reading reports and deferring all field assignments to more experienced agents. Now, more than ever, he was in the thick of it.

He scanned the halls of their temporary headquarters in the bowels of Toulouse's football stadium. It was located on a small island in the middle of the Garonne river, not far down from where the shooting took place under the Rue de Metz overpass. The small island was vacant except for the stadium, which provided much-needed logistical assets such as landing space for a helicopter on the pitch to ferry them back to the airport. Pierre-Emmanuel had worked magic with the local police, flashing all kinds of documents and making phone calls. His sway allowed Hart and Magali to go free after a short discussion of what happened under the darkened overpass. No bystanders were hurt, and since the victim had purported a crime against a French agent, as Pierre-Emmanuel had explained, the gendarmes were more than happy to abide quietly.

Palmer put his glasses back on and longed for a Mountain Dew, or something much more substantial, and several of them. Their makeshift command center had a few fold-up tables and computers, where had been Kelly monitoring proceedings. The closed concession stands providing the only lighting in the corridor. They'd decided to stay in Toulouse because the shooting would take a bit of time to clear up, but the more pressing reason in Palmer's eyes was that they didn't know where next to go. Hart hunched over the tables, jumping from screen to screen, trying to connect the dots of the financial transactions linked to a few new bankcards found on Diego's person. They were associated with aliases and a plane ticket to Marrakech from Toulouse Blagnac, but that was all.

He heard a soft "ahem" before he felt a gentle tap on his shoulder. Palmer turned around to find Kelly glancing towards Hart, who hadn't noticed her leave her station and report to Palmer.

"Clara's tracker…" she started, ensuring Hart couldn't overhear them. "It's *gone.*"

Palmer felt his heart catch for a split second before beginning to beat again. When it rains, it fucking pours. He feigned ignorance. "What do you mean? We lost the signal because she's too far away?"

Kelly shook her head, her ponytail bouncing. "I don't know what happened. When she went past the Portuguese

Azores, the red light died. It vanished. We had a strong signal, but..." She stopped, as if debating whether Palmer wanted her theory or not. He gave a nod of encouragement. "It's as if they found the device and destroyed it. There's no other explanation. It's waterproof to five hundred meters and incredibly resilient, even through signal jamming devices."

"But the general direction remained the same?"

"Correct." Kelly nodded. "I've forecasted the route based on the tracker's current speed and heading. It's not perfect, but it looks like anywhere from Nassau, Bahamas to the top of Venezuela is plausible."

He let out a huff of air as Kelly returned to her computer.

The following required conversation would not be enjoyable. Palmer flicked a glance at Hart, whose face was mere inches from the monitors. Palmer buried his head in his hands but decided against looking too melancholy and slapped his hands on his knees instead to prepare himself.

Palmer crossed the narrow corridor in a few paces. The tunnel out to the pitch gave the only indication they were in a soccer stadium. He wished he could hide amongst the crowd in different circumstances, but he had no such luxury this evening.

Hart was busy studying bank statements on Kelly's monitor.

Palmer put his hand on Hart's good shoulder, and when his protégé turned, Palmer nodded back to the pitch-black tunnel. Reluctantly Hart followed. When Palmer felt they were far enough from George, Kelly, and the team, he began, but Hart immediately interrupted.

"Any update on Lucas?"

"There were no casualties from the explosion, thank God." Palmer watched as Hart sighed in relief.

"How's your back?"

Hart shrugged. "Twelve stitches. Nothing a few Tylenol can't fix."

Palmer nodded. He was buying time, wishing he didn't have to say the next part.

"I do have some bad news. You're the first to know." He paused, recognizing the fire starting to build in Hart's eyes. Before he could complete his thoughts, Hart let loose.

"What, these bastards think they can keep us here? Pierre-Emmanuel with the fancy French cuffs can't get us out of this? We need to keep moving. We just lost our best lead to finding Clara. There was the attack on the Seine this morning and the hotel explosion tonight—we can't afford to sit still. It's all connected." Hart threw his arms out in annoyance, waiting for Palmer's rebuttal.

Palmer shook his head as if he couldn't believe he was about to admit to this. "We lost her signal, Paul. She's off the map."

Hart took in the information as if he were translating it from a different language. He searched the ceiling and then the floor, shifted his weight before frowning in confusion. "Weak signal? International-waters bullshit?"

"No, as in the signal is completely gone." Palmer waited while Hart turned to lean against the tunnel wall to catch his breath. After a moment, he turned back and crouched on the ground next to a plastic folding chair.

"It means," Palmer continued, "and I'm saying this to be perfectly honest with you. It means they most likely found and destroyed the tracker."

Hart buried his head in his hands. Palmer looked past Hart into the stillness that reigned over the corridor. The team behind them could sense the tension emanating throughout the stadium. The stadium was silent except for the dull electric whine of the hallway lights. Palmer turned to find Kelly spectating from the analyst table.

Suddenly, Hart sprung to his feet, grabbed the chair, and smashed it into the cement wall until it disintegrated. Hart tossed the rest of the cheap plastic back down the tunnel and stormed off onto the pitch.

Palmer tolerated the hush as long as he could and stared into the black abyss of the football pitch. Then, he silently prayed for a miracle.

Hart marched through the tunnel and out into the black night air. The stadium walls blocked the evening breeze, the only reprieve from the heat of the Sud-Ouest. He stopped and craned skywards to the stars in contrast against the black sky, hiding behind thin clouds that listlessly floated by. He stayed staring at the sky, wondering if Diego was somewhere above him now, but prayed the bastard was somewhere else considerably less enjoyable. He stood still for what felt like hours until he heard a noise behind him. Hart was ready to pour out all the frustration of the past week onto Palmer, but instead, he found Magali sitting on the ground smoking a short distance from him.

She gave a slight nod. How long had she been watching him? The thought crossed his mind to leave. He wanted to be alone with his anger. He started back towards the tunnel, but he decided that it was Magali's fault there was nowhere left to turn. She'd killed the man, their only lead to intercepting the sale of the nuclear plans, but more importantly for Hart, getting Clara back. He covered the short distance to Magali.

"You just had to kill him, didn't you? Couldn't wait to get him back for screwing you over, quite literally, is that it?"

Magali opened her mouth to speak but instead took a pull on her cigarette as if to calm herself. She flicked it away towards the tunnel and stood. "I saved your life! What choice did you give me?"

"What choice?" Hart felt his voice shaking with emotion and ignored his impulse to control it. "You didn't have to kill him! You were selfish, you wanted revenge, and now we might never get..." He trailed off, too afraid to utter the thought he feared might come true.

"It isn't my fault. I protected you. Don't blame others. You think I've killed someone before?" There was a fire that had built in her eyes, a rage from the challenge Hart had issued. "I killed a man to protect you! Do you think I wanted to take his life? *Non!* I did it for you, and I get thanked by being accused of selfishly murdering him?" She took a step closer to Hart.

"I had it under control. You did what you wanted." Hart closed the distance so he could smell the cigarette smoke from her mouth.

"Without me, you'd be nowhere! You would have never found him if I hadn't helped you."

"And without you, I never would have lost Clara in the first place, and Antoine wouldn't have died. You're to blame for all of it as far as I'm concerned."

Magali reached out and slapped Hart. "Take it back. You shouldn't blame me for your mistakes. You're an asshole, and I am the one struggling here."

Ignoring his stinging cheek, Hart began to walk away. He stopped after only a few steps. "Everything I've been doing is to get her back. And I won't apologize for any of it. I'll do everything in my power to find her."

"What is the point of finding her if you are ruining the lives of others?"

Hart began to open his mouth but closed it without speaking. He headed back off into the bowels of the stadium. He didn't care that he'd almost died because, at the moment, he didn't see how he had any future worth living.

46

Atlantic Ocean

Clara lay still, the swell of the ocean causing her to rise and fall. The ninety-two-meter Italian-made superyacht had stabilizers to keep its passengers as comfortable as possible, but the sea often had different ideas. The slap of the waves against the hull clawed at Clara, keeping her awake, working against the ship's soothing rocking. She wanted nothing more than to sleep, to wake up in several days at a port, and subsequently be rescued, but she feared this would never happen.

Her thoughts drifted to Paul, but she had a hard time picturing him. It had been nearly a week since she'd last seen him. She wondered how he was handling their separation. It wasn't the first time they'd been torn apart by circumstances out of their control. Or maybe he'd been told to sit out the investigation because he was too emotionally involved, although she knew better. Her professional experience told her the higher-ups would not compound the mistakes of losing one agent with one whose decision-making wouldn't be rational. Clara doubted Paul would agree to stand on the sidelines. There were additional possibilities, some much darker and scarier than the openness of the dark ocean she was trying to sleep upon. She couldn't allow herself to explore the upsetting alternatives. The reality was she would likely never know. Until she learned otherwise, she'd believe he was alive and well.

She'd felt uneasy for much of the past few days, thanks to Greta. The late-night visit and her finding the tracker in the necklace left Clara off balance. She touched the empty place on her chest where the chain used to lay. Did he give it to her to keep an eye on her? Did he know she was in danger? The thoughts danced around in her head endlessly. Once again, she was resigned to the ambiguity.

Clara imagined a scenario where it was just her and Greta, the evil bitch who needed to be taught a lesson. Clara pictured herself inflicting terrible pain on the woman. Anger swelled inside of her, blinding any other emotion she had. Fear, loss, pain, longing were all replaced with burning anger.

She snapped her eyes open and calmed her breathing. The things she was capable of thinking of doing to another person made her nauseous. This wasn't her; she wasn't an evil person. Something stirred inside, reminding her of the animals she'd grown up with, the dogs and cats her family had that had always been sweet, but when they were scared or injured, they could turn cruel without a moment's notice. A wounded animal was a dangerous creature.

She pushed the anger away, and as if dragged to the deepest darkest corners of her mind, she fell into a dreamless sleep.

Clara awoke, startled by heavy breathing.

Before she could fully wake up and say 'come in,' Greta knelt next to the bed, grinning. Clara fought every impulse to give her captor satisfaction from surprising her.

"Your presence is requested in the upstairs salon immediately. Please come." She bit her lip and slowly lifted the cover to look underneath when Clara grabbed at it, hiding her modesty.

Greta giggled and left towards the open now. "Now!" she barked.

Clara dressed slowly, a minor act of defiance. She gradually worked her way upstairs under the careful watch of Greta, who escorted her to the salon. The carpeted staircase led her to the fourth level on the ship, finding a new space with tufted-leather furniture, a telescope, and several bookcases lining the walls. Portholes lined the starboard wall. Under them sat two oversized leather chairs, and in one of them was Farhad. On the side table next to him was a mirrored tray with two small tea glasses and a teapot. Greta took a seat on the couch on the far side of the room.

Greta held out her hand and proudly smiled like a bird dog showing off its latest caught pheasant.

Farhad stood and slightly bowed. "I must admit it is quite nice having a guest on this journey."

Clara politely smiled, intent on lulling her captors into ease. "But the guest doesn't know where we are going exactly."

Farhad shrieked with laughter and motioned for her to sit on a chair next to him. He painstakingly poured tea into her cup. Clara could smell the strong apple flavor and assumed it was exported from Turkey. He seemed a man of tradition, another piece of intelligence she could put away in the back of her mind.

"We are going to deliver a gift to a friend of a friend." He smiled and handed Clara a teacup. After clinking their cups together, he sipped his tea and hummed.

Clara raised the glass to her lips and paused. Was she the

gift? Who was the friend? She decided that whatever was going to happen would happen, and she'd be damned if she lived driven by fear.

She sipped the tea.

Farhad was silent for a moment, and when Clara didn't offer a follow-up question, he sat forward.

"Don't you want to know what the gift is? And who it's for?"

Clara suppressed the urge to smile. Men were too easy. Always eager to share their masterful plans and feed their egos. Show some disinterest, and one could learn anything they wanted, just by being quiet rather than asking outright. She offered a face that said, *Pourquoi pas*, why not, and shrugged. The truth was, she already had it figured out.

"Well," Farhad began, setting his tea on the tray. "First, you must understand my humble career." Clara cringed when he gave his odd chuckle. "I manage money for those who, let's say, are in delicate circumstances. For instance, take a country under severe economic sanctions. How does that country grow, or even access their money? How do they pay corporations who are still bold enough to offer them products or services? What about the individuals inside that country that have significant amounts of money? I'm talking hundreds of millions if not billions of dollars that they cannot use to buy goods. So, I arrange access. It's a bit complicated but in essence, I am the banker of the world's most hated or persecuted as I think of them. My clients don't need lucrative profits, but rather access."

Clara smirked. "So complicated that I wouldn't understand? I think you may have been misinformed about me."

Farhad studied her for a moment and brushed his mustache with his fingers. "Well, this vessel is my means of transportation around the world. And this yacht is owned, through a series of convoluted holding companies and contracts, by some vital people in Iran, and it's worth, realistically, several hundred million dollars."

He left the fact to linger, allowing Clara to interrupt.

"So, you use your yacht as collateral to borrow money to negotiate and arrange other transactions that move money around for sanctioned countries and individuals under scrutiny. Is that the complicated part?" Clara tilted her head, waiting for Farhad to explain more to her. "Or do I still not get your very complicated ways?"

Farhad smacked his lips in appreciation. "Very good." He paused and raised one of his fingers with a gold ring on it. "But you're missing one important piece as to why this is even more complicated."

Clara took a sip from her tea. "Well, of course, there is the sale of the nuclear plans you've been brokering. And to ensure your transaction is allowed to proceed, my involvement has become necessary."

Farhad bowed his head in approval. "Precisely."

"And what is it exactly you are expecting to do with me?"

Farhad polished off the remnants of his tea. "You're insurance the transaction will go without issue. Otherwise, there will be consequences. If you are by my side, I'm untouchable because you're a valuable asset yourself to me personally. You see, you can cause pain to an old friend because of your relationship with his young protégé. Funny how the world works, isn't it?"

What protégé? Clara ignoring her confusion, pressed forward. "And after the transaction finishes? What then?"

Farhad smiled and was about to speak when a member of the crew entered the salon and spoke with Greta. Farhad watched intently as Greta then made her way over to him, whispering in his ear. Clara strained to listen but couldn't make out anything.

Greta finished and Farhad sat stone-faced. He slowly began to shake his head in disgust.

"Do you remember the man who brought you to us?" Farhad asked as he rose from his chair.

Clara nodded that she did. How could she forget the bastard?

"Well, your boyfriend found Diego and killed him. Pity— he was a useful assassin, one I had high hopes for. Guess that means Paul Hart is out for blood. I thought this would be civilized, but I think not." Farhad left the room swiftly with Greta at his side, gliding over the ivory carpet.

Clara allowed the information to sink in. Paul was alive. Her heart pounded while accounting for the reality that Farhad could be purposefully misleading her. But if it were true, Paul wasn't idly sitting by letting others look for her. He was fighting for her like she knew he would. But killing? She shuddered at the thought. That didn't sound like Paul or Pierre-Emmanuel at all.

But then again, she recalled, a wounded animal was a dangerous creature.

47

Kelly raised her hand at the analysts' table. "I might have something here."

It was the middle of the night, and a few people, George among them, had been asleep. Palmer slowly unwound himself from a steel bench where he had been lying and shuffled over to Kelly.

Hart watched on from a distance, slumped against the far wall, up the entire night racking his brain trying to think of other ways to move forward. What did they want with Clara? Why her and not him? Every time he had a thought that seemed logical, several more would spring up, frightening the hell out of him. Pushing off the wall, Hart headed over to see Palmer and Kelly.

"I've been researching this for the past hour and didn't bring it up because I wanted to make sure it was solid." Kelly explained to Palmer, his eyes bloodshot and his hair unkempt.

Palmer acknowledged Hart with a grunt. "Kelly's caught wind of a local bank branch that created a suspicious activity report on one of Diego's accounts. Banks all over the world create hundreds of thousands of these reports daily. If a banker believes there's unlawful activity in an account, they send the account information up the command chain. But, these reports usually aren't investigated for at least a few weeks while they are processed."

Kelly sat upright, taking her hoodie off. "Exactly, so I ran an algorithm searching for specific keywords in an alert. Since Diego wasn't using his real name, I tried several IDs associated with his other accounts and got lucky. There's a match." The young analyst beamed.

Hart felt the faint ping of optimism. He nodded towards Kelly. "Nothing lucky about it. Pure talent. What did we learn?"

She glanced at Palmer to ensure it was okay to divulge. He nodded in affirmation. "Several wire transfers came in straightaway from the Cayman Islands but under a holding company. I couldn't get much, the Grand Cayman banking systems and laws don't help. The information cannot be accessed or stored even, and certainly not shared." Kelly's voice trailed off. "But we have ways of tracing the wire transfers' electronic signatures. It is rather genius. Instead of following the money, we follow the IP's original starting point. It's given us a physical address."

Hart began to ask a question when Palmer held up a hand to cut him off. "So, couple options here. We won't get the information we're looking for unless we are on the ground in the Caymans. I can scramble agency resources to go, or we can continue to investigate in France and try to pick up another lead. But if we go and it's a dead end, we've stepped in it. Kelly, thoughts?" Palmer asked, ignoring Hart as he once again was about to speak.

Kelly drew a sharp breath. "The banking privacy laws are brutally tough. Even if you were to get there, I don't know how you identify the accounts. And even if you do, finding

Miss Nouvelle and whoever is brokering this deal for the plans might not be a slam dunk." Kelly paused to glance at Hart. "But her tracker was last pinpointed as heading towards the Caribbean."

Palmer craned his neck to the ceiling as if the correct course of action was sketched on the cement above. "We can't forget this isn't just about the agent. Who is brokering the deal? What exactly is for sale? We might have to explore alternative avenues to stop this sale. We've already seen how sanctions and diplomacy work. Apparently, politicians advocating them get murdered on the Seine."

Kelly began to nod in agreement before Hart interrupted.

"You're not going to ask me what we should do?" Hart was incredulous, his face flushed.

"I already know what you'd say. I don't have to ask you. But if it makes you feel any better—"

Hart cut him off. "Damn right it does. We gotta go there now. We take off soon as we can."

Palmer sighed. "See, I knew you'd say that." He took a phone from his pocket. He walked over to George on the floor and playfully nudged him with his foot. "Saddle up."

The sun was creeping over the horizon as Hart and the team walked across the tarmac. The hazy morning light reflected off the chrome accents of the bright white Gulfstream G550, its winglets reaching up to the sky. The pilots were making their rounds, inspecting the fuselage. The engines were spooling, the front staircase lowered.

Palmer led the way, with George and Hart following suit. The former soldier had a large bag with his gear, while Palmer carried a briefcase. Hart had nothing but the same dirty clothes—his blazer, chinos and chukkas—he'd been wearing for the past twenty-four hours. He was looking forward to the feeling of peace on an airplane, the quiet helplessness he always felt while flying. Hopefully, it would put him to sleep, a temporary reprieve from his nightmare.

Once onboard, surprisingly, Hart heard a familiar voice. Pierre-Emmanuel stood at the back of the plane and greeted the men. Next to him, slumped in the cream leather bucket seat, was Lucas. Hart and his old friend made eye contact and shared a solemn nod. The man's face was bruised and his left arm in a sling thanks to the blast from the hotel. Hart felt terrible for the man, then he remembered Lucas's charge sent the mission into a death spiral. But he was here to make amends; Hart was glad to have the man back.

Palmer spiked his briefcase on a seat and sneered. "Nice to see you, but what the fuck are you doing on my plane?"

Pierre-Emmanuel winced, his arms at his sides as if pleading for patience. "You're still in my country, and after all, we are allies. Lucas and I want to help."

"Lots of people want to help, but that doesn't mean they always do." Palmer swayed in place as he made up his mind.

"May I remind you that Clara is our agent." Pierre-Emmanuel stepped forward. Hart knew him as a man not to beg. Instead, he pleaded with his brown eyes. "Please, Stephen. We can help. I assure you."

Palmer ignored Hart behind him and nodded and the two French men sat quietly in the back of the plane. He turned to George. "Wojtek, find out who the hell let them on my plane." George hurried off to speak with the pilots.

Hart found a seat at a four-person table, the smoothly polished mahogany complete with gold-accented drink holders. The plush seat seemed to pull him in, his exhaustion already clawing at his body like gravity. His stitches still ached, and he knew it'd be a long, uncomfortable flight. But he'd survived.

The Rolls Royce engines roared to life and screamed down the runway. Once airborne, the plane tipped its wings to the west as they waved goodbye to the La Ville Rose before heading to cross the Atlantic.

As Hart drifted off, he couldn't help but think of Magali and their hurried goodbye. He'd tried to make things right but couldn't find the words to apologize for blaming her. She saved his life, and she was the reason they had any hope of finding Clara. Deep down, he believed she knew he was grateful, but then again, maybe he was lying to himself. He hoped to see her again and explain it all with Clara by his side. They would walk her through the investigation, his and Clara's past, and detail their reunion. He did, however, need to accept that this might never be the case. No matter what was next, their lives had all changed dramatically during the past week. Clara, Magali, Hart, Lucas, and most regrettably, Antoine.

Magali had played a crucial role in leading them to where they were off to now. The lingering effects of an adrenaline-packed night and subsequent day had developed a strange bond between them. There was a certain sadness that settled over Hart as he closed his eyes, thinking of his last conversation with Magali. He'd miss her poise, intelligence and her courage. In fact, she reminded him of someone he loved very much.

"You'll get her back. I can feel it," Magali had said as they stood saying goodbye on the runway. One leaving, one staying, both heading off into the same hopeful direction.

"Thank you for it all." Hart had offered a sad smile.

She leaned into him, burying her head in his chest. He

fought off the emotion swelling his throat and held her tightly. He'd said that they'd meet again. Then he turned and got on the plane, not looking back.

But Hart wasn't sure he believed he'd ever see her again. He wished for it but didn't quite believe it.

Palmer thudded into empty seats across from Hart, shaking him from a light slumber. The sleepy fog from his head cleared and at once Hart registered the pain from his stitches. He glanced at the TV screen showing the plane flying over the middle of the Atlantic; déjà vu of the map he watched Clara's tracker drift across.

Just an hour had elapsed since leaving Toulouse. The rest of the plane was quiet; everyone was sleeping except Pierre-Emmanuel in the back, busy on his laptop.

"Want something to drink?" Palmer glanced towards the back of the plane and the galley. "Scotch, coffee, wine?"

Hart shifted in his seat. "Probably a bit too early for scotch."

"Hmm, I agree. Maybe some wine?"

"Coffee's great."

Palmer shuffled to the back of the plane and returned several minutes later with a French press and two mugs and two mini bottles of bourbon.

"How you holding up?" Palmer asked as he began to fill Hart's mug with coffee.

Hart ignored the question and, when his mug was halfway full, told his boss to stop.

"Not a big coffee drinker, eh?" Palmer emptied a bourbon into his own mug and topped it off with coffee.

"No, just small pours save more for later." Hart stared at his mug, his thoughts back to Clara, the safe house, and

Paris. If only he had stayed with her, protected her like he should have done. Palmer's attention settling on him shook him from his daze. The man probably was wondering what Hart was so deep in thought about.

"You know my mother lived to be ninety-eight years old. Did I ever tell you that?"

Hart shook his head from side to side. "Stephen, you've barely told me anything about yourself, and other than what I've deduced, that you enjoy Mountain Dew, intelligence gathering, and terrible plaid shirts, I got nothing."

Palmer blew on his coffee and smirked. He took a moment to watch the passing clouds from the starboard side window. "The last few years were tough on me caring for my mother. She was there, but not entirely. I'd go and visit, less and less every year, but still, you know, she's my mother, so you do what you have to." He took a pull from his mug. "One time, towards the end, I'd gone to visit her on a brutally hot New York City summer day. The type of day where the pavement is cooking, the city's smells strong of sweat and hot dogs." He reached over to close the window blind. "So, this scorching hot day, I'm at my mom's apartment and we're talking about summers growing up at the Jersey Shore. I can barely remember but she's going on and on, and we're talking about ice cream. She tells me her favorite is peach ice cream. So, on and on we go until I leave, and suddenly get this brilliant idea. I'll bring her some peach ice cream. So that very day, I went all over the city, but I couldn't find peach ice cream in a shop, grocery store, anywhere to save my soul. Drove me crazy. But I figured I'd find it the next week. Well, I hunted for that damn ice cream every day, every place I could think of for a week. I would stop at a different store, still never found it. You believe that?"

Hart straightened up. Maybe Palmer had had a few bourbons before joining him? "I'm not sure I'm following here."

Palmer held his hand up like a tennis player winning a point after their ball clipped the net and nodded. "Thing is, Paul, I hunted for this peach ice cream and I never found it. I didn't want to go back to my mom until I did, but the thing was, she died a week later. I never made it back with the ice cream. That shit eats me alive today. Peach ice cream. I want you to know, regret will eat you up, consume you, and change who you are without you even knowing it until it's too late. If you go looking for something hard enough and don't find it, it'll will stay with you forever. You might miss what's right in front of you. Are you sure you want to live with that?"

"I don't see that I have an alternative."

Palmer nodded slowly for a moment. "Then live with that. Own it, because I want you prepared if this doesn't turn out the way…" His voice trailed off. They ignored one another for a moment while Hart contemplated the worst-case scenario.

Palmer began again. "I am trying not to let bad things happen to you. I've lost good men, I wouldn't even call them assets because first and foremost, they were people, and I ruined their lives." Palmer let out a sad chuckle and downed his coffee. "I live with a lot of regrets as you can tell Paul. Right now, my focus is trying to make sure you don't do anything that you'll regret. I'd give fucking anything to be able to give my mom that damn peach ice cream. I regret not being able to everyday. You understand?"

Hart placed his elbows on the table and leaned forward. "I'm okay living with regrets for things I've done. But I'm not going to live wishing I could have done things differently. I'm putting everything on the table."

Palmer smiled despite himself. "You've come quite a long way since I met you. Never thought you'd change from the naïve banker, but here you are. Don't want to be remembered like that I take it?"

"I don't care about anyone remembering me. You said I had one job and I'd get my freedom with Clara, and all of that ironically has caused us to lose everything. I get her back, and then we're out. I'll give anything, and do anything, to get her back, you understand? Just like you would give anything to get that peach ice cream to your mom in time."

Palmer smacked his lips and sat back in his seat. "Well, if you don't want remembrance, you're certainly in the right line of business." He gave a toothless smile. "If we get her back and stop this madness, you'll have your wish. I promise."

Hart narrowed his eyes. "*When* not *if.*"

48

Grand Cayman Island

The Gulfstream touched down with a soft squeal of the tires and taxied to the far end of the runway. Hart had watched the approach to Grand Cayman's international airport from his window seat, the island lush with green vegetation but much flatter than he would have guessed. Once parked outside the terminal, a white van pulled up next to the plane. Without direction, all the passengers filed out and into the awaiting van. Palmer and Hart, the last ones off, stopped at the cockpit to chat with the pilots.

"Appreciate the lift as always, Captain Scott," Palmer said to the younger-looking pilot with his blonde hair parted neatly, flicking off a series of switches.

The pilot craned his neck back and said to Palmer, "I'll catch a few winks, then I have to get out of here. Going to be in some deep trouble for flying you across the pond."

Palmer shifted his briefcase from his hands and sighed. "I owe you one, but so does he." Palmer pointed over his shoulder at Hart.

"No worries, but you're on your own now." With a casual wave over his shoulder, Scott turned around.

Palmer placed his hand on Hart's back and guided him down the steps out of the plane.

"Where exactly did we get this plane?" Hart asked, confused by the conversation.

"It's an agency bird that I use. Technically speaking, this trip was probably frowned upon because I didn't ask permission. But better in life to beg forgiveness than ask permission." He laughed at his own advice, leaving Hart proud of his boss.

"So, basically, we stole the plane?"

"I'd rather live with regret for things I did than didn't do, but that's just me." Palmer winked. "Anyways, quit asking questions. We're here, aren't we?"

The van cruised out of the airport, past the tiny terminal building with tour buses stacked up at the curb. Hart sat in front, the rest of the crew crammed into the last three rows and drowned out by the van's loud engine. He had the ideal vantage point, even if they drove on the opposite side of the road to America or France. British rules still applied evidently. The van sputtered down the brand new six-lane highway, stretching from the airport into the island.

"It used to be just one lane each," the driver said. Hart turned to give her his full attention. She was in her early thirties, with thick brown hair, freckles and light green eyes. "Name's Francesca. I'm the local agency contact. I run the safe house, but it's more like a timeshare." She laughed for a second, then glanced at the rearview mirror. She was experienced enough not to ask Hart's name. Pointing to her right, she showed Hart what sat not two minutes away from the airport: an office complex with several glass buildings, stretching several stories into the air, banks' names, accounting firms and legal services plastered to the sides of the brilliant blue glass. Grand Cayman, well known for its privacy regarding banking, was not shy about the stereotype. Hart was shocked at how blatant they were about advertising privacy. It was as if a sign was literally posted next to the airport. *Welcome, hope you had a pleasant flight. Now, please leave your money with us before heading to the beach.*

"There are more than fifty thousand registered companies at those buildings' addresses."

Hart wasn't surprised. His banking background told him that while these companies were registered here, they were not all nefarious, but rather searching for tax savings.

"Been on the island long?" Hart asked as the offices faded away behind them.

"Several years. Lots goes on here, but at the same time, nothing ever changes. It's a spy's perfect vacation spot. Quiet, with lots of secrets and sun."

Hart sure as hell didn't feel like he was on vacation. He'd been wearing the same clothes for some time, was exhausted, his stitches ached like hell, and he was in dire need of a shower. Hart was anxious to get to their safe house to begin prep work, not take an island tour. He planned to visit the address associated with the wire and start asking questions.

Francesca pulled into a small half-circle drive after a row of palm trees in front of the tall grey stucco building. Hart caught the sign: *Welcome to the Ritz-Carlton Residences.*

Francesca noticed his apparent apprehension. "Perfect cover for Americans to be here, lots of rentals with tourists too sunburnt or hungover to ask questions. The best part, though, is they do room service." She smiled and leapt from the car.

As he left the car, the intense sun and humidity smacked Hart in the face like the first jab of a fight. But with it came newfound energy. It was time to get to work.

They'd set up an office on the twelfth floor, in a three-bedroom suite held by a series of vacation rental companies, but truly owned the agency. Francesca had hurriedly stocked the fridge with essentials, purchased new clothes, told the neighbors and staff that her cousins were coming in town for a fishing trip for a few days. Palmer had George bunked in a room with Hart, gave another bedroom to the French duo, and the veteran spy took the couch, leaving the master for the owner Francesca. After an hour, which everyone showered and changed, they gathered in the main room.

On the coffee table was Palmer's computer, which he pointed to for Hart to grab.

"We have our assignment."

Hart scanned the document from Kelly. The wire transfers emanated from a holding company registered in Grand Cayman, then passed through several offshore accounts in South America until they landed into the Toulouse account, raising alarm bells with the bank manager. Kelly had found addresses associated with the originating wire account, pulled real estate documents, and learned the holding companies actual physical addresses. One of which was a hotel and restaurant just down the street.

"How'd she find this so quickly?" Hart was impressed.

"We might have bent a few laws." Palmer waved the notion off and stood addressing the room. "We've hunted down the location from which Diego received his payments. It's just down the road. We're going to run surveillance starting tonight. We'll do several waves. First up will be Wojtek, Hart, and myself tonight at the restaurant. It'll give us a chance to case the place, find the offices, see the staff, and observe from the ground. We'll place cameras and cloning devices to get into their internal network and see what we can learn for two or three days. Any questions?"

Pierre-Emmanuel and Hart nearly shouted over each other at the exact same moment. "Three days?" Hart spoke to the room. "You can't be serious! There may be no connection whatsoever, and we're just going to park it here?" Hart searched for agreement and only found it in his French colleagues.

A large hand then clamped on his shoulder. It was George behind him. "Settle down, cupcake. This is how things get done in the real world, we can't snap our fingers and get results."

Hart spun around and squared up the larger man. George still had it out for him since Hart threw George to the police. George was calm and had a broad smile, infuriating Hart even more. There wasn't time to surveil a place for days. If they failed, the global ramifications were monstrous, but most importantly to Hart, Clara needed them. He wouldn't let protocols get in his way. Deciding he wouldn't win the battle for urgency, Hart shook off George's hand and focused on Palmer.

Palmer began again, addressing Hart. "Now that our temper tantrums are out of the way. Wojtek—or George to you—and I, seem to be going along tonight so we can babysit you." Palmer paused and turned his attention away from Hart. "The next group will visit the hotel tomorrow morning for breakfast and then get a room. We have a credit card on file embedded with a financial tracking Trojan horse. It'll zip through their system and tell us what interfaces, like the banks or card processing services, the hotel uses. The program will go in any direction the information is sent and back-channel to any interfaces, like personal computers, on the network once card info is sent. Any questions?"

The room was quiet, apart from several seagulls cawing

as they flew past the glass sliding doors of the large terrace.

"Good. The first group will case the beach and surrounding grounds of the hotel before dinner. Until then, you're all on your own." Palmer clapped his hands and headed straight to Hart. "We're not going to have any problems with you, right?"

Hart shook his head to dodge the suggestion. "I'm focused on learning what we can from our visit."

Palmer put his hand on Hart's shoulder. "Remember what I told you. Hunting for peach ice cream can kill you."

Hart smirked as his boss left the room. He wouldn't forget. There'd be no regrets he'd be stuck living with. There was nothing he wouldn't do to get Clara back.

Nothing.

49

Atlantic Ocean

The wind whipped across the bow of the yacht, the forward flag frozen stiff in place. The sky turned slate gray, thoroughly washing out the sun and the remnants of an earlier blue sky. Clara watched the yacht cut through the ocean from the bridge, focused on the horizon, wherever that might lead. Greta sat close by, keeping a watch on her prisoner.

They'd been at sea for seven days; at least that's what Clara thought. She could barely remember the first day, the effects of the drugs heavy on her. While she loved the sea, being a prisoner wasn't one bit appealing. Forced to cross one of the most treacherous oceans on Earth, it was not a leisurely voyage. The simple pleasure of going for a walk around the gardens of Paris, stopping for a *café au lait*, or sitting on the beach with Paul, nursing glasses of Tariquet as the sunset on another day, were memories of another life. Those were the things she dreamed of every night. Would she ever have them again?

The familiar view of the horizon lost her interest, so Clara left the bridge to return to her cabin. Greta, surprisingly, seemed content enough to let Clara go alone and stayed on the bridge.

Clara thought of finding a book to dig into once back

in her cabin, either that or lay on the bed staring at the tufted-leather ceiling. She was beginning to feel the onset of madness, the same daily routine weighing heavy on her. While the yacht had a gym, sauna, card room complete with a billiard table, and a movie theater amongst other extravagant amenities, how could she enjoy them? She still didn't know what fate held. Why go through the effort to kidnap someone and keep them confined to luxury? It didn't make sense.

Perhaps this very dilemma caused her to pass the usual staircase down to her cabin. Instead, she continued straight back through the heart of the ship. The narrow winding hallway with lacquered dark wood banisters led her towards the same open salon with bookcases against the walls she'd been in the other day. She entered the room and recalled her earlier conversation with Farhad when he was told of Diego's death. Good, thought Clara, she was glad he was dead.

She was about to turn around to leave for her cabin when a faint cough caught her attention. She spun back into the room and hesitantly scanned around, even checking behind the sofa to see if anyone was hiding. But the room was empty. Deciding to move on, figuring Greta was probably hiding in her closet or some other twisted ruse, was when Clara noticed one of the bookshelves seemed slightly out of line with the wall.

Approaching the bookshelf with caution, Clara realized its significance before she confirmed her suspicions. It was a secret door. The bookcase hung slightly ajar from the wall, revealing a dark tight passage with only a faint of blue light at the end. She could only make out one side of the room— what looked like servers stacked against the wall. She listened for a moment, took care to look over her shoulder for Greta, and steadied her breathing to not give herself away. After a moment, she heard the familiar sound of a dial tone. Whoever was in the room was making a call.

After taking a quick shower, Stephen Palmer threw on his new ill-fitting chinos and a hideous orange resort shirt with sea turtle depictions. He'd asked Hart to take a walk with him around the resort to not only stretch their legs but also check on his protégé. There was only so much advice Palmer could offer, and inevitably of Hart losing his rose-colored view of the world during the operation left him exhausted. He'd managed to protect Hart once months prior, but now for lack of better judgment, Palmer had pulled him back into dark waters, risking consequences even worse than what they'd faced before. Was he making the same mistake he had all those years ago when he lost his asset? Could atonement blind him to the possibility he was repeating history? Hart was his redemption, and he couldn't afford to fail twice. It would ruin him. His motivation for his career and life was keeping Hart from the same disastrous fate. Palmer found that the best remedy for his anxiety was keeping an eye on his protege. Keep him close, protect him from the wolves.

Palmer found a spot in the shade near the pool, the late-afternoon sun peeking out from in between the hotel's grand towers. A few families were splashing about the pool, mystifying Palmer as to why they weren't at the beach, less than one hundred yards away. He caught sight of Hart making his way through the bar on the far side of the pool; he'd at least found some respectable clothing—navy-blue pants and a simple cardinal-red polo. Hart, for one, didn't look like he'd come from an overpriced cruise ship gift shop.

His phone rang as Hart approached. "This is Palmer," he said to the unlisted number. He'd been expecting a call from Washington to chew him out about taking the plane. It would be impressive timing-wise, but bureaucratic efficiency didn't surprise him anymore when it came to money and wasting it.

"Hello, old friend," the voice hissed.

Suddenly the world melted away. The screaming of children around the pool, the crashing of the waves from the beach, the music from the poolside bar, all ceased to exist.

It was as if he'd heard from a ghost. But dead men don't talk. "Who is this?"

"I know you recognize my voice, even though it has been a long time."

Palmer felt his face flush. He glanced at Hart, who had registered something was wrong. He began to run towards Palmer, even though several staff members urged him to refrain from running by the pool.

"Wh-what…" He fought with great difficulty to stop from stammering. "What? How?" His words slapped together without coherence.

"I'm glad to see my call has had it desired effect already, old friend."

Hart finally reached him, worry on his face.

"But how are you…" Palmer's voice trailed off as he held up a hand for Hart to be quiet.

"It's a story for some other day, which may be sooner rather than later. But what you need to understand now is that I am in control. I am the one who is running you now." Farhad chuckled. "Your new little toy has lost his lover, I understand?"

Palmer fixed his eyes on Hart and hoped he didn't betray the sheer terror he felt. He tried to push the fear from his mind and grabbed Hart by the shoulders, leading them towards the beach and relative quietness.

"I'm listening," he responded happy Hart could only hear one side of the conversation.

"Strange how easy it was to take her. For me, the hardest part was waiting to tell you. I'd envisioned a grand reveal, but unfortunately, you've ruined my plans. Killing one of my assets was brash. But now, I must say I can sympathize with you—it is not a pleasant feeling having poured time, and more importantly, money into him. Then unceremoniously, you kill him like he was some animal. But he served his purpose because he put you on the trail."

Palmer closed his eyes and cursed at having invited Hart. He would much rather have this conversation alone. He was being baited but knew there was a reason for the lunacy besides gloating. There was no choice; he had to further the conversation. "What have you done with her?"

Hart tensed and snapped his attention towards Palmer, his eyes filling with intensity.

"She is safe." Farhad paused before continuing. "For now. Just know once her time comes, it will hurt, or better yet, maybe I will cash in on my investment. How much do you think a beautiful young Frenchwoman would go for on the black market? I could use the money since you've frozen most of my clients' accounts. I need to find creative ways to get it back." Farhad laughed once again.

Palmer felt his chest pound like a war drum. "Listen to me, if you lay one finger on her I swear I'll bring the entire United States Government down on your—"

"Tsk, tsk... Really, that is the best you can do? A tired cliché? I think I am quite safe. You have no idea where we even are, do you? Or what am I even doing? It will be evident in due time, but you are to stop your investigation immediately or there will be consequences."

"Investigation into you?" Palmer stopped himself from shouting the truth. The harsh reality that until two minutes ago, he'd thought his Pakistani asset was killed in a plane crash many years ago. His world wasn't just spinning out of control like Farhad's plane had been. It was crashing and burning.

"Do you understand? Should I send you a picture of her foot missing toes? Would that suffice as encouragement for you to listen more?"

"No!" Palmer nearly shouted, trying to control his tone and appearance. He watched Hart continuously regard him with a certain terror. His world flipped upside down. The things he believed all proved wrong. "You'll get what you want. Let's come to an arrangement, okay?"

Hart lunged for the phone, wrestling it from Palmer's grip. The two men fought on unsure footing of the sandy beach. Finally, Hart had it and spoke.

"Who is this?"

Farhad hummed. "Ah, the new voice must be of the famous Paul Hart."

"Tell me who the hell this is?"

"Oh, not wanting to introduce yourself? Perhaps I should invite Miss Nouvelle to ensure it's really you, Paul."

Hart pushed Palmer's hands away, his boss fell to one knee as if he had a heart attack.

"What do you want?"

"For your boss to watch his country, and someone he cares about, lose. Goodbye, Paul."

The phone went dead. Hart yelled into it still, mad with rage and confusion.

Palmer managed to collapse on a nearby chair.

The sun beat down on the beach. The guests lounged as servers hustled about carrying fruity drinks with umbrellas were in stark contrast to the pain and confusion the men now felt. How could it be possible? The reason Palmer spiraled into a dark place for many years, the reason he saw redemption in Hart, was not only alive but had somehow become hell-bent on seeking revenge.

Hart shook him by the shoulders trying desperately to interrupt Palmer's stupor.

"I know who has Clara," Palmer managed to mutter. "I know who has her."

Clara fought to catch her breath. From inside the narrow hallway outside of Farhad's hidden office, she'd heard one side of the conversation. She'd heard him talking to Paul.

Her adrenaline mixed with the anxiousness made her nauseous. *"How much would a beautiful young Frenchwoman go for?"*

Is that what Farhad was? A human trafficker? She had been taken care of so pleasantly, had that been the reason? Not to damage the product?

The narrow passageway felt like it was closing in on her. She began to panic, her breath catching in her chest and not making it to her lungs. Clara stumbled out back into the living room.

This nightmare kept evolving, slowly seeping into her mind until this moment, when the dam finally broke, fear and anxiety cascaded over her defenses. Paul will come, she reminded herself. He's already on his way.

50

Hart watched his boss sitting outside on the balcony, head in hands, rocking back and forth. He'd been like that ever since they'd come back from the beach and the fateful phone call. *"I know who has her."*

Hart had badgered Palmer relentlessly since he got off the phone for answers, but the old spy was silent. Thinking of it as a good thing, Hart reluctantly gave his boss space to sort the pieces to the proverbial puzzle alone. Suppose he knew the identity of Clara's captor. In that case, they could go to work learning everything there is to know about them—finances, medical prescriptions, magazine subscriptions, how they liked their coffee, online profiles—everything. Instead, Palmer had spoken few words, exiling himself to the balcony.

He felt a presence at his side. "I see it's going to be one of those days," George said.

"Meaning?" Hart glanced at the man. He wore a black polo and folded his thick arms across his chest.

"He's in one of his moods. Some days are much worse than others, but by the looks of it, he's going through something." George pointed with his chin. "What happened when you two left?"

Hart shrugged. "He got a phone call from someone and

it spooked him pretty good. The caller said they had Clara and then Palmer's face turned white like he'd heard from a ghost."

George seemed to soak in the details before speaking. "I bet you didn't know that Palmer has had somewhat of a mythic career at the agency. A career of what-ifs. He has had some brutal luck, always managed to find himself in hot spots. Rumor has it that he had one of the most important assets in the early days of Operation Enduring Freedom, a guy who tried to warn of bad WMD intel. He once had an asset set to break into the tribal area of Pakistan for a lead on the world's most wanted. That poor bastard died, though. Rumor was a plane crash, never confirmed. Just spook gossip. Apparently, Palmer hates flying, so he sent the guy by himself, but who knows. But that is why he's a myth. If he had done what he had the potential to do, he would have been legendary. Instead, he lives with the stigma of what could have been. Maybe that's why he likes you. Not sure what is worse—the failure, or people thinking you were something special but never living up to it."

Hart chewed the inside of his mouth. "How do you know?" He felt his question was too probing, but it was natural that people who work together hear things—everyone gossips, especially spies.

George grunted. "I've worked with him for years. He has never shared much. Others do. Some even believed you were his redemption project—not sure exactly how well that is going, though." He spun and patted Hart on the shoulder. "We have a long evening of surveillance ahead of us. You should get ready, buttercup."

Hart called over his shoulder. "Hey, George, question."

The man stopped and squared him up, then nodded.

"Why does he call you Wojtek?"

The man's dark features shifted into a soft smile. "Wojtek was a name of a bear cub Polish soldiers adopted during World War Two. The soldiers had traded for the cub after being released from a prisoner of war camp. Wojtek was raised by them, and fought next to the soldiers in battle, carrying artillery shells. He was treated as an equal. The soldiers even enlisted him as a private. He was big and dark, and adopted, just like me. Polish family in Minnesota." He held up his left hand and Hart noticed the small signet ring with a bear. "Wojtek means *happy warrior* in Polish. But don't think you can call me by that name yet." He winked and disappeared into the confines of the safe house.

Hart softly chuckled to himself. Some nicknames were just too perfect, although he agreed with the "happy" part.

Hart grew tired of staring at Palmer, still slumped in a stupor facing the ocean. Forgetting his boss, he made his way into the kitchen where their host was making espresso. Francesca smiled politely at Hart, torqued the handle, pressed a button, and stepped back. The machine growled and hissed, pouring espresso into two separate cups.

Handing one to Hart, she said, "It looks like you could use one."

"Thank you, is it that obvious?" He tried to smile but was left feeling like his life was a tsunami; events were crashing out of control and all hell would break loose when it finally hit land.

Francesca let his question lie. "There are some things you should know about the restaurant and hotel you are going to tonight." She paused to blow on the espresso. "I've heard many rumors. It's a boutique hotel, some forty rooms, a pool, and a restaurant, but yet the hotel manager lives like a king. He often wears smoking slippers, suede blazers, cravats and sports an impeccably shaped beard." Francesca giggled but quickly stopped when she recognized the humorless expression from Hart.

"Go on," he implored, draining his espresso in several gulps.

"Well, I just saw the report that Kelly had sent to Stephen via our secure network, but I haven't been able to speak with him since you've returned. The report said the hotel makes hundreds of millions of dollars annually based on some financial statements. Not to mention, they also spend hundreds of millions per year. This has never raised an eyebrow but logically, the basic math of the hotel room rates versus nights in a year plus expenses... How is that even possible? The answer: It isn't."

Hart nodded in agreement. He'd thought the same when he read the report. He craned over his shoulder to the terrace where Palmer was now pacing back and forth. It seemed they were walking into a hornet's nest of activity, and to make matters worse, they didn't seem to be at full strength.

Hart turned back to Francesca. "What else do you know?"

Luke Darlington stretched out on his balcony overlooking the turquoise sea. He'd felt a bit jet-lagged and taken the edge off with some Mount Gay and Sprite. He tried to relax. There were still hours to kill until he'd meander downstairs to dinner. Then early the following day, he'd clear out his bank account and safety deposit box at the bank downtown.

He had no choice but to run. From Farhad, the fear, the phantom agents he imagined breaking his door down. At least he consoled himself by thinking that while he poured himself another drink. First, the Renard murder in Paris, then Diego had gone rogue and killed the man's attorney despite Darlington's insistence not to. Then the subsequent kidnapping of a French agent, to which he was left in the dark. If Diego had simply stolen the documents and kept the attorney alive, would they be in the mess they were in? He doubted it. His agent, Diego, was no longer his own. Diego was a loose cannon, true, but he was anything but stupid. Farhad was Diego's master puppeteer and all of it added up to Darlington playing the fool. He was on the outs, and that was reason enough to run.

He'd checked into the seaside resort just after lunch, under the watchful eye of the manager. The name he'd used to check in with was a call sign of Mr. Neptune—a reference to a code signaling an in-person money exchange. The chic manager had stroked his neat beard while Darlington checked in, offering a sterile smile with watchful eyes. Darlington didn't mind the attention. If anything, he would be ensured more protection and respect. He had calculated the risk and thought it better to hide in plain sight. When animals sensed danger, they often made for familiar places. The island where he frequented for holidays and initially set up the shell corporations, laying the foundation for their vast money-laundering network, now became his launchpad to freedom.

He sipped his drink, the shrunken ice clinking against the glass the only sounds Darlington heard other than the crash of the ocean. He wondered where he would escape to next with all his money. He'd heard many nice things about South America; Argentina with its culture, or perhaps Chile with its wine. Only time would tell where he would end up. His only goal was to stay alive long enough to find out.

51

Grand Cayman Island

The front entrance to the hotel was unimpressive. The driveway was just off the main road; a short and steep incline slightly hidden behind withering palm trees. The hotel was yellow, not unlike the color of a baby duckling. White shutters and tinted sliding glass doors framed the main entrance. There were no cars parked out front, only a bellhop more consumed by his smartphone than the four approaching men.

Hart led the way with George at his side, Shayne next to Palmer, who seemed to watch his shoes in consternation more than where he was going. Ignoring the bellhop who hadn't bothered to look up, Hart lead them through the black-and-white-tiled lobby, with eccentric abstract paintings lining the white walls. Towards the back of the space, past a vacant reception desk, was the restaurant.

Palmer grunted, confirming they'd come to the right spot. The restaurant was in stark contrast to the vibrant lobby. Through the glass doors, Hart saw dark wood covering the space from the floors to the walls, and a glass wine cellar surrounded the room, housing thousands of bottles. The bar against the far wall to his right was well stocked; shelves of bottles lit up by backlighting and a mirror gave the illusion the room was grander than it was. Only two patrons were at the bar, seated at opposite ends, heads down in their massive goblets of frozen drinks. There were twenty tables in the main dining room, but only three were occupied. A small terrace stretched out towards an oval pool.

Upon entering, a smartly dressed man asked them if they had a reservation, to which George said no. With a slight bow, the host brought them to a four-person table near the patio. If anyone inquired, their cover story was simple. An annual guys' fishing trip brought them to the island, searching for tuna, barracuda, and a good time. George had even insisted they get a local boat and captain name just in case inquiring minds checked.

"What do we think?" Hart inquired once the waiter came and topped off their glasses with water and left a wine list.

Palmer touched his ear and appeared to be listening, then looked up. "Sorry, I thought it was the other team trying to reach us."

Hart felt a sinking feeling. Palmer wasn't on his game. Pierre-Emmanuel and Lucas had stayed back at the safe house, monitoring the hotel via a tiny drone that Francesca had pulled from a plastic briefcase. Palmer wore an earpiece and microphone, disguised as a hearing aid, if anything urgent should come up. Hart inquired again about the group's thoughts. George was the first to offer his opinion.

"Doesn't look much to me. Seems like a regular, ugly hotel with guests having too much money to spend." He shrugged. "Pretty boring menu, too, if you ask me too."

Hart shook his head. "Now I regret asking. Stephen?"

"Uh," Palmer glanced around the room to look for anyone close enough to listen, then looked up at the ceiling. "We'll know much more in a few days. But shit, Paul, we just got here."

The group browsed over their menus and when the waiter swung by with open disinterest, they ordered dinner. Hart ordered a bottle of red wine he knew well, 2015 Peter Michael Les Pavots. Without a smile, the waiter disappeared behind the glass walls of wine to find the bottle.

Hart eye's swept across the restaurant, over the empty tables, past the lonely patrons at the bar, following the massive mirrors to the ceiling and noticed the many half-moon smoked-glass camera lenses as if they were floating on the ceiling. Quite a bit of security for an empty restaurant at a quiet hotel, thought Hart as he remembered Francesca's warnings. *"There are rumors."*

The restaurant was a far departure from the fine dining he'd had in France or the US. When one could spot them, the staff lazily hung around the bar chatting amongst each other and rarely to any patrons. He couldn't shake the feeling of unease. There were things about the restaurant that didn't add up for him. However, he couldn't quite justify his feelings based on lackluster service and a quiet clientele. If that was the barometer for money-laundering operations, then most of the restaurants he'd ever been to were guilty.

Hart's attention shifted back to the table where George and Palmer were in discussion about the current state of the NFL, although Palmer looked like he'd taken one too many Ambiens before dinner. Hart was about to engage them in conversation when the waiter appeared with the bottle of wine already open and plopped three glasses on the table.

The broad-shouldered waiter poured Hart's glass with the delicacy of someone pouring out the remnants of spoiled milk. Hart gave the glass a twirl on the table and lifted to smell the wine. He'd had the exquisite cabernet blend many times before; it had been a favorite of his former boss James

Hutchens and he couldn't resist ordering it, partly because he wasn't paying for it, and as well as an ode to his former life. While it had been at least a year since he'd had it last, Hart immediately knew something was amiss. It tasted like the wine had been left out in the sun too long. The nose was severe and sour. Hart sipped the wine and dragged his attention from the glass up to the waiter. He was about to complain when he saw the death glare on the man's face. Hart lowered his gaze as he pretended to taste the wine again, swirling it in his mouth. The bottle the waiter carried caught Hart's interest, the tinfoil wrap at the top of the wine was gone, and the front label from the wine slightly dog-eared at its corner, revealing copious amounts of glue. It appeared to be a fake.

Hart felt his chest pound with a surge of adrenaline. He was far from a wine expert, but after dozens of the same bottle drunk over many years and the poor quality of the presentation, he was easily convinced. Usually, he would have complained the wine had spoiled, but the state of the actual bottle, which seemed forged, evident by the poorly glued on label and missing foil told him it was deliberate. A fine way to launder money, sell bottles of wine that are fake for exorbitant prices, well surpassing the overheard cost of mixing various other wines to recreate a taste that to novice drinkers would appear the same.

"Is there a problem, sir?" The waiter spat out in his thick Italian accent.

Hart took stock of the situation. He felt he was onto something in the restaurant, but he'd lose it quickly if he drew too much attention.

"It's great!" he said as cheerfully as he could muster. George grunted in amusement as the dark purple wine was poured into everyone's glass. Hart was anxious to examine the bottle, but the waiter had clumsily, or perhaps purposefully, emptied the contents with three monstrous pours and took off towards the bar with the bottle in hand. Hart called out for the bottle but was ignored.

The others around the table grabbed their glasses and Hart watched George slug back a good portion of the wine and set it back on the table without a reaction. Palmer had yet to try, but Hart couldn't wait any longer.

"The wine's a fake," he said in a low hush that he was confident the closest table of retirees ten paces away couldn't hear.

Palmer sat upright and lifted the glass, regarding it as if it would spill its secrets on his lap.

George scoffed. "And Monsieur Connoisseur," he started, mockingly pronouncing the nickname, "how did you come to this conclusion?"

Hart took a deep breath and explained his knowledge of the wine, and the poorly faked bottle. While he spoke, he was met with skeptical looks but pressed on. "It's simple really, and a known practice, yet not many people can catch it. You take a cheap bottle of wine, similar blend, pour out the contents and then soak the bottle in warm water for some time, then label easily peels off. It's easy to fake an expensive label. The wine itself usually is a mix of several cheaper wines to resemble the original. *Viola*, you have counterfeit wine that costs you practically nothing to make, yet you can sell it for the cost of a real bottle, which can be hundreds of dollars! No one would stop to think of it being a fake or risk telling a restaurant that their five-hundred-dollar bottle of Brunello is bad."

"Who the fuck pays five hundred dollars for wine?" George frowned and shook his head.

The table was quiet for a moment. The dull clatters of silverware from the nearby tables and the faint music of *Turandot's* "Nessun Dorma" filled the silence.

Suddenly George burst out in laughter, smacking the table and doubling over, his face turning red. Hart anxiously looked around and was for the moment, pleased to see no servers in the main dining room, only the bemused look of several patrons.

"You idiot," George managed to get out between howls of laughter. "You're something else, man. I'll give you that! Think you got the case cracked because you don't like the wine." He smacked the table once more, causing all their glasses to jump and clink into each other. "Well, we might as well call this a day. I think Sherlock Holmes over here led us to victory with his palate."

Hart sadly shook his head. They were supposed to be on the same side, the team who could find Clara, yet at every turn, he fought him. George didn't accept him, but why should he? Hart wasn't a hardened soldier who served for years to one day become a well-paid and experienced mercenary. He didn't cut his teeth spending years in subbasements pouring over intel and crafting his geopolitical knowledge or risking his life anywhere. All he did was manage to be in the wrong place at the wrong time. Fate had worked everything else out. Did he curse his past? No, because it had brought him Clara. But it had also cruelly taken her away.

"Shut the hell up." Palmer reached over and pointed a finger in George's face. "He's the only one of us giving a shit. So, the next time you have something to say, don't. Understand?" Flecks of spit formed around Palmer's mouth like a rabid dog.

George lifted his hands, trying half-heartedly to stop laughing. "Okay, boss."

Hart pushed back and stood from the table. He needed to cool down for a moment and get away from George and his irritating laughter. He passed through the restaurant out into the lobby, seeking the men's room. Signs pointed left and he swung around the restaurant's outer kitchen wall, finding a narrow hallway with bathrooms off to the right side. However, the glasswork door at the end of the hallway with a view of palm trees and the beach behind captured Hart's attention. Seeking a moment of solitude, Hart made towards the view before a nondescript door on his left burst open, hitting him square in the shoulder. Hart cursed out loud, his shoulder on fire from the heavy door.

According to his gold name tag, the manager of the hotel, Gianluca, stood and frowned at Hart. Hart wasn't hurt, but his anxiety level had shot through the roof, not expecting to be hit with a door as he sought out the serenity of the ocean-view window. His eyes met the manager's as the man shot his cuffs and regarded Hart as if he had just parked his bicycle too close to the man's Ferrari. Sweeping his gaze past the well-tailored manager, Hart saw through the open door down the hallway. There was a series of dark-gray steel doors lining down the corridor. One of them was open, and inside it on a foldable card table, Hart recognized cash-counting machines.

The manager looked over his shoulder towards the cash room and then back at Hart. Smirking, he gently closed the door behind him, "I think that you did not like my wine, at least this is what I hear?" He spread his arms to welcome the truth.

Hart stood taller, thrown off by the man's brashness. "No problem with it."

The manager stepped into the hallway, closing the distance between the two men. He reeked of too much cologne.

Notes of cinnamon and sandalwood stung Hart's nostrils.

"Maybe you enjoy the wine and leave. We can call it a day, eh?"

"Is that your apology?" Hart inclined his head. The manager, clearly not the hospitable type required in hotels.

"Sure. You and your friends finish the bottle. No need to settle up." He slapped Hart on the shoulder and headed off into the lobby.

It was at that moment that Hart knew what he had to do.

The manager left his irksome guest in the hallway. He made his way to the elevator bank and took the lift to the fifth floor. There he walked until the end of the green-carpeted hallway, finally reaching his room. The corner suite had been designed to be more apartment than hotel room, but still the kitchen sink overflowed with room-service deliveries.

He kicked off his cherry-red suede smoking slippers and shuffled to the balcony. The man pulled his mobile from the inside of his red velour blazer and opened the encrypted application.

Your contact has arrived. I assume he is here to make a physical pickup? Plus, there are some out-of-towners here that seem too interested in the hotel.

While waiting for the checkmark next to the message to turn from delivered to read, he watched the beach below. The hotel's pool was barren of anything exciting, but several barefoot women ran on the beach. The manager sighed.

He was busy daydreaming about the barefoot runners when his encrypted app chimed with a new message.

What contact? Don't mind the guests. Leave them be.

He rolled his eyes at the organization's clarity, or lack thereof, and ignored the directions about the guests. Instead, relaying that the contact was an Englishman. The reply came soon after.

Ah, brilliant. Give the Englishman as much as he can carry and tell him to bring it to the St. Lucia house. ASAP.

The manager threw the phone onto his bed and slid back into his smoking slippers. He had a message to deliver.

52

Hart knew what was required. But his former life as a banker cried out in protest, it's too risky. Instinct told him he needed more time and more intelligence to satisfy the suspicions he harbored. But he didn't have the luxury of time. His hunch made him recall what Clara taught him: if things don't feel quite right, they usually aren't. He was going to trust his gut. After all, he'd left logic behind in Paris when he made his desperate pleas for Magali's help, ignored it in La Rochelle while trying chasing down Clara amidst a hail of gunfire, and once again in Toulouse, tracking and attacking an assassin without backup. Now halfway across the world, he was sure logic and reason weren't going to return to him. He was on his own.

Hart thundered back into the dining room, after pacing the lobby to unsuccessfully try and cool down, causing the silverware to clatter on the tables. He'd seen the manager return and found him leaning on the far end of the bar, his red-bottomed smoking slippers visible from the front door. Hart went back to his table in the middle of the restaurant and sat down with a thump.

"There's a room full of cash in the back. Stacks of it. Could they be more obvious?"

Palmer scratched his beard. "It's a restaurant and hotel, Paul."

"I don't see thousands of dollars of cash spent here tonight, do you?"

George shrugged and then leaned closer to Hart. "What are your spidey senses telling you?"

Hart ignored him. "It's so blatantly obvious these bastards are shady. Why wait days to sort this out?"

Palmer dropped his head into his hands. "We need facts here, Paul. Do this by the book, for once, will you?"

Hart pushed back from the table. He didn't realize how angry he looked, only registering the vein popping in his forehead when he heard Palmer mutter an audible, 'Shit.'

Hart stormed towards the bar. The manager looked up from his phone and craned his head over his shoulder to watch Hart approach. The man didn't bother to turn around but spoke with his back to Hart.

"Going to take me up on my offer? No need to settle up. Just leave."

Hart had trouble speaking, his throat tight with fury. "I'm going to ask you politely, so that we can do this as gentlemen." He looked the man up and down, the suede blazer probably stifling in the incessant heat of the island. "Which you clearly aspire to be."

"Oh." The man turned and tossed his phone on the bar. He rubbed the corners of his mustache for a moment. "What are you proposing?"

"Tell me who you're getting all that cash to and why you're paying off people via private accounts in the south of France and we'll leave here without any trouble."

The man threw his head back in mock laughter and spun around, putting his right hand studded with rings on Hart's left shoulder. "And why don't you fuck off."

At that moment, a swinging door behind the bar opened and three tall servers stepped out. They'd been watching Hart and the manager through the service window. Hart carefully brushed the man's hand from his shoulder, aware one aggressive move could trigger a brawl.

"How about we try this again, okay?" Hart offered a sarcastic smile.

The manager began to laugh, the servers behind the bar did not. Hart wasn't bothered by the confrontation, a gift from his Irish ancestors. He had a moment of consciousness, thinking of Clara, and where she might be. He pictured her strong, and steadfast. Maybe she didn't even need him, but he was coming for her.

Hart took a deep breath and noticed he was flexing his fists. "One more time, asshole. Where's the money going?"

The manager smiled and mouthed, "Kiss my—" but before he could finish his insult, Hart grabbed him by the suede lapels and hurled him over the barstools and dragged him on top of the wood bar.

Darlington had finished his third neon-blue Sea Breeze when an argument at the end of the bar caught his attention. An American with dirty-blonde hair had a rather terse exchange with the manager. *Must have been a hell of an overcooked steak*, Darlington mused to himself, eager to track down the barman for his fourth cocktail, when all hell broke loose.

The American grabbed the manager and half dragged, half lifted him onto the bar. The manager flailed to stay grounded, sweeping several wine glasses from the countertop, shattering onto the floor. He rolled off the bar awkwardly and threw a knee in the stomach of the American. The man grunted in pain and reared back as if to throw an hook. One of the servers from behind the bar jumped into action. He locked up the American from underneath his shoulders, and dragged him away as shocked patrons gasped. The manager stood and threw two jabs into the stomach of the man being held, the gusts of wind escaping his lungs audible from where Darlington sat.

Darlington's attention switched to a clattering of chairs from the dining room and saw two men running towards the action. The first man, probably in his fifties, with glasses and a thick peppered beard, tackled the manager into the bar with a loud crack. The second man to arrive looked the part of a brawler. He was bald, with broad, mean grin. He freed the blonde American from the grasp of a server and proceeded to land a vicious headbutt against the man.

Then chaos.

Servers and chefs poured from the kitchen, some carrying meat cleavers and wearing their aprons, began attacking the three Americans around the bar. But it was the Americans who held their own, and to Darlington, seemed to be protecting the blonde-haired instigator. The bald man had taken it upon himself to face three challengers, grabbing an empty wine bottle from atop the bar and smashing it into the head of the burliest server he could find. Suddenly, a dozen people brawling in the bar.

An opportunity presented itself to Darlington; he could not allow himself to hesitate.

He'd been told to gather money by the manager, on the orders of their mutual employer, and bring the cash to St. Lucia. Simple enough, thought Darlington. He would make sure he completed at least half of the request. He'd steal the money and run. There was no honor amongst thieves.

Unsteadily Darlington jumped down from his barstool

and made for the front door, pausing only when a server had tried to run past him, only to be grabbed once more by the paws of the bearded American and thrown back into the dining room like a rag doll. Ignoring the fight and playing the part of a scared observer, he bumbled out into the lobby, his vision slightly blurring from the Sea Breezes, and headed for where he knew they kept the cash. It was helpful that he originated the plan to launder cash in and out of the country from the restaurant and hotel. So, in effect, he felt he was owed a cut anyway. Screw waiting until the next day for the bank to open. He could grab hundreds of thousands of dollars' worth of cash and be gone by sunset, all under the guise of following orders.

Hart took another jab to the chin but redirected the follow-up, enough to leave his attacker off balance. The man was tanned, a product of too much time spent on the beach, will a pencil-thin jet-black mustache and gelled hair; more mob hitman than server. While the man's momentum carried him forward, Hart pivoted to the side and swept his leg across the server's ankles, tripping him into a vacant table.

Hart surveyed the battlefield. George was holding his own against several servers, working his way into enemy territory behind the bar. But Palmer was nowhere to be seen, so Hart distanced himself from the action to seek him out, finding him wrestling just off the terrace with the manager.

What have I done? Hart thought the surrealness of the chaos surrounded him. He watched his boss take a shot to the ribs then heard him howl in pain. Hart sprinted out to the terrace; the manager had Palmer pinned to the concrete. The man lifted his hands together, forming one massive fist, ready to bring them down onto Palmer's face when Hart speared him clean off his boss. The two rolled away from the terrace, down a short grassy incline towards the pool. The manager was the first to his feet, pure rage burning in his eyes. Then a flash of metal in the man's hand.

The manager lashed wildly at Hart with the blade, aiming for his midsection. Hart sprung backwards and to the side, allowing the man's arm to come perpendicular to him. He clamped down on the man's wrist and in one motion twisted him clockwise and brought his elbow down into the man's forearm. The knife clattered to the pavement. The manager fell to a knee and then dove at Hart's ankles. Landing a knee on top of him, Hart wrestled the man, the four-inch long blade lying several feet away. But they both froze when the gunshots rang out.

53

Grand Cayman Island

The cracks of gunfire pulled Hart out of his adrenaline-fueled rampage. He kept his weight on top of the manager, ensuring he couldn't slip away or get to the knife that lay nearby. Looking up past the grassy slope to the terrace, he caught Palmer sucking wind on one knee. Next to him, still in her billowing orange pants, Francesca. She held a Berretta pistol pointed straight up in the air.

George strolled out of the restaurant, looking worse for wear with ripped clothing. His usual broad smile replaced with a frown. Francesca trained the gun on the waiters and herded them out onto the deck.

Building on her cue, Hart lifted the manager to his feet and growled, "Now, tell me where the money goes."

Darlington wiped the sweat from his brow. The room was so stifling he could hardly breathe. *Too many Sea Breezes, you dunce.* It was supposed to be a smash-and-grab. But he'd reckoned that he fucked that up. Royally.

He'd managed to sneak into the cash room amidst the chaos in the dining room, providing him the perfect cover. Had he been thinking straight and not through the fog of four strong cocktails, he would not have shut the door while he packed duffle bags full of cash. But he'd realized his fatal mistake too late. There was a keypad on both sides of the door. The room, and his murky career for that matter, had a price to get in or out.

He attempted several offensives at the door, but throwing his shoulder into it had left him dizzy and sore. The room was small, just large enough for a card table, a tall safe and a foldable chair. He couldn't tell if the place was hot or if the alcohol and anxiety were causing him to overheat, but for the first time in his life, he desperately missed the London rain.

Darlington searched the ceiling for a vent to try to climb through but quickly gave up on the idea when he found the small vent in the corner far exceeded his athletic limitations. *Bollocks,* he thought, throwing a full duffle bag of money at the door. Trapped like a rat. However, what was worse was the realization of whoever found him, surely wouldn't take kindly to him stealing their money. He would explain to whoever found him that he was working on direct orders from the boss. That was truthful enough.

Still, panic gripped him when he heard American voices from outside his prison door. He listened to the Italian accent of the manager in protest, then howl in pain. Next, beeps from the keypad code told Darlington they were coming.

He missed the rain of London, he thought as he wrestled with consciousness.

Hart tried to shove the uncooperative manager down the hallway. George helped by smacking him upside the head to encourage out the code to unlock the steel door.

"Business must be stellar and crime pretty severe to have this many security cameras and a steel door, huh?" Palmer remarked, flexing and shaking his battered hand.

Francesca appeared behind them and Hart watched her eyes sweep over the steel door with excitement. "Okay, I can manage to keep the local police busy for a few moments in the front. But you must leave quickly via the back door," she said, pointing to the glass door that overlooked the beach. "Head back to our safe house through the beach and..." Her voice trailed off for a moment as if a stark realization crossed her mind. "Do whatever it is you need to do to these men, but quietly." She scampered off to run interference as the sirens approached in the distance.

"If you go in there, you must know it'll mean you've declared war on us. Vendettas for life." The manager spat out with his thick Italian accent. Hart found that the man had lost his arrogance somewhere amongst the spilled chairs and bloody dining-room floor. He swayed in place, his right eye swollen shut.

Hart nodded. "Yeah, I'll keep that in mind." He shouldered the steel door, which lethargically groaned open.

The stale air from the small room blew out and, with it, the thick body odor. An ashen-faced man, drenched in sweat, sat slumped in a plastic chair next to the counting table.

The manager kicked out at the man and screamed, "Stealing my money, you fool!"

George and Hart, who had been holding his arms behind his back, pulled him out of the room.

"George, can you go lock this guy in the bathroom so he can't bother us. Make sure the cops can find him at some point," Palmer said, eyeing the bags of cash spilled on the floor.

The man inside whimpered for a moment and looked as if he was on the verge of unconsciousness. He raised his hands in defeat.

"Who are you?" Hart asked. The man answered incoherently.

Palmer nodded towards the exit. "We need to go." He pointed to the man hunched in the chair, taking once last look at the messy makeshift vault. "Take him with us."

They'd tied him up in the bathroom. The coral-and-white tiled bathroom was the most secure place in the safe house. The man hadn't yelled for help, but became resigned to the fact he was without chance of escape. After some air conditioning and water, he introduced himself as Luke Darlington.

Hart paced around the connecting bedroom, skirting the massive four-poster bed taking up most of the space. On the bed were two kitchen knives Hart had grabbed if his subject needed inspiration, along with some duct tape he'd found under the sink. He was chomping at the bit to begin his interrogation. He waited for Palmer, who had been debriefing Pierre-Emmanuel and Lucas since they'd come back. Their hotel surveillance was now off, blown quite spectacularly, but the operation itself seemed to progress thanks to Hart's initiative. He knew he'd overreacted, but then again, it had produced results. All's well that ends well, he reasoned. After what felt like hours but had been mere minutes, Palmer appeared through the double doors of the bedroom.

"We ready to do this?" Hart half turned towards the bathroom to begin when in a flash, Palmer was on top of him, grabbing him by the shoulders and forcing Hart back against the thick corner pillar of the bed.

"Listen to me very, very fucking carefully. You were irresponsible beyond measure back there. Don't for one second think just because you got lucky that it was worth the risk. This isn't a game."

Rage burned in Palmer's eyes. It wasn't the first time lately that Hart had caused that. But he wasn't going to apologize for his actions. He believed they'd lead them to the cusp of a breakthrough.

"Without me, we'd all still be over there having tiramisu like it's some damn holiday. I did what I thought was best and I'd say it's going to work out. Now can we get on with this?" Hart tried to push away the bear paws gripping his shirt.

"No!" Palmer's face flushed red. "The things you're doing, the places you are willing to go…" His voice trailed off as he saw the knives and tape on the bed. "Goddammit, Paul, you're going to have to live with your actions. Don't you get that? I've been trying to warn you. You don't want this eating you alive. You're going to have to live with this." Palmer relaxed his grip and shook his head in dismay.

"I'd rather live with this than live without her."

Palmer let out of a huff of air as if trying to calm himself. Hart pushed off the bedpost and pointed to the bathroom and Darlington behind the closed door. "We doing this?"

"Let me talk to this idiot first, alright? I have experience. Give me fifteen minutes, then we can try it your way." He glanced at the objects on the bed and sighed. "He's already singing like a songbird, and you want blood."

Hart went to the kitchen for a late-night espresso. The Darlington character they'd found stashed away in the vault room seemingly had information. Otherwise, what was he doing with bags of cash, and where was he taking them? It could be a long night, but well worth it. Hart mentally prepared to squeeze every bit of intel he could from the man like the last stubborn remnants of toothpaste from the tube. Hart felt Darlington knew something to get them a step closer, but they didn't have the time to waste.

He found Francesca nursing a cup of tea, held in both her hands, and wrapped in a red shawl, sitting on the far countertop of the kitchen. She watched him find a Nespresso machine in the corner of the kitchen.

"You're back quite soon," he said while opening cabinets to find the pods and cups.

Francesca pointed to the cabinet above the machine. "Helps that I habitually paddleboard with the police chief's daughter. Proximity to power is power." She smiled.

Hart paused while he searched for the words. "Thank you," was all he could muster. He thought of all the help he'd gotten from Magali, how poorly things ended, and now how Francesca had allowed him to continue unburdened by police. They were both owed a world of gratitude, but he couldn't slow himself down to think more about it.

Francesca cleared her throat. "Pierre-Emmanuel told me what you are all doing here. I didn't ask, he brought it up, but I want you to know, I believe that you will find her."

Hart was quiet for a moment. The dots were connecting in his mind. "Can I ask you a question?"

"Of course." Francesca sipped her tea, and Hart felt her dark eyes studying him as he made his coffee.

"Did you speak with Pierre-Emmanuel about why we are here, before you spoke to me about the hotel and its rumors?"

Hart turned to see a thinly veiled smile crossed Francesca's face. She tried to hide it with another sip of tea. "I thought everyone could use a bit of encouragement."

Hart didn't bother responding. He realized Francesca had manipulated him into going to the restaurant searching for a fight. He opened his mouth to speak but closed it, locking eyes with the safe house manager.

As if Francesca read his mind, she pushed off from the counter. "You don't have time to waste spending days watching a place we all know is dirty. It wasn't a good use of your time. This way, she'll have a fighting chance." She set her mug in the sink and left the kitchen without another word.

Hart punched the button on the Nespresso machine and leaned on the countertop. Waves of frustration, sadness, and hope poured over him. The blistering pace of his life was exhausting, but it would only gain speed now. He had no choice. Without Clara, what was it all for? Clara had been everything for him, the one who made sense of it all, who gave him comfort to leave his old life behind. He had left a trail of destruction from Paris searching for her. But what did he have to show for it? She was still missing. The insidious seed of doubt began to sprout in his mind.

His trance broke when he heard Palmer shout from the bedroom. "Paul, you need to hear this."

54

Saint Lucia

The clanking of the anchor dragged Clara from her shallow sleep.

Unsettled by the unfamiliar noise she hadn't heard once while at sea, she sat upright in bed. Was she dreaming, mistaken, or had they finally arrived at their destination?

She leaped from the bed and raced to the window. Before she even raised the blinds, she heard a sound that filled her heart: a birdcall.

Land.

With a surge of excitement, she pulled on the blinds so hard they crashed upwards, breaking off the hinges. Clara lost her breath at what lay before her. *No Good Deed* sat anchored in turquoise waters that lead straight into a bay some several hundred yards away, where white-sand shores met the sea. Clara's eyes swept from the beaches surrounded by lush green vegetation of palm trees and bright orange and yellow flowers upwards as the land rose in a gentle slope towards a wide white colored hotel with a terrace overlooking vast green gardens stretching to the beach. The land's slope drew her vision to the left, where the steep gradient rose higher to the top of a mountain with coarse black rock populated by stubborn vegetation that grew out at extreme angles at near impossible heights. The mountain overlooked the bay, shielding half of it from the rising sun. Clara felt she could reach out and touch the rock. Turning away from the mountain and back down across the white sand beaches, she saw a line of luxury modernist homes that fringed what looked to be a private beach. Beyond the beach, which stretched for miles, a more massive twin mountain overlooked the bay from in the distance. The two mountains framed the tropical beach like sentries.

A distant bell rang in her mind. She knew where she was.

They'd passed the Azores islands of Portugal, which meant they had been heading southwest as the crow flies. If they'd kept the course that Clara believed they had, they would have arrived near the top of South America, generally the Caribbean. If they had ventured further north, they would enter US waters, which Clara was frankly suicidal, needlessly risking intercepting. No, she knew where they were because she recognized the one-of-a-kind UNESCO World Heritage site. They'd arrived in Saint Lucia, under the Piton mountains, guarding Sugar Bay.

She cracked the window and breathed the fresh air. In an instant, she had an idea. The beach seemed so close she could swim to shore, run to what looked like the hotel and be free. The sun hadn't fully risen; only a few hazy orange rays fought the revenants of the night sky. She had to act now or never. Going through the window was out of the question as it didn't open nearly far enough. But she could perhaps set off from the back swim deck, slipping into the water without a sound. She estimated shore was three hundred yards, a quick swim, she told herself. All she had to do was find a covert way into the water.

Clara grabbed her boots, left her cabin, and walked barefoot down the dim hallway. Instead of cutting through amidships, Clara darted to the port side and found the heavy sliding door that led to the promenade deck. The fresh humid air of the island hit her with unexpected force. An overwhelming crispness replaced the stale salty air from the ocean she'd come to know. She fought from the urge to cough and willed herself to be silent. She stayed still, breathing slowly into her lungs, feeling her heart rate slow before she began to move aft. If she could make it to the swim deck and sneak into the water, she liked her chances. The memories of swimming with Paul in Noirmoutier's frigid Atlantic water motivated her. Swimming to shore for her life would be nothing for a girl who spent summers in the ocean.

Clara made it to the back deck unseen, and peered around the corner from her walkway. No one was on the stern. Her boots would be hard to swim with, but judging by the terrain and the likelihood that she'd need to sneak ashore via the mountain base instead of exposing herself on the beach, meant she needed them. Clara put her hands inside each of the boots so that her arms would be free to swim, and she could kick her legs for propulsion. She deliberately crept to the back of the ship and heard the water gently lapping against the hull. Her body already sensed it would soon be in the water, her heart hammering uncontrollably. She had one foot down the staircase when the sound of a voice turned her blood ice-cold.

"So glad you're up early to see the view. Breathtaking, isn't it?"

Clara craned skyward to the third level of the ship and saw Farhad leaning over the banister with Greta at his shoulder.

"I am pleased you didn't sleep in and waste such a view." He grinned.

Putain de merde, Clara thought.

"Oh, and Mademoiselle Nouvelle, we have some guests coming this evening, and then we will be going to shore. Do please enjoy your last full day on the ship." Farhad threw a lazy wave at her and disappeared. Greta remained in place, an evil smirk across her square jaw.

Clara sat down on the back deck and watched the dark mountain welcome the morning sun.

Part IV

The Kill

55

Grand Cayman Island

Hart barely had time to register what Darlington had spilled before the team began packing. Palmer landed a credible lead before Hart ever had the chance to use his alternative methods. The information came hurriedly, and the team relayed it back across the ocean to Kelly, who verified everything. Darlington didn't precisely know the location of Clara and the weapons plans, but he knew where they were going.

George threw their gear into black duffle bags while Palmer kept squeezing Darlington, learning about the structures of shell companies and Farhad's massive cabal.

"You see, Farhad isn't just a banker. He's a broker and an insurance policy. He's an assured mutual destruction tool. Just like the Cold War's nuclear proliferation, Farhad maintains peace by ensuring chaos." To Hart, it sounded as though Darlington was pitching Farhad's services. Palmer remained stoic while taking copious notes. The bathroom smelled of sweat and lavender bath bubbles, some of which Palmer had poured into the tub to rid the odor of their subject's fright.

Darlington paused with the firm rap on the door. Hart and Palmer both turned to find the tall, hawkish profile of Pierre-Emmanuel and Lucas hiding behind him. To Hart, the French intelligence man looked disheveled out of a suit. His white T-shirt hung loosely from his thin frame. The prior week's stress appeared on his face, crow's feet forming around his eyes and cheeks. Hart could tell there was still a frost in the air between the intelligence chiefs.

"I understand Clara is in St. Lucia?" Pierre-Emmanuel spoke his words deliberately, trying to hide the slight tremor of emotion.

Darlington blurted out, "Yes, that is correct! They will anchor at Sugar Beach between the Pitons! It's quite lovely, I've never been but there's this massive house and—"

Palmer hushed him. Darlington scoffed in offense he couldn't elaborate further.

"I asked Kelly to pull up our satellite imagery, and it appears that the yacht we had been watching cross the ocean several days ago matches the current ship recently moored in St. Lucia."

Pierre-Emmanuel leaned against the doorframe. "The island is quite far south within the Caribbean, only a relatively short distance from Venezuela. It's somewhat remote; there is an international airport but only a few flights daily. At least that is what it was when I visited years ago."

Palmer took off his glasses and vigorously rubbed his eyes. Hart thought of ways to get to the island, he'd swim there if he had to, but time wasn't on their side. Outside of another private charter, there weren't many options. Lucas offered a quick calculation that Grand Cayman was roughly a thousand miles from St. Lucia. It was by far too great a distance by boat. Especially considering Darlington's admission that Farhad wouldn't be on the island for more than two days at most. By then, the weapon plans, and Clara, could disappear forever.

"Any suggestions?" Hart looked pleadingly around the room.

"Well," Palmer put his glasses back on and stood with his hands on his hips. "Here's the deal. We have a tip that a French agent is being held on a ship by terrorists. She is miles from US jurisdiction, and frankly, our resources won't scramble on the intelligence we've uncovered. Even if I could persuade them, the best-case scenario is at least twenty-four hours until help arrives. Plus, we can't forget this is basically off the coast of Venezuela. Those weapon plans make it into Venezuela, and there's no getting them back without risking war. The mission maybe be too risky. Bureaucratic suits might advise against it. So, while we are still quite some distance from the island, we're in the best position to help." He sighed and regarded the small team. There's only a few of us. Not to mention the three of us," Palmer looked at Pierre-Emmanuel and Hart, "aren't exactly field operators. We could get our hands on some weapons but planning and executing an assault without additional resources is jumping off a cliff without looking what's below first."

Hart wasted no time lobbying his position. "We have to try. This could be our only shot. We made it this far." He looked for support around the room, only to receive a bemused look of wonder from Darlington.

Palmer shook his head. "We don't know how many people are on that ship, or how they are armed. There might be a handover with some unfriendly Venezuelans, which proses additional problems. We are speculating here. Even if we can get there on time."

Pierre-Emmanuel lifted off the doorframe and with the most excitement, Hart had ever seen the man muster. "I know a captain."

"That's great," Palmer said mockingly, "What are you talking about?"

Pierre-Emmanuel grinned. "My brother's good friend is a yacht captain in the Caribbean. He has a large seventy-foot yacht that we could use to approach St. Lucia. I believe he is in Martinique, which is the French island just north of St. Lucia."

"We still need to get there," Hart said, starting to get the sense they were treading water. Eventually, all their plans could sputter and drown.

"I need to make a phone call." Palmer left the room while Pierre-Emmanuel did the same. Lucas and Hart were left standing in the room with Darlington, who seemed to be enjoying the theatrics.

"I am sorry about Toulouse," Lucas offered, his eyes tightening as if the words were inflicting pain.

Hart recalled the fateful night on the banks of the Garonne, the knife coming at him, Magali's screams. Diego's face frozen in death.

"I understand why you did it." Hart put a hand on the man's shoulder.

Lucas turned from the bathroom and their prisoner. He met Hart's blue eyes. "We're going to get her back. You believe that, right?"

Hart heard the man but he'd listened to the words all too often lately. The reassurance had become numb to the notion they could be wrong. He managed a toothless smile. Then he heard Palmer bellowing from the other room.

"Saddle up! Our bird is on the way!"

The sun was peeking through the morning cloud cover when they arrived at the airstrip. Francesca dropped them off in the same van they had driven in only the day before and hurriedly said goodbye to her guests. She had no choice but to stay thanks to a heavily sedated prisoner back at the safe house, who would be transported back to the UK. Then she would have to answer an abundant amount of questions about how he came to be in her possession. Her employers wouldn't be happy renditioning a British citizen, but Palmer said he would take the heat on her behalf.

Parked on the tarmac only a few yards away sat a Cessna Denali, different than the jet they'd flown in on. Its chrome silver turboprop's reflecting the rising sun. Palmer embraced the pilot, who Hart recognized as Captain Scott from their cross-Atlantic flight.

"Where'd you get the wings?" Palmer asked, running his hand along the fuselage of the white aircraft.

"Probably best if I don't tell you. But let's say time is of the essence." The captain tossed Palmer a bottle of Mountain Dew, then pointed to the open cargo door for George to store their gear and went back to visually inspecting the outside of the aircraft. "Also brought some presents for you, boys. Figured maybe you'd need it where you're going."

Palmer barked out thanks midway through a gulp of his soda and climbed aboard.

At the staircase, Hart looked back at Francesca. Leaning against her van with arms crossed, her tanned faced was a mixture of relief and fatigue. He jogged back over to her while the rest of the crew was loading their bags.

"Do you have a phone?" Hart asked, looking back over his shoulder at the plane.

Francesca handed him one and he pulled up the number he was looking for on Google. He just hoped he'd called at an opportune time.

"*Bonjour, c'est* Le Figaro," a smooth French voice said.

Hart asked to connect to the desk of Magali Martin. The request seemed to trouble the operator for a minute, but soon the line began ringing. It was early afternoon in Paris and Hart prayed she was at her desk.

She answered on the first ring.

"It's Paul," he started. "I'm going to be off the grid for a little while, but I had to speak with you."

The line was silent for a moment; he could only hear the clicking of keyboards and yelling in the press bureau. He pressed his free hand to his other ear to suppress the engines starting.

"Hello?"

"Okay, you can go ahead." Magali sighed.

Hart detailed the past twenty-four hours and developments over the past weeks, from the death of an attorney on the quiet streets of the seventh, to telling Magali that she should look into Darlington's bank and offshore company based out of a hotel in the Grand Cayman as quickly as he could. But the real scoop, Hart revealed, was that Iran was flexing its muscles globally. Pierre-Emmanuel believed they were behind the Seine boat attack. They were currently trying to get nuclear weapon plans into Venezuela, a significant play that could change the game in the western hemisphere.

Magali stopped him. "Paul, why are you telling me this?"

"We have a lead on Clara, but it's dangerous. I don't know what will happen, but what's important is that you have the facts to write a story if anything does. I've realized some good people have been helping me, and maybe this is my way of telling you thanks. For everything."

"This is you saying sorry?"

"Yes, it is. You've saved my life, and I owe you. Now we're even. *Merci beaucoup.*"

"Paul," Magali began. There was silence on the line as Hart saw Palmer appear at the plane's door and tap his watch. Hart held up a hand. He strained to listen to the reporter back in Paris. "You're going to get her, and then you're going to come here and I'll get the full story from the both of you."

Hart couldn't help but smirk at the thought, but the truth was he couldn't be so sure. "I'd like that. But if you don't hear from me in forty-eight hours, write the whole damn thing. Promise me you'll run the story?"

"*Oui, Paul. Bonne chance.*"

Hart hung up without another word. He thanked Francesca with a strong hug.

"When you get her back, you're both welcome here to visit."

Hart smiled and jogged onto the plane.

Once he boarded, Hart took the seat across from Palmer.

"We land in Martinique midday. We should be in St. Lucia by nightfall. I assumed you made whatever peace you had to out there." Palmer glanced at the van and Francesca, who offered a wave.

Hart reached out and slapped his employer on the knee. "Let's go get that peach ice cream, huh, boss?"

Palmer rolled his eyes and then shouted towards the cockpit. "Let's roll."

56

Martinique

The wheels gave a sharp bark as they gripped the tarmac on landing. They taxied with pace to a small private hangar where Pierre-Emmanuel and Lucas jumped out and spent several minutes talking with French border personnel. Hart watched the animated conversation through his window. In his dark blue pants and baby-blue short-sleeved uniform, the border official with a silver mustache and attentive eyes didn't seem back down from Pierre-Emmanuel to at first. He made several phone calls before finally bounding up the steps of the plane. He glanced inside at the remaining passengers, "Welcome to Martinique. But remember, you were never here." With a slight bow, the man disappeared into the back of the hangar.

The team piled out of the aircraft. Hart and Palmer were the last ones off the plane and stopped by the cockpit to thank the captain. "Everyone needs some help every once in a while. Unless you're Stephen over here, he needs lots of help all the time." Captain Scott belly laughed as Palmer playfully shook his head.

"I'd say see you around but who knows. You might get arrested for stealing an aircraft, and I might get killed," Palmer joked as he headed off the plane.

Hart shook the pilot's hand and jumped down onto the dark tarmac. Inside the shade of the hangar, the men piled into a waiting van. Hart and Palmer followed suit and found Pierre-Emmanuel behind the wheel.

"We are heading to the marina ten minutes away. There is a yacht that we will then take down to St. Lucia. It's a cruise of a little more than three hours."

The trip seemed straightforward enough, but Pierre-Emmanuel held up one of his long fingers. "*Mais*, the ship's crew doesn't know the nature of our mission or the gear we're bringing on board. We can either be honest with them or use other means…" His voice trailed off.

Palmer spoke up from the front passenger seat. "We will cross that bridge when we get to it. The priority is getting to St. Lucia."

"Any update on the ship anchored there?" George asked, surprising Hart with his interest.

"I have a call with Kelly in about thirty minutes via the sat phone. She'll provide additional information pulled from an Indian telecom-provider satellite that recently passed over the Caribbean. We didn't have any agency resources available, so we improvised." Palmer threw his hands up in the air.

Hart watched the passing palm trees out the window and couldn't help but worry about their strategy. It wouldn't be as simple as just getting close to the ship, especially with their small force. Clara's safety was paramount and could be jeopardized if they haphazardly approached the yacht. They needed to be precise and their mission planned out.

Before anyone had the chance to get comfortable in the hot van, they'd arrived at Marina Etang Z'abricots. The marina consisted of a few rickety wooden docks, with several sad sailboats moored in place. One yacht tethered to the end of the extended dock had a sparkling navy-blue hull. Inside the marina's metal chain fence, a man wearing khaki shorts and a white hiking shirt stood nearby with a broad smile and hands on his hips. He was thickly built with tanned skin, although most of his features were hidden behind his gold aviator sunglasses.

With speed Hart had never seen before, Pierre-Emmanuel raced out of the van and over to the captain. After the traditional *bise*, the captain and the French intelligence man spoke quietly as the team unloaded their gear.

"If you boys are going fishing, there are some better boats I know for that. I could get you in touch and have you sailing by this afternoon." The captain gave a professional smile and turned towards Pierre-Emmanuel, guiding him away by the shoulder to chat in private.

Palmer and George seemed to notice Hart's interest in the interaction.

"Nothing strange about two Frenchies and three relatively fit Americans unloading a bunch of heavy duffle bags wearing tactical gear for a yacht charter," George said, his voice dripping with sarcasm. He grinned. "The relatively fit descriptions were for you new field operators, Paul and Stephen, of course."

Palmer grunted. "Thanks, Wojtek. Anything else?" Hart ignored the slight. He was anxious about their predicament. If the captain disapproved, they were stuck in Martinique, with miles of ocean between them and St. Lucia.

"We'll be fine," Palmer said, noticing the terror on Hart's face.

"Yeah, worst-case scenario, you're decent at swimming, right, Paul?" George laughed and grabbed two duffels, taking off towards the yacht, not awaiting the captain's invitation.

Hart took in the 1953 Burger at the end of the dock, proudly highlighted by the captain. They had walked in a group towards the ship, which sat high in the water, its navy hull cleaned bright, in contrast to the white topside and burnished wood railings and doors. Across the stern read *Bonaparte*.

"Gentleman, welcome." The captain smiled, his tanned face creasing with a casualness that suggested he was nearly always smiling. How could you not be with this setup? Hart checked out the yacht while the morning sun inched higher in the sky. Crystal-clear blue water surrounded the marina. A few hungry seagulls floated overhead in the breeze, cawing for leftover scraps from a nearby fish-cleaning station. What a life, thought Hart, imagining himself laid out on the deck reading a book. Maybe he'd do that with Clara after they were reunited? No, he stopped himself, focus on the objective: the weapons plans and Clara. Everything else, including daydreaming, would have to wait.

The crew materialized from the ship's interior and moved along the starboard gunwale as they waved to their new passengers. The captain procured a stubby half-chewed cigar from his shirt pocket and plopped it into his mouth, waving them down to the dock to meet their new guests.

The captain's smiling facade slipped ever so slightly as he spoke through the stubby cigar between his teeth. "I know this isn't a fishing trip, and while my good friend Pierre-Emmanuel has assured me that nothing dangerous will happen to my crew, I run a tight ship, where the safety of my crew is the priority. So, it needs to be put to a vote."

"What is this?" George motioned towards the three additional crew members coming down the gangplank onto the pier. "A vote for what?"

"Whether or not we take you." The captain offered a reassuring smile and turned to the crew.

"Captain, *s'il vous plaît*, is this necessary?" Pierre-Emmanuel pleaded, his voice steady but Hart could see the fear in the man's eyes. "I've told you things in confidence, I wish you to respect that."

The captain nodded as the crew stood in a straight line as he addressed them. "These men wish to sail to St. Lucia, only a few hours south. But once there, my understanding is there is the possibility of danger to our ship and, thus, you, the crew. The target ship is anchored between the Pitons. There is no space in which to run should we need to. This gal," the captain pointed at the ship, "is strong but she isn't fast. If we need to outrun danger, we won't. Now Pierre-Emmanuel has told me what we are sailing for, and I am grateful for the honesty. But while I understand the sensitivity to the information, I won't set sail without my crew being one hundred percent committed to it."

The captain turned to face his crew. There were two women, dressed in blue skirts, white shirts and linen scarves tied around their necks, one wore an apron, the other a look of sudden worry. The man standing next to them looked stoic, his thick dark beard and tanned skin the only dictations of what he looked like, his eyes covered by thick sunglasses and a hat pulled low.

"There's a kidnapped woman who needs rescuing, and there's also some weapon sales with plenty of bad guys. These men behind me are the best hope for her safety and that of this region. Those in favor, say aye."

Hart looked over the crew.

The two women exchanged glances, and both said "aye" while the man was slower to answer. He shifted his weight for a moment before the shorter of the two women slapped him across the midsection. "David, you know the answer."

A small smirk appeared in his beard, followed by a deep voice that said, "Aye."

Pierre-Emmanuel offered a small clap, "That is great. Can we get on the ship now?" He gestured toward the gangplank.

"Just because my crew voted doesn't mean this is final. I haven't given my vote, which as captain, I'm entitled to."

Hart impatiently looked from Palmer and Pierre-Emmanuel, both seemingly at a loss for words. Out of the corner of his eye, he saw George slowly reach behind him into his waistband and casually keep his hand there. This wasn't the time for democracy, but as much as Hart hated to admit it, things could get dangerous. This was their livelihood, and in the case of a catastrophe, the crew's lives could be on the line.

"Please," Hart interjected into the awkward silence on the dock. "Your ship is our only option, we have no backup and we're the closest help to getting Clara back and stopping some evil people. Without you, we are screwed. Just get us there—nothing more, nothing else. You can slip away into the night, none the wiser. Please."

The captain's shoulders dropped. He glanced at the crew, then past the black duffle bags piled by the gangplank, to the hard stare of George along with the worried faces of Hart, Lucas, Pierre-Emmanuel, and Palmer. The captain pulled the stubby cigar from his mouth and extended his paw of a hand. "Welcome aboard the *Bonaparte*."

57

At an hour before sunset, a jet-black Zodiac swung a tight arc around *No Good Deed*. Clara watched from the porthole window in her room as the menacing boat cut through the water like a shark fin. Two large men dressed in fatigues were onboard the Zodiac, and after circling twice, they sped off the way they came, their destination hidden behind the Gros Piton.

Her door burst open a short time later with no courtesy knock from Greta. Her eyes narrowed, and her lips curled into a twisted smile. "Time to go." She didn't carry a weapon, but Clara had come to know the lady. Her frosty demeanor meant she wanted to provoke Clara so she could have the chance to lay her hands on the prisoner. There might still be time for that, Clara thought as she trudged from her room.

Clara offered no resistance. She steadied her breath in anticipation of the end possibly nearing. What it meant, she didn't know. They climbed the carpeted stairs, passing the ornately decorate living rooms and bridge. Appreciation for the refined luxury of the yacht had worn off long ago for Clara. She longed for simple pleasures, such as a gentle breeze through the open windows of the house in Noirmoutier or takeout in Paris shared over a bottle of wine with Paul.

Clara picked up her pace. She was anxious to smell the fresh air and feel the sea breeze above the deck.

When they stepped outside, Greta snarled. "Oh, I wish you'd try and make a run for it."

Clara ignored her, once again reminding herself to steady her breathing. *You're a fighter*, remember that she told herself, *but you choose the time and place.*

"You've been too well behaved, but I know what you are. Eventually, I'll get my shot, won't I?" Greta shoved Clara in the back as they walked on deck.

Clara spun around to square up to Greta. The two women came within inches of each other. Greta coiled like a snake, ready to strike.

"Try it. Right now." Greta growled, her hands at her sides.

Instead of reacting, Clara willed herself to relax. *She is trying to tempt me into doing something stupid. She must think she will not get another shot at me.*

Clara sighed and disregarded Greta's manipulation. But her coolness appeared to have dumped gasoline on Greta's burning desire to start a fight. She grabbed Clara by the shoulder and pulled back. "You think you are better than me? Let's prove it here and now!" Greta cried through clenched teeth.

Clara's heart pounded. But then, she heard the familiar shrill of laughter from Farhad.

"Ladies, please." He stepped in between the two women ready to face off. He raised his palms to the sky as if imploring for a reason. "I know that the land being so close has made everyone jumpy." He looked at Greta and Clara. "Which is fortunate for you because we're leaving the ship soon." He chuckled and walked back to the end of the aft deck. Clara followed tentatively, confused by the meaning of his message? Was she being freed? Or were they taking her somewhere else?

"The crew has been making runs back and forth all morning, preparing the compound for arrival. We will be comfortable and safe inside."

Clara's fears were only momentarily quelled before Farhad pointed to a rise in the hillside. "It's up there."

"What is?"

Farhad clapped his hands together and looked out to sea. "You will find out in time."

Clara turned and saw four Zodiacs cruising towards them across the bay. The lead Zodiac she'd watched earlier circled their yacht. Behind it the other Zodiacs ferried men who, at a distance, Clara could tell were killers. They were soldiers, mercenaries, or thieves. She'd been around enough types to recognize the bravado and posturing from afar. The question was, who were they, and what the hell was going on?

The *Bonaparte* bulldozed through the sea at fourteen knots. The old ship wasn't nimble, but it was sturdy. According to the captain, she hadn't been pushed this hard in several years. Hart watched the horizon from the bridge, searching for the Pitons, which would be hard to miss. They would be approaching St. Lucia from the northwest, trekking down its west coast, past the old fort of Castries. There the coastline rose high above the ocean, skirting until they'd be round the Gros Piton then into Sugar Beach cove, where the ship was anchored, according to Kelly.

The sun was melting into the horizon, its bright orange glow washing over the entirety of the sea. Hart took in the light playing on the clouds above, making shapes out of them in his mind.

The captain grabbed the intercom and with a matter-of-fact voice said, "Approaching St. Lucia. ETA is twenty-five minutes."

Hart grabbed a pair of binoculars off the wall and caught sight of giant shapes in the distance. Almost there.

He left the bridge to find the team assembled on the rear deck, huddled around a polished wood table. Sitting on the far side, Palmer glanced up from his tablet and motioned for Hart to sit on the cushioned bench next to him. The stern had enough space for everyone to gather around the table. The air was crisp, and there was only a hint of wind rolling across the deck.

Hart overheard Lucas. "What's our weapon situation? Do we have enough tactical gear?"

George looked at Lucas and shrugged. "We have some gear that Captain Scott brought for us, but besides that, not much. Current inventory includes one MP5 with three clips; two MP7s with silencers, three clips each; four P226 SIG Sauers, two mags each; two NVGs; some comms equipment; and a few blocks of C4, but enough to blow through some heavy steel doors."

"Anything else?" Pierre-Emmanuel asked, sounding somewhat disappointed.

George rubbed his bald head and chuckled, "Nope, as always with this crew, ill-planned and duck taped together. We're all we got."

Hart watched Palmer look up from his computer and shoot George a dark look.

George corrected himself. "But we're all we need. It'll work, no doubt."

"It damn well better," Palmer growled, smacking the table. "Need I remind you that we have a foreign agent's life at stake, not to mention if we fuck this up, we'll have allowed terrorists the means to have God knows what capabilities? I don't want to imagine what failure is like, so it's success or die trying as far as I'm concerned."

Hart's eyes shifted to George, who nodded solemnly. There was also a barely perceivable nod from Pierre-Emmanuel to Palmer. Across the table, Palmer's tablet was open to a satellite image of the house Darlington must have mentioned. George and Lucas busied themselves studying several satellite photos of the compound and surrounding terrain.

The door to the main salon opened and the captain stuck his head out to the gathered group. "We will anchor out of sight at the edge of the mountain. I'll get the Zodiac, *Li'l Napoleon,* ready to go. Once we round Gros Piton, it'll be game on. We'll be visible to the entire cove."

Pierre-Emmanuel stood. *"Merci, mon ami."*

The captain shifted in place. "I'm quite capable at managing in swallow waters, so regardless we'll make a quick approach. I figured it may be best to swing around the entire perimeter of her. We can drop some of you into the water to climb the anchor line. Others can board from the stern if we can get close enough to tie up."

Hart visualized the attack in his mind. The sun had nearly set, the stars blanketing their cover. Presumably, the resort and the target itself would be lit up. He imagined they'd make a mad dash around the 110-meter yacht and drop them in the water for a nautical assault. It seemed like suicide considering he suspected the crew was heavily armed. They wouldn't make it within shouting distance before being shot like fish in a barrel.

"Once we drop into the water, we need to be lightning fast. I assume your vessel has snorkeling gear? We can put on some fins and make a quicker approach. If we all have to swim up, we'll make for easy targets," Hart offered, registering the look of annoyance on George's face.

Palmer searched for his colleague's approval. Pierre-Emmanuel had his arms folded, drumming his fingers against his chin.

George cut in. "If you're planning this operation, do you maybe want some actual operator advice?"

"Any help is appreciated," Hart responded, wary as to where George was going.

"This plan for the yacht is last minute and frankly suicidal. The fact is we don't know what we're walking into, what the enemy has prepared, we don't have an exfiltration plan, and we don't have a quick-reaction force on standby. We only have five guys, most of whom haven't been in a gunfight in years, if ever, and trying to board a ship that we don't have the internal plans to. We're going in blind. Not to mention the narrow hallways on a ship are death traps for directing fire. No place to hide in a hallway."

"Can you make your point? Or would you just rather not go?" Hart objected, getting wearier by each word the man said.

"I'm getting there." George placed his hands flat on the table and stared at them for a moment. "We have to hit them and disorient them. Speed will be key. I can sweep the decks with the MP7s, which will do fine close range, but we need people to watch our six from a distance and only have one weapon, the MP5, for that. Who wants it?"

Lucas lifted his chin as if to accept the challenge. "I can manage."

Palmer and George exchanged looks. "Not with a broken wing you can't. Sorry, bud. You're staying on the Zodiac."

347

Hart hesitated. He hadn't handled a submachine gun before; the thought of wielding it gave him pause. But these men needed to see him seize the initiative. Hart could be brave too. Before he could respond, however, another volunteer stepped up.

"I'll do it," Palmer said, his face expressionless. No one objected.

Palmer shot Hart a glance. The men sharing the same thought, he'd taken the pressure off his agent.

"Okay, but how are we going to divert their attention?" Hart asked, trying to forget his moment of hesitation.

George smiled and smacked Lucas on the arm. "Buddy here has got an idea."

58

St. Lucia

They'd gathered on the back deck, clad in all black, the same color as the sky. George went over the MP5's mechanics with Palmer while vigorously applying black face paint all over his bald head.

David, the first mate, lowered the Zodiac smoothly in the water from the top deck, gently guiding it down to the stern so the team could board. The other crew members stayed inside the cabin, their faces barely illuminated by the light of the bridge. Their hands covering their mouths, probably whispering to each other how crazy the mission was, or perhaps Hart hoped, offering their prayers.

Without another moment's hesitation, he boarded *Lil Napoleon* and received a curt nod from the captain, who chewed nervously on his stubby cigar. Hart sat at the front, bobbing and swaying as each man climbed aboard. George, Pierre-Emmanuel, and Lucas, who'd shed his arm sling and looked in dire pain, left Palmer the position next to the captain.

"Listen, just do me a favor." The captain's blue eyes shone in the absence of the sunglasses. He pointed at the MP5 in Palmer's hands. "Just don't let that thing go off, or you'll sink us!" He laughed at Palmer's stoic face. Only George chuckled along.

They pulled away from the ship as David waved them onwards from the stern. *Lil Napoleon* and its cargo motored towards the other side of Gros Piton.

Hart was amazed at the blackness of the night. Light pollution was all but nonexistent around the island, the sea only reflecting the dim stars. As fate would have it, a wispy stretch of clouds rolled in for additional cover.

Palmer asked for the team's attention. "They'll know we're not friendly once we get within two hundred yards, but keep your weapons hidden. The captain will swing wide, drop the swimmers, then push to close distance to the ship fast once we're made. Could get spicy fast, but we're hoping our speed and surprise catches them off guard." Hart could barely hear him at the front of the Zodiac. Instead, he was focused on the edge of the mountain, gradually coming into view, his heart pounding. He'd traveled across the world, and with every second, he was getting closer. Clara was waiting. He would be there for her. He had to be. Failure wasn't an option.

Hart grabbed hold of the rubber handles on the edges of the boat as *Lil Napoleon* skipped across the sea. *Lil Napoleon's* pitch caused the Zodiac to catch some air every few yards, nearly sending Hart overboard. He bounced down into the seat, the barrel of the SIG Sauer P226 digging into his thigh. He'd often been frightened by guns, but now something was comforting knowing that he had one. He would use it soon against the very bastard who'd taken Clara.

Behind him, Pierre-Emmanuel, fighting the stiff wind plastering his grey hair straight back, leaned forward and placed a hand on Hart's shoulder. "Paul, I know we have never seen eye to eye, but I want you to know I want to get Clara back safely as much as you do."

Hart was taken aback by the man's sudden contrition. So much of what he'd done, whether out of helpfulness or spite, had made Clara and Hart's lives more difficult. He'd given Clara difficulties, and conspired with a journalist. Although Magali happened to be quite resourceful, Pierre-Emmanuel had started the avalanche of their problems. Regardless, the man was in the boat, literally in harm's way, trying to make amends.

"Merci." Hart managed a nod. "We'll get her soon."

Pierre-Emmanuel straightened up as if moved by the words and offered no response, but Hart knew he'd given the man what he wanted. Forgiveness.

"Two minutes!" The captain shouted.

The spray of the seawater had gotten more intense as they'd moved closer to land, the waves crashing into the side of Gros Piton. It was so close Hart could make out the vegetation hanging on the rocky cliffs, the thick trees making a dense canopy that swallowed up the dark, hiding what lay underneath.

As if the ocean and mountain had taken everyone's attention, no one spoke or moved. What lay on the other side of the colossal rock, no one knew. Hart's eyes never left the edge of the mountain, watching Petit Piton's massive dark shape appear in the distance. Steadily, a long stretch of beach materialized. A few homes on the land sloped upwards between the mountains and the sea, which he could make out. Their dim lights speckled the forest like fireflies.

Lil Napoleon pushed on. The captain had her at full throttle. Hart's position in the front of the boat rose ever so slightly as they flew towards the bay.

As if a mirage on the horizon, he saw purple lights picking out the monstrous silhouette, the bow of *No Good*

Deed reflected off the smooth glass water of the cove. Hart's primal urge to hit them fast and board the ship took over. "Charge them, head for the stern!" he shouted into the wind, his hand subconsciously grabbing the SIG from its holster.

He looked back at the captain. The man was now standing, one hand on the throttle and the other on the wheel, his jaw set in determination, ready for action. But then something flashed in the man's eyes gave Hart a moment of pause that caused him to turn around. Fear.

They were going to be in for a battle none of them were prepared for.

59

St. Lucia

Darkened shapes of Zodiacs circled *No Good Deed*. The ship was immense. Its underwater purple LED lights menacingly lit up the bay. Hart cursed under his breath, recognizing they'd just swam into a shiver of sharks. George pulled on his night-vision goggles and thumbed the side knob to zoom in.

"We have four tangos, military fatigues, but no flags or other identifying markers. Circle formation around the main target." He growled. "Two of the Zodiacs have fifty-cals mounted on the back!"

Hart snapped his head towards the rear of their boat, making out the worried face of the captain and Palmer.

"Who is that?" Palmer shouted towards George just as the captain throttled down.

They were within two hundred yards of *No Good Deed* and Hart could make shapes out on the deck. The dim lights from inside the cabin illuminated several red shirts running around onboard.

"Let's just stroll by and take a closer look!" Hart searched for an ally amongst the shocked faces of the team. No one had been expecting a naval force.

"Cross in front of the ship on the ocean side, but keep it

wide," Palmer directed, hoping they could skirt by the circle formation of the heavily armored Zodiacs.

After a moment's hesitation, the captain, nervously chomping on his cigar, pressed the throttle forward, the sea once again beginning to part in front of Hart at the bow. They sped forwards in the direction of the purple-hued water around the yacht but took a wide enough angle to ensure the Zodiacs paid them no attention. Hart squinted into the darkness, trying to make out the shapes on the increasingly busy deck. It seemed one of the Zodiacs had broken from the circle formation and was moored at the stern of *No Good Deed*. Hart could see a bevy of activity, red shirts running from the cabin, along with a few heavily armed figures posted on the stern deck.

"George, give me your goggles!" Hart pulled at them.

George reluctantly gave them over. Hart thumbed the side dial to focus.

At first, he thought his eyes deceived him, then he recognized the way she stood, her hair tied up but a few loose strains blowing in the evening breeze. Her profile was unmistakable. Then she turned to listen to a man speaking near her. The little bit of light from the cabin illuminated her face, defining her features on the night-vision goggles.

Clara.

An animalistic instinct took hold of Hart and before his mind could process what he was doing, he found himself ready to stand and shout her name into the wind. Hart began to stand on the bow of *Lil Napoleon* when a strong force pulled him back down into the boat.

"You trying to get us all killed?" George was on top of Hart, holding him down. "We're almost there, don't fuck it up now."

Hart nodded and George smirked, sitting back upright.

The Zodiac kept cruising in a wide arc. Hart's pulse was racing, and he tasted the sweet metallic twinge of adrenaline. Then chaos.

"Incoming!" George cried out, popping back on top of Hart as 50-cal rounds pounded the water around them. The rest of the team on *Lil Napoleon* dove for cover as seawater spray from the rounds rained down on them.

The deck buzzed with activity, crew hurriedly shouting into their radios. Clara stood still while the bizarre scene unfolded. She wore the clothes she was kidnapped in, freshly washed—her light jeans, an oxford shirt and her leather jacket on account of the cool evening breeze. She remained under the close eye of Greta who had put on a black sleeveless mock turtleneck, with her hair pulled back.

From the rear deck, Clara could easily make out the resort just tucked away behind the beach. The main building's terrace full for dinner, with the dim lights and the volume of numerous conversations carrying out to sea past *No Good Deed* like whispers. The bliss those people had, Clara thought. She'd been trapped on her golden prison for more than the past week, what she wouldn't do for a breath of freedom.

She noticed several duffle bags brought out from the cabin by the crew members and stacked at the stern. For the past fifteen minutes, she'd become accustomed to the buzz of Zodiacs racing around the ship. They were the same kind as the one earlier in the day, completing the same circle formation around *No Good Deed*.

"They have come to collect." Greta sneered and took a step closer to Clara.

"Who?"

Greta scoffed and looked off into the distance as if she were debating what to divulge.

Clara didn't take the bait, instead choosing to ignore her captor. After a moment of awkward silence, Greta spoke again.

"The Venezuelans are here to collect the ship, and with it, the value of over four hundred million dollars and the servers in Farhad's office that detail the weapon plans we've ferried across the sea. But not you, my dear. Although, I suggested we give you as an added bonus."

"Where are we going?" Clara asked, uneasy about her immediate future.

"Farhad showed you. The compound." Greta held Clara's gaze.

"For how long?"

Greta rolled her eyes as if bored by the questions. "You're insurance. Because until this ship safely makes it into Venezuelan waters, you'll be kept as leverage. But it should only be a matter of hours. Then…" Greta's voice trailed off, replaced by a knowing grin.

For a mean bitch, she sure likes to smile a lot, Clara thought.

It was then that she heard the boom of a .50 caliber. She spun to her right and saw a dark Zodiac zip by and followed it in the direction it headed. The man on the fifty-cal stood tall on the bow, swinging the cannon-sized gun out to sea. Clara saw the weapon's target, a smaller white Zodiac racing towards their ship.

Even from a distance, she could make out Paul Hart's features and sandy-blonde hair.

Before she could shout in warning, the .50 cal thundered. Paul disappeared behind a wall of seawater from where the heavy rounds had crashed.

"Time to go." Greta grabbed Clara by the arm and dragged her towards the stern.

60

St. Lucia

"Get down!"

Hart couldn't tell who shouted, but it might have been everyone. The boom from the .50 caliber, even at a distance, was deafening, but the water exploding around them was terrifying.

Hart's body, tucked tightly to the floor, absorbed every shockwave from the incoming rounds slicing into the ocean. The captain turned them out to sea, away from their target, away from Clara.

Had Hart's mind played tricks on him or had he seen her? All he had to manage now was fight through several heavily armored boats and an armed crew to free her. Great.

In a lull from the .50 caliber fire, Hart raised up to observe their situation. They were cutting straight out to sea, the captain hunched over the steering wheel, looking behind him at the pursuing Zodiac. He shouted to anyone who would listen. "They're following us! We won't be able to outrun them and I'm not leading them back to my ship!"

Pierre-Emmanuel craned his neck to check their pursuers' position. "They are probably a hundred meters behind us, closing fast."

The captain cursed and cut back towards shore, arching

back on the other side of *No Good Deed*, on a line between the lit-up houses on the darkened hill and the yacht.

"I have eyes on another Zodiac launching from the back of the yacht!" George barked out.

"Another one? Shit." Palmer cradled his MP5.

"Negative. This one appears to be a shuttle to shore—lots of crew members in red polos and I can make out a couple of female passengers."

"What the hell are they doing?" Lucas stood to get a better view and quickly ducked as their pursuers fired off a few small-caliber rounds at them.

Palmer shouted over his shoulder. "George, update?"

"Zodiac left the ship but is heading to shore, further down the beach. They are hauling ass. Tango on our tail's job seems to be keeping us away from the yacht. It's protecting the cargo."

Hart leaned over the side to check on the Zodiac following them. They were sandwiched between the Zodiac leaving the yacht and the immediate threat of the one closing in on them fast, now within thirty meters. But with the yacht in front of them, their pursuer didn't have a clean shot with the .50 caliber. At least for the moment.

A volley of small-arms fire from a distance cracked the water beside them, causing the captain to snap the wheel to the right, closing the distance to shore.

"Everyone hang on. I have an idea!" The captain hollered as *Lil Napoleon* turned portside, zig-zagging out to sea and then straightening back out towards the shore and the fleeing Zodiac. Now he'd set them further from the beach. The throttle was opened to the max, the propeller adjusted to deliver a higher pitch so that it was barely in the water, raising the front of the boat while giving maximum speed.

They raced perpendicular to the beach, a long wooden dock and behind it, a jetty extending out into the water.

"We're going to jump the sandbar!" The captain leaned forward on the steering wheel, willing his vessel to go faster.

The Zodiac following them began to swing wider out to sea, away from the shore, taking a different line than following the captain's ploy. Hart grabbed the SIG from his waist holder and fired at the bow of the pursuing Zodiac. George followed suit, strafing them with fire from his MP7 and forcing them back in line directly behind *Lil Napoleon*.

Before anyone could protest the captain's plan, the bottom of *Lil Napoleon* lifted as if an unseen force from under the sea raised it out of the water. The captain had cranked back to pull the prop entirely out of the water. It skimmed the sand as the boat caught air. Hart hung in the air for a moment before strong hands grabbed him and pulled him back into the boat. From the hard bottom on the craft, now once again skipping across the water, he looked up at Pierre-Emmanuel, who held him tightly. "Careful, my friend." The Frenchman smirked.

Behind them, the boom from the .50 caliber continued to rip through the night air. Suddenly the .50 caliber ceased, replaced by screams echoing off Gros Piton, then a loud thud. Hart rose up to see the pursuing Zodiac turning in the air, a trail of smoke following the motor, which had struck the sandbar. The smoking Zodiac awkwardly landed on its side, but not before throwing its passengers overboard.

Hart's eyes met the captain's. They shared a grin.

"I have eyes on the Zodiac pulling to shore. Looks like there are three off-road vehicles on the beach. The yacht is turning tail." George narrated from the bow. The yacht had begun to slowly creep away from the cove, like a shark heading out to open waters. The remaining three black Zodiacs tucked in formation behind *No Good Deed*.

They all turned to watch the massive yacht make its silent escape to sea.

"We can't let that boat get too far! This was the exchange," Pierre-Emmanuel called out.

"On it!" Palmer grabbed his sat phone and held it tight to his ear as he shouted orders to Kelly. His face grew red. "I don't care whose door you have to kick in or whatever the hell you have to do. We need to stop that ship!"

At this point, everyone recognized they couldn't stop it themselves. The yacht was heavily guarded and nearly out to open sea, *Lil Napoleon* had no chance to break through the armed escort and stop the ship. They now only had one mission left: rescue Clara.

Palmer barked a few more commands and threats into the phone before he hung up and huffed in anger. "Wojtek, did you bring the drone?" he asked, his head inclined towards the sky and the soft blanket of clouds covering the stars.

"Never leave home without it," George said, pulling a small hard case from his backpack.

"Good, let's see where these bastards are going." Palmer re-gripped the barrel of his MP5.

Pierre-Emmanuel, Lucas, and Hart all exchanged glances as if the men were all thinking the same thing. They were close.

"If I may," the captain spoke up, the Zodiac now trolling at slow speed as the threat had moved out to sea and the escaping crew were far enough away to pay them no bother. "There is a small inlet that runs into the island. The water is deep enough to pass through, and we can stay there while the drone finds them. Then it's an easy hike for the most part, or we could make it to the main road for a vehicle."

George tossed the small drone into the air. "I'll tell you where they're going in a minute."

The drone, the size of a baseball, hummed softly as its motor revved up. Then with speed like a line-drive home run, it took off into the night sky without a whisper of sound. Everyone onboard watched it in wonder as it climbed towards its target.

Off in the distance, the engines of the off-road vehicles fired up and took off. The Zodiac left behind, tethered to stake on the beach.

"The inlet is here. What's the call?" The captain asked, pointing towards land.

Hart followed the direction, finding a small break in the tree line between the stretch of beaches. There was thick foliage concealing it through the dense canopy of trees—a perfect spot to hide and wait.

"Let's do it," Palmer said, making his way towards the front of the boat to sit next to George, who was focused on a tablet device watching the drone's live feed.

"Anything?"

Hart caught a glimpse of the green camera feed, the drone's night vision coming in handy.

"Yeah, they didn't go very far, and you won't believe the setup they've got." George toggled through the camera modes, showing the thermal imaging, as a dozen shapes sprung up around a massive house tucked into the hillside. Hart could see several red lines in the land surrounding the house that the thermal imaging picked up.

"What's that?"

"The lines are wiring, probably power for the pressure plates and sensors spread out around the house to signal intruders. This sure is some compound. They are going to be tucked in nice and tight."

Hart brushed away some of the foliage as *Lil Napoleon* entered the small inlet. "Better get a move on then."

61

"What's happening?" Clara demanded. She sat wedged in the second row of the off-road vehicle between Greta and Farhad. When she received no response, she demanded answers again.

Their off-roader grunted with effort while crawling up the rocky path. Farhad slapped his hands on his knees and bellowed like a petulant child, "We're going to the compound! The ship is gone, okay? Traded, bartered, sold, but most importantly lost, as part of the ludicrous circumstances you and your friends put me in."

The fog in Clara's mind began to lift. They'd frozen assets when they started investigating the attorney's death, and Farhad had admittedly needed hundreds of millions of dollars transferred. So, what better way than to bring a monetary vessel, quite literally in the sense of *No Good Deed*, directly to the party? The bonus was the weapons plans. She imagined the servers in his office filled with millions of weapon plans files, ensuring Iran's proxy in the western hemisphere; Venezuela, would be feared.

Clara angled for a view through the trees to the cove but couldn't make out anything. She held on tight to a nylon strap that hung from the vehicle's steel frame and realized the unmistakable booming of the .50 caliber had ceased. Had they run out of ammunition? Or to her relief, maybe Paul and his crew had escaped? Her stomach flipped with dread at the possibility the firing stopped because the target had been destroyed.

The vehicle lurched to a stop on a flat spot ten meters from a cement structure Clara found remotely similar to Nazi bunkers on the beaches of Normandy. The building's dark façade dulled what little light came from the moon peeking through listless clouds. Built into a steep hillside and supported by enormous cement pillars in the front and under the structure for support, Clara assumed it had an impressive ocean view. A trickle of light emanated from a long and narrow window that ran the length of the front of the house.

Greta pulled Clara by the arm.

"Come!" Greta snapped.

Broken out of her awe of the structure, Clara felt the buzz of activity around her. Farhad was shouting at the crew who were ferrying bags from the convoy of vehicles. Like ants, they scurried up the central staircase to the house, returning the same way. Several of the crew carried submachine guns, straps slung over their shoulders. They were moving with urgency, a good sign that Paul and whoever he was with were still a threat; she comforted herself with the thought.

Greta spun and glared at Clara. Not wishing to be dragged up the steep cement steps, Clara followed her guard to the house cautiously. A central staircase under the home brought her up into a room as opulent as it was wide. The room was aglow with soft yellow lights from crystal chandeliers. Walnut floors led to crisp white walls with simple murals of ocean creatures, dolphins jumping out of the water, a starfish, and some stingrays in between floating bookshelves. The long window that ran the expanse of the front of the house framed the dark cove. Several Herman Miller lounge chairs and a bar cart faced the ocean view. Clara could faintly see the lights of the resort through the palm trees some distance away.

Farhad materialized from the kitchen, and beelined to the bar cart, placing a silver bucket filled with ice on top.

"Care for a drink, mademoiselle?"

Even in the relative nightfall that the house sat in, she could see the mischief in his dark eyes.

Clara declined, although she could have used one. She'd seen Paul at the most inopportune time when the gang of Zodiacs had come to take the yacht. The brokered exchange, along with seeing Paul, had left her shaken. The strangeness clung to her like the cold after getting out of a hot shower.

"Are you sure? It's going to be quite entertaining. I'm making myself a negroni. It's gin, Campari and vermouth with an orange peel. Delicious. In fact, I'll make two. It'll help you cope with everything that's about to happen."

Clara raised her eyes from the wooden floor. "What do you mean with everything about to happen?" Her stomach twisted in a knot.

"Oh my dear," Farhad began as he dropped several ice cubes into a crystal glass, "only everything I've crossed the ocean for!"

George twisted and turned, mimicking the flight of the drone he piloted. It hadn't taken long to find the convoy of taillights scuttling up a narrow path towards a monstrosity of a house on top of the hill. The drone settled high above the house and hovered in place. Its rotary blades softly humming at one hundred meters in the dark sky.

"What's the situation?" Pierre-Emmanuel asked, his long boney hands drumming on the tubing of the dingy.

Lucas shimmied over to the screen, conferred with George for a moment before turning to the group. "We have a heavily guarded compound, *beaucoup* bad guys. Looks like one main staircase that runs under the house. There are no other visible entry points at ground level."

"From under the house?" Palmer asked.

George grunted. "Yeah, the house is built into the hill, propped up by some thick cement pillars. There's a staircase that runs up from under the raised portion into the main house."

"That is common on the island." The captain spoke as if engaging in casual bar talk. "They build them like that for the views, but in reality, it's easier to build them into the mountainside with the front raised like that."

"How many enemies we talking about?" Palmer shifted around on the craft, causing it to sway in the swallow water.

George pointed his chin towards Lucas to answer. "I'd say a dozen from when they were unloading, but we don't know if anyone was there already. Thermal has a hard time penetrating the concrete walls."

The team stayed silent for a moment, weighed down with their dire situation. They'd escaped their pursuing Zodiac, while the others ferried the yacht away, but it appeared that the hard part was just getting started.

Hart recognized the dangerous, if not suicidal, operation to rescue the woman he loved and take down a significant broker for terrorists and corrupt countries alike, and, likely, it would come at a severe cost. It was an uphill battle. They were heavily outnumbered, outgunned, out-positioned, and without reinforcements. But, in his heart of hearts, he knew this was the only chance to get Clara and capture Farhad.

"How long can it stay in the air for?" Lucas asked, nodding towards the controller in George's hands.

"She'll stay up there for close to another twenty minutes without a problem."

Palmer jumped at the idea. "So, we'll leave it up there and see what materializes?"

There was some murmuring from the team, but no one spoke up. They all knew that time wasn't a luxury they could afford.

Pierre-Emmanuel cleared this throat. "I will go scout ahead. I am the reason Clara was taken, therefore it's only right that I am the one to go."

"Bullshit," Palmer growled. "We need decent intelligence, we can't send you alone—you won't even know what you're looking for."

"I'll have you know that I served in the French Army, deployed to Mali and Burkina Faso, so don't trouble yourself thinking I am some office suit who sat at a desk his entire career."

Hart turned his head back towards Palmer, as did the rest of the team.

"I know the island. I'll go along," The captain said.

"No, you stay with the boat in case we need a quick getaway." Hart threw his legs over the side and slid into the knee-high water. "I'll go with him." He began to drag the boat several yards towards the grassy bank.

"Everyone, just calm the fuck down with this *Rambo* shit,

huh?" Palmer spat into the darkness. The bluntness of his comment hushed the team. Only the croaks of frogs and insects buzzing filled the silence. "Here's what we're going to do. Paul and Wojtek, you two are going on recon. The rest of the team will stay back, providing support if need be. Get in close and take a look. Only a look, George—don't let Paul be an idiot. I want details about this compound before we raid it."

George grinned. "I love *Rambo*. But anyway, we won't get enough details to plan anything because we'll have no idea what's inside. It could be a maze, there's no telling, and even if there are two entrances, can't we hit 'em at the same time? We could be right in each other's sight lines."

"Well, shit ain't perfect, Wojtek, but it's time to cowboy the fuck up. The Marines aren't coming. It's just us. We all know what we signed up for." Palmer looked each team member in the face, minus the captain who scoured the landscape, already stoic in his duty of watching the boat.

"Yippee-ki-yay." George winked.

Palmer sighed, "That's *Die Hard*."

Grinning, George threw his legs over the boat, grabbed the duffle from the front of *Lil Napoleon*, and joined Hart on land. There he gave Hart a quick crash course of a series of hand gestures. "If I do this"—he held up a fist— "you hit the deck and don't breathe. If I do this"—he twirled his finger in the air—"you move like a banshee to cover. Got it?"

Hart didn't bother responding. He just started ahead.

Before the rest of the team was off the boat, George took off after Hart into the jungle.

62

The steep hike over the rugged hillside took them fifteen minutes to reach a flat rocky plateau. There, George and Hart both decided to track westwards to the house. They clung to the side of the rocky path that was the road, hiding the best they could from the sparse moonlight under the thick foliage and sacrificing stealth for the sake of speed. They passed mostly nothing for several hundred yards, a few desolate houses, marked by trail breaks in the lush forest. They didn't hear a car or see any patrols, and the only noises they heard were the faint flapping of bats overhead.

According to Hart's watch, they'd been jogging along the road for eight minutes when George threw his fist into the air. Hart hit the deck. He laid still, his heart pounding off the hard earth. Had they been spotted? Could their rescue operation be foiled already? He pulled his SIG from his hip holster, and death-gripped it. The sheer thought of failure gave Hart a glimpse of dread he never knew existed, even worse than the night of her kidnapping. Now it was different. He'd fought his way halfway across the world and was so close to her that if he shouted her name, she could probably hear. *If it's the last thing I'm going to do, I'll see her again.*

George was crouched, frozen in place, several feet ahead

370

of him. He had tucked into the branches of a low tree. After a moment of stillness where mosquitos started to pick at Hart's exposed skin, George finally pivoted to Hart, the shadows of the forest obscuring his face. He placed his finger over his mouth. At a much slower pace, they began moving again and approached the nearest tree line. Fruit trees had been planted and spaced out several yards apart as a makeshift property boundary. Hart gently moved some tall grass and immediately saw the massive structure ahead. His initial thought was how could cement pillars hold such a formidable house built like a war bunker?

They observed no activity near or around the house.

George belly crawled over to Hart. "It seems too quiet. We need to scout the target. I'm thinking that staircase is the only way in by design."

"Agreed." Hart had an idea. "Just like defense theory in jiujitsu, green-red-green. We need to get as close to it as possible to cancel their advantage. The closer we are, the less danger because we'll be under the house."

George lightly tapped him on the arm. "Now you're thinking. I'm going in for a closer look. Stay here, wait for the others."

Before Hart could voice his protest, his companion took off around the back of the house, using the forest as his cover. George bear crawled along the tree line, flanking the house. He finally ducked further into the brush and out of sight. Hart strained to listen but couldn't make out any sounds of the seasoned professional. It was only after a few short minutes that he heard loose gravel and trees rustling nearby. The faint footfalls marched up behind him. His heart caught with worry.

Peering out into the blackness of the jungle, he couldn't

make out any shapes. Then, he caught the flash of a small flashlight focusing on a pile of foliage about ten paces from where he lay. Guards were sweeping of the perimeter, and naturally, George had left him at the most inopportune time.

He tightened his grip on the SIG, forcing himself to recall the instructions he'd learned: safety off, aim, squeeze, don't pull, repeat. He felt exposed, like any moment they would stumble upon him. Lying on his stomach instead of the crouch he'd been in for the better part of the past ten minutes, he slithered into the cover of a nearby bush. His knees thanked him as he stretched out on the cool earth and tried to burrow into the ground. With great care, he aimed his SIG towards the guards. If he was going to be spotted, he wasn't going without a fight.

The flashlight extinguished, the sound of boots over the coarse ground replaced the silence, and then without warning, the flashlight beamed once again, this time settling on the undergrowth just two yards from where Hart lay. His throat tightened as he thumbed the safety off his weapon.

The flashlight extinguished once more, the guards, two by the sounds of their footsteps, approached his bush further. Then they stopped. Hart could now make out their large shapes in the darkness. He felt one guard step closer, then the metallic click of the flashlight. The light blinded him, but before he could raise his gun blindly, a shadow flashed in his peripheral vision, then grunting, followed by two thuds on the hard ground. The flashlight fell with the guards, and the faint trickle of light from under the fallen guards illuminated the dark-painted face of George. He stood panting, a long jet-black tactical knife at his side.

"Had that under control, did you?" He winked and crouched down to turn the flashlight off. He then crawled towards Hart, who was left shaken from his near-death encounter.

"I'm only going to be able to watch your six for so long during this fight. You need to know that."

"Thank you, Wojtek," was all Hart could manage.

George grinned. "You can save your thanks for when we're done and heading home." George paused then smacked Hart on the back. "With Clara, of course."

63

St. Lucia

The fluidity from which the crew from *No Good Deed* switched to a defense force impressed Clara. The red-polo crew took up positions on the outer walls with precision, having clearly trained for such a situation. Several screaming radio communications Clara overheard made it evident the departing Venezuelans were not happy that they'd lost a Zodiac. Whoever Paul had with him had survived and were presumably on their way to finish their job. While the cavalry had arrived, they'd have to overcome a substantial disadvantage against a well-armed and organized force of twelve, including Greta and Farhad.

Farhad had ordered the chandeliers off, bathing the light interior in darkness.

"Keep an eye on the infrared cameras. We want to know when they come. Draw them in close." He sipped his red drink, the ice clicking against the crystal.

Clara reminded herself to breathe. She glanced at Farhad, then to the chair opposite him at Greta's square face, whose only hint of emotion was the wild anger that danced in her hollow green eyes. Clara got the feeling it was because Greta knew something she didn't. She spun around the room. At every window, the crew crouched low out of the moonlight.

A pair took off down the staircase leading outside. They'd set up the perfect trap, and the realization was not lost on Clara. She was bait.

Stephen Palmer rested his MP5 on his knee as he crouched and looked around at their assembled team. Hart and George had picked them up on the road and let them back to the tree line on the property's perimeter. There Palmer made the call to split into two teams: the French and the Americans. They synchronized their watches and agreed to move on the house on precisely the stroke of eleven.

"Want to walk us through the plan of attack?" Palmer asked George.

A smirk appeared on George's jet-black face. "Boys, we're in for it. There's only one way into the house—the staircase under the main structure. Behind the house is only rock and the hillside." He paused to wipe sweat from his brow. "The tree line is about twenty yards from the house. You all should be able to clear that space in about five seconds tops. But until we're under the house, we are exposed in the open." He stopped at looked at Hart. "It's green, red, green on this one. We need to get under the house for cover. Then we'll breach and clear inside. The C4 is ready to go." He patted his vest. "I have the detonator. I'm not sure what resistance we will face, but eyes up."

"Anything else, Captain Inspiration?" Palmer asked in a mocking tone.

"Yeah, I have an idea for an insurance policy to cover our retreat."

The group exchanged a few fist bumps, and the teams tore off. George, Palmer, and Hart flanked around the side of the house and were to take it from the west, while the

French team would proceed from the current position they'd all mobilized from in the east.

They would form a bracket and advance like hell on the main staircase. Once there, the heavy weapons with the professional room clearer, George, would lead the charge.

Hart glanced at this watch; its hands illuminated neon green in the dark. They had thirty seconds to go. He turned towards Palmer and started to open his mouth, to say thank you, but it was as if Palmer knew what he was going to say, and his boss wasn't having it.

"It can wait until after."

Hart liked his boss's optimism.

The second hand swept past eleven, and with impressive synchronization, Hart, George, and Palmer burst through the tree line. Immediately, Pierre-Emmanuel and Lucas came into their vision from the right. They all covered ground quickly. It was eerily quiet, so much so that Hart felt his pace slow, his instincts crying out for caution.

Suddenly, floodlights illuminated the night.

Then the windows on the structure flung outwards, bright muzzle flashes raining hot lead down on their positions. The earth around them exploded. It was as if God had opened the heavens. It rained fire. The gunfire pushed the Americans towards Pierre-Emmanuel and Lucas, driving them in a semicircle as they raced to get under cover.

"Aim for the lights!" he heard Palmer shout.

Hart didn't bother to fire his pistol at the lights or the muzzle flashes; rather he ducked his head and sprinted towards the house. Towards Clara.

Palmer returned fire to little effect, the 9mm rounds from his MP5 nicking the house's concrete exterior and missing the lights. The deafening noise of larger caliber weapons firing from the windows boomed off the mountain, disorienting Hart as time melted into a blurry reality. He was steps away from the safety of the house when he heard the first scream. Spinning right, he saw Lucas take several shots to his left leg, crying out in pain as his weapon clattered from his hands. Hart changed course to cover Pierre-Emmanuel, who had dropped to a knee, returning fire calmly, with several clustered shots from his handgun, before hauling Lucas onto his shoulder.

"*Allez! Allez!*" Pierre-Emmanuel shouted when Hart caught his eyes. He waved him forward as he began to drag Lucas.

Hart ignored his French colleague and grabbed Lucas by the shirt, pulling them under the structure. Several yards behind him, he heard another shout. Hart spun, terror gripping him, the adrenaline of battle blinding his vision. Palmer had been shot. Judging by the blood pooling towards the upper part of his shirt, he'd taken one in the shoulder. Hart pushed Lucas and Pierre-Emmanuel in the direction of the house and leaped back into the fray, grabbing his boss by the belt and dragging him under the house. They all fell to the rocky earth, exhausted and badly injured from their charge. George moved with fluidity, taking care to put his shots on targets rather than spraying the structure.

Once under the house without issue, they regrouped with the rest of the battered bunch.

The rocky earth surrounding the house had been annihilated. The air was thick with chalky dust that hung like fog. The massive concrete structure they laid under gave them no clue as to whether anyone was moving about upstairs, that's if they could even hear over the loud gunfire. The staircase led to a nondescript door, which was closed. George kept his weapon trained on the door for a moment.

Then Pierre-Emmanuel relieved him of the watch as George began to rummage through the bag slung over his shoulder, finding three small brick-shaped cubes. "Paul, take the first aid kit out from my bag. We need some wraps and clotting powder on those wounds."

George then jetted and attached several C4 charges to the pillars supporting the house. Hart began to work diligently, first tending to Lucas, who was in much worse shape than Palmer. He was groaning into his sleeve to muffle his painful cries as Hart secured a tourniquet six inches above the gunshot wound on his leg.

Hart placed his hand firmly to the entry wound. The bullet had ruined Lucas's leg. His eyes swept from the dark crimson blood that covered his hands to the sweat-streaked faces of the others. As a team, they were banged up but as close to their goal of getting Clara back as they'd ever been. However, like rats, they were trapped under their objective. Hart never felt further away from Clara.

While Pierre-Emmanuel took over for Hart on Lucas, Palmer waved off any treatment.

"Everything works, flesh wound," he said to Hart, eyes trained on the door.

George then raced to each of the three outermost pillars and attaching the C4 bricks to their centers. When he returned to the group, George met Hart's quizzical look. "To cover our retreat." He tried to smile, but everyone understood their dire situation.

Suddenly, he felt a surprisingly firm grip on his arm. Looking down, he saw Palmer, his face dirty from falling on the rocky earth and glistening with sweat. "I'm sorry, kid."

"For what?" Hart ignored him for a moment and looked out at Palmer's MP5, lying just out of safety of their cover.

"I'm serious. Look at me." Palmer gritted his teeth with effort as if he was willing away the searing pain in his shoulder. "We need to move."

Hart had just opened his mouth to ask George what to do when a column of light filled the darkened space beneath the house.

He heard the clang of metal on the rocky earth before George dove at him and Palmer. The blast reverberated off the concrete structure through his bones, pounding his head as a blinding light, bright as a thousand suns, overwhelmed his senses. Hart fell into a dark abyss.

He had tried to stir awake, pushing against the bodies on top of him. He couldn't guess how long he'd been out or if he had been at all when the butt of a rifle crashed into his forehead, spending him spiraling back into darkness.

64

The pounding headache he woke to told Hart he was still alive. It felt as if there were an entire marching band trapped in his head, banging on drums, pleading, and searching for a way to get out. He'd never experienced a searing migraine like it, but at least he was alive—for the moment.

Tied to a chair, Hart's hands were behind his back, his chin lying on his chest. There were voices around him, but it sounded as if he were underwater. He couldn't make out any particular words. At first, he tried to move his fingers, then wiggled his toes, until he found the resolve to lift his right eyelid. For some unknown reason, he had trouble opening his left. Sticky wetness covered half his face. Blood.

Additional senses slowly came after that. His vision cleared slightly, just enough to know he was in the center of a dark room that smelled strongly of sweat.

Then he heard his name. Someone was pleading, begging him to wake up. Clara.

"Paul.. Paul… *Paul!* Please!" The voice cried out in pain to his left.

He rolled his head to his left as far as he could, his right eye-straining to see more than a few feet in front of him. But

380

even with one eye barely functioning, he would recognize Clara anywhere.

There she was, tied to a chair like he was, in the same leather jacket she wore the night she was kidnapped. Her green eyes were swollen with emotion. Full of fear. But dammit, she still looked at beautiful as ever.

"*Coucou,*" Hart managed to whisper.

She responded with a shuttered half-smile, and then a single tear fell from her cheek. "Paul, you shouldn't have come."

Before he could answer, a strong hand slapped him across his face. The severe impact made his head feel as if someone had put it into a washing machine.

"Enough talking!" A thick accent shouted at him. He recognized the voice—the same from the arcade in Paris.

Hart looked up at a blonde-haired woman with a square jaw and fierce eyes. She stood with her feet set widely apart and her hands atop her hips. For a moment, she was all Hart could see in the room until another voice called her off. "That will be enough, Greta."

When she cleared, Hart managed to take in his surroundings and immediately felt a fool for their haphazard rescue attempt. Standing some distance away from him at the large glass windows that overlooked the bay, Stephen Palmer had his hands tied, held in place by a man with a broad mustache. At their feet, dirtying the light-colored wooden floors lay George, Pierre-Emmanuel, and Lucas. They all laid sprawled out at different angles, but the commonality was their burned and ripped clothing.

Hart tried to recall what had happened, then remembered the blasts. There must have been several grenades, meant to disorient and incapacitate their targets, dropped down the staircase just as they'd planned to go up. Speed hadn't been an option; they took several knocks during their ill-fated charge. George had tackled him thinking they were grenades instead of flashbangs. Regardless of George's valiant effort, the result were the same.

Hart hung his head and let out a sigh. Footsteps grew closer, and a hand grabbed his still stinging cheek. "Mr. Hart, I need your full attention. Are you listening?" The hand shook his cheek from side to side, the pounding in his head nearly causing him to pass out once more.

Hart managed to grunt, and the hand let go. "Good, because you are required to pay attention during the crescendo of my performance. After all, my friends, leading this hopeless orchestra has been amusing, but all good things must come to an end."

Palmer caught Hart's eyes; the man's chest heaved with bated breaths. His eyes swept back and forth between the mustached man pacing about the room and Hart.

"You, Mr. Hart, are my nemesis's"—he ran a hand filled with gold rings over Palmer's head—"secret weapon? Rather more like a pebble in my shoe. Constantly annoying, difficult to eradicate. Yet, I have finally found your weakness." Farhad walked over to Clara and put the back of his hand against her face. Instinctively, she moved her face away, but it only drew him in closer. Enraged, Hart fought against his restraints, but only manning to cause the chair to wobble in place.

Farhad let out a low chuckle and stepped away. "You see, I shouldn't even be here, in this beautiful house, with all these expensive decorations, these men and women who protect me." He spun around in a circle with his hands out as if showcasing his team. "But I was thrust into this life, given no choice, and I must say, I've waited for this day for many,

many years." He walked over to Palmer, who seemed to be breathing heavier with every word uttered. Farhad suddenly grabbed the bottom of Palmer's beard and lifted his chin to the ceiling.

"But you see, old friend, we can't escape our pasts. Sometimes our best intentions cause the exact opposite desired effect. You wanted to stop terror, to eradicate it, and you used me as a tool. Yet instead, I grew to become the very thing you wished to destroy. I am the living, breathing mistake you created, left for dead, cast aside like a child's unwanted toy. Now you must atone for my creation."

"He's behind it all, the bombing, the money, the weapons." Clara burst out, pleading with the eyes of Pierre-Emmanuel and Palmer for understanding and help. As if they could do anything about their current predicament.

"She's right! And may I add, an exceptional house guest. Such a shame we'll never get the pleasure again." Farhad smirked at Hart.

Once again, Hart fought against his restraints. "So, all of this, all the pain and killing is because you feel sorry for yourself? You poor bastard," Hart shouted sarcastically.

Farhad was quiet for a moment as if reflecting on the observation. "I must confess, after a while, I started to enjoy my new lifestyle in death. I even made an effort for people to think I was dead. Can you imagine the satisfaction of rising to power from nothing, becoming the broker to, and friends with, the most influential people in this world? It's invigorating."

"With friends like you…" Hart started but stopped when he saw the blonde woman fashion a gun in his direction.

"What…" Palmer began to speak and stumbled over his words. "What's it all for? All this running halfway across the world? What's the point of it?! I would have saved you had I known you were alive!"

"Ah, but you see, my old friend." Farhad brushed his mustache. "For me to do good with the life you've given me, I needed to sympathize with evil. In the end, it was simple because the countries you Westerners bankrupt with economic sanctions don't provide for their everyday citizens. Sanctions ensure the rich stay rich, and the poor get poorer. Average families fight to put food on the table, just like mine did. Without me, they were hopeless. So, I merely ensure that others are provided for by procuring and safeguarding the necessary funds to those corrupt bastards in charge. They know they won't get their money from me for their defense and pleasures, without at least some of it going to those in need." Farhad spread his hands and smiled, expectant of praise.

Hart noticed slight movement on the floor behind Farhad. His focus on George attempting to sit up caught Farhad's attention. "Ah, I see we have some true warriors here!" He flipped his hand towards Greta and nodded.

Greta walked over to George. She kicked out at him twice, landing two crunching blows to his face.

"You motherfucker!" Palmer stammered, trying to throw a shoulder at Farhad until Greta elbowed his back, sending him face-first onto the floor.

Hart's mind worked feverishly. They needed a miracle.

Most of the defense force was standing near the terrace watching over the prisoners, while only two remained behind them in the room. *Think, dammit.*

"Now." Farhad clapped. "Before we have any other rude interruptions. Stephen, I'd like to finally allow you the second chance you never thought you'd have." Farhad walked over and stood in between Hart and Clara, facing Palmer and the windows. "You made a choice years ago to sacrifice your agent, *moi*, forfeiting my life, my career, and my future. So, tonight, you shall have the choice again, but with your new agent." Farhad's small hand gripped the back of Hart's neck. "You get to choose, kill your agent again, or save his life, but ensure him a lifetime of pain as he watches his lover die in front of his eyes."

He nodded at Greta, who raised her silver pistol at Hart.

Farhad walked back to Palmer with a broad grin on his face. "The choice is yours, Stephen, you have five seconds to choose, or they both die."

65

Time stood still. Hart could feel his heart pounding, but it felt hollow. As if he was in a nightmare, one where he just needed to scream and wake up in a cold sweat. But there was no escaping what he faced with Clara. He silently prayed. It's not supposed to end like this. Hart willed himself to turn his good eye to Clara. Her skin was smooth under the harsh white lights of the room. Sweat glistened on her forehead.

"It's going to be okay. *Ça va allez,* I promise." Hart offered a crooked smile to reassure Clara but realized she didn't need his sympathy or support.

"Why give him the decision?" Clara asked, much to the apparent surprise of Farhad.

"Excuse me?" He cocked his head to the side like a dog recognizing a word.

"You heard me. Why? He didn't give you a choice. And you had me for more than a week to yourself. Could have killed me and made for Stephen and Paul to find out, but you didn't. Which means you didn't think you'd eventually be found, but now that you have been, you're improvising." Clara raised her eyebrows as she waited for his rebuttal.

Farhad snickered. "That isn't a bad theory, but there's one problem with it. Halfway across the ocean, I realized that I needed this. Why else would I have one of my biggest idiots, Luke Darlington, on the same island where I assumed these men would look?"

"Bullshit," Hart cut in. "Darlington was running away. You're just using this as a convenient cover."

Farhad seemed to consider this for a moment. "And how has that worked out for you?"

Hart dropped his head. Clara's attempt to stall and distract Farhad only lasted so long and not nearly long enough to come up with any plan to escape.

Hart cast a glance at the prisoners. George laid near the far windows on his side, left alone due to his rough shape. There were several guards on the deck facing the cove and two behind Farhad against the walls.

"So, what will it be then, sir?" Farhad walked back across the room and stood next to Palmer. "Your agent or his woman?"

"*The* woman, you asshole." Clara spat at Farhad, who brushed away Clara's correction with a wave.

The fear on Palmer's face was evident. He had perspiration dripping down his nose. His hair was wet, his eyes nervous and darting across the room as if searching for the answer he didn't have.

Hart drew a deep breath and once again looked at Clara. She was still as beautiful as the first day he'd seen her in that Paris bistro. It felt like years ago. Time and circumstance had thrust them together, both their lives had changed dramatically. Now those circumstances lead them to the very room where they faced death, once more, together.

"Paul," Clara whispered, not out of secrecy, her voice cracked with emotion.

"*Oui*." Hart offered a smile, trying to coax Clara into a calmer state as if that were possible facing death.

"I want you to know." She paused, the corners of her green eyes welling with tears. "I love you."

As if a knife drove through his chest, the words struck him at his core. The words he longed to hear, the joys he felt, were short-lived. He'd been close to having it all, but quite literally, he was staring down the barrel of a gun. At that moment, it wasn't important what he had, where he lived or worked, but rather who he knew he couldn't live without. Clara. The small consolation prize, was that he got to say goodbye.

"Enough! Enough of this! I'll give you five seconds to choose, or they both die!" Farhad marked the time on his watch.

"No, no!" Palmer protested as much as he could muster, but it was of no use.

"Stephen," Hart shouted to his boss, the man a shell of himself, jolting the man from a dazed slumber. "Looks like we finally found that peach ice cream, didn't we?"

Palmer squinted at him for a moment as his brain connected the pieces, and when it fell into place, his eyes grew wide.

"Three seconds," Farhad interjected.

"Remember I told you I'd give anything to find her. I meant it. I'd give anything." Hart stared hard into the man's eyes, willing him to understand.

Clara watched on as Hart spoke to Palmer, piecing the cryptic language together herself, realizing what Hart was demanding.

"Paul, you can't!" Clara cried out, lunging out against her ties.

Hart knew their time was nearly up.

"Two seconds!" Farhad screamed.

"Clara." Hart turned in his chair and, with as much strength and ability he could muster, leaned over and kissed her lips. It wasn't the goodbye kiss he expected, as she pushed him away almost immediately.

Palmer shouted. "Take Hart, take him!"

Hart looked down at the floor. Pierre-Emmanuel and Lucas were on the main room's cement floor, just off to the side of Clara and Hart. George, half his face covered in dried blood, lay motionless. Farhad began clapping and pacing the floorboards next to the terrace. Just behind him, Hart caught the slightest of movements from George.

Hart tried not to focus his attention and willed himself to look away. After a second, he looked back over at George. The white of his eye was visible through the dried blood on his face. He and Hart made eye contact. George had always been the harshest on him, but perhaps for just reasons. After all, Hart had led these men into the trap, faced with the unthinkable, and he was about to die. He'd failed.

"You choose the man!" Farhad shouted, furious he wasn't getting what he wanted from Palmer, who'd retreated further into a shell. "No, you must cause him pain! Death is too kind, you fool."

Hart briefly met the dark eyes of Farhad, pools of black, like staring into an oil drum. He spun to Greta and motioned for the pistol. Hart was watching their hands exchange the weapon when behind them he saw George stir once more.

This time George held Hart's gaze for a moment, then, with his eyes, directed Hart to look at what he was holding. Hart caught a glimpse of George's hand wrapped around a cylinder-shaped object. A grenade? A knife? Then he recalled the charges set on the pillars of the house. George was holding the detonator. For the first time since he'd woken up tied to a chair, he had hope.

But George was directly over the pillars, surrounded by the guards, in the heart of the blast zone. He was lying just feet away from Farhad, Greta, and most of the armed thugs they had about. Hart widened his eyes at George, who was sweeping the room with one eye open.

"Time is up!" Farhad took the pistol and pointed it at Hart.

"No, no," Palmer stammered, not offering anything other than basic protest.

Hart felt the sights of the gun settle on his chest. He turned to look at Clara. He thought of the nights they'd spent on the beach in Noirmoutier, wrapped up in blankets and each other. It was what he wanted to think of to give him peace.

Suddenly, out of the corner of his eye, Hart saw Farhad change his aim and direct the gun towards Clara. "I get to choose who dies." A sinister smile crossed his face. Hart looked hopefully back towards George. The men's eyes connected. George winked at Hart and lifted his arm.

Hart burst upward with all the strength his body could produce. Still attached to the chair, he swung towards Clara, blocking her from Farhad and toppling her over, back into the cement expanse of the house.

Amidst the first shouts and a wayward gunshot, a grumbling and muffled explosion ripped through the front of the house. The pillars outside exploded simultaneously, brought down by solid punches to the outside of the house. The structure swayed in place for a moment, like a dazed fighter about to hit the mat. Then the outside terrace began to crumble, screams from the guards outside were quickly drowned out by the house breaking in half, taking with it anyone near the balcony.

Hart laid on Clara; the impact of hitting the ground splintered the chairs they were tied to, allowing him to wriggle free. He was busying, untying Clara when one of the guards, bloodied by the crumbling cement, landed on the ground next to him. Then Pierre-Emmanuel appeared with a gun, and Lucas by his side, holding a table lamp like a bat, providing them cover.

"Get her up. We have to get out of here!" Lucas shouted, scanning the smoke-filled room.

"Clara! Clara, are you alright?" Hart leaned in close to her ear. She was face down on the floor.

"Yes! You're just crushing me! Can we get up?" she complained, rolling around, trying to rid herself of the remnants of the broken chair.

Hart fought the ringing in his ears from the explosion. He tried to focus on their immediate environment. The interior of the house filled with dust and smoke. The structure torn in two, the night sky revealed right through the open living room where the large windows once were.

"Where is everyone?" Hart asked, lifting Clara to her feet.

"I can't see anyone else." Lucas turned and headed off towards the hole in the front of the house.

"Find Palmer!" Hart yelled after him, then pointed at Pierre-Emmanuel. "Help me get her out of here!" Hart swung his arm around Clara's shoulder and shepherded her towards the stairs with Pierre-Emmanuel providing cover.

"I can walk, you know!" Clara shouted.

As a group, they began shuffling through the haze and coughing from the dust. The staircase was partially blocked due to the structure collapse. Hart led them to an outside wall in the main room that had begun to break apart. He threw his weight at the wall several times, the broken concrete slightly budging. Pierre-Emmanuel also lent a shoulder and finally, the wall fell outwards, creating a hole large enough for a person.

"Lucas back yet?" Hart glanced over his shoulder into the darkened room.

"I don't see him," Pierre-Emmanuel muttered, seemingly out of breath.

"I'm not leaving Clara. You need to find him. We have to get back to the boat."

"I'll be fine. Go find Lucas." Clara offered as Hart began to help her through the hole. When she was barely stepping into the hole, the wall above her head exploded, causing Hart to crash to the floor. He spun as a bloodied Greta unloaded her pistol towards Clara.

Hart was too far away to get to scramble back to Clara in time. She slowly turned to face her former captor's gun, and Greta pulled the trigger.

66

St. Lucia

Hart, too far away to do anything, could only watch in horror as Greta fired at Clara.

The crack of her shots thundered in the enclosed space. Pierre-Emmanuel spun and shielded Clara from the barrage of bullets. He took two in the back and fell.

Clara caught her boss before he could hit the ground.

Hart expected the next barrage of bullets, but turned to find Greta was nowhere to be seen. She'd fled through the smoke-filled house.

He crawled over to Clara, who held her dying mentor in her hands. Pierre-Emmanuel couldn't speak loudly, expressing his shock in his gray eyes. Clara leaned in, cradling his head, and whispered in his ear. Hart saw the man's lips move as he spoke to Clara. Hart put his arm around her and felt her shudder with emotion.

Then, the French intelligence man's eyes closed, his hawkish features fell lifeless. After his last breath, Hart gently tugged at Clara's arm. "We have to go." The house was continuing to crumble. The outdoor terrace had now wholly collapsed, exposing the house to the full view of the bay.

"Where is she?" Clara's eyes were hard as she searched through the smoke.

"She's gone," Hart said softly, reaching down and grabbing a gun from the fallen man's waistband.

Clara tenderly laid Pierre-Emmanuel back on the ground, placing his arms across his chest.

"Let's go find this bitch."

Carefully, Hart climbed through the hole in the wall after Clara, navigating the loose rebar. Nothing moved below or outside the house from his vantage point, and he couldn't make out any other noises of anyone around. Wanting to make for the quickest getaway, Hart guessed that Greta and Farhad would head for the beach. He took Clara's hand and, through the rugged terrain of the jungle, guided her to the beach.

Cutting in front of the house, Hart saw the full-on destruction of what the collapsing pillars caused. He could see clearly into the living room, the moon lighting up the white walls. His eyes swept downwards towards the mangled pile of cement blocks and twisted rebar; a dust cloud settled over the mess. There he recognized the shapes of Lucas digging through the rubble. Palmer was next to him, his head pressed close to the chest of a body Hart couldn't make out.

Palmer looked up to see Hart and Clara, shouting after them, "The bastard is heading towards the beach! Cut him off before he gets to the boat!"

Neither Clara nor Hart bothered responding. Instead, they put their heads down and plowed through the jungle. Hart's instincts screamed for him to go back, but he couldn't leave Clara's side. They could reach the shoreline and follow it to the inlet where *Lil Napoleon* was hidden and escape, but they weren't finished yet. He and Clara needed to get Farhad and Greta.

Some distance away from the house, at about thirty yards,

one of the red-polo-wearing crew members was struggling to their feet. They must have been on the balcony when the explosions tore the house in two, and rolled further down the hill. While he was on all fours getting to his feet, Clara ran by and kicked out at the man's midsection, propelling him upwards into the air as she then brought an elbow down hard onto his back. An audible gust of air shot from him as the man collapsed onto the rocky earth.

"I bet that felt good," Hart threw over his shoulder at Clara. She didn't bother responding. Only a flash of satisfaction flickered across her face.

"Where are we going?" Clara finally said, the fog of what they just went through lifting.

"They have a boat, and I'm not letting them go."

"No, we need to stop that yacht. It can't reach Venezuela. If it does, no one will be able to stop what could happen next. I'm talking weapons, dirty bombs. Paul, we have to stop them!"

"Clara, that's our mission and what we're doing! But we already called in support for the yacht. Now we need the assholes responsible."

They finally cleared the jungle, stumbling onto several hotel huts spread tastefully on the beach. They maneuvered through the structure and then through a maze of beach chairs until they reached the shoreline.

The silhouette of the Zodiac Farhad, Greta, and Clara had taken from *No Good Deed* was racing off in the distance, already a hundred yards from shore.

Hart kicked at the sand in disappointment.

Clara tugged at Hart's arm. "Who's that?"

Further down the beach where she was looking, Hart recognized the captain.

A wave of worry washed over Hart. "What are you doing here? The boat okay?"

The wide-eyed captain nodded, taking in the scene just up the hill. "I heard the explosions and followed the shoreline to get a better view. I wanted to know if I was needed."

"Yes, get us back to the boat." Hart nodded towards the tree line and held his hand out for Clara.

The captain waved them over, ready to take off back towards the boat. "Where are the others?"

Hart shook his head, the chaos that swirled around him clouding his thoughts. Their plan had gone so terribly he didn't know how to salvage it. Somehow having Clara next to him, without any other single member of the team, tore at his heart. He made a promise to himself that he wouldn't let her out of his sight, but the guilt of leaving everyone in unknown conditions was too much. George had sacrificed himself. Without him, they would have lost everything. Hart prayed the man could have somehow survived.

Clara grabbed Hart's arm. "Do you hear that?"

He closed his eyes and strained to hear the noise of another engine approaching across the bay.

67

St. Lucia

The captain stood at the shoreline alongside Hart and Clara. Next to them, beached to ensure it didn't float away, was a Sea-Doo. The first mate, the man aboard *Napoleon* named David, had ridden in on the two-person Jet Ski. He registered the worried faces and noticed several of the group missing.

"We heard explosions and gunfire from the other side of the mountain, and I couldn't hail you on the radio, so I came to check. We need to go."

"That bastard is getting away," Hart managed, squeezing the hand of Clara. "I have to go." He waded into the water dragging the Sea-Doo. The Zodiac Farhad and Greta fled on was now a tiny dot racing at the horizon in the direction of Petit Piton.

Everyone watched Hart turn the key and press the engine starter. "I'm going after them!" He wasn't letting Greta and Farhad make their escape. Not without justice.

Suddenly the Sea-Doo sunk further in the water. He turned to find Clara had hopped on board, wrapping her arms around his waist, and pointed in the direction of the getaway boat.

"*Allez*, Paul! This is my fight."

Hart turned the Sea-Doo against the crashing of the

waves. Without hesitation, David sprang into action, running into the water to push the powerful craft into deep enough water to open the throttle.

"Plenty of gas!" David yelled out as Clara gave a quick glance back at the men on the beach. Hart didn't waste a second and smashed the throttle so hard he nearly threw himself off. The battered team stood on the beach and watched the Sea-Doo disappear into the blackness of the night.

The wind whipped his face as it swirled off the ocean, but the bay was much calmer than it had been earlier in the evening. Hart hammered the throttle to make up the distance. He could see the faint glow from the running lights of Farhad's getaway Zodiac far away as it headed towards the southern tip of the island. From his memory of the island's layout, he recalled that was where the nearest airport was. He'd be damned if he let Farhad get away. The man was going to pay. People had given their lives trying to help; Antoine, Pierre-Emmanuel. Hart didn't want to speculate about anyone else. Don't let it be for nothing. He would offer the same commitment as the fallen.

The engine growled as it sucked in and propelled out the seawater, whining in a high pitch whenever he caught air.

He had Pierre-Emmanuel's weapon, a Glock handgun, and Clara with him. He thought of George's words. "*You can thank me when this is over, and we go home, with your girl.*" He sure as hell would as soon as he got the chance. He'd only seen Lucas and Palmer at the house, digging through the rubble. It had all been a blur. Everyone could reunite when he'd taken care of Farhad. So many had sacrificed for the mission. Pierre-Emmanuel paid the ultimate price to save his agent, and Hart was going to enact revenge for Clara as much as himself.

The ocean sprayed in his face, water fogging his vision. It was difficult to see with the only light provided by the moon. Hart focused on the running lights in the distance and glanced at the shoreline to make sure he was safely in deep water. He couldn't afford to bottom out. He couldn't afford to lose Farhad.

They closed the distance to about a hundred yards, the nimbler and quicker Sea-Doo navigating the sea with ease. There were three successive flashes from the boat, and Hart felt the shockwave from the bullets whizzing overhead. He, in turn, navigated the Sea-Doo out wider than the wake, making themselves a moving target.

Pop! Pop! Pop!

Three more shots missed them, one striking the water in front of his craft. Greta fired from the stern. She was zeroing in on them but dispensing of ammunition foolishly.

Hart cut back over, directly behind the boat once more into the wake, and closed the distance so that they were no less than forty yards behind.

Clara pulled the pistol from his waistband and fired off a volley of shots, nearly deafening Hart. Greta ducked behind the engine.

Continuing to squint through the water covering his face, his ears ringing, he willed his eyes to focus. Farhad was standing at the helm. Suddenly, Greta sprung up to fire. Hart letting go of the throttle, yelled, "Get down!" crouching low behind the bars as several shots screamed past them.

He looked up to find the boat cutting to his left, towards land and the second Piton Mountain. Just beyond it was the southern point of the island. Far from shore, the black sky met the ocean, striking terror in Hart. Did he have enough gas? How would he get back to the others? He quickly dismissed the worries and focused on the task at hand. *Don't let the sacrifices of others be for nothing.*

Punching the throttle, the Sea-Doo responded, leaping nose-first into the air like a whale breaching the surface. The wind began to blow harder as it whipped around the mountain in front of them. Greta fired two more shots, this time one of them nicking the front plating of the Sea-Doo. It sputtered for a moment, then continued to slice through the sea.

They got within twenty yards, and the gunfire stopped. He could see the scowl on the woman's face as she helplessly watched the Sea-Doo approach. All her rounds were spent.

Clara stood, leaning forward onto Hart's back, and pumped the rest of the Glock's rounds into the fleeing Zodiac. Greta cried out and arched in pain. Clara caught her once more in the torso, sending her overboard and into the ocean.

Clara attempted to fire again, but the gun was empty. She cursed, checked the chamber, then threw it into the water.

"Keep going. I need this!" Clara shouted.

"Need what?" Hart asked, but it was already too late. She had jumped from the Sea-Doo, curling into a ball before hitting the water. At the speed they were going, it would sting, but he knew she would handle herself just fine.

Clara splashed into the water and immediately kicked to the surface to find Greta's bobbing body. As she approached, there was no movement from her former captor. Regardless, she was going to make sure the bitch was dead. She swam close to Greta and grabbed her to roll her over when Greta quickly clamped onto her. The woman pulled Clara under, the unexpected attack catching her off guard. *Focus, Clara, you're a fighter.*

She fought off the urge to panic and swim for the surface. Instead, she found Greta's face with her hands and began pushing on her eyes. Greta screamed underwater, a terrifying gurgled sound to Clara's defensive maneuver. She released Clara from her bearhug. Breaking the surface, Clara took in as much air as she could and readied for another attack. When she saw Greta breach several yards away, she dove underneath the water and attacked her from below.

Clara wrapped her legs around her and felt for the gunshot wound on Greta's torso. Below the water, Greta continued to cry out in pain while Clara dug a fist into her open wound. Greta thrashed back and forth, desperate to free herself from Clara's vice-like leg lock, but it was no use. Clara's head remained above water, her hold on the bitch who killed Pierre-Emmanuel was firm. Greta was fatigued and heavily wounded. She thrashed less and less violently as Clara calmly kept her grip and breathed in the fresh night air. After several moments, Greta stopped moving entirely. Clara gave her a swift kick and sent the bitch to the bottom of the ocean.

Hart glanced over his shoulder, but it was of no use. The ocean surface behind him was blacker than black. There was no sign of Clara anywhere. He trusted her to finish the job but being without her again only reminded him of how far he'd come. He wasn't going to stop now. Not until he had Farhad dead to rights.

He tried to map out his next move. Pull alongside and try to jump onto the fleeing boat? Foolish and an arrogant idea, he told himself. No, he would have to be drastic.

Riding directly in the middle of the wake behind the boat, he fought the sidewalls that pushed to keep him in the lowest part of the water. Farhad was at full throttle, the Zodiac's nose pitched high, Farhad standing to see over it.

They were cutting towards the shore, the ominous shape of the Piton Mountain growing more visible as they drew closer.

Hart steadied his breathing. He squeezed the throttle with all his might. The Sea-Doo squirmed for a moment in the wake behind the boat, then found purchase, speeding towards Farhad.

Don't let it be for nothing.

He held down the throttle and braced himself.

The Sea-Doo raced forward and caught the deep middle wake from the motor on Farhad's boat. The speed shot his craft into the air, the boat momentarily under him, just like he'd planned. The crunch was sickening, and scrapping of fiberglass of the Sea-Doo and the boat's helm was violent. Gravity clawed at the weight of the Sea-Doo, bringing it down directly over the middle of the boat. The Zodiac shifted its pitch downward and the motor burst out of the water. The sudden weight shift to the portside flung Hart from his craft and into the sea.

Hart found himself tumbling through the warm water, surrounded by darkness. He kicked hard and found the surface, the cuts, and scrapes he had stinging like mad. He first heard the chaos before he saw it. The motors on both crafts were revving high. He could see Farhad pinned under the Sea-Doo, not moving. There was smoke pouring from the boat's motor, and before he could even think to swim closer to inspect the damage, it caught fire. He thought he could hear Farhad laughing for the briefest moment, but then, like the wind carrying the laughter away, the explosion ripped through the air. The shockwave jolting him from under the water.

He fought hard to stay above the surface and watched the burning boat and Sea-Doo sink to the bottom of the ocean as exhaustion began to take hold.

He bobbed in the water for a moment, catching his breath. Then he heard a deep rumble overhead, one that he felt shake the ocean.

Overhead several F/A-18 Super Hornets ripped by at impressive speed. Hart knew precisely where they were headed. A moment later, far away on the horizon, an orange fireball flickered. Then, as quickly as it appeared, it disappeared once again.

Exhausted, he began to swim back to where Clara had jumped off. The night was black, and for the moment, things were still. He was swimming hard towards Clara's last position when he heard her calling out his name.

It was the sweetest sound he'd ever heard.

Epilogue

10 Days Later

Cahors, France

The Sud-Ouest was a welcome change from the bustle of Paris for Lucas Locatelli.

He parked near the Pont Valentré, the impressive bridge finished in 1378 AD. Built over seventy years, it had withstood the test of time. The bridge, made into a UNESCO World Heritage site in the 1990s, was comprised of three main towers that stood over the cobblestone base that spanned the Lot River. As Lucas walked parallel to the Lot, he could just make out the small devilish shape on the second tower. Legend had it that the architect made a pact with the devil to finish construction. A bronze devil was installed high in the corner of the tower overlooking the town in his honor.

It was fitting, thought Lucas, as he crossed the road into the main square of the medieval town. We're all prisoners of our past, our triumphs, and failures alike. After all, as far as he was concerned, it was why he found himself in Cahors. Atoning for his failures, reminded by his limp from his gunshot wounds.

He passed through the town square, a gleaming white stone promenade that led to a statue of Léon Gambetta;

behind it, water fountains highlighted the faded bronze statue of Cahors' native son. Reaching Boulevard Gambetta, Lucas checked his watch. It was 1 p.m., the streets busy on a weekday afternoon. While shops closed for lunch, all the locals gathered at the several cafés that faced each other further up the street to his left. He stopped at a small kiosk and bought a copy of *Le Figaro*. Without a better place to wait, Lucas found himself a corner table on the sidewalk at Bistro de Lisa.

He faced the street and ordered a *café allonge*. He checked his watch once more and dug into the cover story written by one Magali Martin. She had an exclusive series of reports about mysterious goings-on around Europe and the Caribbean. According to Mme. Martin, it appeared that a luxury yacht had been sunk twenty miles off the coast of St. Lucia by US Navy aircraft. International security services, who didn't wish to comment on the record, indicated the yacht had been carrying weapon plans and systems, to a rogue foreign county. However, they had all been accounted for and subsequently destroyed.

Furthermore, the recent attack in France was a part of a small cell, since eliminated in a shootout and controlled explosion in a hotel in Toulouse. The article alluded that these related events were all started with the murder of a respected Parisian attorney. Sources close to Magali Martin would confirm as such. At the end of the article was a picture of a man in a grey suit, his hair brushed straight back and his hawkish features striking. Lucas had a pang in his chest and read the inscription.

French intelligence officer Pierre-Emmanuel Dubois was killed in action during the investigation. The president will bestow the Légion d'Honneur posthumously at the Élysée tomorrow.

Lucas folded the paper and laid it flat on the table. He drank his coffee slowly, watching a group of young students pass by the bistro and stand in the long queue at the kebab stand next door. It made him think of Antoine. His partner would never get to see his child grow old. The events he was going to miss—the first steps, first words, the first day of school, the ice cream runs, the family dates—the blessing of watching your own children grow into adulthood. No, thought Lucas, this wasn't possible for Antoine, nor the wife and child he left behind, to shoulder alone. It was what partners were for, to be there when the other needed them. It was the promise he'd silently made to his gone but not forgotten partner. *I will not forget you in death.*

He checked his watch once more; now it was one thirty. He dropped a few euros on the table, left Magali Martin's front-page story there as well for the next passerby, and walked down the cobbled street. Cutting over onto Rue Maréchal Foch, Lucas regarded the grand Cathédrale Saint-Étienne de Cahors at the end of the block marking the medieval quartier of town. It was the neighborhood where Antoine and his wife Eva lived and where their young son, who he still hadn't met, would grow up. It was a convenient place to live for Eva, who ran a small women's clothing boutique right on the narrow pedestrian street.

Lucas touched the envelope in his jacket pocket to ensure it was still there. It was apparently a small gesture that Pierre-Emmanuel had seen to. Lucas was sure it had already been in the works, but he would never get the opportunity to ask his old boss where the money for Antoine had come from. It would be the first of his many visits, Lucas thought to himself as he steadied his nerve. After all, it was his duty to watch his partner's back, in life or death.

The store was quaint; the lower level of an old building was covered in light stone. Lucas made his way down several stone steps into the shop, passing several mannequins dressed in colorful chic linen jackets and scarves.

Eva was behind the counter when he entered.

"Lucas..." Her voice cracked.

The baby behind the counter must have sensed his mother's emotion and started to stir. She smiled down at him with a mother's loving look and turned back to Lucas.

"Would you like to meet my son?" She asked, brushing a strand of dark hair behind her ear.

"Of course." Lucas took a few steps, unsure of himself.

Eva picked the baby up and stepped out from behind the counter.

"Antoine wanted to name him." She smiled and began to cry as she rocked the baby back and forth in her arms. "Meet my baby boy. We named him Lucas, after you."

Fort Snelling, Minneapolis, Minnesota

The early morning dew settled amongst the white headstones that stretched out as far as the eye could see. There was a somberness to the grounds, balanced out by the pure beauty of the gently rolling hills, thick oak trees, and pristinely manicured green lawns. Several jets flew overhead from the nearby international airport, their engines droning from takeoff, filling the space with white noise as if to drown out all the melancholy thoughts of its visitors.

Paul Hart, dressed in a dark charcoal suit, a navy-blue silk knit tie, and a blue raincoat, stood under an oak tree observing the service taking place a hundred yards away. He was brought to the cemetery by Stephen Palmer to witness the twenty-one-gun salute for Lieutenant George Kaminski. His family had been told that a traffic accident claimed the life of the former Green Beret and foreign service officer, but the two men standing at a distance from the service knew the truth and had come to pay their respects.

Clara Nouvelle stood behind the men, next to the black estate car they'd taken directly from the private airport. She'd insisted that Hart stand alone with Palmer, the two men who knew George more than she did. Hart had brought up the trip and told her not to worry about traveling from Washington, DC, where they'd remained since the St. Lucia rescue, but she told him she was coming to pay respects and it was her damned decision, nothing he could do to stop her.

Hart watched on in silence as the small family faced the honor guard. He thought back over the past few weeks he'd had with the man; their fractious relationship, the constant tension. Perhaps it was that history that ate away at Hart. Wojtek, or George, did the most selfless act possible, sacrificing his life so that others may live. Without George detonating the explosives under that house, they wouldn't be alive. He owed the man his life. Perhaps even more importantly, he owed him Clara's life. George had said he could thank him after they got back with Clara, and now Hart was doing just that.

The first seven shots cannoned through the still air of the cemetery. Even after the gun battle more than a week ago, the shots from the honor guard, Hart would swear, were the loudest he'd ever heard. Absolute silence reigned after the third and final round when all guns fell silent. The honor guard folded a flag and presented it to an older woman, sat in a wheelchair, which Hart presumed was George's mother. The men saluted the family, turned on a heel, and headed off to fulfill their duty of honoring another fallen soldier elsewhere.

Hart and Palmer stood in silence until all the family had departed. Palmer was the first to speak. "Thank you for coming. George was originally from Minnesota, and we made damn sure he got the burial he deserved."

Hart noticed the emotion in the man, not from teary eyes or a weak voice, by the pained lines on his face. "I'm gonna miss Wojtek."

The feeling of guilt that Hart was still here, yet George wasn't, overwhelmed him. He could only manage a nod, his throat too tight to speak. Clara offered the men a somber smile and then slid into the car's back seat, ensuring Palmer and Hart a private moment.

"Did he say anything to you?" Hart asked, the question seeming to catch Palmer off guard.

"When? Who?" Palmer stalled, as if he hoped his protégé would drop it.

"At the house, before he passed. I think I saw you in the rubble with him. I assume you were talking."

Palmer took a deep breath and looked over Hart's shoulder to where the black-clad family had offered their final goodbyes to George before climbing into their cars.

"He made me make him a promise."

Hart was quiet. He didn't want to press the man, but he didn't know how many times they would ever speak again. What was to happen to him now? Would he and Clara go back to France and lead a quiet life? Could they stay in the US, and he could start work again? The ambiguity of his future left him at a crossroads without a purpose.

"Tell me this, at least, did you keep that promise?"

Palmer smirked, a mix of sadness and hope in his eyes. "I am trying to. Every day, by working on you."

"Me? How can I help keep the promise if I don't know what it is?"

Palmer waved away Hart's concern. "What matters is that you honor the men that died for the cause. George, Antoine." Palmer paused, a small smile forming on his face. "Pierre-Emmanuel. These men gave their lives for you, their countries, and for Clara. The promise you can make to them is to make your life worthy of their sacrifice."

Hart was silent. Almost immediately, he could feel the weight of the responsibility Palmer had just laid on him. Make your life worthy. What did that mean? Perhaps different things to different people. He didn't even know what it meant to himself.

A hush settled between the men like the morning fog as the last few cars of funeral attendees drove down the oak-lined roads of the cemetery towards the front gate.

Palmer cleared this throat and glanced at the car in which Clara sat. "I have an opportunity for you."

Hart watched a plane take off overhead, wondered where it was going, and if he could soon be free enough to do such things once more. "I'm listening."

"We work well together. Obviously, you and Clara make a strong team. We've managed to align our governments on some serious issues facing us both and decided to create a global task force to actively shut down serious threats before they materialize. Whatever threat comes up, anywhere in the world, we act. In fact, I could use you in Italy immediately."

Hart rubbed his stumble and craned his neck towards the sky, trying to catch a glimpse of the plane that had flown overhead before it disappeared into the clouds. "You said if I came back last time, that was it. I was free to live my life after. Now you're telling me I have to keep working for you?"

Palmer grabbed Hart by the shoulder and led him to the waiting car. "No. You are free. I am simply asking if you want to."

The car took them on the short ten-minute drive to the private hangar at the Minneapolis St. Paul airport, where two Gulfstream G550s sat on the runway. The three of them climbed out of the car, Hart offering a hand to Clara, who took it and held onto Hart as they walked towards the airplanes.

"Why the two planes?" Clara asked, a subtle flash of worry across her face.

Palmer pointed to the right one. "That's your ride. Captain Scott will be flying you. I have some urgent business that I must attend to. But the captain will fly you anywhere in the world. The least we could do for you two. Just tell him where you'd like to go."

Clara smiled and leaned in to give Palmer the traditional French *bise*. "Thank you for everything. I'll never forget what you and your team did for me."

Palmer gave a slight bow. "Until next time, *mademoiselle*."

Clara turned towards the plane, grabbing Hart's hand and giving it a gentle squeeze. "See you onboard."

She climbed the stairs, met by Captain Scott, who offered a wave to Hart and Palmer before disappearing back inside.

"What will you do?" Hart asked, suddenly all too aware this could be the last time he saw Stephen Palmer. The man had been a guardian, a mentor, a sometimes-silent presence who guided Hart through the most challenging circumstances of his life.

"What I've always known. Watching the world from the shadows."

Hart smiled and then sighed. "I never thanked you."

Palmer held up his hand to interrupt him before he could finish. "You know how to thank me. Keep that promise."

The men fell silent, the reality of their separate paths seemingly settling in. They shook hands awkwardly for a moment before Palmer pulled Hart in for a hug.

"You'll think about my offer, right?"

Hart laughed. "I'll need to speak with Clara." Both men turned and headed towards their separate planes. Hart turned to see Palmer throw a wave over his shoulder.

Once on board, he found Clara sitting on a butterscotch leather couch.

"*Ça va?*" she asked, rising to meet him with a kiss.

"Where should we go?" Hart took her hands in his and sat down.

"Good question. Definitely not an island. It would be nice to see someplace new, but maybe we should just head back home to Paris?"

Hart smiled. "It's funny. I actually feel at home right now."

"In Minnesota?" Clara pretended to shiver and looked out the window at the gray weather.

"No." Hart laughed. "With you. That's home."

"Then we can go anywhere." Her green eyes danced with enthusiasm.

Hart sat back and closed his eyes for a second. He had always trusted his instincts, and over the past weeks, learned to do so even more. The life he had never wanted had become the life he knew best. The purpose and challenge felt right.

He could go back to a comfortable life, a job, traveling, and living with Clara. It would be good, safe, perhaps even easy. But was safe and easy, worthy of the sacrifice's others had made for him? Hart already knew the answer before he asked himself the question.

"Clara." He sat up and grabbed her soft hands. "Have you ever been to Italy?"

Stephen Palmer's plane had taken off within two minutes of him boarding. The Gulfstream was just passing through the first cloud layer when his phone rang.

"Palmer, it's Captain Scott."

"Hopefully, you didn't take it too personally that I requested you fly them and not me."

The captain laughed. "No, but I called to say you were right. I asked Paul and Clara for their preferred destination, and at the same time, they both said Italy."

Palmer smirked as he looked out the window. "Well, I'll be damned. The lovebirds want to stay around."

"Do I have your clearance to fly them there?" Captain Scott asked.

Palmer was quiet for a moment. He'd gotten a glimpse of the bright sun and blue sky that rested above the thick gray cloud cover. It was so different from what they'd experienced that morning that he needed to remind himself where he was. It had turned out to be a beautiful day. All that was required was a different perspective.

"Stephen, do I have your clearance?" Captain Scott once again asked, shaking Palmer from his thoughts.

"Of course. Ceiling and visibility unlimited, Captain."

The End

Acknowledgements

Southwest of France

Spring 2021

Chasing a dream is never a sole endeavour. It's an effort sustained through the support of so many people. This book took over three years in the making, through a Pandemic, an international move, and plenty of challenges, and with the help of friends and family, *Where the Wolf Hunts* finally came to life.

I'm forever grateful to the medical professionals, front-line workers, scientists, and everyone who saw us through COVID-19. Thank you.

To my mother and father, Tim & Susan, thank you for always believing in me, even when I gave you plenty of reasons not to. The values you taught me of determination and following my path have guided me every step of the way. My love of storytelling comes from both of you. I can still remember watching *Singin' in the Rain* with my mom, or *Top Gun* with my dad, thinking how much I loved a great story. I am thankful for your love.

To my love Marie, who puts up with the focused writer in me nearly 24/7, *merci beaucoup*. (You can choose the next research trip location, I promise!)

For Laura and Rory, thank you both for your thoughtfulness and support. Hopefully, one day in the future your, little boys will enjoy these stories.

To Daniel, Fabienne, Florian and Romain, *merci beaucoup*!

To my family, who have been there every step of the way, encouraging a writer's dreams, thank you. Grandma and Grandpa Flynn, thank you for setting a great example!

To Scott Corrick, one of my oldest and best friends. Thanks for pushing me to chase my dreams. Megan and Phoebe, thank you.

Liz and David Reynolds, your encouragement is so much appreciated.

To Phil Wagener, who's been a true friend in every sense of the term. *Danke.*

Phil Titcombe and Francesca Rossi, your support and enthusiasm has meant the world to me. Pizza together soon!

To Head Coach Glenn Caruso and the St. Thomas Football team. My time with UST football had a profound impact on my life and as a man. I've forever grateful for the thoughtful leadership of Coach. Roll Toms.

To Kathleen and Steve Peterson, thank you for always being there for the family come hell or high water.

To Colin and Lisa Peterson, Skol!

To Shayne and Callie Driscoll, you guys have always been there. I'm forever grateful. Fitz too. Cheers.

To Lindsay and Anthony Locatelli, thanks for the copious amounts of Rosé and laughs.

Magali and Florian, I hope I did your city proud!

To Ryan Steck, in the words of one of my favorite films, "I think this is the beginning of the beautiful friendship." Thank you, excited for what's ahead!

To Rebecca Millar, who's been the professional alongside me since the start of this adventure years ago. Thank you for challenging and teaching me along the way.

To JD Smith Design for always coming through clutch! Thank you.

To Patrick Boylan, the star of the Audiobook narrations, you have captured Paul brilliantly. Well done, cocktails on you soon!

To Patrick Kang for the fantastic cover art, thank you so much.

To NYT Bestselling author Harvey McKay, thank you for taking the time to speak to a young writer.

To Michael Weill, thank you for providing a beautiful home while I finished WTWH. Not only did we find peace, but also a friend.

To Steve Syvrud and Aaron Fisher, thank you both for taking a chance on me. I'm forever indebted to you both. We need to tee it soon!

To Kyle Hanson, thanks for helping me find the balance. You're a good man and friend, cheers.

To my former co-workers in the health field, thank you for holding the line, so appreciative of our time together.

I'm tremendously grateful for the support of Marana, Arizona and my hometown of Minneapolis, Minnesota. Thank you from the bottom of my heart.

To my Scottie Mac and rescue kitty Gaia, you both bring me so much joy. Since you both can't read, at least everyone now knows!

And in memory of Marcus Trower, the first editor I ever worked with who sadly passed away at the release of *Where the Wolf Lies*. His kind words and patience always have stayed with me. A portion of the proceeds from this book will go to charity in honor of Marcus. May he rest in peace.

To the late and great Vince Flynn. Thank you for setting the bar so high and inspiring a young boy to become a writer. Finding your books in my dad's briefcase after work his trips was my first introduction to thriller novels. Vince is the reason I began to write and love the genre. Thank you, Vince and Lysa.

And in memory of my grandparents, who cultivated my love of history and cinema. I fondly recall listening to stories from my grandfather about his time flying B-29's in the Pacific theater during World War Two as a Captain. From a young age, he and my grandmother introduced me to a love of history, Westerns and the classic movies that I firmly believe laid the groundwork for my passion for storytelling.

Finally, to you, the reader, thank you. To all who have been on this adventure with Paul and Clara, I'm eternally grateful. There's no better way to promote a book by way of mouth, so please recommend to others and leave reviews if you've enjoyed the ride. Until next time.

-Tyler

Made in United States
Orlando, FL
17 October 2022

23526980R00257